"So You Mind Telling Me What You're Doing Running Around Half Naked?"

Shirlene took a steadying breath that didn't do much to steady her pounding heart.

"Only if you answer my question about where you've been the last three days. Of course, it's probably not that hard to figure out seeing as how Billy Wilkes is only interested in three things—hunting, fishing, and women. And since it doesn't look like you're dressed for the first two, I'll have to go with the last."

His hand tightened on her arm. "If I said I was with a woman, would you turn back around and go home?"

"Yes."

"Fine. I was with a woman."

She might've believed Billy if he'd released her arm. But instead he pulled her closer. With her heart banging out a polka, she reached up and smoothed down the collar of his shirt, her fingers brushing the soft curls at the back of his neck.

"Liar." She licked his earlobe before sucking it into her mouth. He rolled his head closer, the brim of his hat grazing the top of her head. His breath fell hot against her neck. She tipped back her head as he kissed his way up her neck...

"It will make you laugh, and then make you sigh content-edly. *Make Mine a Bad Boy* is a highly entertaining ride."
—RomanceNovelNews.com

Going Cowboy Crazy

"Romance, heated exchanges, and misunderstandings, combined with the secondary characters (the whole town of Bramble) who are hilarious...This is the perfect summer read. Katie Lane has a winner on her hands; she is now my new favorite author!"
—TheRomanceReadersConnection.com

"Entertaining...[with] a likable and strong heroine."
—*RT Book Reviews*

"Ah, I want my own cowboy, tall, dark, and handsome, but alas he is only between the pages of the book, a good book at that. Katie Lane knows how to heat the pages and keep you burning for more. Romance, steamy love scenes, humor, witty conversation with a twang, all help the pages keep turning. I'm looking forward to reading other books written by Katie Lane."
—BookLoons.com

"An enjoyable romp...a fun, down-home read."
—*All About Romance* (LikesBooks.com)

"I enjoyed this book quite a bit. It really reminded me of an early **Rachel Gibson**...or early **Susan Elizabeth Phillips**. Faith became a sassy, intriguing heroine...The chemistry between these two ratchets up to white-hot in no time." —TheSeasonforRomance.com

"Frequently amusing...The lead couple is a wonderful pairing while the third wheel hopefully gets her own tale." —*Midwest Book Review*

Catch Me a
Cowboy

Also by Katie Lane

Going Cowboy Crazy
Make Mine a Bad Boy

Catch Me a Cowboy

KATIE LANE

FOREVER

NEW YORK   BOSTON

Copyright © 2012 by Cathleen Smith
Excerpt from *Going Cowboy Crazy* copyright © 2011 by Cathleen Smith
Excerpt from *Make Mine a Bad Boy* copyright © 2011 by Cathleen Smith

Forever
Hachette Book Group
237 Park Avenue
New York, NY 10017
www.HachetteBookGroup.com

Printed in the United States of America

First Edition: April 2012

10 9 8 7 6 5 4 3 2 1

Forever is an imprint of Grand Central Publishing.
The Forever name and logo are trademarks of Hachette Book Group, Inc.

The Hachette Speakers Bureau provides a wide range of authors for speaking events. To find out more, go to www.hachettespeakersbureau.com or call (866) 376-6591.

The publisher is not responsible for websites (or their content) that are not owned by the publisher.

To my brother, Ronny Roy.
I miss you, Bubba.

Acknowledgments

It takes a team of hard-working, dedicated people to get my Bramble stories out to the public:

My agent, Laura Bradford. My editor, Alex Logan. My editorial director, Amy Pierpont. My publicity crew, Jennifer Reese and Brianne Beers. Summer book club sweetie, Lauren Plude. My subrights guru, Salvatore Ruggiero. And all the marketing geniuses, cover designers, copyeditors, proofreaders, and retailers who help get my books into readers' hands. Thank you for all your hard work and the pride and dedication you have for your jobs.

Speaking of dedicated people, I'm amazed by the bloggers I have met in the past year. Thank you for your love of reading and reviewing—and for putting up with a new author who stumbles around on your websites trying to figure out how to leave a comment. LOL!

And last but not least, I'd like to thank my readers. You are the ones who bring me back to my computer time and time again. The ones who send me sweet e-mails, tweets, and Facebook posts that get me through those days when I think everything I put down on paper is a pile of cow manure. Y'all are just the best, and I love you!

Catch Me a
Cowboy

Chapter One

WHOEVER CAME UP WITH THE SAYING, *"You can never go home again"* was loonier than a snakebit coyote. You can go home. You just shouldn't.

Ever.

This became crystal clear to Shirlene Grace Dalton as she stared out of the windshield of her Navigator at the beat-up trailer she'd been born and raised in. Not that her mama had done much raising. Abby Lomax preferred raising a bottle to raising her two children. And even though her mama had been dry for over eleven years, it was hard to hang on to forgiveness when memories swept through Shirlene's mind like the west Texas wind buffeting her childhood home.

But Shirlene had never been one to live in the past— a philosophy that had gotten her through the trials and tribulations of the last year. She believed in living in the present. And at the present moment, she needed a place to sleep for the night.

"Just what kind of a low-down ornery scoundrel would evict a poor widow from her home without one word of warnin'?" she grumbled.

At the snuffled snort, she glanced over at the pig who sat next to her in the front bucket seat. The beady eyes over the soft pink snout held not one ounce of sympathy. In fact, they looked almost reproachful.

"Okay, so maybe there had been a few words of warnin'," Shirlene conceded. She reached down and grabbed her Hermès Birkin handbag off the floor and scrounged around until she found the Snickers candy bar. Since she had gained a few pounds over the last nine months, she probably shouldn't. But willpower had never been one of her strong suits.

"But for the love of Pete, how can that new bank owner expect me to know about managing money when Lyle," she glanced up, "God rest his soul, took care of all the financial details? I never had to worry about late fees and overdraft charges . . . and eviction notices." Her green eyes narrowed as she peeled off the candy wrapper and took a big bite. "*Eviction*. Even the word sounds like it comes straight from Satan himself."

A high-pitched squeal resounded through the interior of the Navigator, and Shirlene pinched off a piece of candy bar and held it out to the pig, who exuberantly attacked the chocolate as if he hadn't just downed two of Josephine's bean burritos and a bag of extra-crispy Tater Tots. Being the other white meat, Sherman was a devout vegetarian.

"You realize, don't you, that Colt and Hope would skin me alive if they found out what I've been feeding you, especially after the fiasco with the margaritas." She shook her head. "As if I were responsible for you helping yourself, or for the drunken rampage you went on afterwards. Considering it took two days for you to sober up, I'm surprised they allowed me to watch you while they're in California."

At the thought of her brother, Shirlene took another bite of chocolate. If she thought Colt would be unhappy about her feeding Hope's pig Tater Tots and candy, it would be nothing compared to how upset he would be when he found out she had blown through the money her late husband had left her like a tornado through the panhandle. Especially after she had insisted she could handle her finances all by herself. She just hadn't realized how bad her compulsive spending had become, and her depression over Lyle's death had only made it worse. But shopping trips to Austin and Dallas hadn't made her feel any better. All they had done was fill her home with a bunch of pretty but useless things—things she couldn't even get into her sprawling estate to see.

Which explained what she was doing back on Grover Road.

Her old trailer was the only place in Bramble, Texas where she could spend the night without the nosy townsfolk finding out and tattling to her brother. And one night was all she needed. First thing in the morning, she was going to pay a little visit to the new bank president and set him straight. By nightfall, she would be right back where she belonged—in a big mansion with a pitcher of margaritas.

But until then...

She opened the door and stepped out. A blast of ninety-degree wind slapped her in the face, and she teetered on her four-inch Manolo Blahniks before she grabbed onto the side mirror and caught her balance. Pushing the thick strands of blond hair out of her face, she staggered around the front of the SUV to let Sherman out. The pig didn't like being out in the wind any more than she did. He took his time climbing down, then huddled against her legs as she walked around the piles of rusted junk.

A few feet from the front door, the Navigator lights clicked off, leaving her and Sherman in thick darkness. Shirlene had never much cared for the dark—or the eerie sound of tree branches creaking in the wind.

She glanced around at the sinister shadows. "This night isn't fit for man nor beast." Sherman grunted his agreement as they climbed up the sloping front steps that looked as if they were seconds away from becoming nothing more than kindling.

Wanting out of the ferocious wind as quickly as possible, Shirlene reached for the battered doorknob. It took numerous twists and a couple of stunned seconds before she realized it was locked. And no one locked their doors in Bramble except the librarian, Ms. Murphy, and only because she lived next door to Elmer Tate, who had trouble remembering where his house was after seven or more shots of Jack Daniel's. Of course, no one had been out to the trailer in years so maybe Lyle had locked it against looters.

The thought made Shirlene smile. Her late husband had been so sure she would want to hang on to her childhood home. So sure that one day the bad memories would be replaced with good ones.

Pushing down the sadness that threatened, Shirlene searched for the key that Lyle had given her on their first anniversary—along with a diamond and ruby bracelet. At the time, the jewelry had been much more appreciated. But now, with the darkness and wind pressing against her, she took the time to be grateful for the gift.

"Thank you, honey," she whispered up at the moonless sky. "You always did know what I needed, even before I needed it."

She unlocked the door, but it still refused to open— almost as if something held it from the inside. Leaning her five-foot-ten-inch frame against the cheap plywood, Shirlene shoved. The door cracked open just wide enough to see a figure in white float past before it slammed shut.

The keys slipped from Shirlene's fingers and clunked on the steps, followed by her purse, as a chill tiptoed down her spine. Frozen in place, she stared at the door with its fist-sized imprint put there by Colt during his belligerent teenage years and tried to figure out what she'd seen. Or what she thought she'd seen.

If she'd had her nightly margaritas, she could've blamed it on Jose Cuervo. But since being evicted from her home, the only thing swirling around in her stomach was Josephine's chicken fried steak—something that could give you indigestion but not hallucinations. Which meant one of two things: Someone had moved into the trailer without her knowing it . . . or her childhood home was haunted. And since very few things happened in Bramble without Shirlene hearing about it, she was leaning toward the latter.

Her heart started to thump like the Bramble High drum corps. There might not be a person on the face of God's green earth that she feared, but the macabre was a different matter. Be it ghosts, demons, or the boogie man, the thought of something she couldn't flirt into submission scared the bejesus out of her. But before she could retrieve her purse and keys and get the hell out of there, Sherman lost patience with the weather and his chicken-livered pig-sitter. With a frustrated grunt, he lowered his head and plowed into the door.

Plywood splintered as the door flew open. With a triumphant toss of his head, Sherman trotted in. Shirlene, on the other hand, moved a tad bit slower. The room was dark but familiar. For a second, she could almost smell her mother's Avon perfume and cigarettes.

She reached for the switch on the wall and released a sigh of relief when the eye-squinting overhead light came on. The living room was smaller than she remembered, especially with the fold-out couch opened up, the couch with the same paper-thin mattress Colt had slept on every night. In fact, with the rumpled sheets and blankets, it looked as if her brother had just climbed out of it.

"Hello?" she said, hopeful that a living, breathing human being would step out of one of the two bedrooms and cordially explain their presence in her trailer.

Sherman had no such illusions. Hopping up on the low mattress, he proceeded to root around in the blankets until he'd made himself a comfortable nest. With one exasperated look from those beady eyes, he flopped down.

"Oh, no," Shirlene whispered. "I'm not staying here after—"

The wind whistled in through an open window, fluttering the dingy sheet that served as a curtain and slamming the door closed. At the loud bang, Shirlene almost peed her designer jeans. But it only took a second for the proof of her foolishness to have her chuckling with relief.

"Silly goose," she breathed. "It was just the wind." She walked over and pushed her phantom ghostly sheet aside as she slammed the window closed. When she glanced over at Sherman, it almost looked as if he rolled his little piggy eyes. "Okay, so I'm getting as nutty as the Widow Jones," she said, as she walked back and opened the door so she could collect her purse and keys. "Pretty soon I'll own twenty-five cats and wear my bathrobe and slippers to Sunday services. But I'll still be the only one who feeds you chocolate and tequila, so I wouldn't be acting too snooty if I was you."

The pig snuffled, then dropped his head down to the blankets and closed his eyes. Shirlene didn't usually go to sleep until well after *Letterman*. But with no television in sight, she resigned herself to an early night.

As she closed the door, she glanced down at the worn carpeting to find the Barbie doll Colt had given her on her sixth birthday. Picking it up, she stared at the wild blond hair and naked body—the type of body she had dreamed of possessing. But the dream of perky breasts and skinny hips died at thirteen when Shirlene started to develop more curves than an Indy raceway.

Carrying the doll with her, she flipped out the lights, slipped off her high heels, and climbed onto the fold-out couch. No doubt there was still a mattress in each of the bedrooms, but after her fright, she had no desire to sleep alone. Even if it meant she had to share a bed with a hog.

"Scoot over, Piglet." She gave him a shove, and he gave her a mere two inches more before snuffling back to sleep. Rolling to her back, she stared up at the ceiling while she stroked Barbie's short, uneven hair. For the life of her, she couldn't remember cutting the doll's hair. Just one more piece of her childhood she'd chosen to forget.

The night was hot and dry and the mattress so thin that the metal frame pressed into her back. How Colt had managed to sleep on it was beyond her. Her brother had

sacrificed so much growing up so she would have what
other kids had—like her own room. Which was why she
wasn't about to let him sacrifice any more. Not when he
had a new wife and baby girl to worry about. No, this
time, Shirlene would fix her own mess. Come hell or high
water—or nasty bank owners.

Despite the bad mattress, it didn't take her long to fall
asleep. It wasn't surprising that she dreamed of Grover
Road.

She was nine years old again and playing in the
broken-down Chevy in the front yard. The day was hot
and, even with the windows open, sweat glued her bright
copper hair to her temples and to the back of her neck.
Regardless of the heat, she refused to climb out of the
rusty car. There were too many places she wanted to
travel to, too many things she wanted to see. It would've
been much more fun if Hope and Colt had been traveling
with her. But Hope had moved into town, and Colt spent
most of his days at Tinker Jones's garage. So Shirlene was
all alone, except for her mama, who was passed out cold
on her bed inside the trailer.

Of course, that was the one nice thing about Grover Road—you were never alone for long. A man suddenly appeared in front of the hood ornament of the old
Chevy, a man with a friendly smile and eyes as green as
Shirlene's. She wasn't surprised to see her daddy. Even
though he'd died in a car accident when she was a baby,
she dreamed of him often. He walked around to the open
window and reached in to smooth back her hair. At first,
his fingers were cool and soothing. But, as with most
dreams, when you least expect it, things could take a turn
for the worst. Suddenly, he wasn't stroking her hair as

much as strangling her neck. As his fingers tightened and she fought for breath, his face turned from her daddy's into her husband's—not the living Lyle, but the dead Lyle. Eyes that were deep holes of nothingness stared out of a lifeless face.

Shirlene woke with a start. Pre-dawn filled the room with grayish light. It sounded like the wind had died down, although it was hard to tell over the wild thumping of her heart and her heavy breathing. The nightmare slowly receded from her mind. But what she couldn't seem to shake was the feeling of icy fingers on her neck. It only took a subtle tightening for Shirlene to realize that the icy fingers were no longer part of a dream.

"Mine," a deep voice growled in her ear.

Releasing an ear-splitting scream, Shirlene jumped from the bed and headed for the door. When her hand closed around the doorknob, she quickly glanced back to see how closely the strangler followed. The room was empty except for a startled pig that looked at her as if she'd lost her mind. Maybe she had. But whether it was a figment of her imagination or not, she'd had enough of Grover Road. Without waiting for Sherman, she threw open the door, only to come face to face with an image straight out of a horror movie.

But it wasn't the hockey mask that held her attention as much as the chainsaw. And having watched the *The Texas Chainsaw Massacre* at least a dozen times, Shirlene knew exactly what happened to the pretty blonde. Luckily, Sherman had no intention of being carved into ham hocks, and with a high-pitched squeal, he sailed off the mattress and charged the door. The short psycho killer stepped back long enough for pig and blonde to hightail it out.

They took the front steps in one leap, Sherman land-ing on all fours and Shirlene going down to one knee. But she got up quickly enough when the chainsaw cranked to life. Since her keys were still in the trailer, she bypassed her SUV and headed for the hole in the shrubs that sepa-rated her lot from her neighbor's. If she had been thinking clearly, she would've run to a trailer that was occupied, but her brain had flown right out of her head the minute the ghostly cold hands had closed around her throat. Add a chainsaw-wielding midget, and her only thought was escape.

Since the trailer next door was vacant at the moment, Shirlene didn't waste any time knocking. She just swung open the screen door and barged right in. She closed the door behind Sherman and fumbled with the lock. While the lock at her trailer worked perfectly, this one didn't work at all. Even locked, the flimsy door would be no match for a chainsaw, something she didn't think about until the front steps creaked and a masked face peered in the kitchen window.

Terrified, Shirlene glanced down at Sherman, who shot her a look that pretty much said *every pig for himself* before he streaked behind a dilapidated recliner. With no room left behind the chair, Shirlene headed for the back bedroom. Unfortunately, the bedroom door didn't have a lock either, and with her heart pounding in her chest, all she could do was listen and wait.

The chainsaw sputtered to a halt. She didn't know if that was a good thing or a bad thing. Maybe the psycho was lulling her into a false sense of security—hoping she'd open the door to peek out so he could decapitate her in one slice. The image of splattered blood and her rolling head was fresh in her mind when someone grabbed her from behind.

Before she could do more than squeak in terror, she was being pulled down. But it wasn't the cold blade of a chainsaw that pressed her into the sagging mattress, but rather a solid chest of warm hard muscles. Shirlene barely had time to suck in a startled breath before a pair of firm lips settled over hers in a deep, tongue-dipping kiss that curled her toes into the sheets and sizzled all thoughts of ghosts and psycho killers right out of her head. Of course, her senses came back quickly enough when the man nibbled his way over to her ear and whispered in a whiskey-soaked voice.

"Now I'm shore not the type of man to look a gift horse in the mouth." A hot palm settled over her breast, and Shirlene sucked in her breath. "Especially a gift that turned out to be more than I expected. But I'm afraid I'm a little too tuckered out from my trip to give you the kind of ride you deserve, Marcy. So if you don't mind showin' yourself out...."

"Marcy?" Shirlene huffed. Suddenly indignation took the place of fear. How could anyone in their right mind confuse her for Marcy Henderson? Marcy had to weigh a good twenty pounds more than Shirlene, with breasts that she was still making payments on.

The lips stilled against her neck, and he pulled back and brushed the hair out of her face. As he stared down at her, his brown eyes appeared to spark with something that actually resembled thought. But it must've been a trick of the early morning light that filtered in through the sheet over the window. Because when she looked again, all she saw was a whole lot of nothing.

Bubba.

Chapter Two

IF SOMEONE HAD TOLD Shirlene that one day she would find herself in bed with Bubba Wilkes, the biggest redneck to ever come out of east Texas, she would've laughed them clean out of town. But she wasn't laughing now, especially when the country hick dipped his lips for another taste. Without fear muddling her mind, his skillet-fried kisses turned into lukewarm milk toast. When he finally came up for air, it took a real effort not to wipe off her mouth.

An idiotic smile split his face. "If I had known you had such a hankerin' for me, Ms. Dalton, I'da been back much sooner."

"I think there's been a mistake, honey," she stated with as much civility as she could muster.

"Not in my book, Honey Buns." His gaze drifted down to her breasts, nuzzled against his chest. "And all I'll need is a couple minutes to prove it."

"I hate to decline such a fine offer," she said between gritted teeth, "but the only reason I'm here is because I was being chased by a psychotic killer."

His forehead crinkled before a light went on. As usual it was the wrong light.

"Now there's no need to come up with whoppers like that one, Ms. Dalton. If you wanted a tour of Wilkesville, all you needed to do is ask."

Shirlene rolled her eyes. Good Lord, it had been so long since his last visit, she'd forgotten what an arrogant hillbilly the man was. A hillbilly who had wiggled his way into the hearts of every man, woman, and child in Bramble. Which was the only reason Shirlene didn't knee him in the family nuggets and be done with it—that and the fact that there was a chainsaw-wielding killer on the loose.

She flashed him a dimpled smile. "Yes, well, I'll have to take that tour another time. Right now, I need you to—"

"You sure about that?" he cut her off. "Because some offers only come once in a lifetime."

"I guess that's a chance I'll have to take." She glanced back at the door. "So do you have a gun?" It was a stupid question, considering that most Texans owned a gun—or two.

"Yes, ma'am." He pressed his hips closer. "Would you like to see it?"

She stared back at him in disbelief. "Do you really get women with these lines?"

"What lines?"

Good Gravy, and she thought dealing with a psycho had been tough.

"Look." She patted his cheek in an attempt to knock a little sense in him. "All I need—"

The front door banged open.

And brains or no brains, she clung to Bubba like he

was a bathtub in a tornado. But instead of the whine of a chainsaw, Kenny Gene's voice drifted in. Which was almost as terrifying, when she realized one of the biggest gossips in Bramble was about to find her in bed with Bubba Wilkes.

"Hey, Bubba," Kenny Gene yelled. "You in here, buddy?"

Remembering the kind of hell her best friends, Faith and Hope, had been put through at the hands of the crazy, matchmaking townsfolk, Shirlene sent Bubba one look of warning before she dove beneath the covers. Not that the man would know a look of warning, but she really didn't have much choice. Especially when Kenny Gene didn't believe in the sanctity of a closed door.

Throwing it open, he walked right in.

"There you are!" Kenny sounded like he had just found his long-lost hound dog. The floorboards creaked as he stepped into the room. "Rossie Owens said you showed up at Bootlegger's last night. And I was damned sorry I let Twyla talk me in to stayin' home to watch that exterminator show—although watchin' that skinny, weird dude flush out them roaches was pretty fascinatin'."

"Hey, Kenny," Bubba drawled. "How you been?"

"Fair to middlin'. I had a bad case of the runs last week, but I feel fit as a fiddle now. 'Course things in town have been a little scary since Lyle passed away and Dalton Oil changed hands. But that C-Corp seems like a good enough outfit, so people are probably worryin' about losin' their jobs over nothin'—" He stopped in mid-sentence, and Shirlene's breath hitched in her chest.

"Hey, who's that sleepin' next to you? By the size of that bee-hind I'd say it was Ernie Clines. You two plannin' on gettin' an early start on fishin'? You mind me taggin' along?"

A squeak of disbelief slipped out of her mouth, and she clamped a hand over it. First Marcy Henderson and now Ernie Clines. Her butt was not that big. She might have a little junk in the trunk, but it was nothing close to Marcy and Ernie's bubble butts. Still, she made a mental note to cut back on the chocolate.

"You're always more than welcome to come along, Kenny," Bubba replied in his thick drawl. "Except I'm not goin' fishin' with Ernie."

"You ain't? Huntin'?"

"Nope."

There was a long stretch of silence before Kenny spoke. "Then why is Ernie sleepin' over? You ain't one of them fellers that—"

Before Kenny could finish and the smirk even began to settle on Shirlene's face, she was pulled, blanket and all, into Bubba's arms.

His deep voice rumbled against her ear. "As much as I like my fishin' buddies, I prefer my bed partners to be of the female variety." His hand slipped down and patted Shirlene's butt. "Even if those females have a little extra paddin'."

Her humor evaporated as Kenny crowed like a proud papa. "Why, you sly dog, you. In town for less than a day, and you already got yourself a woman—a pretty blonde by the looks of that hair." The floor creaked as he backed out of the room. "Well, I'll just leave you to it then, Bubba." But before Kenny left, he added, "You want me to let Slate know you're here so he can bring by your truck?"

"I'd shore appreciate it," Bubba said.

"Call me if you change your mind about that fishin'."

The front door banged closed, and Shirlene pushed the blanket back and glared at Bubba.

"You can let me go now."

The dark brows over his deep-set eyes lifted. "You shore you haven't changed your mind about Wilkesville?"

"Get. Your. Hand. Off. My. Butt."

A grin tipped up the corners of his wide mouth. "Yes, ma'am," he said, although those warm digits didn't seem to be in any hurry to comply. It took Sherman's earsplitting squeals of pain to get him to release her.

"What the hell?" Bubba sat straight up, almost dumping her to the floor.

In her desire to get Kenny out of the trailer without recognizing her, Shirlene had forgotten all about Sherman—and the psycho killer. Although Kenny had more than likely scared the killer away. Still, she wasn't taking any chances.

"Where's your gun?" she said as she jumped up from the bed. When he continued to sit there with a stunned look on his face, she yelled, "Your gun, Wilkes!"

He rolled to his feet, giving her a glimpse of Wilkesville as he slipped into a pair of Wranglers. If Shirlene hadn't been so worried about Sherman getting carved into Sunday dinner, she might've been impressed by the lean muscled streets and the half-mast flagpole in the center of town. Instead, she didn't even wait for him to cover that fine butt before she hurried out the door.

Fortunately, she didn't find Sherman sliced into a hundred pounds of bacon. But she did find his head caught in the springs of the overturned recliner.

"Oh, Piglet." She hurried over and sat down next to him, trying to soothe him until she could figure out how to get him loose.

"A pig?" Bubba stood in the doorway of the bedroom, wearing nothing but his unbuttoned jeans. Distracted by the lean stomach and defined chest, it took her a moment to notice the revolver he held in one hand.

"I gotta tell you, Ms. Dalton." He rubbed his whiskered jaw. "I like my pork about as much as any man. But I don't much care for shooting defenseless animals." He nodded at the door. "Now if you was to let him loose, it might be a little more sportin'."

"I don't want you to shoot Sherman," she snapped. "I want you to shoot the maniac with the chainsaw who was trying to kill us. Now could you put that thing down and give me a hand?"

Bubba hesitated. "Does it bite?"

She glanced up. "Don't tell me that a good ol' country boy like yourself has never been around a pig before."

"We didn't have pigs," he stated as he set the gun down on the counter in the kitchen right next to a bottle of tequila that Shirlene could've used a few minutes earlier. "We had passive cows. Not some squealing overweight animal."

"Sherman is not overweight," she stated. "He's a perfect weight for his species and height."

Bubba nodded. "Sorta like you, I suppose." He knelt down next to her and brushed her hands away. "Pretty soon you'll have him so tangled up I'll be forced to keep him as a conversation piece."

"What do you mean sort of like me?" She bristled. "Are you comparing me to a pig?"

"No, ma'am," he said, but his smirk said something else entirely.

She wanted to wipe that stupid country grin off his face with her fist. And seeing as she was not a violent person, she wondered where the powerful reaction had come from. The man was nothing to her. In fact, she'd only been in his company a couple of times. But both times she'd gotten the distinct feeling that Bubba Wilkes didn't like her. And maybe that was where her animosity for the man came from—very few people disliked Shirlene and none of them were men.

After taking his good sweet time assessing the situation, Bubba gripped the coils on either side of Sherman's head in his lean hands and, with a simple flex of muscles, set the pig free. Sherman shook his head a few times before he nuzzled against Shirlene and received her sympathy scratches.

Reaching into the springs of the recliner, Bubba pulled out a half-eaten bag of Doritos. "Was this what you were lookin' for, Pig?"

Sherman leaned over and sniffed the bag before very delicately taking it out of Bubba's hand.

"See," Shirlene cooed. "He's as gentle as a lamb." At which point, Sherman proceeded to rip the bag to shreds trying to get to the last of the crumbs.

With a wary look, Bubba sat back on his heels and watched the animal scarf up the cheesy chips. "So is this maniac with a chainsaw the same psychotic killer you were telling me about? Or are they two different fellers?"

Having lived in Bramble most of her life, Shirlene had developed a tolerance for the country psyche. But after being evicted from her home, choked by ghosts, and chased by psycho killers, she wasn't about to be made fun of by a redneck from east Texas. So she shot him a look she gave very few people and climbed to her feet.

"Come on, Sherman," she said. Before she headed out the door, she took a detour to the kitchen, where she slammed down a shot of tequila and picked up the gun.

The sun had crested over the horizon, but Shirlene didn't stop to enjoy the mellow pinks and oranges of the beautiful sunrise as she trotted down the steps with Sherman close on her heels. She had some things to get accomplished, namely talking to the new bank president so she could get back to the lifestyle she was used to. Not this crazy trailer trash nightmare she had stepped into. And in order to do that, she had to face whoever—or whatever—had taken up residence in her trailer long enough to retrieve her purse and keys. After that, the ghosties could have the pile of aluminum for all she cared.

"Would you slow down," Bubba said as he followed her through the opening in the hedge. She accidently released a branch, and it slapped him in the face. Or maybe not so accidently. But what was a branch in the face compared to all the butt pats and heinous pickup lines? He was lucky she didn't turn the gun on him. Although the women of east Texas would probably thank her for ridding them of such a distributor of bullshit.

"Now just hold up there," he said. As they weaved their way through the junk maze, he reached out and grabbed her arm and pulled her to a stop. He was careful to grab the arm that didn't hold the gun. "You can't just run around shooting at anything that moves."

"I can if they're on my property."

He released her arm and glanced around at the pathetic lot. "This is yours?"

"Since the day I was born." She continued to the front steps, but when she reached the door, she hesitated. The door looked even worse than it had to begin with. The plywood was splintered and cracked, and the hinges sagging.

Bubba came up behind her, and she couldn't help but be comforted by his presence, especially when Sherman had refused to climb the steps and was now cowering beneath an old, metal lawn chair with the remnants of the Doritos bag still clutched in his mouth.

"The psycho?" Bubba asked when he noticed the battered door.

"No, the pig," she answered as she pushed the door open.

Before she stepped over the threshold, Bubba reached down and took the gun out of her hand. "Wouldn't want you shooting off your toe by accident—or other important body parts."

Shirlene rolled her eyes as he preceded her into the room. Except for the bright sunlight shining in through the thin sheets that covered the windows, the room looked much as it did the night before—the couch was still pulled out and the sheets and blankets still rumpled. When she saw her purse and shoes sitting on the floor, she heaved a sigh of relief.

Bubba might be an annoying redneck, but he wasn't a coward. He boldly checked out the rest of the trailer while she followed more cautiously behind him. After looking in the tiny bathroom, he stepped back out in the hallway where she stood. The narrow space seemed much smaller with his bare chest so close.

His eyebrows hiked up over those deep-set brown eyes. "No maniacs or psychos that I could find."

"And you expect the villains to stay at the scene of the crime after the sun comes up? What horror movies have you been watching, honey?" She shot him a skeptical look before she headed back to the living room, where it was much easier to breathe.

While she sat down on the edge of the couch and put on her shoes, Bubba walked into the room and flopped down next to her. "I don't watch horror movies. Those things scare the hell out of me—even if it's only Hollywood magic."

It was difficult to concentrate on fastening the tiny little buckles with his body stretched the length of the mattress and then some. Her gaze couldn't help wandering over to the flat stomach with its slit of a belly button, or his muscled-coated ribcage, or the deep brown of his small nipples. But what really had her stomach fluttering was the patch of dark hair under each arm. She couldn't ever remember looking at Lyle's underarms—or any man's for that matter. And seeing the contrast of the white skin with the rest of his tan body had her face flushing as hot as Main Street in late August.

It took his eyelids sliding open and a very quizzical look to get her attention back to her shoes. It took a couple moments more before she could speak.

"Well, the thing that chased me this morning wasn't Hollywood magic."

"Are you sure it wasn't your imagination?" He sat up, and she released her breath. "Sure you didn't have yourself a little happy hour last night?"

"No, I did not have myself a little happy hour," she said.

Although as she looked around the dismal but ordinary room, she had to wonder if maybe the cold fingers and chainsaw-wielding horror star hadn't just been figments of her imagination—the remnants of her nightmare. But if that was the case then what had scared Sherman?

Bubba rolled to his feet and tucked the gun in the waistband of his jeans. "Well, I don't think it was a psycho killer. Probably just some fool tryin' out his new Craftsman eighteen incher—you know how we Texans love our man-tools." He pulled a can of chewing tobacco out of his back pocket. After unscrewing the lid, he pinched out some tobacco and placed it in his mouth.

As far as Shirlene was concerned anything that involved stained teeth and streams of disgusting brown spit was a nasty habit that needed to be outlawed. But she didn't expect anything less from Bubba Wilkes.

"At five o'clock in the morning?" she asked.

Using his tongue, he maneuvered the tobacco down to the corner of his mouth before he spoke. "Which brings up a good point. What is the privileged Ms. Dalton doing out on Grover Road so early?"

"I was just looking things over before I sell it." It was a pretty good lie if she had to say so herself. And it wasn't so far from the truth. After her night of hell, she had no intentions of keeping the trailer.

The dark eyes stared back at her for only a moment before he grinned and pointed a finger mere inches from her nose. "You had me goin' there for a second. But there's no way a person would want to sell such a prime piece of real estate. Which leads me to believe that I was right in the first place; you *do* have a hankerin' for a little Bubba lovin'."

Shirlene stared back at him for only a second before heading for the door. It wasn't Bubba lovin' that she had a hankerin' for as much as her Tempur-Pedic mattress and down pillows. "I'd tell you thanks for the hospitality, but an uninvited mauling isn't what I consider being hospitable."

"As hospitable as a woman breakin' into someone's huntin' lodge without an invite? 'Course I figure Ms. Dalton can stay just about anywhere she pleases." The way he said it sounded almost sarcastic. But since Bubba wouldn't know sarcasm if it bit him in the behind, she figured she was mistaken. Or maybe just exhausted from her harrowing night.

"See ya around, Bubba."

"More than likely, Ms. Dalton." He followed her out.

Wasting no time, she hurried down the steps and hollered for Sherman. Never in her life had she been so happy to slip inside the plush leather seats of her Navigator. And Sherman looked about as happy as she did when she cranked on the air conditioner full blast. He stared back at her with relief in his beady eyes and orange Doritos cheese dust on his upside down heart-shaped snout. As she backed out into the road, she glanced back at the trailer. Bubba still stood on the steps, the pinks and oranges of the sunrise gilding the wavy dark strands of his hair and the hard rippled plains of his body.

Wilkesville was sure nice to look at. Too bad once you got there, it was nothing more than a ghost town.

Chapter Three

"Bubba" Billy Wilkes waited until the black Navigator had disappeared from sight before he leaned over the steps and spit the wad of tobacco out of his mouth. Still, the strong flavor stayed with him as he wiped off his chin and looked around.

It wasn't the first time he had seen the lot, but with his mind preoccupied with other things, it was the first time he'd really looked at it. It was a pathetic sight. The yard was so cluttered with trash and junk he couldn't even see the ground. Water-stained mattresses stuck out of piles of garbage, treadless tires were stacked haphazardly next to rusted-out car and truck frames, and dilapidated couches leaned against dinged-up appliances.

It had to be the biggest pile of crap Billy had ever seen in his life. Even Aunt Mildred and Uncle Fin's yard didn't come close, and people had long confused their double-wide for the town junkyard. But it wasn't the magnitude of junk that surprised him. It was the fact that Mrs. Lyle Dalton owned it. Something he hadn't discovered from the talkative townsfolk on his visits to Bramble. Of course, he hadn't been interested in the wife as much as he was in the husband.

Still, Billy didn't like unanswered questions. Good thing all it would take to find out why a flashy blond gold digger, who clothed herself in diamonds and designer denim, owned a rundown trailer on Grover Road was a trip to the town diner. And since his stomach was touching his backbone, he could kill two birds with one stone.

Padding down the steps, he weaved his way through the junk toward the high hedge. But before he slipped through, he noticed the old '55 Chevy sitting under an elm tree in one corner of the lot. Compared to the rusted-out, weathered frames of the other vehicles in the yard, the car looked to be in excellent condition.

Billy had always preferred trucks to cars. But his big brother had a weakness for antiques, so he walked over to check it out. The paint had a few rust spots, and the tires were all flat. But the windows were still intact, although the back one had a long spidery crack—

A head popped up and two bright eyes stared back at him through the dirty glass. Before Billy could get over his surprise at seeing a little kid in the backseat of the car, an engine cranked to life and a chainsaw-wielding psycho-killer came charging out from behind the trailer.

Now Billy had never backed down from a fight in his life. But the scary mask and haphazard way the psycho swung the chainsaw had him rethinking his position. Except before he could make a run for it, two things caught his attention: One, his assailant was no bigger than a Munchkin, and two, there was no blade on the chainsaw. Still, the metal arm hurt like hell when it came down on his shoulder. And pain wiped out all logical thought.

"Why you little shit!" Billy dodged the next swing, then brought his arm down and knocked the chainsaw out of the kid's hands. The kid turned and tried to make a run for it, but Billy easily grabbed the neck of his Batman t-shirt and jerked him back.

"Let me go!" The kid fought like a little demon.

Billy tightened his grip as he reached out and pulled off the mask. The defiant redheaded imp that stared back at him caused Billy's temper to cool, although he refused to let the struggling kid go.

"You better let me go!" the boy yelled. "'Cause if you don't, you'll be sorry. My daddy is the sheriff of this town. And when he finds out you've been threatenin' me, he'll shoot you dead."

"Considering Sheriff Winslow doesn't carry a loaded gun, I'm not real scared," Billy stated. "Besides, who was threatening whom?"

The kid stopped struggling and glanced down at the gun in the waistband of Billy's jeans. "Then what are you doing with that?"

"I was planning on using it on a psycho killer who likes to scare women with his chainsaw. Seen any of them around?"

The kid's brown eyes didn't even flicker. "Nope, I sure ain't."

Billy chuckled before he released the kid. "So what's your name, son?"

"I ain't allowed to talk to strangers," he said sullenly.

Billy shrugged. "Then maybe I should get Sheriff Winslow out here, after all. I'm sure you'll have no problem explaining yourself to your daddy."

"Jesse," the kid said in his belligerent tone.

"Nice to meet you, Jesse." Billy stuck out a hand. "I'm your neighbor, Billy Wilkes. 'Course most folks call me Bubba."

The boy's eyes widened. "You're Bubba? You sure? Because the Bubba I heard about sounded a lot younger— and a lot more fun."

Billy scowled. "I'm not in my grave yet. And as for fun, I'm always in a better humor when I'm not being threatened." He glanced down at the chainsaw. "You do realize that doesn't have a chain, don't you, son?"

"Mia won't let me have one with a chain," he groused. "She thinks it's too dangerous."

"Is Mia your mama?"

"Nope, my sister." Jesse shot a quick glance behind him before he lowered his voice. "But she acts like my mama, always harpin' at me for one thing or another. Geez, a guy can't even catch a break."

It was hard to stay mad at such a sassy kid, and Billy found himself smiling. "So I guess you live around here?"

"A couple over. You gonna be livin' next door for good?"

"No." The word came out a little too fast, and Billy backpedaled. "I'm just here for a little fishin' and huntin', is all." He looked back at the Chevy and the child who still watched him through the cracked window. "You know that kid?"

"That's my little brother, Brody. I'm babysitting him while my sister went into town."

Unless it directly affected him, Billy believed in staying out of other people's business. Still, he couldn't stand the thought of a kid getting hurt.

"Listen, you and your little brother need to find another

place to play. This yard has way too many dangerous—"
His words were cut off by a deep, familiar rumbling, and
both he and Jesse looked out at the road as a huge monster
truck drove past.

"You better get on home, Jesse," Billy said as he
turned and headed for the hedge. He had barely gotten
through when the beast of a truck turned into his lot, its
huge deep-treaded tires flattening the waist-high weeds
as the mud-splattered chrome grill stopped within inches
of him. The diesel engine cut off, and the door swung
open.

"You plannin' on shootin' me for keepin' your truck
for so long?" Slate Calhoun said as he hopped down from
the truck.

Billy cocked a hip and rested his hand on the revolver.
"Only if you brought her back empty. Of course, even
then, you'll have to wait here while I run into the house
for bullets." He walked over and grabbed Slate's hand in
a firm shake. "Good to see you, man."

"Same here." Slate thumped him twice on the shoulder.
"I thought you'd run off and forgotten about Bramble."

"Nope, just been too busy for recreational sports. So
what's this I hear about you gettin' hitched?"

Slate's smile spread from ear to ear. "Married with
child."

"No kiddin'?" He shook his head. "Sounds like you've
been busier than a four-legged bee."

"A little." Slate leaned up against the truck and crossed
his arms. "So I take it the farm equipment business is
going well."

"Good enough." Billy looked away from Slate and
stared out at the road. "I heard about Dalton Oil."

"Yeah, it sure came as a surprise. Not just the company doing so poorly, but Lyle dying of a heart attack. He was a good man."

"So I hear."

"But things are looking up," Slate continued. "C-Corp hasn't laid anyone else off. And we have some other businesses thinking about making a home here in Bramble."

Billy's gazed snapped back over to Slate. "Really? Anyone I know?"

"Colt Lomax for one—Shirlene Dalton's brother."

"Is that so?" Billy shook his head. "Well, I guess I need to catch up on all the town gossip."

"I'll have to fill you in another time, buddy," Slate said as a Yukon pulled in behind the monster truck. "Right now, I've got early mornin' weight-training with the team." He placed a hand on Billy's neck and herded him toward the SUV. "But come meet the family."

Billy barely had time to flip the gun in the bed of the truck before he was being introduced to a pretty brunette with big blue eyes.

"This is my wife, Faith," Slate said. "Faith, darlin', this here is Billy Wilkes," he paused as if waiting for a drum roll before he finished, "Bubba."

If possible those blue eyes got even bigger as her lips formed a perfect O.

Grinning, Billy stuck his hand in the open window. "I'm sure pleased to meet you, ma'am."

Her mouth snapped closed as her soft hand slipped into his. "And it's a pleasure to meet you...Bubba. Or would you rather I call you Billy?"

The prim and proper manners coupled with the eastern accent took him by surprise, but he recovered quickly and gave her hand a gentle squeeze. "A pretty lady like yourself can call me anything she wants."

"Be careful, Bubba," Slate cut in. "This one's taken."

Billy winked at Faith. "Only because I didn't get back sooner." He tipped his head at the car seat in the back. "And I suppose that's little Slate Junior."

"More like Faith Junior." Slate walked over to the back window and poked his head in. And Billy couldn't help but squint his eyes at the cooing and babbling idiot the head coach of Bramble High's football team had turned into.

"Why, hello, daddy's little dumplin'. Did my Daisy have a good ride with her mama? Yes, you did, didn't you?" His head popped back out. "Take a look, Bubba, isn't she the cutest thing you've ever seen?"

Realizing there was no way to get out of it, Billy walked over and leaned down to take a look at the tiny little body completely engulfed by the car seat's shoulder harness. Big blue eyes stared back at him from beneath a crop of silky brown hair. Unwilling to babble like her father, Billy kept it simple.

"Hey, there."

The baby studied him so intently that Billy had trouble holding her gaze. Then as if she didn't like what she saw, she scrunched up that chubby face and let out an ear-splitting scream. Billy couldn't get away from the Yukon fast enough.

"I told you she was a genius, Faith," Slate said, while flashing a teasing grin at Billy. "At a little over a month, my daughter has already developed good taste."

"Slate," Faith chastised as she reached around to soothe the child.

"It's the truth, darlin'. And once you've been around the man for awhile, you'll understand what I'm talking about." He headed to the passenger side. "Stop by the stadium later on, Bubba. That's if an East Texan can stand to see what a real football team looks like."

Billy snorted. "I heard about that state championship trophy, but I didn't realize they handed those out for flag football."

"Flag, my—" Slate glanced at the backseat, "butt." Still grinning, he climbed into the SUV.

"It was nice meeting you, Billy," Faith said. "We'd love to have you over for dinner sometime."

Slate leaned across her. "She's only saying that because she's never seen you eat."

"It can't be any worse than you with a plate of ribs, Calhoun," Billy shot back before he returned his gaze to Faith. "I'd love to come for supper, Ms. Calhoun. You just say the word."

"Friday?"

The quick reply took Billy by surprise. And before he could think up a good excuse, Slate jumped in. "We'll see you on Friday then."

"Damn," Billy muttered under his breath as he watched Faith carefully back out. When she reached the road, she waited for the non-existent traffic for what seemed like a good five minutes before pulling out. But instead of telling her to get a move on like Billy would've done, Slate just sat there grinning like a fool. Obviously, the man had fallen hard. Billy was happy for him. Slate was good people.

When the Yukon was finally gone, Billy turned back to the trailer. The truck caught his attention, and he couldn't help but smile. From the floodlights to the American and Texan flags that hung from poles on either side of the back window, the monster truck screamed redneck like a flashing neon sign. The weathered stickers plastered on the huge back bumper didn't hurt: DON'T MESS WITH TEXAS; REBEL BORN AND REBEL BRED AND WHEN I DIE I'LL BE REBEL DEAD; I LIVE BY THE THREE B'S: BEER, BRAWLS, AND BROADS; CRUDE RUNS THROUGH MY VEINS.

And Billy's favorite: IF YOU THINK MY TRUCK IS BIG…

It was male Texan philosophy at its finest. And Billy ate it up like a slice of apple pie à la mode.

"Hey."

Billy glanced away from the truck and over to the redheaded kid who had just slipped through the hedge. And Jesse wasn't alone. He held the hand of his little brother. Although Billy figured he'd misunderstood Jesse when he noticed the naked doll clutched in the child's fist.

"Sorry, kid." Billy headed for the door. "I don't have time to chat."

But Jesse was a quick little pain in the butt, and before Billy could reach the steps, he had dropped his sibling's hand and raced over.

"So you ain't gonna call the sheriff on me about the chainsaw?" he asked, his face wary. "Not even for chasin' Ms. Dalton?"

Billy looked down at the kid with his mussed hair and dirty, freckled face and didn't hesitate a second before answering.

"Nope." He reached in his pocket, pulled out a ten dollar bill, and handed it to Jesse. "In fact, keep up the good work."

Chapter Four

THERE WAS SOMETHING NICE about growing up in a small town. Something nice about driving down the one main street and being greeted and waved at by the people you'd known since you were in droopy diapers. But the flipside of that coin was that sometimes people knew you too well.

"Either I'm gettin' senile, or I need to go get my eyes checked," Moses Tate said as Shirlene hopped down from the Navigator. "Because I sure ain't never seen Shirlene Dalton in town before noon."

Since Moses had to be close to a hundred and never remembered to wear his hearing aids, Shirlene yelled back as loudly as she could. "No need to waste your time at the doc's, Mr. Tate. It's me in the flesh." She shot him a wink as she walked around to the passenger door to let Sherman out. "Pig-sittin' is keepin' me from gettin' my beauty rest," she fibbed. "But I guess a pig's got to eat when a pig's got to eat." As if to confirm her words, as soon as Sherman hopped to the ground, he trotted over to the gutter and started sniffing around a candy wrapper.

Moses slowly pushed himself up from the bench in

front of Sutter's Pharmacy and shuffled out to the curb. "I guess Colt and Hope got off okay."

"Dropped them and little Daffodil off at the airport in Lubbock yesterday," Shirlene yelled. She pulled the leash out of the truck and walked over to snap it on Sherman's collar. Cattle, sheep, cats, and dogs were allowed to roam free on the streets of Bramble, but pigs had to be on a leash. Which seemed like the worst sort of discrimination to Shirlene.

"How long they gone for?" Moses asked. Without teeth or dentures, his mouth resembled a puckered peach left out in the sun too long.

"At least a week or two. Colt's got a lot to do if he wants to get his motorcycle shop moved here by winter."

Moses nodded. "Always knew that boy would turn out all right. A person don't watch out for their mama and sister like he did and not have a good heart. 'Course you can't tell the people of this town anything. They still think Colt spent time in prison." He shook his head. "Durn fools."

Moses was right. The folks of Bramble might have their noses in everyone's business, but rarely did they get their facts straight. Something Shirlene had given up trying to change a long time ago.

"See you, Mr. Tate." She tugged the disgruntled pig away from the wrapper. But she only made it halfway down the block before Kenny Gene's girlfriend Twyla came trotting across the street, her over-processed hair teased higher than a Jersey girl's.

"Hey, Shirl. Missed you at the Founder's Day decoratin' meetin'."

Shirlene shot her a big smile. "Well, I'm sure you got things figured out just fine without me, honey."

"We shore did. Darla's takin' care of all the decoratin' and Josephine the food." Her gaze wandered over Shirlene's hair. "I'm havin' a special on cuts and dyes this week."

Since the woman could destroy hair better than nuclear fallout, Shirlene kept her mouth shut and continued to smile. The smile drooped when Twyla continued.

"Did you hear the good news? Bubba's back in town. I guess he just strutted right into Bootlegger's last night as if he'd never been gone." Her face turned all dreamy. "Wish I'd been there. Cindy Lynn said he was flirtin' and dancin' with all the girls like there was no tomorrow."

Fortunately, about then, Sherman spotted a paper cup blowing in the wind and took off after it. Glad for the excuse, Shirlene let him tug her down the street, waving a hand behind her. "Take care now, Twyla."

Like most of the other buildings on Main Street, the bank stood two stories high and was made out of red brick. It sat on the corner of Walnut and Main, its large maple doors facing out at an angle. Thanks to her industrious friend Hope, who had organized a painting party in early April, the wood trim was freshly painted a bright Bramble High purple. Shirlene had to admit that it looked real nice. Of course, she'd always loved purple. What she didn't love was the fact that the bank doors were locked.

"What in the world is goin' on in this town?" she grumbled under her breath as she tried the other door.

It was locked as well, which just didn't make any sense. Shirlene knew it was early, but the bank manager, Luther Briggs, was always at his desk by seven. And even if he was late, The Bank of Bramble didn't keep their front doors locked—that was what the huge gray vault was for. Of course, there had been that one time when the bank teller, Ruby Lee, had an affair with that Coca-Cola distributor. When her husband found out, he'd come to the bank with his shotgun and filled the Coke machine with buckshot, forcing Luther and two other employees to drag him out and lock the doors.

But since Hank had long since forgiven Ruby her infidelity, Shirlene figured the locked doors were a mistake so she lifted her fist and knocked. After only a few minutes, the door was thrown open. Except it wasn't Luther that greeted her, but a short skinny stranger with eyes beadier than Sherman's and a skinny, black mustache above a thin, sweaty lip.

"I'm sorry," he stated in an uppity voice with not an ounce of Texas charm, "but the bank doesn't open for another two hours." He pointed a finger at the schedule posted on the window, a schedule that hadn't been there when Lyle was alive.

Confused, Shirlene stared at it for a few seconds, just long enough for the man to start to close the door.

"Now wait just a minute." She pushed it back open, which wasn't difficult with such a scrawny man holding it. "I realize I'm here a little bright and early, but I need to speak to Luther."

His thin eyebrows arched. "Are you referring to Mr. Briggs?"

"That would be the one." Shirlene slipped inside, Sherman close on her heels.

"Have you lost your mind?" The little man stared down at Sherman, who started licking the solid wood floor like it was coated in honey. "You can't bring that filthy animal in here."

Now Shirlene had always believed in being cordial, especially to a stranger who didn't have a clue who she was. But she couldn't let the slight go, not when Sherman was extremely sensitive. Still, the best set-downs were done with a smile, and she flashed him one of her better ones.

"What's your name, honey?"

"Mr. Reginald Peabody the third," he sputtered with indignation. "But it doesn't matter what my name is, young lady. You can't just bust into a bank that is not open for business—especially with a...pig!"

Shirlene's eyes narrowed. "Well, Mr. Peabody, I think that's exactly what I did. And Sherman's not just a pig. He's our new town mascot." She flapped her hand as the man started to speak. "Yes, I know that we're the Bramble High Bulldogs. But since Emmett died a few months back at the ripe old age of fifteen, Sherman here is filling in until we get us a new bulldog. And let me tell you, that little purple sweater with the 'B' on it looks breathtaking against all that pink skin."

"B but," the man stammered.

"No ifs, ands, or buts about it, Reggie. School pride is school pride. But if it will make you feel any better, Sherman and I don't plan on staying very long."

"Just because he has a name," Mr. Peabody groused, "doesn't mean he can be in my bank."

Shirlene's eyebrows popped up. "*Your* bank?"

"Well, not mine exactly." His pointy chin came up. "But I'm the new bank manager. So therefore, I'm the man in charge."

Shirlene knew that the bank had been sold—just another one of Lyle's assets that had been auctioned off to the highest bidder after his death. She just hadn't considered the fact that Luther Briggs would no longer be working there. But now that she thought about it, it made sense. Luther would never have repossessed her house without talking to her first.

"And if you don't take that animal out of here this instant," Mr. Peabody continued, "I'm reporting you to the authorities."

It was a lame threat considering Sheriff Winslow had absolutely no authority over anyone—not even his wife. But regardless, Shirlene didn't want the sheriff knowing about her situation so she tried to smooth things over.

"Now there's no need to call Sam. If you'll just give me the keys to those new locks you've put on my door, I'll be out of here in a jiffy."

The man looked confused for only a second. "Ms. Dalton?" he asked.

"That would be me." She held out a hand. "Keys?"

"I'm afraid I can't do that."

Her smile slipped. The little man had really started to try her patience. "And exactly why is that?"

"I gave you plenty of warning, Ms. Dalton. And a banking institution will never survive if they don't collect the money owed them. You had an obligation to make your loan payments, and you defaulted. Therefore, your house reverts back to the bank."

"Reverts back to the bank?" Shirlene's eyes narrowed as she took two steps closer. "Are you trying to tell me that you own my house?"

The man stepped back and nervously straightened his tie. "If we don't receive payment in thirty days, that's exactly what I'm telling you."

"But how can that be, when my house is paid for? The payments I missed were for one of Lyle's loans he took out to help folks with their severance pay after the layoffs at Dalton Oil."

Reginald nodded his balding head. "Exactly. And your house was what he used as collateral for that loan."

Whoever said *the truth hurts* had hit it right on the money. Shirlene was devastated. Still, she wasn't about to let this little pipsqueak know that.

"Well, of course, that makes sense. I assume you take credit." She opened her purse and searched for her wallet. Most of her credit cards had reached their limit, but there were one or two that might work. Except her wallet wasn't there. Not under her sunglass case, or her makeup bag, or her half-eaten Snickers bar. It wasn't anywhere.

"Why that dirty little chainsaw-wielding midget," she hissed under her breath.

"Excuse me?" Mr. Peabody's beady eyes widened.

Shirlene tried her best to smile, but it was getting harder and harder to do. "Nothin'. I was just talkin' to Sherman." She pulled out her checkbook. "On second thought, why don't I just write you a check from my bank in Austin?" She quickly signed and dated a check before she tore it out. "I'll just let you fill in the blanks."

The man glanced back at the bank schedule on the window, and finally conceded that she and her pig weren't going anywhere. Taking the check, he nodded at a chair. "If you'll just have a seat, I'll be right back."

Once Reginald disappeared into the back, Shirlene flopped down in the chair and covered her eyes with her hand. The check was only a Band-aid. With very little money in her account, she was just robbing Peter to pay

Paul. Sooner or later, it would catch up with her. She just hoped it was later. All she needed was a couple weeks to come up with another plan. She would have to sell the house, something Colt had wanted her to do since Lyle's death. And he was right; the sprawling estate was way too big for just one person.

The upkeep on such a big place was more than she could continue to pay. Just that morning, she'd had to call her cook, housekeeper, and gardener and make up a far-fetched story about a rat infestation to explain why they shouldn't show up to work.

Of course, it wasn't really that farfetched. Only a rat would force a woman out of her home.

The bell over the door jangled. Shirlene turned just as a tall cowboy stepped in, the kind of cowboy that made a woman take another look—even a tired widow with a bad credit score. The man was as fine a cut of prime as Shirlene had ever seen. A lean muscled body was covered in starched cotton and worn jeans, and topped off with a sexy black Stetson pulled low on his forehead. He held a cell phone to his ear as he headed toward the back offices, moving with the type of confidence that left little doubt that this was a man used to being in charge.

"I've checked out every cemetery within a hundred miles and have come up empty-handed. And even if I do find it, I think you and Brant are grasping at straws. Do you really think it will end the curse—"

Sherman snorted, causing the man to cut off in mid-sentence and turn to Shirlene. Even though the hat shaded his eyes from the morning sun shining in the windows, Shirlene had little doubt they gave her a thorough once-over. Suddenly she wished she'd taken more time to touch up her makeup and fix her hair after her harrowing night in the trailer. Still, she wasn't one to waste time on regrets.

She eased into a smile. "I think it's only fair to warn you that cursin' is frowned upon in this town."

It only took a second for the phone to be hung up and the Stetson to be whisked off; exposing a face that was as fine as the body it was attached to—even if it was a little pale. But it wasn't the man's strong features that caught her attention as much as the silver hair that reflected the sun coming in through the windows like a shiny new dime. Premature was putting it mildly, considering the man looked much younger than herself. Still, the hair color fit him and made those pretty blue eyes stand out like Shirlene's sapphire earrings. All in all, he was one sizzling stick of Texas testosterone.

Too bad her sex drive had died with Lyle.

"Good mornin'." He flashed a smile that rivaled Slate Calhoun's. "And I thought we grew 'em pretty in Houston."

"Why, thank you, honey. Nothing like a little sweet talk to get the day started out right." Shirlene rose from the chair, taking great pleasure in the way his eyes widened when she reached her full height—and with the Manolos a smidge more.

"Lord have mercy," he breathed.

Her libido might be on the fritz, but her ego wasn't. Shirlene couldn't help but enjoy the appreciative gleam that sparked in his eyes. She held out the hand that wasn't attached to a pig.

"Shirlene Dalton."

Surprised flashed, but he recovered quickly. Taking her hand, he bent over it and placed a chaste kiss on the back.

"A pleasure, Ms. Dalton." He lifted his head and

grinned back at her. "I was christened Beauregard, but I'd sure be obliged if you called me Beau."

Shirlene laughed. "Beau it is. So what brings you to Bramble, Beau?"

"Vacation."

She arched an eyebrow. "You always spend your vacations in graveyards of podunk towns?"

A hint of a blush stained his cheeks. "My family's into genealogy."

"My husband, Lyle Dalton, was into oil," she said, pronouncing the word like any true Texan—"awl."

His gaze dropped, and he smoothed out the brim of his hat. "I was sure sorry to hear about his death, ma'am." A strained silence followed before he finally spoke. "I hate to cast aspersions on your pet, but is that a pig?"

She glanced down at the pig, which had given up on finding anything to eat and was now scratching his ears against the leg of a chair. "Sherman."

Beau didn't hesitate to kneel down and help the pig out by giving him a good scratch behind his floppy ears, which earned him Sherman's immediate devotion and Shirlene's immediate like. Too bad old Reggie came out and rained on her happy parade.

"Ms. Dalton, I'm afraid your account in Austin had insufficient funds—" His beady eyes shot down to Beau. "Oh, good morning, sir, I didn't realize you were here." He straightened the lapels of his ill-fitting gray suit. "Let me just show Ms. Dalton out, and I'll be right with you."

Beau stood back up. "No hurry." He nodded at the row of chairs. "I'll just make myself comfortable while you help this pretty lady."

"Of course, sir." But when Mr. Peabody turned back

to her, he didn't look all that pleased to be helping her. And if the truth was known, Shirlene wasn't that pleased to have her dirty laundry aired in front of a handsome stranger. Even if that stranger had sat down and appeared to be preoccupied with his cell phone.

"Insufficient funds? I'm sure there's been some kind of mistake." Shirlene accepted the check with as much dignity as she could muster. "Just how much do I owe in back payments?" When he told her the amount, she thought she might pass out. "You've got to be kiddin'."

Mr. Peabody shook his head. "With penalties and interest, that's exactly the amount."

"Then I guess I'll need to speak to your boss, Reggie." She tried to flash another smile, but it fizzled when Mr. Peabody spoke.

"I'm afraid that won't be possible, Ms. Dalton. Mr. Cates is on vacation."

"Mr. Cates? As in one of the owners of C-Corp?"

"That would be the one." The man smiled smugly.

Shirlene knew the Cates brothers had bought Dalton Oil. She just hadn't realized they had bought the bank as well. "I'm sure Mr. Cates wouldn't mind speaking with the wife of Lyle Dalton—vacation or no vacation."

Mr. Peabody shook his head. "He left express instructions not to be bothered until next week."

"So that's it?" She hit a high note that had Beau glancing over. She lowered her voice, but her temper still sizzled. "You're just going to throw a poor widow woman out on the streets?"

Mr. Peabody's beady eyes wandered down to the three-carat diamond on her finger. "I'm sure you won't be out on the streets, Ms. Dalton."

That violent feeling reared its ugly head again, and she really wanted to shove the diamond straight up the snooty little bugger's nose. But instead she reached out and patted him on the bald head. "Hang on to that title, honey, because I'll be back." Lifting a hand, she waved at Beau. "Nice meetin' you." Then with a tug on the leash, she swept out the door.

The sun had inched higher in the sky. Heat already rose from the sidewalk in suffocating waves. At least it felt suffocating to Shirlene as she strode back to her Navigator. All it would take was one telephone call to her brother, and she would be back in her house by sundown—one quick call and she'd be sitting on her opulent white couch with a margarita in one hand and a remote in the other.

Except no matter how wonderful the image was, she couldn't bring herself to grab her cell phone. Partly because she never liked to eat crow, and partly because she hated disappointing Colt. In the last few months, she'd done her best to convince him that his wild, impulsive sister had grown into a strong, independent woman who could handle her own finances—and the death of a husband. Too bad it was all a lie. A lie she wasn't ready to own up to. At least, not yet.

"Ms. Dalton!"

The sexy drawl stopped her in her tracks, and she turned to see Beau hurrying toward her, his long-legged strut eating up the sidewalk.

When he reached her, she cocked her head. "Did I forget something?"

"Yes," his smile almost blinded her, "my invitation to dinner." She opened her mouth to decline the offer. But before she could, he held up a hand. "Now it wouldn't be like a date—more like a charitable woman helping out a stranger that doesn't know a soul in town."

She laughed. "A charitable woman? Honey, you don't know me at all."

The smile faded. "I'd like to change that."

She had to give it to Beau, he was charming. Still, she didn't have time for cute young cowboys. Except before she could decline, her stomach growled.

Beau's eyebrows shot up, along with his smile. "Should we make that breakfast, Ms. Dalton?" He glanced over at Josephine's Diner, where it looked like the entire town was standing in the windows, watching them.

Shirlene waved at the townsfolk, realizing she wouldn't make it back to her Navigator without half of them stopping her. And she wasn't in the mood to dodge all their questions.

She turned to Beau. "There's this little truck stop right outside of town that serves up a mean flat-iron steak and eggs."

Beau winked. "Now how did you know I was the steak-and-eggs kind of guy?"

"Possibly because I'm a steak-and-eggs kind of woman."

He tipped back his head and laughed before he held out an arm. "Ms. Dalton, I think you and I are going to get along just fine."

Shirlene slipped her arm through his. "I think you might be right, Beau."

They were still smiling at one another when a loud rumbling broke their eye contact. Having heard the noise before, Shirlene wasn't even fazed by the large monster truck that rolled into view. Its big, black, deep-treaded tires ate up the asphalt as the flags fluttered out behind the cab. The mud-splattered chrome grill grew closer, and the truck slowed down, giving them both an unobstructed view of the man who slouched in the driver's seat.

The stupid-looking redneck in a camouflage John Deere hat sat behind the wheel. A hat with a brim so curled it almost came full circle. As he passed, he lifted the bare arm that stuck out of the ripped-off sleeve of his shirt in a greeting Shirlene completely ignored.

"A friend of yours?" Beau asked.

Shirlene watched the truck with its offensive bumper stickers rumble into the parking lot of Josephine's Diner.

"Not even close, honey. Not even close."

Chapter Five

BILLY WASN'T IN THE BEST OF MOODS when he walked through the door of the bright pink train caboose that served as Josephine's Diner. He needed a cup of coffee badly, something it didn't look like he was going to get any time soon. Not with the waitress, and every person in the diner, crammed up against the glass of the front windows. With their attention focused elsewhere, he took the time to observe the group of townsfolk. He couldn't remember all their names but there were a few he couldn't forget.

Like Harley Sutter, the town mayor, with his handlebar mustache and huge belly that sagged over his belt buckle. Sheriff Sam Winslow in his stiff, khaki uniform shirt with the shiny star and so many law enforcement gadgets attached to his black belt that it turned his jeans to hip-huggers. Rachel Dean, a big-boned waitress with hands that could easily palm a basketball and a flirty tongue that could make a man feel ten feet tall. Twyla, who ran the local beauty shop and dated Kenny Gene—the skinny black cowboy who rarely stopped talking long enough to take a breath and who had become Billy's main source for information since arriving in Bramble.

Kenny glanced over and noticed Billy first. A wide smile creased his face.

"Hey, Bubba!"

Everyone turned and the room erupted in warm greetings, although no one seemed to be in a hurry to leave the window.

"I thought you'd still be busy with that gal you picked up at Bootlegger's last night," Kenny said, but before Billy could even open his mouth to answer, Twyla chimed in.

"Bootlegger's! You went to Bootlegger's last night? I thought you went straight home, Kenny Gene Guthrie."

"I did go home, sugar," Kenny defended himself. "It was this mornin' that I saw Bubba. Sonofagun already got himself a woman. A big ol' blond gal from the looks—"

"Would you two shut up?" Cindy Lynn glared at Kenny Gene with eyes that were coated with more makeup than a television evangelist's wife. "I'm tryin' to concentrate on what Shirlene is doin' with the new stranger in town."

Billy glanced out the window and his brow knotted.

"Well, it ain't that hard to figure out." Rachel Dean wiped her big man-hands on the soiled apron tied around her waist. "It looks like Shirlene has decided to come out of mournin'. And who better to do it with than a handsome cowboy?"

Sheriff Winslow spoke up. "Shirlene shore does go for the older men. Look at the gray hair on that one."

"Age is a matter of mind," Rachel stated. "If you don't mind, it don't matter."

"Well, I don't think we should be worried about the man's age as much as his moral integrity," Harley Sutter said. "We can't just have some stranger wander into town and take off with our womenfolk."

"He ain't no stranger," Kenny Gene said. "I just got finished talkin' to him in front of the pharmacy and he told me his name was Beauregard Williams from Houston."

"Did he tell you what he's doin' here?" Harley asked.

"Nope, but he shore is interested in the town. Must've asked a hun-nerd questions."

Rachel turned to Harley with a worried look. "You don't think C-Corp brought him in to lay more people off, do you?"

"I sure hope not. We're already strugglin' to find jobs for the people who got laid off before Lyle sold the company."

"Isn't Colt's business gonna help with that?" Twyla asked.

Before Harley could answer, Billy took the opportunity given him. "Slate was tellin' me somethin' about that. Some feller named Colt Lomax is startin' up a company?"

"Shore is," Sheriff Winslow said. "Buildin's goin' up right next to Jones's Garage."

"No kiddin'." Billy tipped his head. "And just what kind of business is it?"

The townsfolk glanced at each other with confused looks until Kenny's best friend, Rye Pickett, spoke up.

"I think it has somethin' to do with choppers."

"Like them choppers on QVC that dice onions without tears?" Rachel Dean asked. "Because I bought one of those things once, and it don't work a'tall—I still bawl my eyes out."

"Not those kind of choppers, woman," Rossie Owens, the owner of Bootlegger's Bar, enlightened Rachel.

"We're talkin' the kind of motorcycles with the long forks and big handlebars—Desperado Customs is what Colt calls it."

The name took Billy by surprise. Anyone with any interest in motorcycles knew of Desperado Customs. It wasn't a fly-by-night operation. Desperado made custom bikes for the rich and famous. A business like that would employ a number of people.

He shook his head. "C-Corp. A new motorcycle shop. Pretty soon Bramble will be as big as Houston, and I'll have to find another small town to do my huntin' and fishin' in."

A concerned look entered the eyes of the townspeople before the mayor spoke up. "Now I wouldn't go that far, Bubba. A few new businesses won't turn us into a big city."

"A few?"

Harley nodded. "Colt and Hope think we need a few more if we want to have enough jobs to support our town. 'Course they haven't had much time to pursue other companies, what with little Daffodil's birth and all."

"Cutest thing you've ever seen," Twyla gushed.

Rachel shot her a shocked look. "Cuter than our little Daisy? Why, shame on you, Twyla. You know full well that Faith and Slate's baby is just as cute as Colt and Hope's. In fact, they look as identical as Faith and Hope do."

While Twyla looked duly chastised, Billy tried to steer the conversation back to the subject he was most interested in.

Pulling his hat off, he scratched his head. "I guess I'm just a dumb ol' country boy, but I don't quite understand why y'all need other businesses when C-Corp took over Dalton Oil?"

Harley grinned at Billy as if it *was* the stupidest question he'd ever heard. "Because Colt and Hope don't think we should have all our eggs in one basket—or depend on oil to keep Bramble afloat."

Billy snorted. "Not depend on oil?" He held up a hand. "Now, I don't mean to be puttin' my nose into other people's business, but isn't askin' Texans not to depend on oil a little like askin' a kite not to depend on the wind?" He shrugged. "I mean, isn't crude what Texas was built on?"

A multitude of eyes squinted in thought until finally Harley spoke up.

"Bubba's right. Why are we lookin' elsewhere when we've got plenty of oil right in our own backyard?"

Rachel Dean nodded. "Oil has sure done right by us."

"Shore has," the sheriff agreed.

"Well, there she goes," Kenny said, drawing everyone's gaze back to the window as the rental SUV drove past with Shirlene and the pig sitting in the passenger's seat.

"You want me to do a background check, mayor?" Sheriff Winslow asked. "The man could have a record."

"No foolin'," Kenny Gene said. "If I'da known that, I'da asked for his autograph. 'Course, they ain't called records no more, Sam. They're called CDs."

The sheriff looked completely exasperated. "Damn, son, if you want the position as my on-call deputy, you're gonna have to use that brain God gave you. I'm not talkin' about a music record. I'm talkin' about a criminal record—a legal document that lists every offense a person has." He looked over at the mayor. "Or I could bring him in for questioning?"

Harley shook his head. "No, let's wait and see what the man's up to first. But we'll need to keep a close eye on him, especially if he's set his sights on Shirlene."

"I won't have a problem durin' the day," Sam said. "But Myra expects me home by six for dinner."

"I can take the late shift, sheriff," Kenny jumped in.

After a full minute of indecision, Harley slapped Kenny on the back. "Give it your best, son. Remember, you're protectin' our little Shirlene." He hitched up his pants. "Welp, I better get back to work if we want a Founder's Day to remember."

There was a grumbling of agreement as the townsfolk moved toward the door.

Once the diner cleared out, Billy flipped over his coffee cup and waited for Rachel to fill it. It didn't take her long. The woman was a whirlwind of efficiency.

"Well, stranger or not, I'm shore happy to see that little gal gettin' back in the saddle," Rachel said as she filled Billy's cup to the brim. "She was shore tore up after Lyle's death."

Tore up? Obviously, Shirlene Dalton had fooled the entire town with her big Texas smiles and pretty green eyes. But she didn't fool Billy. From the first moment he'd been introduced to her, he'd had her pegged. No woman who looked like that would be married to a man almost twice her age unless she wanted to get her hands on his money.

Billy added some cream to his coffee before taking a sip. "Funny thing," he said as nonchalantly as possible. "I thought I saw Shirlene this mornin' out on Grover Road."

Rachel laughed. "That's doubtful, sugar, seein' as how she hasn't lived out there for over ten years."

"She grew up out there?"

"Born and raised." Rachel grinned. "But she shore moved up in the world. She married Lyle just a couple years after high school and has been livin' the high life ever since."

"Really?" Billy set down his cup. "So I guess Dalton Oil's problems haven't affected her lifestyle."

A confused look settled over Rachel's face just as Moses Tate, who sat two barstools over, spoke up.

"You fishin' today, boy?"

Billy tried to steer clear of Moses. While the rest of the town saw only what they wanted to see, Moses' aging eyes missed very little. Even now they were pinned on Billy with an intensity that had him fidgeting.

"Yes, sir."

Moses spit a stream of tobacco in the plastic cup he always carried in his front shirt pocket. After he wiped off his mouth, his eyes narrowed on Billy. "For fish?"

The laugh Billy forced from his mouth sounded as fake as it was. "What else would I be fishin' for, Mr. Tate?"

After a breakfast of light, fluffy biscuits and thick, rich country gravy, Billy was ready for a nap. Between Bootlegger's and the surprise visit from Shirlene Dalton, he hadn't gotten more than a couple hours' worth of sleep. Still, the thought of heading back to a hot trailer and a lumpy mattress didn't appeal to him. Instead, he headed over to the town library, a pretty, single-story brick building that sat right next to the park.

He pulled open the glass door to a blast of refrigerated air that was a welcome relief from the scorching July heat.

Inside, the library was like all libraries, rows of books surrounded by hushed silence—a silence suddenly broken by the tap of fingers on computer keys.

Pulling off his cap, Billy followed the sound to the checkout counter in the center of the library. Behind the desk sat the librarian, Ms. Murphy, her attention intent on the monitor before her.

After he'd first met Ms. Murphy, Billy had relegated her in his mind to the position of the town's old maid. But studying her features behind the wire-framed glasses, he realized he'd made a mistake. Despite her calf-length skirts and buttoned-up blouses, Ms. Murphy looked no older than he was.

"Howdy, Ms. Murphy," Billy said as he leaned across the desk.

And even though his words were whispered, the woman almost shot out of her conservative black heels. Her butt did leave the chair. Unfortunately, when it came back down the caster-wheeled chair was no longer there, and she sat down hard on the floor. Since there didn't appear to be an opening in the counter, Billy vaulted over it and crouched down next to her.

"You all right, ma'am?" He tried to take her hand and help her up, but she jerked away.

"I'm fine, Mr. Wilkes," she said in a tone that had more than likely reprimanded an entire town's worth of overly loud library patrons at one time or another. But Billy had never been one to pay much attention to authority. As she started to get to her feet, he reached out and took her elbow and helped her back into the chair.

"Thank you," she said with just a slight quiver in her voice, although Billy wasn't so sure if it was the fall or his touch that had her nerves scrambled. She appeared visibly relieved when he released her.

"I assume you're not thanking me for scaring the daylights out of you," Billy teased.

She glanced up and took note of his grin. A blush heated her cheeks before she smiled back. It was a nice smile, and unlike a certain blonde he'd run into that morning, this smile was genuine. "No, I'm thanking you for helping me off the floor after I made a fool of myself."

"And here I thought I was the fool for sneaking up on a pretty lady when she's busy." Her blush got as red as the apple on her desk. Not wanting to embarrass her any further, he changed the subject. "What had your deep concentration anyway, Ms. Murphy?"

Before he could turn around and look at the computer screen, she dove for the mouse and clicked the window closed. "Just research," she blurted out.

His grin deepened. "Research, huh?"

"You know how we librarians are," she cleared her throat, "always walking around with our nose in a book."

Billy's eyes narrowed, but he decided to let it go. What Ms. Murphy did in her little fortress was her own business. He was here on his.

"Speakin' of books," he shot a glance around at the shelves, "I was wonderin' if you could help me out with some readin' material while I'm here in Bramble."

Ms. Murphy got to her feet and smoothed out her beige skirt, one that looked more appropriate for winter than the heat of midsummer. "What types of genres do you prefer, Mr. Wilkes? Mysteries? Westerns? Bestsellers?"

"Actually, I was thinkin' more of history, ma'am."

Her big brown eyes widened only fractionally. "Of

course." She opened a hinged section of the counter. "If you'll just follow me, I'll be happy to show you where we keep all our history books."

On their way through the book-stuffed shelves, Billy took note of the gentle sway of Ms. Murphy's hips. They weren't as skinny as he thought they would be, nor were they as curvy as Shirlene Dalton's. Of course, few women had a body like Ms. Dalton's. That woman was built like a brick shithouse. And it had taken every ounce of willpower he had not to succumb to the soft give of her butt beneath his fingers or the crush of her breasts against his bare chest. But he wasn't stupid enough to dip into that kind of trouble. He preferred his women low maintenance, unlike the flashy Ms. Dalton.

"Here we are," Ms. Murphy said. Billy was so caught up in his thoughts he almost ran smack dab into her.

She turned, and when she saw how close he was, she took a few steps back. "Is there anything you're particularly interested in—the old west? Alamo? Civil War?"

Billy glanced at the titles and tried to appear nonchalant.

"Actually, I'm interested in Bramble history—mostly, the late 1800s."

Chapter Six

SHIRLENE'S CHILDHOOD HOME didn't improve in full sunlight. In fact, the opposite was true. The sweltering sun only served to illuminate the pathetic state of the trailer and intensify the smell of the stinky garbage that surrounded it. Fortunately, Shirlene didn't plan on staying long. Just long enough to find her wallet.

After enjoying a hearty breakfast with a sizzling hot cowboy who understood just how to treat a lady, Shirlene had come to a couple realizations: One, extra weight or no extra weight, she still had it. And two, it was very unlikely that a chainsaw-wielding midget had taken off with her wallet, especially when he had left her checkbook, her expensive cell phone, and a wad of cash. Which meant her wallet had probably fallen out when she dropped her purse on the front steps.

All she had to do now was find it.

"Come on, Piglet," she tried to coax Sherman out of the SUV. "Bubba was probably right. It was just some neighbor trying out his new chainsaw."

But being that Sherman was smarter than the average

pig, he saw straight through the lie and, with a grunt, refused to budge from the seat.

"Some watch pig you are," she huffed. Still, she left the door open just in case the pig decided to come to her rescue if she screamed.

Shirlene's wallet wasn't under the front steps. Or anywhere in a ten-foot radius. She really didn't want to enter the trailer, but her credit cards were the only things keeping her from abject poverty. The locked door surprised her yet again, especially in its current condition. But she figured Bubba had locked it when he left as some kind of east Texas joke.

As she searched through her keys, an image of Wilkesville flashed through her mind—something that had happened frequently that morning. It annoyed the hell out of her. Why in the world would her mind be stuck on Bubba Wilkes when she had better things to think about? Like a pair of laughing sapphire eyes. And a lean torso covered in the smooth cotton of an expensive western shirt. And a sexy smile that spoke of naughty thoughts and steamy nights.

Beau might be young, but he was twice the man Bubba Wilkes would ever be. Unfortunately, it didn't seem to matter. Like a two-headed cow in a carnival freak show, the image of Bubba's naked body seemed to have burned itself on Shirlene's retinas.

Frustrated with her thoughts, she didn't waste any time unlocking the door. The sooner she found her wallet, the sooner she could drive to Midland and spend the next few days in an air-conditioned hotel room while she waited for the bank president to get back from his vacation. Her plan was to try and convince the man to let her live in her house until she could sell it. Then with the proceeds, she would pay off the loan and have enough left over to last her a while. Since it was a win-win for both her and the bank, she didn't see how the president could refuse her.

Unless he was as ornery as Mr. Peabody.

But her plans evaporated when she couldn't find her wallet inside the trailer either. Feeling slightly hysterical, she jerked out the sofa bed and was in the process of searching beneath the thin mattress when a thought struck her. Who had folded the sofa bed back up? She couldn't see Bubba doing it. Not unless he was some kind of closet neat freak. Of course, Lyle had been a little anal, so it was possible. It was also possible that Bubba had found her wallet. Although why he hadn't said anything when he drove past her earlier was beyond her. Still, he wouldn't be hard to track down, not when he lived at Josephine's Diner during the day.

Resigning herself to a few more hours in day-old clothes, she turned back to the door. Her gaze swept to the small kitchen and the old card table she and Colt had eaten all their meals on. Two paper plates sat on the scarred top, along with two cans of grape soda. On each plate were remnants of peanut butter and jelly sandwiches and Cheetos crumbs. A kid lunch if ever Shirlene saw one.

Suddenly everything made perfect sense. The locked door. The cold-fingered strangler. The chainsaw-wielding midget. Kids were using her trailer like a summer playhouse, no doubt having a ball with sleepovers and picnics, and scaring gullible women.

She smiled at the thought of how much fun she and Hope would've had in a vacant trailer. But the smile faded when her gaze drifted down to the floor. Lying on its side by the leg of one chair was a baby bottle. Not a play one, but one that dripped milk onto the faded linoleum. Swallowing hard, Shirlene picked up the clear plastic bottle with the bright pink butterflies and watched as the drop of milk on the end slipped down the nipple to the pink rim.

A wall of sadness swept over Shirlene, a sadness that had her fingers tightening around the bottle and her chest tightening around her heart. She wasn't surprised by her reaction. Baby things always made her sad. But for once she didn't try to hide it. There was no one there to notice her pain. No one there to realize how devastated Shirlene Dalton was over her childless state.

Of course, Lyle had known. Sweet, even-tempered Lyle who had put up with sex by the calendar, fertility doctors, and boxes upon boxes of over-the-counter pregnancy tests. He had put up with it all and never once complained. And Shirlene couldn't help but wonder if the pressure he'd felt to give her a child hadn't been partly to blame for his heart attack. Lyle had always worked so hard to give her everything she wanted.

But guilt was a useless emotion. Lyle was gone, and she had no baby to comfort her. It was sad, but she wasn't going to let it turn her into a bitter woman who couldn't enjoy her sweet niece and goddaughter. She was stronger than that.

Of course, she re-evaluated her strength when a lusty cry had her almost jumping out of her Manolos.

With her heart thumping, she turned to the closed bedroom door. Between a chainsaw-wielding midget and a screaming baby, she'd choose the midget every time. Unfortunately, it didn't look like she had much of a choice. The cries were so pathetic she couldn't help but answer them.

She opened the door to find a baby girl sitting in

the center of the sagging mattress, her chubby cheeks streaked with tears and her blond hair sweat-matted to her head. Shaken, it took a moment for Shirlene to react, but in that moment someone hit her in the back of the knees and knocked her down to the stained carpet.

"Mine," the same deep voice from the night before growled.

"Hold her, Brody! I'm comin'!" another male voice joined in. This one was higher and most definitely belonged to a kid, a kid who dove on Shirlene's back like a WWF wrestler. She reached back to push him off, but that was a mistake. The kid looped a rope around her wrist, and within seconds had her hands tied together. She kicked at him, but he lassoed each of her ankles. With a hard pull, her heels snapped up to meet her hands.

It was the most stretching Shirlene had done in years, and it hurt like hell.

"Time!" the kid yelled and jumped off her as if she was a rodeo steer and he an expert roper. A pair of beat-up cowboy boots appeared in her line of vision. A pair of cowboy boots she recognized immediately.

"Jesse!"

The boots jumped back out of view, but not before he'd picked up the baby bottle. The springs of the old mattress creaked, and the crying stopped immediately.

Jesse Foster had moved to Bramble about a year earlier with his mother and three siblings. The boy had befriended her brother, Colt, but Shirlene had yet to warm up to the kid. And right now he wasn't making it any easier.

"Let me go this instant, you little delinquent!" Shirlene yelled as she struggled to get free. But the little delinquent had done a great job of hog-tying her.

"Too bad, so sad," came his sassy reply.

Shirlene scooted around so she could see the boy. The redheaded brat sat on the mattress holding his little sister and feeding her the bottle. His demon eyes twinkled back at Shirlene as he showed off his chipped front tooth.

"Why, you little ornery punk," she said, "when I get untangled from here, I'm going to blister your butt—something your mama should've done a long time ago." She pulled at the ropes and rocked back and forth, but all it did was make her neck ache and give her a Charlie horse in her leg.

"My mama don't believe in spankin's. And you won't get untangled," the ornery kid said. "Kenny Gene taught me how to tie a rope, and everyone knows that he used to rope in the rodeo."

Great. Shirlene rolled her eyes. When she got a hold of Kenny Gene, she was going to blister his ears with a long list of reasons why you should never teach a kid rodeo skills. While she was mentally cussing Kenny, a pair of chubby legs came into view. They folded right in front of her, and she found herself staring into a pair of bright brown eyes beneath a fringe of uneven bangs.

"Mine," he growled in his unusually deep voice before he cracked Shirlene right in the head with the naked Barbie doll he held in one fist. Not just any Barbie, but Shirlene's.

"You," she hissed, and Brody scuttled back a few feet as she lifted her head and turned to look at Jesse. "It was you and your little brother who scared me and Sherman the other night."

"It wasn't that hard to do. You're the biggest chicken-livered girl I've ever met—even more than Mia."

If she could've gotten loose at that moment, she

would've easily paddled the kid. But the rope was too tight, and the position too awkward, to do more than rock back and forth like a fishing bobber on a line. Finally accepting defeat, she flopped back on the floor. Brody stared at her, his mouth smeared with jelly and his eyes big as saucers. Realizing that anger was getting her nowhere, she tried a different tactic.

Lifting her head, she flashed a smile at Jesse. "Now, sweetie. I realize I surprised you and your siblings, but I'm not mad at you for usin' my trailer as a playhouse—although your baby sister really needs to be watched by someone a little older."

Jesse glared back at her. "I'm old enough."

Not wanting to rile the kid, she let it go. "Now, that's not here nor there. What I'm trying to say is I'm not gonna tattle on you to your mama. This little mishap will remain between you and me. In other words, if you'll untie me, I'll just be on my way, and no one will be the wiser."

Jesse's eyes narrowed as he stared back at her. Finally after several hamstring-stretching minutes, he spoke.

"You mean you'll leave and never come back?"

Seeing how the trailer was hers, the little brat was asking a lot, but with her toes and fingers going numb, she really didn't have much choice. Besides, she didn't have any plans to return to Grover Road. Ever.

"That's exactly what I'm saying." Since her neck was killing her, she rested her head back down on the floor. Time ticked by, punctuated by the baby's gentle sucks. Finally the mattress squeaked, and Jesse's boots appeared in front of her.

"You'll need to take a blood oath."

"A what?" She lifted her head and tried to look Jesse

in the eye, but all she could see was his baggy jeans and stretched out Spiderman t-shirt.

"A blood oath," Jesse solemnly stated. "I won't believe you if blood's not involved. Go get your scissors, Brody."

The little boy jumped up and disappeared from sight.

Scissors? Blood?

Shirlene quickly tried to get control of the out-of-control situation. "Now, wait a minute, Jesse. I don't think scissors are such a good idea. Besides, a man is only as good as his word, and I'm more than willing to give you my word."

"But you ain't a man."

Damn.

"No, I'm not," she conceded. "But I'm an honest west Texas woman. You can ask anyone in town."

He flopped down in front of her. "Honest ain't a word that comes up when people are talkin' about you."

"And just what words come up?"

His freckled face scrunched in thought for only a second before he spoke. "Wild. Im-puss-ive. Gold digger."

Shirlene's mouth dropped open. "Why, that gossipy bunch of—"

"Where do you dig for gold around here, anyway?" Jesse cut in.

"Never you mind," she huffed. "And I'm not doing any blood oath, either. I give you my word I won't be back, and I won't. In fact, I'm selling this place just as soon as I can."

"Selling it?" Jesse yelled as he jumped to his feet. His loud voice set the baby to crying again. Brody walked back into the room holding out the scissors, but Shirlene had already screwed up the blood oath, and Jesse slapped them out of Brody's hand as he screamed. "You can't sell it! You can't! Where would we live?"

Before Shirlene could even digest that piece of shocking information, Jesse raced out the door like the hounds of hell were after him. And if Shirlene ever got loose, they would be. But for now, she was stuck with two screaming kids, for as soon as Jesse disappeared, Brody started crying in his deep wail.

Flopping her head back to the floor, Shirlene rested there for a minute with her ears ringing while she tried to figure out what to do. Since she couldn't do anything trussed up like Thanksgiving dinner, she figured that was the place to start. Lifting her head, she tried to speak over the cacophony, and at the same time keep her voice soothing.

"Brody. It's okay, honey. If you can just come over here and untie Shirlene, everything will be all right."

Brody stared back at her and let out another bellow, which set his sister into a higher-pitched mode. Shirlene might've joined in if she hadn't spied her purse lying on the floor.

"Candy, Brody," she yelled. "Do you like candy?"

Brody's crying fizzled, although the baby kept screaming. Still, it was enough to give Shirlene hope.

"If you help me get untied, Brody, I'll give you a candy bar."

The little boy stared at her for only a few seconds before he scooted across the dirty carpeting and leaned over her back. But the knots proved too much for his little fingers—that and the fact that he refused to let go of the Barbie. Shirlene had almost called it quits when she noticed the pair of scissors on the floor.

"Brody, honey, see those scissors? Get the scissors, Brody."

The kid took directions well. But once he had the scissors in his little pudgy hand, Shirlene had second thoughts.

"Do you know how to cut, honey?" she asked as she stared at the ends that no longer looked so blunt. "Maybe it would be better if you just ran and found a grown up. Kids your age probably shouldn't be using scissors—"

Before she could even finish the sentence, he reached out and lifted the strand of hair that had fallen over her face. And with one efficient snip, he cut it off.

Too stunned to speak, Shirlene could only stare at the lock of hair the child held up triumphantly. But when he reached for another strand, Shirlene screamed louder than the baby. Unfortunately, it didn't stop the little hair-cutting tyrant from wielding the scissors like Edward Scissorhands. Two more chunks fell to the floor before Sherman came charging through the door, scaring the kid so much that he dropped the scissors and began to wail again. Not more than a second later, both Brody's and the baby's wails suddenly cut off.

Shirlene dropped her head down to the carpet that was now strewn with her silky hair. How did her life get to be such a mess? A year ago, she had been the wife of the wealthiest man in town without a worry in the world. Now, here she was in a rundown trailer with more problems than she could deal with. She had no money. No credit cards. No house. And now no hair. She might've cried right then and there if a pair of scuffed cowboy boots hadn't appeared in her line of vision.

Except these boots didn't belong to a little delinquent.

These belonged to a big one.

Chapter Seven

"WHY, MS. DALTON, if I had known you was into bondage, I would've pulled out my handcuffs last night," Billy drawled as he stared down at the woman, who was tied as snug as a rodeo steer awaiting the buzzer. He smiled as his gaze swept over the sexy-as-hell, sky-high heels that were pulled back against the generous curve of her bottom.

"Bubba," she groaned. And his smile got even bigger.

"I'm glad you're so happy to see me." He glanced first at the baby who sat on the mattress watching the pig, and then over at the little boy who cowered in the corner watching him. "'Course, if we're gonna have any fun, we'll have to figure out what to do with your rug rats."

"Would you stop messing around, Wilkes, and untie me?" she commanded.

For a moment, Billy considered leaving her right where she was. But then his gaze got snagged by the little boy's big brown eyes, and he knelt down and picked up the scissors. Although he couldn't help but throw a little fuel on the fire.

"You're probably right. With a sassy woman like you, it would take all night to properly instruct you in the basics of servitude."

"Just cut!"

"See what I mean?" Billy teased as he leaned over her. The scissors were blunt, but fortunately the jump rope was weak. Once she was free, Ms. Dalton's legs dropped to the floor, and she moaned in pain.

Billy might not care for the uppity Ms. Dalton, but he wasn't completely immune to her suffering. Reaching out, he slipped off first one high heel and then the other before he started to massage the feeling back into her feet.

"God, that hurts," she mumbled into the piles of blond hair that had fallen over her face.

"Give it a minute," he said as he worked.

Like the rest of her body, her feet weren't petite. But they weren't ugly either. They were long and narrow with a high arch and a perfect row of toes that were painted a bright red. Billy had never much cared for red, so he couldn't explain the sudden desire to bend down and suck the sweet little pinkie toe into his mouth.

What the hell?

He dropped the foot like a hot potato. It thumped down to the floor accompanied by a gasp of pain.

"Gee, thanks," she grumbled as she rolled to her back and sat up.

Always observant, he noticed two things: one, the swell of her breasts against the soft material of her shirt— which considering their size didn't make him all that observant—and two, the blond hair that remained on the floor. His gaze snapped back up to the short cropped hair that stuck out by her temple.

"Don't you dare say a word," she hissed.

He didn't even try to bite back the smirk. "I wouldn't dream of it, ma'am."

Her hand lifted to her hair, and her eyes narrowed on the little boy who still stared at Billy as if he were the Big Bad Wolf.

And maybe the kid wasn't too far off.

Billy's gaze shifted back to Ms. Dalton, who was waggling her hands to get the feeling back into them. It must've worked because she stopped after a while to reach out and grab her purse. After digging around in it, she pulled out a half-eaten Snickers bar. But before she even got the wrapper off, the pig let out a squeal and jumped up on the mattress. Startled, the baby started to cry. This in turn caused the little boy to bellow in a deep wail that sent shivers down Billy's spine. The racket of screaming kids and squealing pig almost had him heading for the door. It was only the enjoyment of watching Ms. Dalton's panicked eyes that kept him rooted to his spot.

When she noticed him standing there grinning, she yelled above the noise. "Don't just stand there, Wilkes! Do something!"

He shrugged. "I'd love to, ma'am, but I've never been much good with kids. In fact, they scare me almost as much as horror movies."

Shirlene shot him an exasperated look before she took action. In a flurry of motion, she pinched off a piece of candy and tossed it to the pig, handed the rest of the candy bar to the little boy, and finally scooped up the baby and silenced her with the bottle. When the room was filled with nothing more than smacking noises, Billy didn't know who was more surprised.

"Well," she breathed as she leaned back against the pillows. "That wasn't so hard."

Since Billy had grown up around plenty of children, he knew that peace was a fragile thing—kids were always just one poopy diaper or empty bottle away from chaos. Still, he kept this knowledge to himself.

"So whose kids are these, anyway?" He moved over to the mattress and pushed the pig out of the way so he could sit down.

"I don't really know the woman. Her delinquent son, Jesse, is the only one who hangs around town much." Ms. Dalton adjusted the bottle in the baby's mouth.

It was strange, but unlike most women he knew, Ms. Dalton didn't cuddle the child close as she fed her. There was no cooing or brushing back the curly hair that fell over the little girl's forehead. Instead she held the baby like she was a stray dog with fleas and stared at the doorway as if counting down the seconds when she would be able to race through it. It was strange. Or maybe not so strange, considering she was a spoiled gold digger who seemed to be worried about only one thing.

Herself.

That didn't explain what she was doing out on Grover Road again. If he didn't know better, he might be worried that Shirlene Dalton was spying on him. But before he could broach the subject, she shifted the baby in her arms and glanced over at Brody, who seemed to have more chocolate on his face than inside his stomach.

"According to Jesse, they live here."

Billy's gaze snapped over to her. "Here?" He pointed down at the saggy mattress. "As in this trailer?"

"Exactly." She glanced around the sparsely furnished

room. "Which is why the door was locked, and why Jesse and Brody tried to scare me off last night."

Billy attempted to look duly surprised. "The chainsaw psycho?"

"The same."

"Well, if that's the case, I guess there's nothing left to do but call Sheriff Winslow."

Ms. Dalton's gaze flashed over to him, and suddenly Billy found himself sympathizing with Lyle Dalton. Ms. Dalton's eyes were the exact color of a meadow in early spring—a vast expanse of crisp, dewy grass that invited a man to leave behind the cold blues and dull browns of ordinary women and lose himself in the lush, vital green of this woman. One glance of those peepers and the poor old coot probably hadn't known what hit him.

"You think that's what I should do?"

Her question jerked Billy out of the meadow and back to the trailer. Except it took a while for his mind to catch up. "Huh?"

"Sheriff Winslow? You think I should call him?" Ms. Dalton glanced down at the baby who had finished the bottle and was now sucking air.

"Who else are you going to call?" He reached over and pulled the bottle out of the baby's mouth so the kid wouldn't end up with a bunch of gas. Didn't the woman know anything about kids?

Once the bottle was gone, the baby just stared up at Ms. Dalton with wide, blue eyes set in a chubby, little face that Billy had to admit was pretty darned cute. Except Ms. Dalton must've had a heart of stone. She quickly handed the baby over to Billy.

"Here, your turn."

He would've handed the kid right back if the baby hadn't started to fuss. And since there was no more milk in the bottle, he figured he didn't have much choice but to comfort her. He tucked her against his chest and patted her back, which resulted in a burp that was louder than Rye Pickett after he'd downed a Dr Pepper.

The rigid lines on Ms. Dalton's face finally eased, and they both laughed. Even Brody giggled. Of course, it sounded more like a deep chuckle.

"Where did that kid get his voice, anyway? James Earl Jones?" Billy asked.

Ms. Dalton's laughter cut off as her gaze lowered to the floor and the locks of blond hair. She reached up and tried to smooth the longer strands over the shorter. It didn't work, and Billy couldn't help grinning at her partial mullet.

"So I'm assuming that James Earl gave you the trim."

She held out a short strand. "You call this a trim?"

Knowing how sensitive women were about their hair, he backed off a little. "It's not that bad—nothin' a couple months won't fix."

"More like a good year," she grumbled. She shot a glance over at the kid, who was licking the chocolate from his fingers. In his other hand, he clutched a naked doll. The same one he'd had that morning.

"I hate to tell you this, son," Billy pointed at the doll, "but you need to change out toys."

The kid hugged the doll closer and yelled in his deep, baritone voice, "Mine."

Billy shrugged. "Suit yourself, but I'm only trying to save you some grief. You walk around with something like that for too long in Texas, and you'll end up in more fights than one of those *Dancing With the Stars* dudes in a biker bar."

"Please don't get him started," Ms. Dalton said. "I've had enough screaming today to last me a lifetime." She looked at the baby who rested against his shoulder, and her eyes widened. "She's asleep."

"No foolin'." He carefully laid the baby down on the mattress. "I guess I'm better with kids than I thought."

She stared at the sleeping child. "So where do you think they'll go?"

"Who?"

"Jesse's family," she said.

Billy shook his head. "I don't know, but Sheriff Winslow probably will." When she shot him a skeptical look, he realized his mistake. "Okay, so maybe he won't know either, but I'm sure he'll figure it out."

She reached out as if to smooth back the hair that had fallen over the baby's forehead, but instead her hand just hung there for a few seconds before it dropped back to the mattress.

"What do they do with homeless people in east Texas?" she asked.

"We don't have any homeless people in Dogwood. No one in their right mind would want to live on the streets in that humidity," he teased. Although why he wasted his time trying to tease another smile out of her was beyond him. He had other things to worry about besides making Ms. Dalton smile, and he needed to remember that.

"My pastor took care of things like that," he said. "I remember him taking up a collection for a family that had run out of gas while traveling through town."

"You attend church?" Her voice betrayed her shock.

"It was either that or get my butt warmed with my daddy's belt. The hard pews and Pastor Miley's hour-long sermon seemed like the least of two evils. Although once I grew up, I became nothing but a big ol' sinner." He winked at her. "You wanna do a little sinnin' with me, Ms. Dalton?"

For one split second, it looked as if she was actually considering it. Her head tipped to one side and those green eyes of hers slithered over his body like a slab of butter on a hot skillet. And he was feelin' hot all right. Even though he had no intentions of touching the woman with a ten-foot pole, his nine-inch pole hadn't gotten the memo.

"I'm afraid I'll have to pass," she said in that throaty voice of hers. While Billy tried to get a grip on his body's betrayal, she looked over at Brody, who was now slumped back in the corner with the Barbie cuddled close and his thumb in his mouth. "I guess it wouldn't hurt anything to leave things like they are."

He blinked. "You mean let these kids live in your trailer?"

"Why not?" She shrugged and looked down at the sleeping child. "They aren't really hurting anything—although I'll need to talk to the mother about leaving a little delinquent in charge of such a precious little girl. And the dangers of letting that delinquent play with a chainsaw."

"It didn't have a chain on it." The words popped out before Billy could put much thought in them, and Ms. Dalton's eyes narrowed.

"How did you—?"

The tinny clang of feet on the front steps cut off her

words, and they both turned to the doorway as a teenage girl raced in. She was a skinny little thing with pale skin and blond hair pulled back in a haphazard ponytail.

She stood there panting, her eyes behind the black-framed glasses tracking to the sleeping baby on the mattress, then over to the dozing little boy in the corner. There was a moment of relief, but it disappeared quickly enough when she looked back at Billy and Ms. Dalton.

"I'm so sorry," she said with a Texas twang, "I've told my little brother not to play in other people's trailers." She pushed back the hair that had fallen from her ponytail and glanced back at the doorway. "But he has a problem listening."

As if on cue, Jesse slunk into the room in his over-sized cowboy boots. When he saw Billy, his eyes narrowed. But he kept his mouth shut while the girl continued to talk.

"So we'll just get out of your hair." She strode to the bed and had just started to pick up the baby when Ms. Dalton stopped her by placing a hand on her arm.

"Why don't you let her sleep, honey? She looks almost as tuckered out as you do."

The teenage girl's entire body tensed, but Billy had to hand it to her. She knew how to hold it together. "I'd really love to, ma'am, but our mama is due back from work anytime. And she'll be real worried if we aren't at home when she gets there."

Billy got up from the bed and removed his hat from his head. "And just where is home, Miss..."

Her unusual violet eyes stared back at him. "Foster. Mia Foster."

Ms. Dalton got to her feet and flashed one of those megawatt smiles. "Well, it's real nice to meet you, Mia. I'm Ms. Dalton, and this here is Mr. Wilkes."

"Bubba," Billy grinned. "So y'all live around here?"

Mia didn't flinch an inch; her eyes behind the glasses were clear and direct. "Just a few trailers down."

Billy hadn't hung out in the trailer park long enough to meet any of the neighbors, but the girl didn't need to know that. "A few trailers down, huh?" He scratched his head in thought. "Now, I thought the Millers lived in that trailer."

"Nuh-uh," Jesse chimed in, "the Walshes do."

Mia shot the kid daggers, and Billy actually felt sorry for him.

"We know that you've been living here, Mia," Ms. Dalton stated. "And I'm not mad about it, honey. But I do need to talk with your mama."

Like a trapped animal, Mia's eyes flickered with fear, and there was a moment when Billy thought she might sprint right back out the door. Instead, her chin hiked up, and her mouth turned stubborn. "It will be a long wait. She won't be home until later."

Ms. Dalton's smile drooped, and those green eyes flashed with indecision. Figuring this was as good a time as any to make his exit, Billy tugged his hat back on. "Well, I'd love to sit and chat, but there's a catfish in Sutter Springs with my name on it."

"Wait a minute!" Ms. Dalton grabbed his arm before he had even taken a step and stared at him with panic thick in those green eyes. "You're not leaving me with..." Her voice trailed off.

Billy smiled. "Why, Ms. Dalton, I didn't realize you'd gotten so attached to me." He removed her hand with a pat. "But you need to remember the first rule in fishing and relationships... Don't cling too tightly or a good catch might get away."

Chapter Eight

SHIRLENE COULDN'T REMEMBER the last time she'd been out to Sutter Springs. Stumbling along the muddy bank in her high heels, she realized why. It was hot and dirty and smelled like dead fish, a perfect place for the man who stretched out under the cedar tree with a sweat-stained camouflage hat resting over his face and a fishing pole leaning against the rock next to him. Fishing line stretched across the bank and into the murky water, the bright red bobber on the end bouncing in the ripples caused by the strong breeze.

It didn't look like he had caught anything, although the miles of sun-bronzed sculptured muscles exposed by the open flaps of his snap-down shirt hooked her gaze quickly enough. She didn't know how long she stood there staring before his voice rumbled up through the dark green mesh of the hat.

"I've gotta tell ya, Ms. Dalton. Your persistence is startin' to wear me down."

Shirlene pulled her gaze away from all that hot, manly flesh and over to where Sherman wandered down to the muddy edge of the water, looking for any dropped picnic foods.

"Do you have my wallet?" she asked.

He removed the hat from his face and, lifting his head, squinted back at her. "That's as good of a lie as you could come up with? Lord have mercy, woman, your mama didn't teach you any man-catchin' skills at all."

Shirlene shot him an exasperated look. "Just answer the question. Did you find my wallet on the front steps this morning or didn't you?"

Bubba's gaze wandered over her body, from the top of her head to the tips of her painted toes. "You might want to start with a change of clothing. There's nothin' wrong with a little sweat, but I prefer women who bathe and put on clean clothes at least every other day."

With a groan of frustration, Shirlene flopped down on the sandy soil and rested her head in her hands. What had she been thinking? The man couldn't count to ten without starting over. He certainly wasn't observant enough to notice a woman's wallet. But he had been her last resort, the thin thread she clung to after Mia the Sullen and Jesse the Delinquent had denied knowing anything about her wallet and credit cards.

Of course, what did she expect from a bunch of little hooligans?

"Now don't be gettin' all teary eyed." Bubba sat up and hooked an arm around her shoulders. "I've been known to overlook a little bad hygiene if the woman has certain skills—"

She elbowed him hard in the stomach, although it appeared to hurt her more than it did him. "Would you please spare me your pathetic hillbilly charm? I have enough to worry about without listening to your idiotic talk."

Flashing her that dopey smile, he rolled to his feet and walked over to his fishing pole. He reeled in the line and checked the bait before he recast and sat down on the rock, his long, bare feet braced on the ground.

"So you lost your wallet, did you?"

"More like stolen by that little redheaded demon."

Billy chuckled. "That kid is a pistol."

She glared over at him. "It figures you'd think so."

"So what did their mama say?"

Shirlene slipped her shoes off and cuffed her jeans. "She didn't come home. And after an hour of being stared at by Jesse and Mia, I decided to check back later."

"Later being a couple months down the road?"

She glanced over at him, and her forehead furrowed. Sometimes the man surprised her. She didn't plan on stopping back by. She'd had enough of Grover Road to last her a lifetime. Of course, she'd let the Fosters continue to live in her trailer. But someone else would have to check up on them. Someone like Faith or Hope. Someone who didn't feel as if they'd been kicked in the stomach every time that sweet, little baby turned those big, blue eyes on them.

"What do you know about their mama?"

Bubba's words filtered into her thoughts, and she turned to find him staring out at the water that glistened in the sun.

"Not much," she said. "I hear she holds down two jobs, which is probably why she's never at home." A trickle of sweat rolled down her brow, and she wiped it off with her wrist. Shooting a glance over at Bubba, she flipped open a couple buttons on her blouse.

"You think she's abusive?" he asked.

"I don't know, although neglect is just as abusive as physical brutality."

His gaze snapped over to her. And even though she couldn't see his eyes in the shadow of the hat brim, she couldn't help fidgeting.

"But you're right, something's wrong," she said. "Even after I made it clear that they can continue to live there rent free, Mia still looked nervous."

"Maybe she doesn't trust you." Bubba reeled in his line. "You have to admit you look a little untrustworthy."

"Untrustworthy?" She snorted. "I look a hell of a lot more trustworthy than a stranger from east Texas."

"Not to someone from Grover Road." His head dipped, and she followed his gaze down to her fingers and the diamond that flashed in the sunlight.

She slipped her hands between her knees. "Money doesn't make you untrustworthy."

"It does to a bunch of kids who don't have two dimes to rub together. To them, you're the kid on the playground who ended up with a big slice of watermelon when all they got were the seeds. The fickleness of fate tends to make people suspicious."

Shirlene stared at him. "The fickleness of fate?"

He grinned. "I read it in a comic. It sounds good, don't it?"

It sounded as ridiculous as Bubba, but it certainly made sense. Why should the kids trust her when she had everything they didn't? When she had busted into a place they thought of as their home as if she owned it. Okay, so maybe she did own it, but that didn't mean she had the right to look down her nose at the kids. Had she spent so much time in her rich little bubble that she couldn't remember what it was like to be poor and scared?

"So what do you think I should do?" She didn't know why she asked Bubba the question. Possibly because she didn't have anyone else to ask, and because, in the last few minutes, he hadn't seemed like such a dumb redneck. Although when a long silence followed, she wondered if she'd made a mistake. After she sat there for a while watching the setting sun reflect off the water, he finally spoke.

"I think you should go back and talk with their mama and offer them a place to live until they get on their feet. Their mama can either take you up on the offer, or not. But at least you've done your best."

His answer made her feel better. And after a while of watching Bubba stand there fishing, she lay back on the cool earth and closed her eyes. Except a funny thing happened; even with her eyes closed, she could still see Bubba standing there. She could still see the way his dark brown hair curled around the brim of his hat and the stubble that covered his square jaw. She could see the rounded bulge of his bicep as he cast the fishing line and the hard ripples of his stomach as he reeled it in.

Then suddenly, that wasn't all she could see. Gone was the western shirt with its ripped off sleeves and the wranglers with the faded circle on the back pocket from his can of chewing tobacco, and there stood Wilkesville in all its splendor.

It was a sight for sore eyes. A sight Shirlene allowed herself to indulge in for more than a few minutes. Which was why she almost jumped out of her skin when Bubba yelled.

"I caught one!"

Sitting straight up, she slapped a hand over her thumping

heart. She looked over at Bubba, relieved to find him still dressed. Still dressed but struggling to reel in whatever was on the other end of the line.

"Don't just sit there, woman," he hollered. "Grab the net!"

Shirlene had never taken orders well, but his excitement had her making an exception. She jumped up and searched around until she found the net. She had never cared much for fishing, so once she had the net, she wasn't real sure what to do with it.

"Bring it over here," he instructed. "Be ready. It feels like a big one." His biceps flexed as he pulled back on the fishing pole that bowed under the weight of the fish on the other end.

She leaned out over the edge of the bank, not knowing what to expect. But it sure wasn't the big muddy running shoe that came out of the water so fast she barely had time to duck. Unfortunately, she didn't think about the return trip, and the shoe swung back and clocked her between her shoulder blades, knocking her off the bank and straight into the water.

And fishing wasn't the only thing Shirlene didn't much care for.

Water filled her nose like ribbons of fire as she tried to fight her way to the surface. Her head popped up for only a second before she went back under. But a second was all it took to hear Bubba's hysterical laughter. She might've been mad at the dumb hick who stood there laughing while she drowned, but death had a way of keeping a person focused. And while she struggled to get back to the surface, she hedged her bets.

Forgive me, Lord, for stealing my mama's cigarettes and smoking them out behind the trailer.

And for sneaking out to meet Tom Riley—and for let-

ting Tom get to third base without a wedding ring. And for putting the live ammo in Hope's prop gun during our high school performance of Annie Get Your Gun.

And for not attending church, even on Christmas and Easter.

And for—

A band of steel curled around her waist and lifted her out of the water. But even after breaking the surface, she still wondered if she might die. Her chest, throat, and nose burned, and she couldn't seem to stop coughing.

"Lord have mercy, woman," Bubba's voice broke through her attempt to get air. "Who taught you how to swim?"

She sagged against his solid chest and waited for him to swim to shore. But instead, he lifted her up in his arms and walked there.

"Three feet of water," he mumbled as he trudged up the bank. "And she was going to drown."

If Shirlene could've talked, she would've questioned his measurement. There was no way she almost drowned in three feet of water. Bubba had to be taller than she thought. And much stronger. He carried her as if she weighed no more than Hope or Faith.

He laid her down on the thick buffalo grass beneath the cedar tree and then knelt over her. His cool fingers brushed her forehead, smoothing her wet, matted hair from her face.

When she looked up, Bubba was close. Too close. The hat was gone, and his wavy hair fell over his high forehead in sweat-dampened ringlets, framing a set of clear brown eyes that looked filled with concern. Although his next words didn't reflect that.

"Please tell me I need to perform some of that mouth-to-mouth?"

When she shook her head, his look of disappointment was almost laughable.

"You sure know how to deflate a feller, Ms. Dalton. Especially one who just saved your life."

She coughed a couple more times. "I thought it was only three feet of water."

He shook his head as if he still couldn't believe it. "And you were drowning in it."

"Because I can't swim."

His eyebrows shot up. "Can you stand?"

It was a good question. A ridiculously good question. And Shirlene couldn't help but smile at the thought of her thrashing around in a couple feet of water like a bass on a hook. A laugh escaped her—followed by another—and another, until she was laughing so hard tears escaped her eyes and her stomach hurt. How long had it been since she had laughed like this? Not the chuckles she gave her friends and townsfolk to prove that she wasn't still hurting for her dead husband, but the kind of out-and-out laughter that made a person realize that life still held humor. That life was still worth living.

Somewhere along the line, Bubba joined in, his deep laughter a perfect complement to hers. Shirlene didn't know how long they laughed. Seconds or minutes, it was just enough. They sobered at the same time and were left staring at one another with satisfied smiles.

"Thank you," she said. When his head cocked in confusion, she quickly added, "For saving my life in three feet of water." Her gaze dropped to his drenched jeans. "And for getting all wet in the process."

"We both look like a couple of drowned rats, don't we?" he teased as his gaze wandered down. Just that quickly, the smile slipped from his firm lips.

Shirlene glanced down, and her own smile dropped. It seemed that while she had been drowning in three feet of water, the buttons of her blouse had come undone, revealing a full-figure bra that wasn't even close to being full-figured enough to cover the mounds of flesh that pressed against its transparent pink lace.

"O-oops" she stammered, trying to make light of the embarrassing situation as she tugged the edges of her shirt closed. But when she glanced back up, Bubba's gaze was still pinned to her breasts, almost as if he was imagining her as she'd imagined him—dressed in nothing but a birthday suit.

When he finally did lift his gaze, it wasn't any better. His deep, brown eyes were steamed up like two cups of hot cocoa. And Shirlene had always been partial to cocoa. And to men who didn't ask permission—who just took what they wanted. Without a by-your-leave, Bubba's head dipped, and those lips scorched hers.

He had either gotten some practice since that morning, or he was more of an afternoon-delight kind of guy. Because this was no sloppy, puppy kiss like he'd given her in his trailer. This was more of a sizzling, expert manipulation of tongue and mouth that left Shirlene slightly dazed and completely convinced that she'd been wrong.

Her sex drive hadn't died with Lyle. It was right there simmering in her belly like a pot ready to boil over. And she wanted it to boil over—to boil over, and catch fire, and burn down the entire kitchen. Especially when Bubba's hand settled over her breast and those long, lean fingers stoked the flame to unbelievable heights.

Things were just getting heated up when Sherman came over and plopped down in the shade next to Shirlene, snuffling and snorting over something he'd found. With the mood broken, Bubba pulled back and stared down at her as if he didn't know who she was or how she'd gotten there. He had a good point. How had she gotten there? One minute she was fighting for her life, and the next, she was kissing Bubba Wilkes. And not just kissing—she glanced down at his hand on her breast—but desiring. That was what really freaked her out. There had to be at least a million eligible men in the state of Texas, and she had chosen a womanizing, tobacco-chewing redneck to light her stove.

Obviously, near brushes with death could really screw up a person's libido.

She tipped her head and hiked up one eyebrow. "You all through, honey?"

Those chocolate-coated eyes blinked, and his fingers flexed a couple tummy-tingling times before he finally released her.

"Thanks," she said with an entire piss pot full of sarcasm. Although it didn't seem to seep into his hillbilly brain. As he rolled to his feet, he winked at her. "Anytime, Ms. Dalton. All you have to do is ask." Without offering to help her up, he wandered back over to his fishing pole with the muddy shoe attached. "Now if this don't beat all." He shook his head and chuckled. "Kenny Gene will never let me live it down when he discovers I caught me a tenny shoe."

"About that," Shirlene sat up and finished buttoning her blouse. "Maybe we should just keep what happened out here at Sutter Springs between you and me."

His gaze shot back to her. "A secret, Ms. Dalton?"

"Exactly, honey." She got to her feet.

"Well, I'll sure try." He scratched his head. "But I'm gonna warn you, secrets ain't my specialty."

It didn't take Shirlene long to herd Sherman back to the Navigator. But the cool blast of the air conditioner didn't cool her down a lick. It seemed Bubba had started a fire that wasn't easily put out. By the time she got back on the main highway, her breast still tingled and her panties were still steamed.

Of course, it probably didn't have as much to do with Bubba as it did with nine months of going without—and if the truth was known, more like a year. Lyle had been so busy the last few months of his life trying to get Dalton Oil back on its feet that he hadn't had much time for Shirlene or sex. Which explained her volatile reaction to Bubba. She was just coming off a dry spell, was all. She would've reacted the same to any man who had saved her from a watery grave.

It was close to sundown when she and Sherman pulled onto Grover Road. Sherman looked about as excited to be back there as Shirlene was. He snorted with disdain as the SUV bounced over every rut and bump.

"This coming from an animal that just ate someone's leftover, sand-encrusted peanut butter sandwich," she said.

At the mention of food, he snorted even louder. But before she could soothe him with the promise of Josephine's tater tots, she noticed the three kids standing by the side of the road. Kids who looked as if they'd just had all their Halloween candy stolen. Dust flew as she pulled to a stop. She barely made it around the front of the Navigator when Jesse met her.

"It's all your fault!" he screamed as he shoved the baby at her. "We don't got a mama, and now we don't got Mia, neither!"

Chapter Nine

MIA WASN'T GOING BACK. She wasn't. She'd done everything she could to try to keep their ragtag family together,
and she couldn't do any more. It was someone else's problem now. Maybe the pretty, blond Ms. Dalton. Although
the woman hadn't exactly looked like she liked kids. The
entire time she had been at the trailer, she'd looked like
she was going to throw up on the stained carpeting. Of
course, it wasn't kids as much as poverty that probably
had Ms. Dalton looking that way.

Poverty could do that to a person. Settle in your stomach and make you feel as if you couldn't keep a thing
down. Mia had felt that way ever since she could remember. Nauseous bordering on deathly ill.

She glanced in the rearview mirror of the Impala
she'd stolen from "Auntie Barb" and eased her foot off
the accelerator. She didn't like to drive the car, which was
why she'd kept it under a tarp and a pile of garbage for
most of their stay in Bramble. Even if she and Jesse had
switched out license plates, all it would take was a cop
pulling her over for her to be sent back to Houston. And

just like she wasn't going back to Bramble, she was never going back to Houston.

She'd been there and done that. All she had was nineteen more months. Nineteen months before she would turn eighteen and could go where she wanted to go and do what she wanted to do without worrying about Children's Services breathing down her neck. But for now, she just wanted to drive and try to forget Jesse's accusing brown eyes. And Brody's tear-streaked face. And Adeline's loud screams.

If she could just get far enough away, she could forget. She knew she could.

Unfortunately, in order to get far enough away, she needed gas. She had hoped she would be able to get out of Bramble before she stopped. Now it looked as if she would barely make it to Jones's Garage. She rolled up to a pump with the car jerking and sputtering.

Stepping out of the car, she reached in her purse and pulled out the brown wallet with the scrolled Ls and Vs. She'd planned on giving the wallet back to Ms. Dalton after Jesse had discovered it on the front steps. She didn't believe in stealing from complete strangers, just from horrible foster parents who had no business taking in kids. But after buying the groceries that morning, she only had a few dollars left.

She pulled out the gold American Express and stared at the name. Shirlene Grace Dalton. One day, Mia would have an American Express card with her name on it. And when she did, she'd pay back Ms. Dalton every cent she owed her.

Until then, she needed to borrow some.

Except when she slipped the card in the slot it was

denied—as were five others. Had the woman already canceled them? Mia glanced around, waiting for a sting operation to jump out and grab her. But no Feds showed up, just the football hero of Bramble, Texas.

Which was almost worse to a skinny girl with glasses and bad acne.

"Hey, you need some help?" Austin Reeves strutted across the oil-spotted pavement in cowboy boots that were too pointed, and a straw cowboy hat that looked as if it had been put through the spin cycle one too many times.

The purse slipped out of Mia's hands and spilled out on the concrete. Completely humiliated, she didn't waste any time shoveling the spilled contents back inside and climbing into the car. But after only one joyous rumble, the engine sputtered and died. A hand thumped on the roof, and Austin leaned down and peered in the window with a cocky grin on his tanned face.

"Did you forget something?"

Mia swallowed hard and tried not to look at the boy who had starred in so many of her daydreams. "Like what?"

"Like gas?"

She blushed to the roots of her hair. "Oh, yeah, I guess I was busy texting and forgot."

She could feel his eyes staring down at her as if she was the dumbest thing this side of the Mississippi, and she hated people thinking she was dumb. Hated it with a passion.

Tipping her chin up, she turned and looked at him. "Aren't you that football player who plays for Bramble High—Avery? No, Albert?" She snapped her fingers. "Alvin!"

His eyes narrowed, but he didn't pull back. Instead he continued to rest his hand on the roof and stare at her. "Austin."

"Oh, right." She gave him a closed-mouth smile.

He continued to study her until she thought she might scream. Then finally he stuck his hand in the window. "If you'll give me your card, I'll fill her up for you."

It wasn't like Mia had much of a choice. Hand him a credit card or sit there like an idiot. She just hoped that he wouldn't take the time to read the name on the card. Pulling out the wallet, she chose the only card she hadn't tried and handed it to him. "So what position do you play?" she asked in an attempt to distract him. Everyone in town knew what position Austin Reeves played.

"Quarterback," he stated as he slipped the card in the slot.

It seemed like a lifetime passed while she waited for authorization. And when the pump beeped its acceptance, Mia finally released her breath as he handed the card back. Although his next words caused her empty stomach to heave.

"I know you."

She glanced up to find him leaning back against the car, his head cocked toward her.

"You're Jesse's sister, Mia."

She was shocked that such a popular boy would know her name, shocked and embarrassed all at the same time.

"I bought a dirt bike from your brother that kicks ass," he continued. "He gave me a sweet deal, although his smart mouth is kinda hard to take."

The mention of Jesse had a lump crawling up the back of her throat. Jesse did have a smart mouth, but it was all a defense mechanism put in place to hide his tender heart. A heart she'd trampled when she blamed him for Ms. Dalton finding out they lived in the trailer. But it hadn't been Jesse's fault. Sooner or later, someone would've found out.

Mia just wished it had been later.

She looked out the car's windshield at the sunset that had exploded across the horizon in deep tangerines and cherry-pink. About now the kids would be eating the boxed macaroni and cheese she'd brought home that day from the Food Mart. Brody would try to whistle through his noodles, and Adeline would get half of hers on the floor. Jesse would've burnt the toast again and wasted too much butter, but it wouldn't matter. She wouldn't be there to scold him. Or to help him clean up and fix the things he'd found in the dump that day. And she wouldn't be there to give Brody and Adeline their baths. Or tell them a bedtime story. Or kiss them goodnight.

"Hey," Austin stood in the window looking down at her. "You okay?"

The lump in her throat that had started out as a pebble seemed to have gotten so big she couldn't get words past it. Luckily, becoming a mute seemed to work in her favor. Austin shot her one confused and slightly scared look before he quickly finished filling the tank and screwed on the cap. Once it was fueled, the car started right up.

Without any acknowledgment or gratitude, Mia pulled away from the pumps. But when she reached the highway, she couldn't seem to get her hands to turn the steering wheel in the direction leading north out of Bramble. Nor could she get her foot to press on the accelerator. She just sat there, uncaring that the most popular boy in town still watched her with his crumpled cowboy hat pushed back on his high forehead. She wasn't sure how long it was before she pulled out onto the blacktop.

Twilight had barely settled against the heated earth when Mia pulled in behind the Navigator. She climbed out of the car and had only taken two steps when Jesse came flying out of nowhere and flung himself at her.

"I'm sorry, Mia." He shoved his wet face into her neck. "I won't ever tell no one nothin' ever again. And I ain't gonna disrespect you, and I'll do my school work and clean up after myself and never sass back—just don't ever leave us again." He pulled back, his red hair standing in mussed tufts on the top of his head and his freckled face smudged with dirt. "Okay? Just don't leave us."

About then, the front door opened, and Brody came racing down the steps, the naked Barbie held tightly in his hand. He hit her full in the legs and almost toppled her to the ground.

"Mine!" he growled. "Mine!"

The steps creaked, and Mia looked over to see Ms. Dalton standing there holding a sobbing Adeline. The baby held out her hands to Mia and that was the final straw. Tears dripped down Mia's face like every leaky faucet in the trailer, and her stomach lurched. She figured she would throw up, but instead, she found the strength to utter three words.

"I need help."

Chapter Ten

THE FIRST THING TO GREET Shirlene when she stepped inside the First Baptist Church was reverent silence. And being that Shirlene was anything but reverent—or silent—she almost turned right back around. The only thing that stopped her was the image of four sets of heart-wrenching eyes. Still, when Shirlene walked through the doors of the chapel and saw the huge gold cross that hung over the altar, she wondered if a telephone call wouldn't work just as well. Death by lightning wasn't exactly the way she wanted to go.

"Shirlene Dalton?"

Her gaze snapped up to the high arched ceiling before she realized it wasn't God talking but Pastor Robbins. He strode down the aisle dressed in his usual weekday attire of running shoes, board shorts, and a brightly colored Hawaiian shirt. His gaze swept from the top of the Texas Rangers baseball cap pulled over her hair to the toes of the flip-flops she'd borrowed from Mia. His forehead knotted, although she didn't know if he was more con-fused by her outfit or by the fact that Shirlene Dalton was standing in his church. Probably both. Shirlene was pretty darned confused herself.

But being the man of God he was, the pastor recovered quickly. With a teasing grin, he waved the paintbrush he held in one hand. "Please tell me you came to help me touch-up the baseboards."

Shirlene flashed him a smile. Not the kind she flashed most handsome men. She was a flirt, but she didn't believe in messing with men who had a direct line to the Almighty.

"If you'd seen my artwork in grade school, Pastor, you wouldn't be askin'," she said.

"Well, you couldn't be any worse than I am. I can't wait for Mr. Sims to get back from visiting his grandkids in San Antonio. Although when he sees my handyman work, he might just quit altogether." He shot her a quizzical look. "So is there something I can help you with, Ms. Dalton?"

"Actually I stopped by to ask you some questions," she said.

Pastor Robbins studied her for only a moment before he nodded and held out a hand. "Why don't we talk in my office?"

His office wasn't what Shirlene had expected. The big desk and richly upholstered chairs fit, but the posters of kite-flying surfers were completely out of place, as was the small, brightly painted surfboard in one corner.

"I take it you like to surf," Shirlene said.

"Kite boarding." He waited for her to take a seat before he sat down in the leather chair behind the big desk. "It's like surfing, but you can stay out for as long as the wind allows."

Her gaze locked on the poster above his head. "So if you don't mind me askin', what's a kite-boarding pastor doing in Bramble, Texas?"

"I guess you could say I was blown in this direction."

Her gaze flickered back to him. "Harsh wind."

He smiled. "Only if you fight it." He leaned up and rested his arms on the desk. "So how have you been, Ms. Dalton?"

It was a question a lot of people had been asking lately, and normally Shirlene lied. But she was still worried about that lightning bolt so she stayed as close to the truth as she could.

"As fine as a recently widowed woman can be." She crossed her legs and flapped a too-small flip flop as she tried to figure out how to get answers without breaking her promise to Mia.

Not that Shirlene had much of a choice. The teenage girl was as devious as she was pathetic. She had no qualms whatsoever about insuring Shirlene's silence with a little blackmail. It seemed Mia was bright enough to figure out that something wasn't right when the wealthiest woman in town suddenly showed up on Grover Road. But it wasn't blackmail that kept Shirlene from calling Sheriff Winslow as much as it was the fear in Mia's eyes.

It was possible that the kid was acting, but Shirlene doubted it. The best actress in the world couldn't put on a haunted look like that. Still, she planned to do a little investigating before she made a decision on what to do.

She flashed a bright smile at Pastor Robbins. "So I was thinking about doing some charity work."

The pastor nodded. "The church can always use volunteers, Ms. Dalton."

"Actually," she smiled, "I was thinking more of orphans."

He blinked. "Here in Bramble?"

"Orphans in Bramble. Now that's funny, honey." Could you call a man of the cloth *honey*? She glanced up at the ceiling before continuing. "I was thinking more of Dallas or . . . Houston."

Pastor Robbins smiled. "I think homeless children are a wonderful charity to choose, Ms. Dalton. Most short-term childcare facilities are busting at the seams and way understaffed."

"So what happens to the kids that are put in places like that?" she asked.

"Ideally, they stay there for only a few months until they're adopted or put in foster homes."

"And these foster homes, are they nice?"

"Most are." His gaze moved to the window. "As with all foster programs, there are abuses—hey, isn't that Jesse?"

Shirlene turned around in time to see a freckled face pressed to the glass. The brown eyes widened before the strawberry-blond head ducked back down. Obviously, her word hadn't been good enough for Mia.

She looked back at the pastor and shrugged. "Kids," she said. "So what if someone wanted to be a foster parent for just a little while—say until the kids put in her care were adopted? How would that work?"

Pastor Robbins's face registered surprise.

Shirlene was pretty surprised herself. It was one thing to want a child of her own and another to be stuck with four ornery kids all at one time—even if it was only short-term. Still, the kids hadn't run away for nothing, and Shirlene couldn't bring herself to send them back to an abusive situation.

It didn't take long for Pastor Robbins to pull himself together. "I guess the first thing a person would need is an information packet from the Department of Family and Protective Services." He swiveled his chair toward a filing cabinet. "I think I have one around here somewhere. Of course, anyone wanting to foster children needs to meet certain criteria—they have to be over 21, have a home and be able to provide for a child, and be in good mental and physical health."

Shirlene frowned. As of now, she had one out of five.

"Here it is." He pulled out a thick package of paper and handed it across the desk. "After the paperwork is filled out, it needs to be processed—which can take up to a year."

"A year?"

He nodded. "They'll have to do a home study. At the earliest, it would be four or five months."

In four or five months, Shirlene hoped the kids would be settled with a nice family, and she would be settled with a nice chunk of money from the sale of the house.

"Is there any way we could hurry that up?" she asked.

Sympathy filled Pastor Robbins's eyes. Shirlene wasn't much on sympathy, but if it helped the kids, she'd live with it.

"I might be able to call a few people and see what I can do," Pastor Robbins said.

"I sure appreciate the help, Pastor." She stood and held out a hand.

He got to his feet and cradled her hand between his. "Anytime, Ms. Dalton. Is there anything else you'd like to talk about?"

She flashed a smile. "If there is, I'll be sure to let you know."

Once outside the double doors, Shirlene hurried around the side of the church just in time to stop a fleeing Jesse.

"Why, you little sneak," Shirlene said as she reeled him back by his Superman shirt, "what are you doing following me around?"

He jerked free and turned on her, his eyes squinty and mean. "Catchin' a big fat liar! You told Mia you wouldn't tell no one!"

"Would you keep it down," Shirlene hissed. She lifted a hand and waved at Sheriff Winslow, who stood in front of the town hall talking to the mayor. "I didn't tell anyone. But you can't expect me to take on four homeless kids without asking a few questions."

"We ain't homeless," the ornery kid huffed. "We had a fine home until you showed up."

"That's debatable," Shirlene said as she walked back to the bench where she'd hooked Sherman's leash.

The pig snuffled as he got up from the shady spot beneath the bench he'd been sleeping under, then he trotted over to Jesse and prodded the kid with his head until Jesse leaned down and scratched his ears. Obviously, Sherman didn't believe in holding grudges. Jesse grinned from ear to ear until his gaze landed on Shirlene's Batman t-shirt, a t-shirt she had been forced to wear when none of Mia's other shirts had fit her.

"You better not stretch it out," Jesse grumbled for the umpteenth time that morning.

"And you better quit following me," Shirlene warned as she tugged Sherman down the street. First things first;

she needed a strong cup of coffee. After she had some caffeine in her system, she'd be able to figure out what to do next. Unfortunately, before she could get to Josephine's, a little pipsqueak of a bank manager came around the corner and almost ran her over.

The pig squealed a warning, and Mr. Peabody jumped back as if bitten.

"I wish you would keep that creature properly penned up, Ms. Dalton," he said in his uppity voice.

Shirlene stared the man down. "And I wish you would give me back my house, Reggie."

He looked thoroughly annoyed. "We wouldn't be in business long, Ms. Dalton, if we forgave every loan."

"I'm not asking for forgiveness. Just a little human kindness, is all."

He cleared this throat. "Well, you'll have to take that up with Mr. Cates."

"And I plan to, Reggie. Just as soon as Mr. Cates gets back from his vacation." She tipped her head. "Where did you say he went?"

"I didn't." The man hurried down the street as fast as his little legs would carry him.

"He stole your house?"

Shirlene turned to find Jesse standing behind her. She might've given the kid a piece of her mind for eavesdropping if a flash of white hadn't caught her attention. As she watched the familiar SUV come down the street toward them, she couldn't help tugging the Rangers cap lower and stepping behind Jesse. Unfortunately, Jesse was no bigger than a gnat, and Beau was more observant then she thought.

The Escalade pulled up to the curb, and the window rolled down.

"Ms. Dalton?"

Since there was no help for it now, Shirlene sucked in her stomach, pushed out Batman, and sashayed over. Except it was hard to sashay in a pair of too-small, worn-out flip-flops.

"I thought we'd gotten past Ms. Dalton."

He smiled that sexy smile. "Mornin', Shirlene. It sure looks like it's going to be another pretty day."

She sent him a sassy little smirk. "Only if you like your days sizzlin' and your nights steamy."

The dazzling smile reconfigured into one a lot more devilish. "A true Texan doesn't like it any other way."

Behind her, Jesse snorted. But she chose to ignore the kid.

"So how's the vacation goin'? Any luck hunting down your ancestors?" she asked.

"No, ma'am, and I've pretty much given up." He stared out the windshield for a few seconds before looking back at her. "You wouldn't know where a man could go for a little fun in this town, would you?"

She rested a hand on her hip. "I guess that would depend on what your idea of a little fun is."

He laughed. "How 'bout a little drinkin', a little dancin', and a little female companionship?"

"Then Bootlegger's Bar is your place."

He squinted up at her. "I don't suppose you ever go there?"

"It's been known to happen."

"You think it might happen tomorrow night?"

Since Shirlene already had more than enough on her plate, she probably should've turned Beau down. But she had always believed in keeping her options open. And an attractive man with misty blue eyes was a nice option to have.

"It might," she said with a slight smile.

Beau grinned from ear to ear before he tipped his hat at her and pulled away from the curb. As Shirlene watched the white SUV drive away, Jesse came up and stood next to her.

"I thought Bubba was your boyfriend."

Shirlene snorted. "Not likely."

"Then how come he looks so pissed at you for flirtin' with that Beau feller?"

Shirlene glanced around, her gaze landing on the man who stood not more than three feet away, his shoulder propped up against the side of the library and his cap pulled low. Jesse was right. Even with the curled brim shading his eyes, Bubba Wilkes looked pissed.

Although his next words were as cool and country hick as ever.

"Why, Ms. Dalton, if I'd known you were interested in baby-faced cowboys," he rubbed the scruffy whiskers on his jaw, "I would've tried out that hot waxin'."

Chapter Eleven

BILLY WAITED UNTIL Shirlene Dalton had tossed him an exasperated look and sashayed down the street before he headed in the opposite direction. The woman annoyed the hell out of him, and it was best to keep his distance. Especially after the kiss they had shared out at Sutter Springs. A kiss that had been a mistake. A big mistake. Billy had too much on his plate to get wrapped up with some woman who flirted with every cowboy who came down the pike—every cowboy but Billy.

And maybe that was what had his back up. Shirlene hadn't flirted with him once, yet she was more than willing to flaunt that killer body and flash that smile at a man she hadn't known for more than a day.

Billy didn't know who pissed him off most—Beau or the woman. But he figured it out soon enough when he crossed the street to his truck and overheard the mayor and Sheriff Winslow talking.

"...couldn't find a thing on a Beauregard Williams from Houston who fits his description," the sheriff said. "Which means he's probably going by an alias."

"I knew there was somethin' fishy about the man." Harley's eyes narrowed as the SUV disappeared from sight. "A name is the most important thing a man has, and someone who lies about it is up to no good. Which means that we need to keep him away from Shirlene."

"It may be too late for that," the sheriff said. "Last night, Kenny Gene followed him straight to Shirlene's mansion. And according to Kenny, the man didn't even wait to be invited inside. Seems he has his own key and just up and let himself in."

While Billy's anger came to a full boil, Harley only shook his head. "I was afraid that somethin' like this would happen. A fine-lookin' widda woman attracts men like buzzards to roadkill."

"So what are we goin' to do, Harley? We can't let some no-account varmint mess with our Shirlene." Sam fingered the gun in his holster.

Harley shook his head. "Nope, we sure can't. 'Course, we can't go runnin' in half-cocked either. Shirlene might not have a temper as bad as Hope's, but she sure doesn't like folks pokin' their noses into her business. Which means, we need to have some hard evidence." He hitched up his pants. "Have Kenny keep watchin', and I'll see what I can dig up." He glanced up and noticed Billy. "Hey, Bubba, you gonna do a little fishin' today?"

Billy plastered on a grin. "Nope, more like a little huntin'."

It didn't take Billy long to get out to Shirlene's mansion. He saw the house long before he reached it. A huge, white, mission-style monstrosity that covered more land than Texas Stadium. Having grown up in a small farmhouse, it seemed like a blatant misuse of space and money.

Especially when the only two people that had lived there were Shirlene and her husband Lyle.

Billy had never thought of Lyle as more than a means to an end. But as he drove down the tree-lined road, he couldn't help but feel jealous of the man. Which was just plain crazy. The man was dead, for God's sake. And even if he hadn't been, he had nothing that Billy wanted. Nothing at all.

The circular driveway was located at the end of the road, but instead of pulling up in front, he pulled around back by the six-car garage. As he climbed out of the truck, Billy glanced around. Sure enough, there was Kenny Gene sitting up in the cedar tree right next to the garage with a pair of binoculars as big as he was.

Billy took a moment to control his laughter before he strutted over. "Hey, Kenny Gene."

"Shhh." Kenny held a finger to his lips. "I'm on duty."

"So I heard." Billy stared up at the man, who was dressed in a camouflage vest and pants that had to be hot as hell in this afternoon heat. "You see anything suspicious?"

Kenny made so much racket climbing down from the tree that he scared a flock of white-tailed doves from the underbrush in the open field next to the garage. They took to the sky in a loud flap of wings.

"As suspicious as a snake in the grass," Kenny said. He had almost reached the ground when he got one boot caught in a branch, and Billy had to grab him to keep him from taking a nosedive into the driveway. As soon as he was on his feet, he grabbed Billy's t-shirt and pulled him around to the side of the garage. "We can't be too careful. The man is up to no good, I tell you."

"So he's in there." Billy leaned around the corner of the garage and squinted at the huge floor-to-ceiling windows.

"Shore is." Kenny gave Billy a pointed look. "And so is Shirlene."

"You don't say?"

Kenny nodded. "Shirlene ain't left the house since I've been watchin'. While the suspect," he glanced down at his watch, "left at 9:15 a.m. on the dot and returned at 10:32. Except this time, instead of goin' through the front door, he just pulled right on in the garage like he owned the place."

"That does sound suspicious." Billy looked down at the binoculars. "So you been here all night?"

Kenny nodded. "Sam was gonna relieve me, but he needed to have a meetin' with the mayor." He perked up. "You didn't by any chance bring me somethin' to eat, did ya? A donut? A Payday? A stick of Trident?"

"Sorry, buddy," Billy shook his head. "I just came out to say 'hey.'" He peeked around the corner again. "But I tell you what, if you want to go grab something and get some shut eye, I'll keep an eye on things here until you get back."

Kenny looked a little doubtful. "I shore appreciate the offer, Bubba. But I don't know if Sam would like me passin' off my official duties to someone who isn't as highly trained as I am."

Billy looked down at the ground and tried not to smile. "Well, there is that. 'Course what Sam don't know won't hurt him. And since Beau just got back, he probably won't be going out again soon. By the time he does, you should be back at your station."

It only took Kenny Gene a second to slap the binoculars in his hands. "Be careful with them. They ain't standard equipment."

Once Kenny had gotten in the truck parked out behind the garage, he gunned the engine and left in a spray of gravel. If the birds hadn't attracted Beau's attention, Kenny's exit sure would've. Billy was still shaking his head when he walked around back to the patio doors. The sun reflected off the sparkling glass, forcing Billy to cup his hand around his eyes in order to see in.

Beau sat at the breakfast counter, a newspaper spread out in front of him and a cup of steaming coffee within reach. He picked up the coffee and took a sip, his gaze lifting from the newspaper and over to the French doors. He choked and came up off the bar stool, spilling coffee all over his pressed western shirt. Billy was still laughing when he pulled open the door and walked in.

"Not funny, Billy," Beau turned and reached for a paper towel. "I could've been scalded."

"I should do more than scald you," Billy stated as he strode into the kitchen. "I should whup your butt. Who the hell told you that you could live in Shirlene Dalton's house?"

Beau swiped at his shirt and yelled like the twenty-five-year old he was. "I made the decision myself! I was tired of driving fifty miles each way to that crummy hotel room, especially when this house was sitting completely empty. And since you and Brant said I was just as much a part of the company as you two are, I figured I had a right."

"Well, you figured wrong." Billy set Kenny's binoculars on the counter before moving over to the automatic coffee maker. "When we said you were part of the company, we meant the part that takes orders, not the part that gives them." He poured a cup of coffee and took a sip.

"Well, I'm through taking orders," Beau said. "You can play the dumb country hick who lives in a beat-up trailer if you want. But if I have to hang out in this Podunk town, I want a little comfort . . . and some fun."

Billy turned and looked at his brother. Beau was the spitting image of their daddy right down to the gray hair. Hair that had been the same color as Billy's before the chemotherapy.

"And just what kind of fun are we talking about, little brother?"

Beau looked away and shrugged. "Just fun, is all."

Billy set his cup down and leaned back against the counter, crossing his arms. "Fun in the form of Shirlene Dalton?" When Beau's face flamed a telltale red, Billy lost his cool and pushed away from the counter. "Over my dead body! I'll not have my little brother taking up with some money-grubbing gold digger."

Beau bristled and leaned toward Billy. "She's not a gold digger. She's a nice lady who didn't deserve to get tossed out of her house."

"A nice lady?" Billy waved a hand around the room. "Take a good look around, Beau. Shirlene Dalton married a man more than twice her age in order to get her hands on this, then turned around and lost it all only months after he died. And I won't have C-Corp falling prey to a woman who runs through money quicker than sand through a sieve. You take up with Ms. Dalton, you'll choose another place to work."

Beau's shoulders wilted. "I wasn't planning on marrying her, Billy. I was just hoping to get lucky. Have you seen the body on that woman?"

Billy had—every luscious curve and sweet valley. If he thought it was hard to keep his mind off Shirlene before he'd seen her soaking wet, it was nothing compared to how difficult it was now. All morning long, images of Shirlene kept popping into his brain—full, sweet breasts spilling over wet, pink lace—and damned if he could stop them. But what he could put a stop to was Beau setting his sights on something he could never have. Not if Billy had anything to say about it.

"Well, look for some other kind of entertainment while you're here."

Beau snorted. "I've tried, but it seems the town doesn't exactly care for strangers. I don't even know why Brant wanted me to come out with you."

"He was hoping you would get some rest and maybe do a little research. But it appears that all you've been doing is panting after Ms. Dalton. Did you even notice you're being watched?"

Beau grinned. "The guy in the camouflage? Yeah, I saw him. But I figured he was harmless."

"He's not harmless if he's spreading rumors around town about you sleeping with Shirlene."

Beau straightened. "Really? They think I'm bedding her?"

Billy rolled his eyes. "Don't get all cocky. They also think you're a low-down scoundrel who is up to no good."

"So that's why they've been treating me so badly." He shot Billy a snide look. "They think I'm you."

"Thanks to your stupidity, they do now." He picked up his cup and walked over for a refill.

"So I guess you want me to pack up and go back to the motel," Beau said.

Billy shook his head. "It's too late for that. The towns-people will figure out soon enough that Shirlene has been evicted, and that you're one of the Cates brothers responsible for kicking her sweet behind out."

"Sweet behind?" Beau smirked. "You sure you don't have a thing for Shirlene Dalton, big brother?"

"Not likely," Billy said. "Women like her will drain you dry and spit you out. Just look what she did to her husband. Poor man worked himself into an early grave trying to keep her in diamonds."

"Diamonds and enough clothes and shoes to fill three closets."

Billy's eyebrows popped up. "You been snooping in her panty drawers, Beauregard?"

"Nooo," Beau said, although his blush said otherwise. Before Billy could try to mentally justify his sudden flare of anger, Beau headed toward the bedrooms. "Besides, I didn't have to snoop to see more than her panties."

Setting down his coffee cup, Billy followed Beau back to the cavernous master suite. The high, king-sized bed was rumpled, but still looked like a sultan's with the rich, brocade bedding and multiple satin pillows. But then it wasn't the bed that held Billy's attention as much as the painting that hung over it.

Even with Beau standing there grinning like an idiot, it was hard for Billy to keep his mouth from falling open. Not with the life-sized painting of Shirlene as naked as the day she was born staring him in the face.

Of course, she wasn't completely naked. She had on a pair of silver stilettos with tiny rhinestone buckles and a necklace with a diamond-encrusted pendant. The pendant hung in the cleavage of her full breasts, breasts with nipples barely covered by the gray fur of the coat she lay across. Over one smooth shoulder, Billy could see the slope of her back, followed by the sweet swells of her hips. Her long legs were bent and crossed at the ankles, the silver heels inches from the shadowy crevice of her ass. But it wasn't the curvaceous body that held his attention as much as the face framed by piles of blond hair—a face that was lit with laughter and a look that could only be described as love.

"Now you see why I was so hot to get her into bed," Beau said.

The words were barely out of his mouth before Billy reached out and grabbed the front of his brother's shirt, jerking him close. "We don't have time for your bullshit, Beau. If standing around fantasizing about Ms. Dalton is what you've been spending your time doing, you might as well get your ass back to Dogwood."

By the angry look on Beau's face, Billy figured he was in for a brotherly tussle. But before Beau could get in the first shove, Billy's cell phone rang, and he released Beau to answer it.

"Hello."

There was a slight pause before a female voice came on. "I'm sorry. I must have the wrong number. I'm looking for a Mr. Wilkes."

Billy quickly slipped into a less intimidating voice. "You got him, ma'am."

"Oh," the woman said. "I didn't recognize your voice at first. This is Ms. Murphy over at the Bramble Public Library."

"Well, howdy, Ms. Murphy. Did you find some more books for me?" Billy asked.

"Not books," Ms. Murphy said, "but I found some *Bramble Gazette* newspaper articles from the late 1800s that I think you'll find interesting."

"Well, I shore thank you for all the trouble, ma'am."

"It was no trouble, Mr. Wilkes." Ms. Murphy laughed softly. "In fact, I enjoyed reading the articles about whose hog took first place at the state fair, or how some young boys got in trouble for sneaking into Bootlegger's Saloon. Of course, one story wasn't quite so humorous."

Billy's eyes narrowed. "And what story would that be, Ms. Murphy?"

"The one about that poor metalsmith from Lubbock being shot dead in the middle of Main Street."

"That does sound sad." He glanced over at Beau, who was listening intently. "I'll tell you what, Ms. Murphy. I have some things to pick up in town so why don't I stop by and get those newspaper articles today?"

"Of course. I'll have them on the front desk waiting for you."

After he hung up the phone, Beau didn't waste any time asking, "What did she find, Billy?"

With anger rolling through him, Billy stared back at his little brother. "A newspaper article about the cold-blooded murder of our great-great-granddaddy, William Wilkes Cates."

Chapter Twelve

THE *BRAMBLE GAZETTE ARTICLE* didn't give Billy much more information than he already had. But it did serve to confirm the Cates family legend.

On August 5, 1892, William Wilkes Cates had ridden into Bramble from Lubbock, Texas, with a shiny dedication plaque for the new town hall. No more than an hour later, he lay dead in the middle of the dusty street. Shot down in cold blood by the sheriff for doing nothing more than demanding the money due him—money the mayor had withheld because the date on the plaque was wrong. But it hadn't been Billy's grandfather's fault that the town hall's completion had been delayed due to bad weather. William had only engraved the date that had been given him.

Billy stared at the faded newspaper print and the one piece of information he hadn't had. Sheriff Wynn Murdock. The man responsible for his grandfather's death and the curse that had followed the Cateses since the .45-caliber bullet had shattered William's heart.

From that moment on, nothing but bad luck had

followed the Cates family. Disease. Dust storms. Drought. Tornados. If a person could name a calamity, they had suffered through it. And it didn't help that Billy's relatives refused to forget. Every male child born from William's only son, William Junior, carried the name William as a first or middle name.

The name was more of a death sentence. The only Cates descendants remaining were a couple of old aunts and Billy's family. Every other ancestor had succumbed to the curse in one way or another. Even Billy's family hadn't gone unscathed. Billy's oldest brother, Buckley, had died in high school when a train demolished his car. Brant's wife and son had lost their lives when a tornado hit Dogwood. And Beau had been diagnosed with cancer just a year earlier.

It was after the cancer diagnosis that Billy had first come to Bramble. He didn't have any particular plan. He was just angry and wanted something or someone to blame. What he found was a town filled with friendly people who thought no more of William Cates than a funny story to tell at Bootlegger's. But it wasn't so funny to Billy. And the more he learned about the incident, the more consumed he became. His preoccupation grew worse when on a trip to Lubbock, he discovered William's wife's diary. It was mostly ramblings from a broken-hearted woman, but one entry intrigued him: William's body had never been returned home.

For some reason, Billy believed that if he could just find the bones of William Cates and take them back to Lubbock to be buried with his wife and son, the curse would be broken. But while looking for clues to where his ancestor was buried, he discovered information about

Dalton Oil. And Brant, Billy's older brother, wasn't interested in bones as much as he was in revenge. He wanted Bramble, Texas, wiped off the map. At first, Billy had wanted that too. But it was hard to live among the friendly townsfolk and not form attachments. And now that Beau's cancer was in remission, he had started to rethink closing down Dalton Oil and ruining an entire town. Unfortunately, it was too late for regrets. The wheels had already been set in motion, and now all Billy could do was sit back and watch the train wreck happen.

He picked up another history book and leafed through it in hopes of finding something he'd missed—a clue that would lead him to his grandfather's gravesite. But after only a few sentences, his mind took a detour and traveled to a place it had gone often in the last twenty-four hours. A place filled with eyes as green and lush as a PGA fairway, lips as sweet as elderberry wine, and breasts as soft and full as his great-granny's featherbed.

When Billy hardened beneath the fly of his jeans, he slammed the book shut and rolled up from the couch. To hell with lying around reading boring books that failed to hold a man's attention. What he needed was some good old-fashioned manual labor. The kind that worked off a man's frustration and energy and left him too tired to think about things he had no business thinking about.

Within hours, he'd pulled a mountain of waist-high weeds from the lot surrounding his trailer, fixed a hole in the back fence, and filled in a pothole as big as a swimming pool. And when his mind continued its slideshow of wet cleavage above a lacy transparent bra, he grabbed a rusted pair of hedge clippers and moved on to the shrubbery.

After only a few feet, he decided manual labor was one thing; heat stroke something else entirely. Still, he had never left a job unfinished. Especially when all he needed was a different tool.

Tossing the hedge clippers in the back of the pickup with the weeds, he headed next door. Since he'd spent most of yesterday holed up with the box of old newspapers the librarian had given him, he hadn't seen or heard much from his neighbors. And he had to admit he was curious about the woman who had borne such a ragtag group of kids. No doubt she was a tired-looking thing, worn down by years of trying to feed four mouths. The thought made him feel slightly guilty for not stopping by sooner and offering the woman some help. Of course, like his mama liked to say, there was no time like the present.

Billy weaved his way through the junk, wondering how to offer help without hurting feelings. He was so wrapped up in his thoughts that he didn't notice the woman who stood at the back of the lot until he had almost passed her. He stopped and studied her as she hung clothes on a wire that stretched between the elm tree and the fence. From the back, she didn't look all that worn out. Her stance was straight, and her body sturdy as she clipped a diaper to the line. A stiff breeze blew her coppery hair off her neck, the thick, shoulder-length strands gleaming in the afternoon sun like a shiny new penny.

She bent over to pull out another diaper, and Billy couldn't help but notice the generous curve of her behind. One white cheek peeked out of the uneven cut-off jean shorts, and Billy felt a swift kick of desire.

Damn, he really needed to get out more. His attraction to women was way off kilter. Maybe he'd head over to Bootlegger's tonight and see if he could find some female company. He hated to get involved with a woman when he didn't plan on hanging around for long, but it was better than attacking a mother of four from behind. Or worse, a gold digger who was only interested in the size of a man's wallet.

"Excuse me, ma'am."

The woman let out a screech and jumped a good foot off the ground. But her shock was nothing compared to his when a pair of angry green eyes flashed back at him.

"What the hell—" Shirlene Dalton slapped a hand over her mouth and glanced around before removing it and hissing under her breath, "What the heck are you doing sneaking up on me, Bubba Wilkes?"

"What the hell happened to your hair?" He didn't even try to keep his voice lowered. How could he keep his voice lowered when he was fit to be tied? He had been sweating his ass off all morning trying to forget the woman, and here she was not more than five feet away from him looking like some kind of sexy Daisy Duke in a pair of cut-off shorts and a Spiderman t-shirt that was shrink-wrapped to those luscious boobs like tin foil on a tater.

"A five-dollar haircut at Twyla's is what happened to my hair!" She shook the diaper out with a snap, then folded the ends over the wire as she continued to rant. "All I asked for was a cut and a root touch-up. And what do I get? A 1970s shag and an entirely different color!"

Her voice grew higher as she did a pretty darned good job of mimicking Kenny's girlfriend. "Why, Shirlene Dalton, I don't know why you're all upset. It's the exact color you was born with." Ms. Dalton jerked up another diaper. "Except I haven't been a redhead in over ten years, for God's sake!"

A smile slipped over Billy's face, and damned if he could help it. "I don't know why I didn't see it before."

She whipped around and stared at him. "What?"

He took a minute to study the coppery mane that fluttered around her face—a face with an angry scowl and not a stitch of make-up.

His gaze wandered over the hills Spiderman precariously clung to. "Just talkin' to myself."

With a roll of her eyes, she turned back to the makeshift clothesline. "I'd love to dive into that east Texas brain of yours, but I just don't have time." She finished hanging the last diaper before she reached down and picked up the clothesbasket, resting it on one curvy hip as she headed to the trailer.

If Billy knew what was good for him, he'd turn right back around and go home. Not to his trailer, but all the way back to Dogwood. Because if he'd realized anything in the last few minutes, it was that no amount of manual labor was going to erase the fresh images of red hair and soft white cheek burned into his brain. But since he couldn't leave Bramble just yet, he figured he'd have to suck it up and deal with it.

"Now don't go runnin' off, Red. At least, not until you explain what you're doing here dressed like that."

She whirled on him with fire in her eyes. "Don't you dare even think about it, Bubba Wilkes." She rammed a finger at his nose. "You can call me Honey Buns. Sugar Stick. Cinnamon Muffin. Or any other bakery item you dream up. But if you call me that again, I'll grab a gun and send you straight to redneck hell via thirty-aught."

He laughed. "I should've known with a temper like yours, that you would be a redhead." When she took a step closer, he held up a hand. "All right, Shirley girl, I'll lose the Red."

Shirlene didn't appear to like her new nickname any better. She shot him a nasty glare before she hurried up the steps of the trailer.

"So what are you still doing here?" he asked as he followed her.

There was only a second's hesitation before she answered. "I'm just helping out while their mama's at work."

Billy laughed at the joke. Except his laughter died when he walked in the door and four pairs of eyes stared back at him and Shirlene—including the beady eyes of the pig, who was stretched out on the couch. Jesse was sitting at the table working on some kind of school work with Mia while Brody sat on the floor playing. The baby was nowhere in sight, although he figured she must be napping in the room with the closed door when Shirlene walked over and pressed an ear to it.

"I told you," Mia said, rather defiantly. "She'll let us know when she's awake."

"Right." Shirlene stared at the door for only a second before she dropped the basket and flopped down on the couch next to the pig.

"Hi, y'all," Billy threw out, although the only response he got was from Brody, who lifted the naked Barbie and shook it at him.

"Mine," he growled.

"Gotcha, brother," Billy held up a hand. "She's all yours."

The answer seemed to pacify the kid, and he went back to playing. Jesse and Mia still watched Billy as if he were a cockroach they couldn't decide if they wanted to let live or squash beneath their boots. After a few uncomfortable minutes of standing in the doorway, Billy figured he wasn't going to get an invitation so he pulled out one of the folding chairs from the table and straddled it.

"So Jesse, you still have that chainsaw?" he asked.

The kid shot a glance over at Shirlene. "Yeah, but I ain't gonna be able to scare her now that she knows—"

Billy reached out and ruffled Jesse's hair before the kid pulled back and glared at him. "'Course you shouldn't run around scarin' folks, which is exactly why I want to buy the chainsaw from you." He sent the kid a warning look. "We can't have a dangerous tool like that in a child's hands, now can we?"

Jesse looked confused, but not so confused that he didn't jump on a money-making opportunity. "Two hundred bucks, and I'll throw in the chain," he said.

Billy cocked a brow. "I can get a new one for less than—" He paused, realizing that this was the perfect opportunity to help out his neighbors without hurting feelings. "Two hundred it is. But if you want cash, you'll have to wait until I make a trip into town." He wiped at the sweat that trickled down his temple. "Dang, don't y'all have air conditioning?"

"Do you think we would be sitting here in this oven if we did?" Shirlene said in her sassy tone.

Billy finally took note of the kids' flushed faces and sweaty heads. This guilt thing was starting to get annoying. "Fine. I'll take a look at it and see what I can do."

Shirlene perked up. "You can fix it?"

"What is a dumb redneck good for if he doesn't know one end of a screwdriver from the other?" He winked at her as he got back to his feet.

Jesse quickly followed suit. "I'll help you."

"Oh, no, you don't," Mia said. "Not until you finish your homework."

"But it's summer, Mia," Jesse whined. "None of the other kids got school work."

Mia shot a quick glance over at Billy. "I just don't want you to get behind is all."

"Listen to your sister, son," Billy said. "Book learnin' is important. Besides, if you hurry, there'll still be plenty of time to fry your butt off on the roof." That seemed to light a fire under the kid, and he picked up his pencil and went right to work.

What with the trailer stifling and the company frigid, Billy didn't waste any time heading out the door. Shirlene was hot on his heels.

"I can help until Jesse gets finished," she offered as she followed him down the steps.

He laughed. "If you're so scared about being with the kids alone, what are you doing here?" He glanced back at her on his way to the hedge. "Especially dressed like Daisy Duke?"

"I am not dressed like Daisy Duke," she huffed. "And I'm certainly not scared of those kids." When he snorted, she surprised him by conceding. "Fine. I'm terrified of the little heathens. And who wouldn't be? Mia's a fifty-year-old menopausal woman in a sixteen-year-old's body. Jesse's an ornery con artist who thinks I'm the devil incarnate. And Brody only says one word and in a really creepy voice. Hey, watch it!" She yelled as the branch Billy had just released slapped her in the face.

He grinned. "My bad, Shirley girl."

"Right," she grumbled under her breath.

But she didn't return to the trailer. Obviously a devious redneck was safer than a group of heathens.

"I noticed you didn't mention the baby." He grabbed the tool belt out of the back of his truck.

"Adeline is the exception."

Billy glanced up after buckling the belt to his hips. "Let's see how you feel after changing your first poopy diaper."

It took a full minute for Shirlene to reply. Her gaze seemed to be riveted on Billy's tool belt.

"Mia doesn't let me do much with Brody or Adeline. She prefers to treat me like a maid without a green card—when did you change a diaper?"

Sharing personal information wasn't a good idea. But Billy figured a little wouldn't hurt. "I have a big family."

"How big?"

"Seven, including my parents." He headed over to the ladder on the side of the trailer.

"That's not big, Wilkes, that's Mormon-sized." She hesitated. "Are you?"

"Nope." He picked up the ladder and started back toward the hedge. "Just country." She hurried in front of him and held back the branches of the shrub, but he wasn't falling for that trick. "I can get it."

"Chicken." She flashed her deep dimples right before she ducked through the hedge.

The afternoon sun was almost unbearable. But so was the view of Shirlene's bee-hind when she climbed up the ladder before him. The woman had curves in places he hadn't even known women had curves in, and it left his body hard and his brain empty, which was why he didn't say much of anything for the next few minutes. Instead he located the swamp cooler and tried to concentrate on the job at hand. But it wasn't easy.

"Geez Louise, it's hot." Shirlene pulled the edge of the t-shirt up and fanned it, revealing a tempting piece of white stomach and a cute belly button.

Jerking his gaze away, Billy knelt by the air conditioner. "So what's up with the shirt? I didn't take you for a superhero kind of girl."

"Really? And just what kind of a girl do you take me for?"

"The kind who enjoys the feel of satin and silk." He pulled off the cover of the evaporative unit and looked inside. It wasn't as bad as he thought it would be. The belt and filter pads needed to be replaced, but the motor seemed to be in good condition. He exchanged the screwdriver for a wrench. After a few minutes of working on getting the belt off, he glanced up at Shirlene who stood there sweltering in the heat.

"If you're plannin' on standing there, the least you could do is block that little strip of sunlight."

She sent him an exasperated look. "I'd be sitting if I had somewhere to sit." She glanced down at the dirty, metal roof.

"Prissy woman," he sighed as he got to his feet. He jerked open the snaps of his shirt and slipped it off, intending to spread it out on the roof for her to sit on. The cool air on his sweaty chest was a welcome relief. What wasn't a relief was the hot, green gaze that settled there.

Damn, the woman's eyes should carry a warning— DANGER, ONE GLANCE COULD FRY YOUR BRAIN CELLS. But it was too late for warnings. His mind was already fried. He just stood there like the dumb country boy he was and allowed those eyes to glide over his bare torso like a curry brush over a horse's back.

"You're sweating," she said as her eyes ate him whole.

"Uh-huh," squeezed out of his tight throat. As he watched, one soft hand lifted and stroked a cool path down the center of his chest.

"Satin and silk," she sighed as her hand trailed down his stomach and back up again. At the top of his clavicle, she spread out her fingers and slid them over one pectoral muscle. It twitched as she cradled it against her palm. The woman was like an electrical current and he the conductor. All he could do was stand there and let her spark straight through him.

"Hey? What are y'all doin'?"

The question had them both jumping back and turning to look at the strawberry-blond head that peeked over the edge of the roof.

Jesse scrambled over the ladder and sauntered across the roof as if he'd done it every day of his life. Billy didn't doubt that he had. Boys wanted to climb on top of any obstacle put in front of them—Billy's gaze slid over to Shirlene—make that boys and men. Never in his life had he wanted to climb on something as much as he did the fiery-haired woman who stood there with her green eyes all steamed with desire.

To ease the sexual tension that arced between them, Billy tried to come up with a stupid hillbilly line. Unfortunately, his hillbilly had been seduced into submission, and all he could do was stare back at her until Jesse spoke.

"So now that I'm here, does she have to stay?"

It took a real effort for Billy to pull his gaze away from

all that green heat. He cleared the desire from his throat. "Well, I think that's up to Ms.—"

Before he could finish, Shirlene started backing toward the ladder. "I-I think I'll just go on inside now." She flapped a hand in a cute, flustered way. "I'm sure you men can handle things just fine without little ol' me."

For some reason, the thought of Shirlene Dalton being as flustered as a roosting hen brought a smile to Billy's face. And fearing she might drop off the side of the roof, he stepped over and took her elbow, guiding her over to the ladder. When she was safely on the ground, he headed back to the air conditioner.

"So what was you and Ms. Dalton doin' up here?" Jesse asked. "Having S-E-X?"

The blush that spread across Billy's face was damned annoying. He squatted down and tried to sound stern. "I think you're a little too young to be talking about things like that. Not that Ms. Dalton and I were even close to having..." He cleared his throat. "She was just swattin' a fly."

"On your titty?"

The wrench slipped out of Billy's fingers and thunked to the roof. He wiped his hand off on his jeans before picking it back up. "It happens. And men don't have titties, we have muscles."

The kid glanced down at his skinny body, then over at Billy's chest. "Well, I ain't got those yet, so what do I call mine?"

After only a few seconds, Billy shrugged. "Titties."

Chapter Thirteen

SHIRLENE DIDN'T KNOW what was worse: sitting in the hot trailer putting up with Mia's silent treatment or standing on a sizzling roof with an even more sizzling redneck. A redneck she had trouble keeping her hands off. What had she been thinking? She had never helped herself to a man in her life. She'd never had to. Men took one look at her body and dove right in. Except as much as Bubba talked a good game, he wasn't the diving type. The kiss out at Sutter Springs had been a mutual agreement, and the body massage on the roof had been all Shirlene.

Geez. She shook her head. Her preoccupation with Bubba's body was starting to become annoying. Of course, it made perfect sense. After being married to a man close to twenty-five years her senior, firm and smooth held a certain appeal. And Shirlene had never been good at resisting things that appealed to her. Even if they weren't good for her.

Bubba wasn't good for her. He was way too cocky. And way too country. And way too...hot for her to handle. Especially now when her emotions were still screwed up

CATCH ME A COWBOY

over Lyle's death. Anyone with half a brain knew that you should wait an entire year after a major tragedy before making any big decisions. Hopping in bed with Bubba Wilkes was a big decision.

As was deciding what to do with four orphaned kids. Unfortunately, she couldn't put that off. The Foster kids needed help now, not three months from now. Not that they seemed real happy about her being there. All four treated her like a bad case of the chicken pox.

Shirlene glanced over at Mia, who sat at the card table working on some problem that had her smooth forehead crinkled with worry. "So what are you working on, honey?" she asked, although she didn't expect an answer. The girl talked less than she ate, which was something that had started to concern Shirlene. The eating part— not the talking. After living with a silent-type brother and a drunk mama, Shirlene was used to keeping up a one-sided conversation.

"I hated homework as a kid," she continued as she adjusted her long legs over Sherman. Given that Mia insisted on closing up the couch every morning, there was barely enough room for a girl and her pig. Not that Sherman seemed to mind. After finishing off the generic Corn Flakes and Cheerios, he was content to sleep the afternoon away just like Adeline and Brody.

Shirlene only wished she was as lucky. Since arriving at the trailer, she hadn't slept more than a wink. Which was just another reason she hadn't been able to keep her hands off a certain country boy. It appeared that all the studies were right: Sleep deprivation not only slowed down your reactions, but it impaired your decision-making skills.

In an attempt to keep her mind off the hillbilly on the roof, she continued to talk to herself. "Lordy, me and Colt used to get into it over my homework. I could think up every excuse under the sun not to do it—or take a bath— or pick up my room."

"I thought Colt was your brother."

The softly spoken words had Shirlene glancing over at the girl. Her glasses had slid down on her nose and those odd-colored eyes stared back at Shirlene.

"He is." Shirlene lifted her legs off Sherman and sat up.

Mia tipped her head, her long ponytail brushing over her arm. The blond hair had Shirlene mentally cussing Twyla all over again. What had she been thinking letting a beauty-school dropout style her hair? Of course, what choice had she had with only twenty dollars and a Brody-cut?

"So why was it your brother's job to get after you?" Mia asked. "Why didn't your parents do it?"

Shirlene wasn't one to air her dirty laundry. The past was the past, and history was best left in textbooks. But there was something in Mia's eyes that made Shirlene make an exception. Something that spoke of times much harder than anything she and Colt had gone through.

"Colt watched out for me just like you watch out for your siblings," she said. "My daddy died in a car crash when I was little, and my mama...wasn't real good with kids." She got to her feet and walked to the fridge. But she had no more than pulled out the orange juice container when Mia stopped her.

"We have to save that for Brody and Adeline." Mia shot a nasty glance over at Sherman. "Seeing as how your pig has already eaten our breakfast for tomorrow."

"Stop worrying, honey. I'll get us more orange juice and cereal." Still, she only splashed a small amount of juice in the Dixie cup.

"With what?" Mia asked. "Your good looks?"

"As a matter of fact...yes." She pulled one of the folding chairs over to the cupboard. "My good looks have done just fine by me. Of course, lately I've run into a bit of a slump."

"You call being evicted from your home a slump?" Mia stared at her as if she'd lost her mind. Since only a few people looked at Shirlene like that—mostly Hope and Sherman—it was a little disconcerting. Especially since Mia was still wet behind the ears. Although wet behind the ears or not, the girl was smart enough to figure things out. Of course, Shirlene would bet that Jesse eavesdropping on her conversation with Mr. Peabody hadn't hurt.

"Okay, so it's more than a slump," Shirlene conceded. She stood on the chair and felt around on the top of the cupboard. The cobwebs creeped her out, but she kept searching. "With my love of the finer things in life, I might've dug myself into a bit of a hole. But it's nothing I can't dig myself out of." Amid the dirt and cobwebs, she finally found what she was looking for. She held the bottle up triumphantly. "See what a little perseverance will get you?"

Mia stared at the dusty bottle of vodka for only a second before she dropped her head into her folded arms. "Just great, Mia Michaels, the one person you ask for help turns out to be a narcissistic alcoholic without a penny to her name."

"Now wait just one minute, sister." Shirlene almost toppled off the chair. "I am not narcissistic!" The dust from the top of the cabinet finally caught up with her, and she sneezed twice before she continued. "Nor am I an alcoholic." She got down and tried to unscrew the lid on the bottle, but it was covered in grime and kept slipping through her fingers. She turned on the faucet, but even after holding it under the trickle of hot water for a good five minutes, it still wouldn't budge.

She grabbed the old dishrag and wrapped it around the top. "I might have a margarita every now and again."

Mia lifted her head. "Every now and again?"

"Every now and again," Shirlene huffed as she placed the bottle between her knees and twisted as hard as she could. When she still couldn't get it opened, she held it out to Mia. "You mind giving it a try, honey?"

The look Shirlene received was one of those teenage eye-rolls she'd seen, but had never had directed at her. Now that she had, she understood why wealthy parents sent their kids off to school.

"Just a couple a night, is all," she defended herself. Except once the words were out, they sounded more incriminating than vindicating. "For the love of Pete!" She slammed the bottle down on the table. "I am not an alcoholic."

"Shhh!" Mia glared at her. "You'll wake the babies."

Shirlene glared back. She wasn't the type of woman to let her temper get the best of her, but she had had about enough of Mia's superior attitude. Who did she think she was talking to, anyway? The girl was living in her trailer, drinking her water, and using the electricity she'd paid for. The teenager had no business pointing out her flaws when she was living off Shirlene's charity.

Alcoholic? As if Shirlene would fall into that trap after living with an alcoholic mother.

Her gaze tracked over to the bottle. A bottle exactly like all the other bottles that her mother had stashed in every nook and cranny in an attempt to keep them hidden from Colt—who, when he found them, would pour them down the drain. Shirlene hadn't gone on the bottle hunts with her brother. She hadn't wanted anything to do with the clear substance that turned her mother into a sloppy drunk.

Until now.

Now she wanted the inch and a half of alcohol left in the bottle more than she wanted a dye job and decent haircut. Just one little drink to make the situation she found herself in more tolerable. One little drink to ease the tension in her shoulders and the throbbing at her temples. But before she could reach for the bottle, her gaze fell on the tablet that sat on the table. A tablet with a long column of figures and a total at the bottom. The total was barely readable, but the negative in front was a thick dark slash. The obvious display of Mia's financial concerns caused Shirlene's thirst to be squelched beneath a heavy dose of guilt.

She flopped down in the chair and released her breath in a long sigh. "I want to help you, Mia, but you've got to quit treating me like I'm a wart on a hog—" she glanced over at Sherman, "present company excluded." She looked back at Mia. "I'll be the first person to tell you I'm not perfect, but I'm the best you got."

"Great," Mia muttered, looking annoyingly defeated.

Shirlene felt pretty defeated herself. But never one to give in to depressing feelings, she forged ahead. "Things might not be great now, honey, but they will be. Just as soon as I get my house back, I plan to make a visit to

Houston and see if I can't get this entire thing cleared up."
When Mia started to argue, she held up a hand. "I know,
I know, you're not going back to your mean foster parents. And I don't expect you to. Lyle had a lot of friends
in Houston so I'm sure I won't have any trouble finding
you and your siblings a suitable home. But until then, you
need to give my wallet back."

The young girl's eyes narrowed behind her glasses.
"How . . . ? I guess Jesse told you."

"No." Shirlene held out her hand. "You just did."

Mia's shoulders slumped, and without another word,
she scraped the chair back and headed for the bedroom
where Brody napped. When she returned, she had the
wallet in her hand. "Here. But I don't know what good
it will do you. Most of the cards don't even work—" She
caught herself. "I mean . . ."

Shirlene's eyebrows lifted. "You been using my cards,
honey?"

"Only for gas," Mia said. "And I plan on paying you
back."

"With what? Your good looks?"

"Very funny." Mia scowled as she sat back down.

Shirlene laughed. "You've got to lighten up, kiddo.
Life's too short to live it under such a dark frown."

"That's easy for you to say." She flopped back in the
chair and crossed her arms over her chest. "And don't
include me in your adoption plans. Once I've made sure
the kids are settled, I'm out of here."

"Got the big city itch, do you?" Shirlene picked up
the bottle of vodka and stared at it for only a few seconds
before tossing it into the trashcan.

"No. I have the anywhere-but-Texas itch." She glanced

around. "I don't know how anyone lives in this godfor-saken state."

"And I don't know how anyone doesn't," Shirlene coun-tered. "But I guess that's just something else we'll agree to disagree on. For now, we need to write ourselves a list." Tearing the top piece of paper off the tablet, she picked up the pencil and handed it to Mia. "Go ahead, honey, write down everything we need from the Food Mart. And I mean, everything. Then write down all the things the kids have been going without—clothes, toys...chocolate."

"But—" Mia started.

"No ifs, ands, or buts. I might not have much credit left. But what I do have, we're going to use."

"And what are we going to live on for the rest of the month?" Mia groused.

"By this time next week," Shirlene winked, "we'll all be livin' the high life in my home sweet home."

Mia's face registered shock. "You're taking us with you?"

"Why not? I have more rooms than I know what to do with." She flashed a grin. "So what do you say, honey? You ready to go on a little shoppin' spree?"

Except thirty minutes later, Shirlene was the only one heading out the door. Mia was a stubborn little thing who had decided that the less the people of Bramble saw of her and the babies, the better. She had a valid point. All they needed was the townsfolk becoming suspicious. Still, Shirlene felt a little guilty about leaving the kids, which was crazy given the fact they barely acknowledged her departure from the trailer. Only Sherman snuffled a good-bye after refusing to leave his spot on the floor between Brody and Adeline.

Once outside, Shirlene couldn't help glancing up at the roof, or the disappointment she felt when the only person there was a freckled-face kid with his legs dangling over the edge. Ignoring Jesse, she made a beeline to the Navigator in the hopes of making a quick getaway. She should've known she wouldn't be that lucky.

"Who said you could wear the Hulk?" Jesse said, his demon eyes blazing in the deep oranges of the setting sun.

The ugly green t-shirt looked ridiculous with Shirlene's jeans and turquoise Manolos. But it was the only clean shirt she'd been able to find after she'd showered. "I promise I'll have it back to you by tonight, honey," she made an attempt at smoothing the kid's ruffled feathers.

"It won't do no good," Jesse grumbled. "You already stretched him out with your big—"

"Watch it, Jesse." Bubba's deep voice had Shirlene's heart thumping against her ribcage. It lodged there when he suddenly appeared around the side of the trailer in all his shirtless glory. Since the air conditioner didn't work, she had figured he'd given up. Obviously, Bubba was more dedicated than she thought.

Dedicated and wet.

Water dripped from his soaked hair and ran in glistening streams down his chest to the waistband of his jeans. He tossed the running hose over to the trunk of the elm before using two hands to scrape his wet hair off his forehead.

"You going into town?" he asked.

It took an effort to pull her gaze away from the sex video that played out before her. Even then, she had trouble figuring out what he'd just said.

"I need you to pick up some parts for the air conditioner at the hardware store," he clarified.

She tried to keep her gaze pinned somewhere above his head. Unfortunately, it worked about as well as trying to avoid the candy aisle at a convenience store. It seemed her eyes had a will of their own. They indulged in the sight of every slick, wet muscle as she tried to get words out of her suddenly dry throat.

"Okay, but I won't be back for a while."

He cocked his head. "Babysittin' again?"

Damn, her preoccupation with the man was really screwing up her memory. She kept forgetting that Bubba didn't know she lived there.

"Well, you know what they say; charity begins at home."

One corner of his mouth hiked up. "It appears that you sure are one charitable woman, Ms. Dalton."

She flashed him a smile. "It does look that way, don't it, Bubba Wilkes?" She went to pull open the door, but suddenly he was right there holding it open for her, his wet chest inches from Hulk's green bulging biceps. She stared up into those deep pools of chocolate, and her stomach clenched with hunger. Or possibly a spot much lower. Then his strong fingers slipped to the small of her back, guiding her in before he slammed the door and leaned down in the window. The look he sent melted her as much as the sun that shone through the windshield.

"Anytime you want to visit Wilkesville, Shirley Girl, you just let me know."

Chapter Fourteen

DUDS 'N SUCH WAS A LONG WAY from Neiman Marcus. Still, it had been such a long time since Shirlene had gotten to spend money—at least four days—that she went a little crazy in Bramble's only clothing store. It wasn't easy considering that the inventory was small and the designer labels nonexistent. Still, Cruel Girl and Wrangler were better than Marvel, and she piled the counter high with jeans and belts and boots. Once she was done shopping for herself, she pulled out Mia's list and started shopping for the kids. The children's clothing had Justin, the sales clerk, looking a little befuddled.

"Christmas gifts," she said as she pulled out the cutest little western skirt for Baby Adeline. Justin nodded, although his confused look didn't clear much, especially when he kept looking down at her t-shirt.

"It's the newest trend in women's wear." She checked the size on a plaid shirt for Jesse. She might not like the kid, but she didn't believe in showing favoritism.

"B-but it's the Hulk," he stammered.

"Exactly," she smiled brightly. "Who doesn't love that angry, green man? You have this in a smaller size?"

By the time she was finished, Shirlene felt like a new woman. It was truly amazing what an hour of shopping could do for a girl. It was too bad that a little thing like a credit limit rained on her parade.

"I'm sorry, Ms. Dalton." Justin's ears turned red. "But this card doesn't seem to want to go through."

"Silly me." Shirlene handed him another card. "I must've given you the wrong one." Five cards later, Shirlene's ears had turned the color of Justin's—thankfully, Twyla had left enough hair to cover the evidence. "Well, isn't this embarrassin'? I guess I did a little too much shoppin' this week." She picked up the pair of Tony Lama boots. "I'll just put a few things back and see if that doesn't help."

A few things turned into the majority of the clothes on the counter. By the time the card finally went through, the only things left were the toy guns in the holster for Brody and the dress for Adeline.

"I'm sure sorry about that," Justin said as he bagged up the items. "I'm thinkin' there must be something wrong with this machine."

"Not to worry, honey." Shirlene tried her best to smile, but her shopping high had long since fizzled out. "I have enough clothes in my closet to dress most of Texas."

Too bad she couldn't get to them.

Once outside the door of Duds 'N Such, Shirlene let her shoulders slump. How was she going to explain this to Mia? The teenager already thought she was the biggest screw-up in the world. And Shirlene was beginning to wonder if she wasn't right.

"Shirlene!"

She glanced up in time to see Faith hurrying across the

street with Daisy dangling from one of those backward backpacks.

"Where have you been?" Faith's big. blue eyes were filled with concern. "I've been trying to call you for days, and you haven't returned my calls."

"I'm sorry, honey," Shirlene said. "My cell phone died, and I couldn't find my charger." It wasn't exactly a lie. She *had* just found her car charger under her front seat that morning.

"Well, you could've stopped by the house—" Faith hesitated as her gaze snapped up to Shirlene's hair then down to her shirt. "What...?"

"Vintage Marvel," Shirlene said as she leaned down and cooed at Daisy. "Hi, precious, how's my little goddaughter?"

But Faith wasn't as gullible as Justin. Her eyes narrowed in confusion for only a few seconds before they welled up with tears. And just that quickly, Shirlene was engulfed in a hug that sandwiched a cooing Daisy between them.

"Oh, Shirl, I'm so sorry," Faith said. "I've been so wrapped up with the baby I didn't realize how depressed you are." She pulled back and stared at the Hulk t-shirt. "But I do now, and I'm going to help you get through this. We're going to get you the best professional therapist in west Texas." Her gaze snapped over to the group of men talking outside of Sutter's Pharmacy. "In fact, there's Doc Mathers, I'll just go ask him who he would recommend—"

Shirlene reached out and stopped her. She hadn't wanted to tell Faith what was going on, not when Faith and Hope did this weird twin-mind-reading thing. What Faith knew, Hope knew. And if Hope knew, so would Colt. But it looked like Shirlene didn't have much of a choice. Not unless she wanted to spend the next few days being mentally evaluated.

She glanced around before leaning closer to Faith. "I'm haven't gone off my rocker, honey—at least, not yet. I had to borrow this shirt because all my clothes are locked up in the house I've been evicted from."

"What?!"

Faith usually had a soft voice. But when she was surprised or angry, she could be as loud as her hog-calling twin sister. She was so loud this time that she woke up Moses Tate, who was napping on a bench a good block away. He sputtered and coughed a couple times before settling back in.

Hooking her arm through Faith's, Shirlene pulled her toward the Navigator. "Would you keep it down, honey? I don't want word getting out just yet."

"But how?" Faith asked. "I mean, the only way a person can get evicted is if they don't make—" She paused and her eyes widened. "You forgot to make the payments?"

"I didn't exactly forget. I just kept putting it off."

Faith's brow crinkled. "So why can't you just pay the back payments and get your house back?"

"Because while I was putting off making the payments, I was spending Lyle's money like there was no tomorrow in an effort to alleviate that depression you were just talking about. And now I don't have enough to cover the payments and late fees."

Faith pointed a finger at her. "I knew you were depressed."

"Well, a lot of good your psychic powers will do me now. I wish you'd stopped my compulsive spending about six months ago."

"I just thought you were doing what you always did. I didn't realize that you had a problem—or a limited amount of funds." Faith's entire face drooped. "But I should've been more attentive."

Unable to take the sad, puppy-dog look, Shirlene squeezed her arm. "Now don't go blamin' yourself, honey. I wouldn't have survived Lyle's death if it hadn't been for you and Hope. Even with weddings and babies, you've always been there for me." She stopped by the Navigator. "Which is why I know I can count on you to keep this little secret between us. If the townsfolk get wind of this, who knows what they'll do."

Humor sparkled in Faith's eyes. "They mean well, but their help always seems to cause more problems than solutions. Look at the craziness that happened when they thought Hope was pregnant and sent out Bear the Bounty Hunter to bring back the father."

Just the thought of the "daddy search" had Shirlene grinning. "Or when they thought you were Hope and stole your car to keep you here in Bramble—of course, if they hadn't, you wouldn't be standing there with that cute baby."

Leaning down, Faith kissed Daisy's downy head of dark hair. Surprisingly, Shirlene didn't feel the stab of envy she normally felt. Probably because she had too many other things to worry about.

Faith looked back up. "But you've told Colt and Hope, right? Colt's probably working on getting you back in your house as we speak."

There was a part of Shirlene that wished that was the case. But the more stubborn part refused to give up.

"Actually, honey," she said, "I don't want them knowing just yet. Colt has watched out for me all my life. I think it's time I started watching out for myself. Which is why I'm hoping you'll keep your crazy ESP away from Hope."

"You don't have to worry. The telepathic connection

Hope and I have doesn't seem to work long distance," Faith said. "But once Hope and Colt get back from California, I can't make any promises."

"I'm hoping the bank president and I will have things worked out by then—that's if he ever gets back from sunnin' himself on some tropical beach." Shirlene reached for the door handle, intending to toss her measly shopping bag on the back seat. But Faith's next words stopped her.

"Why don't you just call him?"

Shirlene turned. "What?"

"Why don't you just call the bank president?" She shielded the setting sun from Daisy's eyes with her hand. "My boss used to go on vacation all the time. But if an emergency came up, we always had a number we could reach him at. And being kicked out of your home should qualify as an emergency—which brings up a good point. If you don't have any money, where have you been living?"

"Out on Grover Road," Shirlene mumbled absently, her mind still wrapped up in what Faith had said about calling the bank president.

"In your old trailer?" Faith sounded shocked.

"Why not? You lived out there in Bubba's." Shirlene looked down the street, her eyes narrowing on the bank. As she watched, Ruby Lee stepped out and turned to lock the door behind her.

"Listen, honey." Shirlene gave Faith a quick hug. "I'll have to talk with you later. Right now, I need to have a little chat with that lowdown scoundrel who evicted me."

"Good luck," Faith called as Shirlene hurried down the street.

"Well, hey, Shirlene!" Ruby Lee greeted her with

a wide smile that showed off the big space between her front teeth. "How you been, girl?"

"I've been good, honey." Shirlene glanced back at the bank. "You workin' a little late for a Friday, aren't you?"

Ruby Lee rolled her eyes before she leaned in and whispered. "The new bank manager's got a bug up his butt about employees stayin' until the last dog is hung. I've worked so much in the last two weeks that my kids are startin' to call their babysitter mama."

"Well, I'm real sorry to hear that, Ruby. Speakin' of the bank manager, is he still workin'? Because there was something I needed to discuss with the man."

"'Course he's still workin'," Ruby said. "I wouldn't be surprised to find out that the little feller sleeps in his office. At least, he's always there to yell at me if I'm five minutes late." She pulled out her keys and turned back to the door. Once the door was unlocked, she pushed it open. "I'll just let him know you're here."

"No need for that," Shirlene said as she stepped past her. "I know where his office is. You get on home and see those kids."

Ruby Lee didn't hesitate to slip the keys back in her purse. "Well, if you don't mind, I think I will. Just have Mr. Peabody lock up after you."

"I'll be sure to do that, honey," Shirlene said as the door shut closed behind her.

With twilight just around the corner, the bank was dark. But Shirlene had been to Luther Briggs's office enough to find her way. Mr. Peabody sat behind the large desk with a pair of reading glasses perched on his small nose as he read through a stack of papers. Shirlene reached into the bag, and at the rustle of plastic, his beady eyes snapped up.

She smiled brightly. "Howdy, Reggie."

He registered surprise for only an instant before his face puckered with annoyance. "The bank is closed, Ms. Dalton. And if you continue to ignore the bank schedule that is posted as plain as day on the front window, I'll be forced—" His voice dropped off, and his eyes bugged out when he noticed the shiny silver revolver in her hand. He swallowed hard before he stammered in a high-pitched voice. "I-i-is this a r-robbery?"

"No, Reggie," Shirlene said as she strolled into the office. "This is a woman who has reached the end of her patience with bad customer service. Now I know I screwed up—and I'm willing to take responsibility for my actions." She waved the gun, and Mr. Peabody's face lost all color. "But would it have hurt you to show a little common decency? To come out to my home and explain the situation instead of sending a few measly letters quickly followed by a locksmith?"

"P-please, Ms. Dalton," he squeaked. "D-don't shoot. It was Mr. Cates who wanted the locks changed. All I was doing was my job."

Since it looked like he was about to cry, Shirlene lowered the gun. "Following orders is one thing, Reggie. Doing it in such a nasty manner is another. And speaking of your Mr. Cates," she pointed the gun at the phone, "why don't you get him on the line. I have a few things I'd like to say to him, too."

"B-but," Mr. Peabody stammered. But all Shirlene had to do was lift an eyebrow before he pulled out a business card from his desk and start dialing. "I'm sorry to bother you, sir," he whined. "But Ms. Dalton is here in my office, and I'm afraid she's going to do something rash if you won't speak with her." He swallowed hard. "No, sir, not to herself—to m-me." Less than a second later, he held out the receiver to Shirlene.

Shirlene took the phone and sat down in the chair across from the desk, hooking a leg over the arm. "Good evenin', Mr. Cates. How's the vacation goin'?"

There was a pause before a voice came over the line. A voice that didn't sound anything like a lowdown, dirty scoundrel. This voice was as smooth as a shot of three-hundred-dollar-a-bottle tequila with just a hint of Texan flavor.

"Good evening, Ms. Dalton," he said. "And the vacation *was* going well. Now I'm a little worried about the safety of my employee."

She swung her foot back and forth. "Nothin' to worry about, honey. I'm only violent when I'm riled. And I'm not riled...yet."

"So what are your demands, Ms. Dalton?" Mr. Cates asked. "A billion dollars and my helicopter on the roof?"

The helicopter surprised her. Lyle hadn't even had one of those. She leaned over and grabbed a tissue out of the box and handed it to Mr. Peabody, who appeared to be sweating profusely. "Actually, I just want my house back."

"So you expect me to just give you your house back and forget all about the loan?"

"Now that wouldn't be fair at all, honey. No, I plan on paying you back every cent with interest and late fees... just as soon as I sell my house." The burst of laughter that came through the line halted Shirlene's leg mid-swing. "Is there something amusing about that, Mr. Cates?"

The laughter died. "You do realize the loan is for close to a million dollars, don't you?"

Shirlene hadn't realized that, but she hid her ignorance well. "And the house has to be worth at least two million."

"In a big city like Dallas or Houston, you'd get that easily. But in a town Bramble's size, there's not a chance in hell."

Suddenly Shirlene started sweating as profusely as Mr. Peabody while Mr. Cates continued ruining her plans.

"Which means I'll be lucky to get enough to cover the loan. And since it doesn't look like you have sufficient funds to make the payments, I suggest you find another place to live. Isn't your brother building a house just outside of town?"

Shirlene was really getting steamed now. She jumped up and walked to the window, waving the gun as she talked. "I am not going to impose on my brother and his family! And how do you know about my insufficient funds?" The chair squeaked behind her, and when she turned, Reggie was long gone.

"It's my job to know," Mr. Cates stated. "And I'm sure you won't have to live with your brother for long—from what I hear, you're very good at finding men to take care of you."

She wanted to call him every dirty name she'd ever heard out on Grover Road. But the thought of her childhood home, and the kids who lived in it, had her swallowing the words. "And what about you, Mr. Cates?"

There was a long pause. "What kind of offer are you making, Ms. Dalton?"

She gritted her teeth. "One that only concerns my house. I'll make you a sweet deal."

He laughed again. It was really starting to annoy her.

"Bramble, Texas is the last place on earth I'd choose to live." He paused for just a heartbeat. "Besides, Ms. Dalton, unless you can come up with some cash fairly quickly, I already own your house."

Chapter Fifteen

"SO WHATCHA DOIN', KENNY GENE?"

The deep voice so close to his ear almost made Kenny wet his Wranglers. But a law enforcement officer needed to keep his cool in tense situations so he pulled himself together. Although he was mighty relieved to turn around and find his best friend Rye Pickett standing there.

"For the love of Pete, Rye, would you keep it down?" Kenny said. "Can't you see I'm workin' surveillance?"

Rye looked duly impressed. He also looked all green and spooky. Kenny pushed up the night-vision goggles that he had gotten in the fifty percent-off aisle at Wal-Mart. Not that he needed them. The sun had yet to disappear over the horizon. Still, they were cool as hell.

"Surveillance on what?" Rye asked.

"Not what, but who." Kenny glanced back over at the Escalade parked in the parking lot of Bootlegger's. "See that man talkin' on his cell phone?"

Rye squinted across the street. "Yeah. He's that new feller in town." He glanced back at Kenny. "But I thought it was legal to talk on your cell when you wasn't drivin'."

"He's not under surveillance for talkin' on his phone," Kenny stated as he leaned against the lamppost and crossed his arms over his chest. The goggles flopped back down over his eyes, but he decided to leave them there for dramatic effect. "He's under surveillance for being a criminal."

"No foolin'?" Rye looked even more impressed.

"Now would a law enforcement officer fool about a thing like that, Rye Pickett?" he said, although he tried not to sound too prideful. Rye had wanted the job of Sam's volunteer deputy almost as much as Kenny had. Since Kenny had gotten it, he didn't want to rub it in.

"So what did he do? Rob a bank? Murder someone? Bring that Mary-juanie over from Mexico?"

"I don't know the particulars, but one criminal is as bad as another."

"Now that ain't always true." Rye shot a stream of tobacco into the bushes. "Colt Lomax was a little bit of a criminal growing up, but he turned out okay. Hey, can I try on them goggles?"

"I'd love to let you, Rye, but while I'm on duty I can't let people be playin' with my special law enforcement equipment. But tomorrow night when we go gopher huntin', I'll let you wear 'em then." Kenny slipped them back up on the top of his head. "And Colt don't count, seein' as he was born and raised here in Bramble. This criminal, on the other hand, could be from anywhere—maybe even New York City. Although I can't see Shirlene shackin' up with some foreigner."

Rye's eyes widened. "You mean, he's the feller Shirlene has taken a shine to? The one who's got a key to her place?"

"One and the same."

Rye glared at the Escalade. "A criminal livin' with our little Shirlene. That just don't seem right. Why don't you go on over there and arrest him?"

No wonder Rye had lost the deputy contest. The man just didn't use the old noggin.

"Because you can't just arrest a man without hard evidence," Kenny said. "It's like fishin'. You tug too hard, and the big one will get away. You gotta let him take the bait first—make him feel like he's just helpin' himself to a nice dinner." He jerked up his hands like he held a fishing pole. "Then you got him."

"And Shirlene's the bait?" Rye asked. "The bait for what?"

It was a good question. Up until that point, the man had done nothing more than stay out at Shirlene's and stop at a bunch of cemeteries—which was just plain creepy. Still, Kenny hadn't just been watching Beau. He'd been thinking. And he thought he had it all figured out.

"I think he's plannin' on connin' Shirlene out of her millions."

Rye looked surprised and then confused. "But how's he gonna do that? Shirlene ain't dumb enough to give her millions away."

Kenny set him straight. "She didn't used to be. But being without a man can do strange things to a woman. Just the other day I saw her comin' out of the First Baptist Church—a place she hasn't stepped foot in since her mama and daddy had her baptized—wearing a Batman shirt and a pair of rubber floppy shoes without a speck of heel."

"No heels?" Rye looked truly horrified. His entire face drooped in mourning. "I loved that woman's heels."

"Which is exactly my point," Kenny continued. "Losing Lyle has taken all the sass right out of our girl and left her prime pickin's for a no-account con artist with bad intentions on his mind."

Rye Pickett was a big dude to begin with. But when he got riled, he could puff up to twice his size. He did that now, his jaw tightening on either side of his goatee. "Well, we shore ain't gonna let that happen to our little Shirlene. But how are we gonna keep the man away from her when she's given him a key to her house?"

Kenny scratched his head. "I haven't figured that one out yet, but I'm workin' on it. In the meantime, I'll be keepin' a close eye on Mr. Beau Williams. And if he makes one false move, he'll be lookin' down the barrel of my huntin' rifle."

Chapter Sixteen

"...SO I JUST TOLD KENNY GENE, if he was gonna work again tonight, I sure wasn't gonna be stuck home doin' nothin'—especially when he's yet to make any kind of commitment."

While Twyla chattered on, Shirlene motioned for Manny, the bartender at Bootlegger's, to pour her another shot. But the smooth burn of her third drink did nothing to dim her anger—or Twyla's annoying voice.

"I mean how many weddin' reality TV shows do I have to force the man to watch before he gets the hint?"

Shirlene set the shot glass down on the bar and released her breath as the first wave of alcohol bliss assailed her. "Well, I sure couldn't tell you, honey. But maybe he thinks after three marriages that you're all married out."

"As if." Twyla lifted her ridiculous apple martini and took a big gulp. "I just love weddin's—especially my own." She shot a glance over at Shirlene. "You wouldn't be thinkin' of tyin' the knot, would you, Shirl?"

The question was so stupid, Shirlene snorted.

Twyla nodded her head. "That's what I figured. The

entire town might be worried about you takin' up with the wrong kind of man. But I knew it was just them horny-mones actin' up. 'Course I should warn you about hop-pin' in bed with the first good lookin' cowboy to ride into town. I let that travelin' nightie salesman sweet talk me into givin' him some sugar and talk about a Slam-Bam-Here's-A-Nightie-Ma'am. Not only was it over before I could hit the high note of the Star-Spangled Banner, but that flimsy piece of lace didn't even hold up a month."

Before Shirlene could figure out what Twyla was talking about, Harley Sutter pushed his way through the Friday-night crowd at Bootlegger's. Given that his stom-ach was the size of a barge, this wasn't that difficult.

"Well, there's my little gal." He gave her a couple awk-ward pats on the back before his eyes scrunched up over his thickly waxed handlebar mustache. "You did some-thin' different."

His observant comment surprised Shirlene.

"I styled her hair," Twyla jumped in. "Don't it look great?"

Harley shook his head. "Nope, it ain't the hair." He leaned closer. "Must've been the lightin'. You still look like the same redheaded, freckled-faced kid who used to tear around town after Hope."

Freckles? She glanced at the mirror behind the bar. Unfortunately, it was obscured by rows of bar glasses. Still, Mayor Sutter had really gone off the deep end if he thought Shirlene had freckles. Maybe in high school when she wasn't smart enough to stay out of the sun. But as an adult, she avoided sunlight like the plague—her mind wandered back to this afternoon when she had stood on the roof of the trailer with no thought in her head about freckling skin. Of course, with sweat trickling down

Bubba's hard, smooth muscles like condensation on glass, her horny-mones had wiped out all logical thought.

Harley reached out and ruffled her hair. "You sure were a sassy-pants back then." His eyes turned serious. "A sassy-pants who was smart enough to steer clear of ornery boys with no good on their minds."

Ever since Shirlene could remember, the townsfolk had functioned like one illogical brain. And being part of that brain, it didn't take Shirlene long to figure out what ornery, good-lookin' cowboy Twyla and Harley were talking about. Obviously, Kenny Gene had figured out who the blonde in Bubba's bed was, and the entire town was now worried she was going to make a monumental mistake. Considering that only that afternoon Shirlene had been worried about the same thing, she couldn't very well blame them.

"Well, it's real sweet that y'all are worried about me." She flashed a smile. "But the only reason we were together was because I got scared."

Harley patted her on the back. "I'm sure it's pretty scary being all alone in that big old mansion with Colt and Hope out in California."

Shirlene only wished she was all alone in her house. But thanks to Mr. Cates, she realized she would never be lonely in her great big, old mansion again. The thought depressed her so much that she waved at Manny for another shot. Fortunately, the owner of the bar had always allowed her to run a tab.

"But no matter how scared you get," Harley continued, "you can't leave your door open for any rascal who wants to walk through it. There are scoundrels out there just waitin' to prey on lonely widda women."

"Amen to that," Shirlene said, thinking of Mr. Cates.

A bigger scoundrel she'd never met. Too bad he hadn't been the one looking down the barrel of her cap gun. She would've loved to see him squirm like Mr. Peabody. Poor Mr. Peabody; no doubt the man had run all the way to the sheriff's office. Unfortunately for the bank manager, Sam took off early on Fridays and was now sitting at the end of the bar enjoying a tall one.

And speaking of tall ones... Shirlene's gaze got caught by the man in the black Stetson standing next to Sam. A man who hadn't been there earlier. She would've noticed that long, lean body and expensive shirt. She smiled a "hello," and he answered with one that had Twyla choking on her Appletini. Shirlene hadn't come here looking for Beau, but suddenly he seemed like a life raft in the middle of a stormy sea.

"But don't you worry about a thing, Shirlene," Harley rambled on. "I'm keepin' a close eye out."

"That sure makes me feel a lot better, honey." She got up and scooted around his big belly. "Now if y'all will excuse me." She weaved her way through the crowd. Beau met her halfway around the bar, his hat off and his smile dazzling.

"You came," he said.

She grinned up at him. "I figured it wouldn't be very hospitable of me if I didn't."

He shook his head. "Not hospitable at all."

They smiled at one another for a few seconds more before Beau held out a hand, directing her to an empty table in one corner. Once she was seated, he took a stool across from her.

"What would you like to drink?" He looked around for the waitress.

Since Shirlene had already had a few shots, she probably

should've ordered beer. But considering her week, she ordered a margarita on the rocks.

"You changed your hair color."

She looked over into a pair of twinkling, sapphire eyes that made her feel better than three shots of tequila had.

"Not intentionally," she said.

He laughed. "My mother had that happen to her a few times, although I think hers was intentional. When I was younger, I never knew what color I'd come home from school to. One time it would be as red as a barnyard hen, another as black as the ace of spades, and the next as golden as our Labrador, Honey. My father liked to tease that she was just trying to give us boys a sample of each so we'd know which color we wanted to spend the rest of our lives with."

Shirlene grinned and leaned her arms on the table. "And which one did you decide on, Beauregard?"

Tipping his head, he studied her. "Red looks awful nice on you, Ms. Shirlene."

"Chicken," she said. "That was an easy out if ever I heard one." She squinted. "Let me see, you look like the type of man to go for deep and rich. A dark brown—no, a thick gleaming ebony."

Something flickered in those eyes—something that looked a lot like pain. But it was quickly covered over with a smile.

"Pretty good. Do you also read palms?"

"Only during the winter solstice."

He laughed, and when he sobered, he glanced down at the floor by her heels. "I'm surprised you don't have Sherman with you."

"He wasn't in the mood for dancin'," she teased, although she couldn't help but feel guilty all over again for leaving the pig—and the kids. But not guilty enough to head back to the trailer. At least, not yet. She needed just a little more fortification before she faced Mia and informed her that, not only weren't they going to live in a big mansion, but Shirlene had also spent the last of her credit on a miniature western skirt and toy guns. Although the guns had been worth every penny.

The waitress, Jenny, brought their drinks to the table. As she took Beau's money, she spoke to Shirlene. "If you're needin' a little company, Shirl, Buddy's cousin is single. Owns a taxidermy shop and everything. He's the one that stuffed that moose over the bar." Both she and Beau glanced over at the moose. It might've been impressive if not for the crossed eyes.

"I'll be sure to look him up if I need any stuffin'," Shirlene said.

Once Jenny was gone, Beau asked, "Has she noticed the eyes?"

"In case you haven't figured it out already, the people of Bramble only see what they want to. John Wayne isn't dead but living on a ranch just east of El Paso. Bullwinkle is a fine example of taxidermy. And I've always been a redhead."

"And a fine lookin' redhead," he teased.

"This coming from a man who no doubt salivates over Catherine Zeta-Jones."

His blue eyes twinkled. "I've seen *The Legend of Zorro* at least a hundred times."

"The entire movie or just the stable scene?" she asked.

"The stable scene, of course."

She laughed, suddenly feeling much better than she'd felt in a long time. And the more they talked, the better Shirlene felt. Even though she had no intentions of taking things further than a little friendly flirting, it felt nice to be courted by such a good-looking man. Of course, the alcohol didn't hurt. After her second margarita kicked in, she was feeling no pain. And when a Tim McGraw song came on, she tapped her foot to the beat.

The action didn't go unnoticed. Slipping his hat back on, Beau slid off the stool and held out a hand. "Could I have this dance, Ms. Shirlene?"

She took his hand. "Only if you stop calling me that. It makes me feel like your first-grade teacher—especially since I'm already feeling a little uncomfortable about our age difference."

"What age difference? And I'll have you know that I had some pretty steamy fantasies about kissing my first-grade teacher," he whispered in her ear as he guided her out to the crowded dance floor.

She swatted at his arm. "Behave yourself, or I'll have to pull out the ruler."

"Lord have mercy," he breathed as he whirled her into a two-step.

Beau turned out to be a good dancer—his steps were smooth, his turns and reverses effortless. They danced a two-step and the western swing before they settled in to a waltz. Beau held her close but not too close, his hand wandering no further than her waist.

He seemed like the kind of man a woman could trust. The kind of man Lyle had been—strong and dependable. Because of that, she allowed herself to relax, her head dipping to rest on his shoulder as she gave herself up to the dance moves.

Just as her eyes slipped closed, Bubba popped into her head. And not just popped, but stuck there. One minute she was enjoying the feel of being held by a trustworthy man again, and the next, she was fantasizing about running her hands over a hard chest and ripped stomach all slicked up with manly sweat. And what made matters worse was when she finally snapped out of it and lifted her head, she discovered her hand cradling Beau's pectoral muscle. She quickly moved it back up to his shoulder, but it was a little too late for apologies or explanations.

His eyes already simmered with heat.

Before she could stop him, his lips brushed over hers. It wasn't terrible. In fact, it was nice. Just not nice enough to continue to lead Beau on. She started to pull back when another dancing couple ran into Beau from behind. His teeth bumped her top lip, and he had started to apologize when an annoying voice cut him off.

"Well, if I'm not as clumsy as an armadillo in a china cabinet."

Shirlene didn't know who pulled back quicker, she or Beau. They both turned and stared in horror at the man who stood there with an idiotic grin on his hillbilly face. But when his gaze slid over to Shirlene, the intensity in Bubba's dark eyes didn't quite match his smile.

"Why, Shirley Girl, I didn't realize you were still babysittin'."

A look came over Beau's face that didn't bode well for the east Texas redneck. Shirlene probably should've let Beau teach Bubba some manners. But the sight of blood had always made her a little woozy. Although right now she didn't need blood to make her woozy.

When she released Beau and stepped back, the room shifted like the bow of a boat, causing Shirlene to teeter on the heels of her Manolos. It appeared that while they'd been dancing, the tequila had finally caught up with her. Before she could fall overboard, both men reached out and steadied her, Bubba sending her a squinty-eyed look from beneath the curled-up brim of his hat.

Once she had her sea legs, she cleared her throat.

"Gentlemen," she looked first at Beau and then at Bubba. Ironically, they were about the same height and build. Both nicely muscled and sinfully good-lookin'. The sinfully good-lookin' part caused her brain to take a detour, and she completely forgot what she had been about to say. All she knew was that she felt happy—very, very happy. She smiled brightly. But the smile slipped when a hand tipped in long acrylic nails painted with little palm trees slid over Bubba's bare bicep.

"Come on, Bubba," Marcy Henderson whined as she cuddled his arm between her silicone-inflated breasts. "I want to dance, not talk—or better yet, we can go back to my place and do a little waltzin'." She batted her eyelashes. "If . . . you know what I mean."

"Well, I can't think of anything I'd rather do, Marcy." He gave the woman an annoyingly lecherous smile. "But it appears that Ms. Dalton here is as toasted as a dropped marshmallow in a campfire. And what kind of man would I be if I let her drive home drunk?"

"Psshht!" Shirlene slapped the air, when what she really wanted to do was slap Marcy upside the head. "As if Shirlene Dalton has ever been drunk a day in her life."

"Well, there was that one Fourth of July," Harley butted in.

"And a couple Christmas parties," Twyla piped up.

"Not to forget Lyle's last birthday when you fell into the swimmin' pool fully clothed," Cindy Lynn said in her normal, gloating voice.

Shirlene had been so wrapped up in her own drama, she'd failed to notice that every patron in Bootlegger's was circled around them like a bunch of farmers at a cock fight. Now that she did, she wasn't about to give them a show. Especially when they seemed to have memories like a bunch of danged elephants and when their eyes were all aglow with the prospect of more juicy gossip.

"If you will excuse me," she sent Beau a bright smile, and Bubba and Marcy the evil eye, "I'm going to call it a night."

Except she should've known it wasn't going to be that easy.

"I don't think so, Apple Dumplin'." Bubba reached out and grabbed her arm. "Not when you're more pickled than a Kosher on rye."

"Let her go," Beau said. "Since she came here to meet me, I'll drive her home."

Bubba's hand tightened, and Shirlene figured she was about to see some blood after all, when Harley jumped back in.

"We don't take with strangers drivin' our drunk women-folk home." He nodded at Bubba. "Bubba here will see she gets there."

Shirlene jerked her arm away from Bubba and, thankfully, only wobbled a little before she caught her balance. "I appreciate everyone's concern. But I'm perfectly able and willin' to drive myself home. And that's exactly what I intend to do."

She turned with every intention of stumbling her way off the dance floor when she was scooped up from behind and flipped over a shoulder as easily as a bag of down feathers.

"Just relax, Shirley Girl, and enjoy the ride."

Chapter Seventeen

BILLY DIDN'T LIKE SCENES. Scenes were for reality shows, Jerry Springer, and his Aunt Flo when the Dallas Cowboys lost. Billy preferred restraint coupled with a few well-chosen words. But restraint and well-chosen words flew right out of his head when he looked up from the conversation he'd been having with Rye Pickett and spotted Shirlene on the dance floor fondling Beau like she'd been fondling him only hours earlier.

Without a word to Rye, he latched on to Marcy Henderson and pushed his way toward the dance floor, only to discover when he got there that the fondling had moved on to kissing. And suddenly causing a scene hadn't seemed like such a bad thing after all. Except now that he had an angry woman hung over his shoulder like a wiggling bag of potatoes and Beau breathing down his neck like a yearling bull in heat, he wondered if he shouldn't have just stayed at home and watched the late news on his 13-inch black and white.

"Let her go." Beau made a grab for Billy's shoulder. But before he could get a firm grip, the townsfolk closed in around Billy, pushing Beau back in the crowd.

"I'm glad you're watchin' out for our little Shirlene," Harley huffed and puffed as he tried to keep up with Billy. "We sure don't want her becomin' easy pickin's for nefarious types of men." He shot a glance back over his shoulder.

"If that's the case," Shirlene hit Billy twice in the butt with her fist—and the woman was no lightweight—"why in the heck aren't you stopping this ornery scoundrel, Harley Sutter!"

Harley grabbed the door and held it open. "Why, Shirlene, Bubba isn't an ornery scoundrel. He's just a good ol' boy from east Texas." He waited for Billy to step outside before he leaned his head out the door. "I'll hold him off for as long as I can. But I'll warn you—he's got a key."

Billy might've laughed at that if Shirlene hadn't bitten him in the butt.

"Oww, woman." He dropped her to her feet. But before she could do more than teeter on those sexy blue stilettos, he had her back up in his arms.

"Would you put me down?" She swatted at his shoulder. "I'm fine to drive."

He snorted. "About as fine as Elmer Tate when he plowed through the front of the post office." He pulled open the door of the truck and tossed her in. By the time he climbed up, she had scrambled across the bench seat to the opposite door. But it only took a tug on her tight t-shirt to reel her back in.

"That's enough, woman," he ordered. "You're not drivin' in your condition, so just give it up."

She fell back against the seat, folding her arms over her more than ample chest. "Then Beau can drive me home."

It took a strong will not to grit his teeth. "Beau's not

driving you anywhere, especially not home—which brings up a good point. Just exactly where is your home, Ms. Dalton?"

She turned and stared at him, her green eyes reflecting the neon beer signs that hung on the walls outside of Bootlegger's. That stubborn chin lifted. "Everyone in town knows where I live."

"Hmmm?" He cocked his head. "Do they now?"

There was a long silence before her eyes narrowed. "Jesse."

"Don't blame the kid." He turned the key, and the truck rumbled to life. "I already figured something wasn't right when the wealthiest woman in town started wearing comic book heroes." He glanced down at her t-shirt. The Hulk had never looked so pumped—or so hot. He cleared his throat and looked away. "And hanging out on Grover Road pretending to be the Super Nanny."

She snorted. "As if Mia would let me touch those kids." She leaned up and looked on either side of her. "So does this bucket of bolts have seatbelts? I'd rather not be caught dead in this blatant redneck excuse for a vehicle."

"Don't tell me you don't like the Bubba-mobile," he made a stab at teasing, even though he wasn't in a teasing mood.

"About as much as I like okra," she responded.

Once they were on the road, he expected her to slide across the seat as far from him as she could get. Instead she settled right where she sat, her head resting just beneath his gun rack and the Hulk much too close to his right arm. They drove like that for a while. Long enough for his anger to recede to a low simmer. And long enough for her scent to fill the cab of the truck. It was a scent he had a hard time defining—a mixture of subtle perfume and earthy woman. A heady combination that made him feel as drunk as Shirlene. Although she didn't appear to be as inebriated as he'd first thought.

"So I guess you think it's funny," she said as he made the turn onto Grover Road. When he shot her a questioning look, she continued. "The fact that a woman who sashayed around town flaunting her wealth is now living in a rundown trailer."

"Now why would you think a thing like that?"

Her head rolled toward him. "Because I know men. And underneath all that 'aww, shucks' country bullcrap is a man who doesn't really like me." Before he could confirm or deny it, she continued. "Don't get me wrong; I don't really like you either. But at least I don't act otherwise."

"So you're saying you don't like me, Shirley Girl?" He covered his heart with his hand. "I'm crushed."

She arched an eyebrow at him. "See what I mean? You're no more crushed than an elephant in a dog pile—which doesn't explain your desire to drive me home. Or was it all just a male-possession kind of thing: He has it—I want it."

He shot a glance over at her. Want? As if he would ever want a gold digger who thought so much of herself. Which didn't explain why he was having such a hard time keeping her out of his mind. And maybe he was just curious. Curious to see if the rest of her body was as sweet as those bee-stung lips.

As curious as a cat in front of a mouse hole.

His grip tightened on the steering wheel. "Maybe I just didn't want you drivin' home drunk, is all."

She snorted. "What a gentleman. Although it wasn't so gentlemanly of you to leave Marcy Henderson alone on the dance floor. The poor girl is probably heartbroken."

"Doubtful. Marcy isn't particular about her men." He

glanced over at her. " 'Course from what I've seen neither are you."

She lifted her head. "And just what is that supposed to mean?"

He shrugged. "That one man's chest is as temptin' as another's."

She sat up, her breast brushing against his bicep. Heat rocketed through him and he jumped, banging his shoulder on the edge of the gun rack.

"Are you callin' me a slut, Bubba Wilkes?" she asked.

Between the pain in his shoulder and the ache in his pants, it took a full minute to find his voice. "What would you call a woman who fondles one man in the afternoon and another in the evening?"

Her mouth dropped open, and her eyes turned mean. "I wasn't fondling you. I was just...." When she couldn't seem to find the words, he filled them in for her.

"Filling the lonely hours with a little slap and tickle since your rich lifestyle got jerked out from under you?"

They had reached her junk-filled lot. But instead of turning in, he proceeded on to his. His anger was back in full force. After he pulled up next to his trailer and popped the truck into park, he turned on her. "Come on, Ms. Dalton, be honest. You've got an itch that needs to be scratched."

"I never realized how crazy east Texans were until you showed up," she said as she slid across the seat. But before she could close her fingers around the door handle, he pulled her back into his arms.

He slipped his hand up under all that soft hair and cradled her jaw. "Crazy? Or just accurate? And I'll be more than obliged to help you out with that itch, Shirley Girl. Much better than any wet-behind-the-ears kid."

He dipped his head and kissed her. She didn't fight him, nor did she participate. When he pulled back, she was watching him.

"If that's what you call a kiss, Bubba Wilkes, then you've got a lot to learn about catchin' a woman."

The words were spoken in the same thick country drawl he used when he teased her. But instead of making him laugh, they lit a fire inside his gut that quickly spread throughout his body. Or maybe it wasn't the words as much as her green gaze that seemed to look straight through him and ferret out all the lies and secrets.

And without his lies and secrets, Billy had no defense against the woman. None at all.

"Well, maybe we should work on that," he breathed in a low whisper right before he kissed her again.

Her mouth was as lush as every other part of her body, her plump lips made for a man to sink into. Billy didn't waste any time doing just that. After only one sip, he deepened the kiss and dove headfirst into all that moist heat. He'd kissed his fair share of women, but all other kisses were obliterated when Shirlene took control.

She slid her hands up his shoulders, her fingernails gently scratching his neck, before they burrowed into his hair and knocked his cap to the floor. Then she proceeded to feast on him as if she was starving and he was the most decadent of desserts.

Billy answered her need, feeding her one hot kiss after the other, while his hand pushed up her t-shirt and skated across the warmth of her stomach to the lace of her bra. He had touched well-endowed women before, but nothing prepared him for the generous wealth of supple softness that filled his palm to overflowing. It was like cradling a piece of heaven, and Billy wondered if he'd ever be able to let go. He stroked a thumb over the very center, and her breath puffed into his mouth before she pulled back.

With his lips free to wander, he kissed a moist trail along her cheek and over to her ear, where he nibbled and suckled until her fingers tightened against his scalp. She tasted as good as she smelled, and he took his time moving down her neck to the sweet cleavage that swelled above her bra. His breath fell in heavy gusts as his tongue took a dip into the deep crevice. He could've feasted on the bounty for a lifetime if her hand hadn't slid over the fly of his jeans, turning the hard knot beneath the worn denim to rigid steel. But before he took things to a new level, he released her breast and lifted his head.

"You're sober, right?" His voice was raspy with desire. He watched her eyelids flutter open and pools of liquid green stared back at him.

"Sober enough," she said before she pulled him down for another deep, mind-altering kiss.

From there, things got completely out of hand.

Shirts were jerked off in such haste that thin cotton ripped and snaps popped. When Billy reached for the button of her jeans, she slid off his lap and helped him out. He started to remove his own pants, but then the pink lace of Shirlene's panties came into view, and he froze with his waistband riding his thighs.

Propped back against the opposite door, she lifted one long leg almost to the roof and tugged on the hem of her jeans. A blue stiletto popped out, quickly followed by the other. Once the jeans were off, she tossed them to the floor and sat back, one heel resting in the seat and the other stretched out toward Billy. With that wild hair tousled around her face and those desire-steeped eyes, she looked better than any Playboy centerfold he had ever seen. Forgetting all about his pants, he considered diving on her like a kid on a slip-and-slide.

But instead, he leaned over and placed a kiss on the skin just inside her left knee that rested against the back of the seat. It was so soft and so sweet that he nibbled his way down her thigh until he reached the piece of lace. She moaned and pushed her hips up as he dampened the material with one opened-mouth kiss after another.

"Bubba," she breathed on a sigh. The sound vibrated through the truck as he slid down her panties and touched his mouth to her hot center.

He took his time, starting off with gentle kisses and working his way up to long, slow strokes. But when her thighs tightened against his ears, he quickly changed to steady flicks that had her head falling back against the window and little breathy moans escaping from her mouth. Shirlene Dalton wasn't a screamer, but when she found her release, her moans were so loud that Billy started to worry about waking the residents of Grover Road.

And the last thing he needed was Jesse showing up.

So after he eased her down from her climax with a few gentle kisses, he quickly pulled up his pants and opened the door. He forgot about the light until it almost blinded him. As quickly as a man could with a raging hard-on, he climbed down and jogged around to the other side. When he pulled her into his arms, she snuggled up next to him and sighed. Why that would make him smile, Billy didn't know. But it did—the type of smile that took up a man's entire face.

"Feelin' pretty content, are we?" he asked as he took the steps of the trailer.

"Mmm-hmm," she hummed against his throat while her fingers played with the hair that curled around the back of his neck.

Inside, he switched on the kitchen light before heading for the bedroom. He stopped in the doorway and stared down at the double mattress. At that moment, he would've given his left nut for his king-sized bed with the nice crisp sheets. But Shirlene didn't seem to mind. Once he set her down on the bed, she stretched out like a cat on plush carpet.

With his gaze pinned to the voluptuous goddess in pink lace and sexy-as-hell stilettos, Billy toed off first one boot and then the other. He had just started pushing down his jeans when a thought struck him, and he pulled them back up and hurried to the bathroom to search through the medicine cabinet.

Ibuprofen. Aspirin. Eye drops. Pepto. Tums. Midol— Midol? He pulled the bottle back out and stared at it before slamming it back in the cabinet and moving to the next shelf. But what he was looking for wasn't there either. Nor was it in any of the kitchen cabinets or drawers. It took him scouring through his truck before he discovered the condom in the visor. With contraception in hand, he didn't waste any time getting back in the trailer. He hopped his way down the hall, jerking off first one sock and then the other. When he reached the bedroom, he stopped and stared down at the woman sprawled across the bed.

In the small strip of light from the kitchen, she didn't resemble the sexy siren he'd left only a few minutes earlier. With one arm and a high heel dangling off the bed and her plump lips slack, she looked like what she was.

Passed out cold.

Chapter Eighteen

THE LIGHT SHINING IN THE WINDOW was blinding. Shirlene really needed to get thicker curtains. She also needed to call for her cook, Cristina, and have her bring in a couple of aspirins and a strong cup of coffee. If the dull ache in her head was any indication, Shirlene had had too many margaritas the night before. Rolling away from the light, she stuffed her head under the pillow. A pillow that wasn't nearly as soft and downy as she'd remembered. Nor did the sheets feel as satiny, or smell like the flowery fabric softener the housekeeper used. Although the smell was rather nice. She took a deep breath and held it into her lungs. It smelled like...

Bubba?

She sat straight up, then groaned as a vise of pain tightened around her skull. She slammed her eyes shut and took a quivery breath. Then one by one she slowly opened her eyelids. But this time it wasn't quick movement or bright sunlight that caused her intense pain. This time, it was the dingy sheets hanging over the window, the exposed insulation dangling from the ceiling, and the mattress sagging beneath her butt. Not to mention the fact that she was wearing nothing but her lace underwear.

She jerked the sheet up over her breasts and glanced around for her clothes. But the only things on the floor were her blue high heels. An image flashed through her mind: an image of those heels resting on a set of broad shoulders while a man with a talented tongue worked his magic.

With a groan, Shirlene flopped back on the bed and pulled the sheet over her head.

Had she lost her mind? What was she thinking letting Bubba Wilkes work his magic? And what else had he worked? She couldn't remember a thing after her explosive orgasm. Other than feeling content. Completely and totally content. But she didn't feel content now. Now she felt like she could throw up. Although that might have more to do with the alcohol than the oral sex.

Realizing she couldn't hide in Bubba's bed all day, she crawled out, dragging the sheet with her. In the bathroom, she studied her face in the mirror. She looked like death warmed over. Her hair was wild, her mascara smeared, and her freckles stood out on her pale face like chocolate sprinkles on white icing. After downing three of the aspirins she found in the medicine cabinet, she washed off her makeup and finger-combed her hair. It wasn't much of an improvement. While she was standing in front of the mirror wondering why she was worried about looking good for a redneck, the redneck walked in.

She barely had time to grab up the sheet from the floor. By the look in those deep brown eyes, it wasn't near fast enough.

"Well, good mornin', Strawberry Shortcake," he

drawled as he propped a shoulder on the doorjamb and crossed his arms over a chest that was only partially covered by the thin white cotton of the sleeveless undershirt.

She didn't know why she suddenly felt so angry. Probably because while she looked like Courtney Love after a hard night of partying, he looked like Hugh Jackman ready to belt out *Oklahoma*. And no woman wanted to be upstaged by a man the day after.

Her eyes narrowed as she gave in to her sour disposition. "You took advantage of me."

Those dark eyebrows lifted. "Advantage? Now, I hate to split hairs, Sugar Biscuit, but at what point last night did I end up with the advantage? Was that during your orgasm or after you passed out in my bed and left me on a hard sofa...with a hard-on."

She flapped her mouth like a bass out of water while he continued.

"Now, it's true that I should've evaluated your condition a little more carefully, but most' the women I date can't hold their liquor quite as well as you can. Although you do look a little worse for wear this mornin', Shirley Girl."

Unable to come up with one thing to say to that, she shoved him out of the way and headed back toward the bedroom, where she searched around for her clothes until Bubba cleared his throat. She glanced up to see her jeans dangling from his finger.

She snatched them away from him. "And my shirt?"

He shook his head. "More shredded than the Hulk's." He walked over and pulled open a drawer. "But I don't mind you borrowing one of mine."

"Don't mind? It's the least you can do considering you were responsible."

"Actually," he turned and held out the shirt, "you were the one that ripped it off—followed by mine." He grinned. "Obviously, patience is not one of your virtues."

She grabbed the shirt. "You're right, and my patience for a redneck has about run out."

Before the words were even out of her mouth, she was in his arms. "You sure you don't want to sample a little more Bubba lovin', Shirley Girl? Because I don't mind, at all. Not even if you look a little like my Aunt Clara after she got locked in the henhouse with a bunch of angry chickens."

The warmth of his chest through the thin, cotton shirt seeped into her weary, aching body like a steam sauna. And for a moment, she actually considered sampling a little Bubba lovin' when she wasn't under the influence. But then he smiled that cocky smile of his, and she regained her senses and pulled away.

"Thanks for the shirt, Bubba," she said as she strolled back to the bathroom to get dressed. But before she closed the door, she peeked her head back out. "And for the orgasm."

When Shirlene was finished dressing, she found Bubba outside working on his truck. If you could call hanging a pair of large artificial bull balls from the back bumper work. Her heels clicked on the front steps, but he didn't come out from beneath the huge chrome bumper to say goodbye. Figuring it was for the best, she headed toward the hedge, although as she walked past she couldn't keep her gaze from wandering over those lean legs.

"I'll take you back to town to get your SUV anytime you're ready," he said.

Consumed by the way the soft denim encased his

hard thighs, it took her a second to answer. "Thanks, but I think I can find my own ride." She didn't know how she was going to do that, but she figured walking was better than driving around in a vehicle with balls.

When she stepped through the hedge, she was greeted by an exuberant pig.

"Piglet." She knelt down to scratch his head, noticing the close-clipped hairs in between his ears. Darn that little Brody and his scissors. But since hair seemed to be the only thing missing on the pig, she counted her blessings. Of course, Sherman was the least of her worries. She had just gotten back to her feet when Mia came out of the trailer with Adeline on her hip and Brody peeking around her legs.

"Where have you been?" Mia asked in a voice that sounded a lot like Colt's when Shirlene had stayed out past curfew.

It had been years since she had to answer to anyone, so Shirlene was more than a little rusty at coming up with good excuses. She hemmed and hawed for a few minutes until she finally gave up and told the truth.

She shot a glance back at the hedge and lowered her voice. "I might've had a little too much to drink last night so Bubba drove me home. And since it was so late, I didn't want to wake y'all up so I spent the night there."

Mia's eyes narrowed. "And the groceries?"

Shirlene swallowed hard. "Uhh...things didn't go exactly as I expected with the bank owner...and there was a little problem with my credit at Duds 'N Such." She held up a hand. "But don't you worry, honey. I plan on callin' my brother as soon as I get to a phone. And I promise we'll figure this thing out."

The look of disappointment and defeat in Mia's eyes caused Shirlene's stomach to tighten with guilt. The entire time Shirlene had been pointing guns and slamming down tequila and enjoying Bubba-lovin', she hadn't given one thought to the kids or how her actions would affect them. All she'd been concerned with was how badly she felt. But her troubles didn't come close to Mia's, and instead of helping the poor girl, she'd only added to her misery. And it didn't look like Mia was going to give her a second chance. Without a word, she turned and walked back inside, slamming the door behind her.

Shirlene stared at the battered door, and the knot twisted. She rarely tossed her cookies—regardless of how much she had to drink—but all of a sudden she leaned away from her shoes and threw up. When she was finished, she staggered over to the shade beneath the elm tree and sat down on the back bumper of the old Chevy. Sherman followed, flopping down only a few feet away.

She wiped off her mouth with the back of her hand, trying not to notice how badly it shook. "Well," she smiled weakly, "I guess Manny mixes his drinks a lot stronger than I remembered."

The snuffle the pig gave her pretty much said he didn't believe her for a second. And when she looked over at him, his little beady eyes were reflections of Mia's disappointment. It was the same look Colt had given their mama every time she'd broken her promise to stop drinking.

A look that held the pain of crushed hope.

The tough façade that Shirlene had been struggling to hold in place since Lyle's death—or possibly since she was born—cracked open, and tears welled up in her eyes. But this time, she couldn't stop them from falling as the truth smacked her square in the face. No matter how much she had tried to distance herself from the pain and poverty of Grover Road, it had somehow followed her.

As she sat there staring through her tears at the broken junk that filled the yard, she realized that it wasn't geological as much as genetic. She could hop in her SUV and drive as far from Grover Road as she could get, and she still couldn't get away from where she came from and who she was. Distance could not change the fact that she was her mama's daughter—a self-absorbed woman with an addictive nature.

She didn't know if the traits had been planted at conception, or if it had been a slow process brought on by years of observation. It didn't seem to matter when Baby Adeline's cry filtered out through the open window of the trailer. Shirlene's stomach heaved again, and she stuck her head between her knees and took deep even breaths until the feeling passed. She stayed that way, staring at the tears that plopped down to the ground between her expensive, ridiculous shoes.

Finally Sherman's cold nose snuffled up against her ear, and he continued to butt up against her until she lifted her head. The disappointment was gone from his eyes, and all she could see was her own reflection in the beady orbs.

She sniffed. "I screwed up, didn't I, Sherman? Mia asked me for help, and all I've done in the last few days is think about getting my house back." She leaned her head on his and took a quivery breath before blowing it back out. "It looks like I stink at being a foster parent."

"You ain't as bad as Auntie Barb or my other foster moms."

Shirlene sat up to find Jesse sitting on a tire not more

than three feet away. His head was tipped, and one eye scrunched up as he studied her.

"How come girls are such cry babies, anyway?" he asked. "Every time somethin' don't go your way, you start bawlin' your eyes out. Mia's in there packin' and sobbin' up a storm, which caused Adeline and Brody to start wailin'. I swear a man can't find a speck of peace and quiet around here."

She swiped at her nose. "What do you mean Mia's packing?"

"She says she don't want to stay in a town filled with stupid people. She thinks we'll do better elsewhere." Jesse's gaze wandered over her, stopping at the snap-down western shirt with the ripped off sleeves. The boy's curious eyes had her face flaming like gasoline-soaked briquettes. "So where's my shirt?"

She ignored the question and leaned closer. "You can't let Mia take you away again, Jesse," she pleaded. "You've got to talk her into giving me one more chance."

He shook his head. "Once Mia gets a bug in her butt, it's not easy to change her mind. She's all worried you're gonna tell Colt, and he's gonna call the sheriff. I tried to tell her that Colt ain't like that, but she ain't gonna listen."

"Calling Colt would probably be the best thing for everyone," Shirlene said, but even as she spoke the words something inside her rebelled at the thought. But now her desire to keep things from Colt had nothing to do with her brother finding out about the house and everything to do with proving something to these kids—and to herself.

"I'm not going to call Colt." She glanced down at Sherman, who seemed to be smiling back at her. The silly pig's affirmation brought the lump back to her throat.

"You ain't gonna cry again, are you?" Jesse said, not looking at all happy about the prospect of seeing more tears.

She laughed. "I'll make you a deal. I won't cry again if you help me keep Mia and the kids here."

His eyes narrowed. "Why? You don't even like us."

It was hard to argue with the truth so she didn't even try.

"Sometimes it takes a while for people to get past that first impression. Take my best friend Hope, for example. At first, I thought she was the biggest brat on the face of the earth, but then she shared her Popsicle with me, and I've loved her ever since."

"We ain't got no Popsicles," Jesse said.

"Well, we'll have to remedy that, but right now we have to figure out how to keep Mia from running off."

Jesse stared back at her for the longest time before he nodded. "Fine, I'll help you. But first things first, we gotta get some money. If anything makes Mia feel better, it's a handful of cash."

"I thought you made money selling junk." Shirlene looked around. "And it looks like we've got plenty to sell."

"It ain't about the amount you got," he said as if she was as dumb as dirt. "It's about how many folks is willin' to buy it. And Bramble's done bought everything they're gonna buy from me. What we need is somethin' really good to sell." He thought for a moment before he looked over at Shirlene. "So you ain't gettin' your house back?"

"No, it doesn't look that way."

"Because of that Mr. Peabody guy with the skinny mustache?"

She really wanted to blame Mr. Peabody, and especially

Mr. Cates, but if she was going to take responsibility for a bunch of orphans, she first needed to take responsibility for her own actions. The truth was that Mr. Peabody and Mr. Cates weren't responsible for her lack of funds—or her lack of house. She was.

"No, it isn't Mr. Peabody's fault," she said. "It's because I can't manage money worth a flip."

Jesse nodded as if he was in total agreement. She really had to stop hanging out with brutally honest children and pigs.

"What about all your stuff?" he asked. "Did you mismanage that too?"

Shirlene hadn't given much thought to the contents of her house. She'd been too busy trying to get back the entire enchilada. But now that Jesse brought it up, she realized that Mr. Cates might own her house, but he didn't own the things inside it. Not the furniture, or art, or her entire walk-in closet of clothes and shoes. The thought made her almost giddy with happiness.

"You're right," she jumped up. "All the stuff inside is mine." When she noticed Jesse's face, she amended her words. "I mean *ours*, to sell." Her eyes narrowed. "Now all I have to do is figure out how to get Mr. Cates to hand over the key so we can get inside."

Jesse shrugged. "Why don't we just ask the man who's livin' there to let us in?"

Chapter Nineteen

"Ms. Dalton, I've got to tell you, I'm getting pretty sick of my vacation being interrupted by phone calls from you."

Shirlene's eyes narrowed as she adjusted the cell phone to her ear. "Believe me, Mr. Cates, not as sick as I am of having to deal with you. Now you want to explain who's living in my house?"

Shirlene had made her own assumptions. But for some reason, she wanted to hear it from this man's lips. Surprisingly, he didn't disappoint her.

"That would be my brother, Beau. And the house isn't yours, Ms. Dalton. It belongs to the bank, unless you can come up with a lot of money real quick."

For a moment, she thought about continuing the charade of being the poor widow woman bullied by the mean bank owner. But no matter how much Shirlene enjoyed acting, she was getting tired of the role.

She released her breath in a long huff. "You can have the house, Mr. Cates."

"Excuse me?" The shock in his smooth voice suddenly made her feel a whole lot better.

"Those ocean waves a little too loud for you, honey?" she asked as a grin split her face.

"They must be, Ms. Dalton. I thought you said I could have the house."

"I did. What in the world am I gonna do with a big old house like that, anyway?" Even as she said the words, her mind filled with images of her propped up on the pillow-topped mattress, soaking in the huge Jacuzzi tub, or basking by the glistening swimming pool. But as her mama used to say, Life is hell and then you die. And Shirlene wasn't dead yet.

"So, Mr. Cates, now that we have that settled, when can I come get my things?"

"And what things would those be, Ms. Dalton?"

She gritted her teeth. "The things inside my house."

"Getting a little upset about going without a change of diamonds, are we?" Mr. Cates's voice was filled with snide humor. "Or is it that nude painting of yours that you miss the most?"

"How did you . . . ?" Shirlene couldn't help but glance up and down the street as if she stood there completely naked. Of course, even if she was naked, no one would notice. Everyone in Bramble seemed to be too caught up in their Saturday morning business.

Moses Tate napped on the bench in front of Sutter's Pharmacy. Missy Leigh loaded groceries and her horde of kids into the back of her minivan. Twyla and Kenny Gene were having a fight outside of Josephine's. And Jesse and his siblings sat in front of the Dairy Treat, eating the ice cream Bubba had bought them. Bubba stood a few yards away, talking on his cell phone. When he noticed Shirlene looking at him, he grinned that dopey grin of his and waved.

She rolled her eyes and looked away. The man was harder to get rid of than head lice.

"So I guess your brother has seen my painting," Shirlene returned to her conversation with Mr. Cates.

"And I'm sure he's not the only one." He paused. "So is the painter a past lover or a present?"

She flinched, but kept her cool. "What difference does it make to you? You waitin' in line, honey?"

He snorted. "Not hardly. I prefer my women a little more modest."

"And I prefer my men with a little more chivalry."

He laughed. "Don't try and tell me that dumb redneck you're hanging out with is your new knight in shining armor."

Shirlene's eyes narrowed. Obviously, Beau had a mouth as big as Texas.

"As a matter of fact, Bubba has come to my rescue a few times," she said. Mostly by dumb luck, but Shirlene wasn't about to let Mr. Cates know that. "So when can I get my things?"

"It all depends on how much I can get for the house," he said in that uppity voice that was really starting to get on Shirlene's last nerve. "If it doesn't cover the loan, I might just have to sell that painting of yours."

"You're not selling my painting!" She was so angry she stomped her foot. Her heel got caught in a crack, and it took a hard yank to get it back out, minus the little rubber tip. "You have no right to anything of mine besides the house."

"I disagree. Until I get every cent of my money back, I have the right to put a lien on anything you own, Ms. Dalton."

Shirlene's stomach tightened, and she wondered if she might get sick all over again. It took a few deep breaths until she was able to speak.

"Does your mama know what a disagreeable man she raised?" she asked.

"She knows exactly what kind of man I am, Ms. Dalton," he said. "Just like your mama is aware of the kind of woman you are."

It was an insult if ever she heard one, but with anger boiling in her veins and her stomach churning, she couldn't think of a snide reply to save her soul. So instead, she ended the conversation. "You haven't heard the last of me, Mr. Cates."

Once she hung up, she released her breath. She still felt sick to her stomach, and she wondered if maybe all the stress of the last week had given her an ulcer. The way her luck was going, she wouldn't be at all surprised.

"So he's not going to give you back your things, is he?"

Startled, Shirlene turned to see Mia standing there with Adeline on her hip. It had taken most of the morning to convince Mia to give up on her plans to leave town and give Shirlene another chance. And it was hard not to lie when the girl looked as if she carried the weight of the world on her narrow shoulders. But Shirlene was through with lying.

"No," she said. "He's not. But I'll figure something out."

Mia only stared back at her with those defeated purple-gray eyes. It was almost a relief when Jesse came shuffling up with Brody in tow. The toddler's face was smeared with vanilla ice cream, and he had the gun holster she'd bought him strapped to his hip. In one side was the gun she hadn't used on Mr. Peabody and in the other Naked Barbie.

"I just got finished talkin' to Darla," Jesse said. "And she said she's lookin' to buy a new couch. You got one of those in that big house, don't ya?"

His red hair shot up straight up from his head and looked like it hadn't seen a comb in a year. Looking for anything to postpone the bad news, Shirlene reached out to smooth it down. But the kid jerked away and narrowed his eyes at her.

"I don't like people touchin' on me."

She pulled her hand back. "Well, I wouldn't be touchin' on you, if you'd comb your hair occasionally."

His face grew more belligerent. "You should talk. At least my hair don't look like it was throwed in a blender."

Criticism about her grooming was a hard pill for Shirlene to swallow, especially when the woman who had always refused to go out of the house until every hair was in place was the same woman who stood in the middle of town in Bubba's tattered western shirt with no makeup and her hair looking like it had been "throwed in a blender."

But her daydreams of hair products and a shower with water pressure would have to be put on hold. She had a family to feed. And if she couldn't keep her promise to Mia, she had little doubt that Mia would take the kids and run, forcing Shirlene to call Sheriff Winslow whether she wanted to or not. Sam was a nice man, but she didn't trust him to make the right decision concerning the kids. Of course, she hadn't exactly been a sterling example of someone making the right decisions either.

She wanted to change that. For once in her life, she

wanted to prove that she was the type of person that people could rely on. The type of person completely different from her own mama. Still, she didn't know how she was going to pull it off without calling Colt. If she couldn't get in her house, she had nothing else of value besides her SUV.

About then Sherman woke up from his nap at her feet and sniffed the air. Like a hound dog on a scent, his head snapped over to Brody, and he popped to his feet. The little boy giggled as the pig licked his face clean. When Sherman got a little too exuberant, Shirlene reeled in the leash and tugged him back. The sun hit her hand, reflecting off her engagement ring in spangles of dancing light. It was like a sign from heaven. Or maybe just a timely coincidence. Either way, Shirlene knew what she had to do.

It took more than a little effort to get the ring off her finger—obviously, swelling was related to stress. When it finally slipped free, she gave the brilliant three carats one last fond look before handing it over to Jesse. "You'd better come back with enough to last us a while."

Jesse's eyes widened for only a second before he spit on the ring and shined it up with his Superman shirt. "I ain't dumb, Shirley Girl." The use of Bubba's nickname had Shirlene sending him a warning look. But he ignored it, and with a lopsided grin, shuffled down the street toward Josephine's.

"You gave up your wedding ring?" Mia's voice was soft and filled with confusion.

"Not my wedding ring, honey," Shirlene reached down and used Brody's shirt to wipe off his mouth. "Just an old ring that didn't mean a thing. In fact," she nodded over at the Food Mart, "why don't you head on over there and fill out that grocery list of yours."

"But what if Jesse can't sell it?" Mia asked.

Shirlene shrugged. "I figure I still have enough clout in this town to get me a little bit of credit." She flapped a hand. "Go on now. I'll be over there in a few minutes."

Mia studied her for only a second before she nodded and reached a hand out to Brody. "Come on, Brody." But for some reason, Brody pulled back and shook his head. Shirlene might've taken it as a sign he was warming up to her, if he hadn't placed one dimpled hand on Sherman's back.

"It's okay if he stays," Shirlene said. "I promise I won't let him run in the street or anything."

Mia glanced out at the street, and doubt settled over her pretty features. But since the traffic in Bramble was pretty much nonexistent, she finally accepted Shirlene's offer and walked away.

When she was gone, Shirlene glanced down at the white line on her finger and swallowed hard. *Forgive me, honey, but I couldn't figure out any other way.* But instead of hearing from Lyle, all she heard was the voice of an arrogant east Texan.

"Does the kid have to carry that doll around with him everywhere he goes?"

Bubba's words caused her to glance over at Brody, who had pulled the Barbie out of the holster and was giving her a Lady Godiva ride on Sherman's back.

"He likes naked blondes," she said. "What man doesn't?"

Bubba took a lick of the chocolate ice cream cone he held in one hand. "I guess it could be worse. He could be totin' around a Raggedy Ann." He reached out and ruffled

Shirlene's hair. "Although I'm kinda partial to Raggedy, myself."

"Funny." Shirlene moved over to one of the benches that lined Main Street and sat down. Her sleepless nights were catching up to her, and all she wanted to do was curl up on the bench and take a nap. She tugged Sherman over and Brody and Barbie followed.

"So where is their mama today?" Bubba asked as he took the seat next to her. "I tried asking Mia, but talking to that kid is like talking to a wall."

The less Bubba knew about the kids' situation the better, so Shirlene stretched the truth. "I don't know. She wasn't there when I got back this morning. Obviously, the woman works her fingers to the bone."

Bubba's eyes narrowed. "Still, it seems strange, doesn't it?" When she didn't say anything, he glanced over. "But no stranger than you spending a good half hour in church. Repenting, Shirley Girl?"

She probably needed to repent. But instead she'd been filling out paperwork. Pastor Robbins didn't even question her rush to become a foster parent, which made her wonder if he hadn't figured things out. The thought had her glancing up at the clear, blue summer sky.

"So what got you all fired up this morning to get back to town?" He leisurely licked at the ice cream.

It was a struggle to pull her eyes away from Bubba's tongue. "I needed to talk to someone."

"I hope it wasn't that wet-behind-the-ears kid you were fondling last night."

"I was not fondling him," she huffed. "And had I known of his sinister nature, I wouldn't have been dancing with him in the first place."

"Sinister?" Billy rested an arm on the back of the bench. "That's a pretty strong word, Shirley Girl. Are you telling me that this Beau feller is responsible for you being evicted?"

"If he's not responsible, he's related to the villain who is—" she paused, putting extra emphasis and hate on her next words, "Mr. Cates."

Billy lifted his eyebrows. "That doesn't exactly sound like a villain's name to me. Lex Luthor or Snidely Whiplash, now those are villains' names." He held out the ice cream cone. "Lick?"

"Which makes Mr. Cates more sinister. At least, Snidely didn't pretend to be anything but what he was." She nodded at the ice cream. "What flavor?"

"Bubbalicious," he said with a sly wink. When she heaved an exasperated sigh, he shrugged. "Rocky Road." He moved it closer. "Here, have a taste."

She really shouldn't take anything else from Bubba— a ride into town and an orgasm were more than enough. But it had been so long since she'd had a chocolate fix that she couldn't help but lean in and brush her tongue around the icy scoop of deliciousness. The rich, cocoa flavor had a party on her taste buds, and she pulled back and closed her eyes in ecstasy. When she opened them, Bubba was watching her, his eyes twin pools of smoldering lust.

Shirlene knew how he felt.

Her gaze slipped down to the firm set of lips with the tiny smudge of chocolate ice cream in one corner, and suddenly chocolate wasn't the only thing she craved. She wanted to lick that sexy mouth clean. And when she was finished, she wanted to wash it all down with more of those sweet Bubba-kisses that she couldn't seem to wipe from her mind.

But before she could make a fool of herself in front of the entire town, Bubba's fingers tightened around the cone, and the soggy wafer crumpled, sending the scoop of ice cream plopping to the ground. The pig bumped against their legs in his enthusiasm to lick up every last drop of Rocky Road, breaking their sexual trance and causing Brody to shriek with laughter.

While Bubba pulled a napkin from his back pocket and wiped off his hand, Shirlene tried to think of something to say to the man that would let him know there would be no repeat of what had happened the previous night. Before she could find the words, Bubba beat her to it.

"I hope you didn't get the wrong idea last night, Honey Buns." He flipped the napkin into a nearby trashcan. "Now I sure enjoyed our time together—well, I might've enjoyed it more if you hadn't passed out, but Bubba likes to spread it around."

She squinted at him. "What?"

The dopey look was replaced with a serious one, or at least as serious as Bubba Wilkes could get. "I hate to bust your bubble, but I ain't a one-woman man."

Her eyes widened. "You've got to be kidding. You're giving *me* the brush off?"

He flashed a wide grin. "Now I wouldn't call it the brush off—I'm more than willin' to take up right where we left off. Just so long as you realize that you can't get greedy with Bubba-lovin'."

Resting her elbows on her knees, she covered her face and groaned.

"Now I realize you're upset." He patted her back as he continued. "But it just wouldn't be fair to the other women in Bramble—or in the rest of Texas for that matter, if I only courted you."

She lifted her head and glared at him. "Have you lost your mind?" Before he could talk any more of his nonsense, she reached over and covered his mouth with her hand. She might've pressed a little too hard because he flinched.

"I don't want you courting me," she spoke slowly and distinctly. "And I don't want a tour of Wilkesville. Or a little Bubba-lovin'. What happened last night was a mistake." His eyes flickered. "A mistake that I don't intend to make again. So would you please keep all your hillbilly euphemisms to yourself?" She hesitated for a moment to let her words sink into that thick skull before she pulled her hand away.

His eyes turned thoughtful. "All right, Shirley Girl. I'll keep it to three other women." When she stared at him in disbelief, he amended. "Fine, two, but that's final, Cinnamon Muffins. You'll just have to learn to share. And speaking of sharing." He pulled his wallet from his back pocket and took out the entire stack of bills. "I want you to give this to the kids' mama. It's a little more than two hundred for the chainsaw, but I figured they could use—"

"I done it!" Jesse came tearing down the street in his oversized boots. "I sold it for a pretty penny!" When he noticed Bubba sitting on the other side of Shirlene, he came to skidding halt and shoved the wad of money in his hand into his jeans pocket. Unfortunately, not before Bubba saw it.

"That looks like a fair chunk of change, son," he said as his eyes narrowed. "What did you sell to get all that?"

"Just some junk," Jesse said with a wide grin.

While Bubba stared at Jesse, Shirlene stared at the money in his hand and tried not to drop to the sidewalk and scream like a baby. Fifteen minutes. Just fifteen minutes earlier, and Lyle's diamond ring would still be on her finger. She glanced back across the street. Maybe it still could be. She jerked the money out of Bubba's hand and jumped up from the bench. "Who did you sell it to—?"

Before Shirlene could even get the words out, Twyla raced out of Josephine's Diner like her teased hair was on fire.

"Lookee, everybody," she screeched, startling Moses Tate from his nap and causing Sherman to look up from his Rocky Road feast. She waggled her hand in the air, the sun reflecting off the huge diamond. "I'm gettin' married!"

Chapter Twenty

BILLY LOOKED OUT the kitchen window toward Shirlene Dalton's property. He couldn't see a thing through the thick hedge, but he didn't need to. For the last two days, his mind had been filled with images of long legs and sweet centers. And breasts so plump and full they made a man want to drop to his knees and beg for death by suffocation. And it wasn't just her phenomenal body that had Billy obsessing about Shirlene. He also couldn't stop thinking about her uncharacteristic behavior.

Why would a woman who lived for the finer things in life sell a huge diamond for the measly five hundred dollars Kenny Gene had forked over? It just didn't fit with the entire gold-digger image he had of the woman. Of course, a lot of things didn't fit—like her sudden desire to live out on Grover Road. He had figured that once Shirlene found out that she wasn't getting her house back, she would be on her way to greener pastures—or wealthier men. But instead, she'd continued to live in the beat-up trailer with the ragamuffin Fosters.

Yesterday morning, he'd been on his way to talk

with a historian in Odessa when he'd heard Brody giggling. Moving just far enough into the hedge to see, he'd watched as Shirlene chased Sherman around the piles of junk with the water hose. She didn't look like a frivolous Texas socialite. With her bare feet, cut-off jeans, and Billy's shirt tied up high on her stomach, she looked like a redneck mama just beggin' for a little lovin' from her redneck daddy. With the sun setting her hair on fire and water dripping down those long, tanned legs, it took everything Billy had in him to keep from playing his own game of chase—one that ended with Shirlene in his arms.

He'd been so distracted by the sight that he'd been late for the meeting. Not that the historian had given him any new information. Still, he wished Shirlene would quit fooling around and get back to the selfish gold digger he expected her to be. He had some bones to find, and he couldn't find his granddaddy's gravesite if she kept distracting him. And maybe he wouldn't be so distracted if he had some answers.

Billy pulled the cell phone out of his front shirt pocket. After only two rings, the other line picked up. He glanced at the clock over the stove and had to smile. The man might be annoying, but he was one hardworking son of a gun.

"Bank of Bramble, Reginald Peabody speaking."

Billy rolled his eyes. "Good evening, Mr. Peabody, this is William Cates speaking."

"Oh, Mr. Cates." A chair squeaked. "What can I do for you, sir?"

Billy paused, suddenly wondering if he'd been a little too impulsive—the less people knew about his infatuation with Ms. Dalton the better. Still, she had a loan with his bank, so his curiosity was easily explained. "Actually, I was wondering if you could look up someone's accounts for me."

"Of course, sir, whose accounts are you interested in?"

"Shirlene Dalton."

There was a swift intake of breath before Mr. Peabody recovered. "I'm assuming we're gathering this information to add to our case against Ms. Dalton." His voice became even more uppity. "I was appalled by the so-called sheriff's handling of the incident—why, he didn't even put that criminal behind bars."

"A criminal is stretching it a little, wouldn't you say?" Billy said.

"I would not say," the little man huffed. "She threatened me with a gun."

"A toy gun that she left on your desk." It took a real effort for Billy not to laugh at the image of Shirlene waving a cap gun at a wild-eyed Reginald Peabody.

"Toy or not," the bank manager continued, "I almost had a heart attack."

"Something you'll be more than compensated for in your next paycheck," he said. That seemed to shut Reggie up, and Billy went back to the reason he'd called the man in the first place. "So can you get the information?"

"You do realize that Ms. Dalton closed her accounts with us after the buyout." The man really did have an annoying manner.

"I'm well aware of that, Mr. Peabody. If she had accounts at our bank, I could just look them up myself, now couldn't I?"

"I'll see what I can find out," Mr. Peabody said. "Will there be anything else, sir?"

"No, I think that will do it for now." Billy hung up the phone and slipped it back in his shirt pocket just as Slate Calhoun's Yukon pulled up in the yard. Billy was out the door before Slate had even climbed out of his SUV. Taking note of his sweaty t-shirt and running shorts, Billy couldn't help but tease him.

"So you still tryin' to whip that team of yours into shape before they have to face the Dogwood Dragons?"

"Funny," Slate said as he slammed the door, "but I didn't see the Dragons in the state playoffs. Did they take the year off?"

Billy snorted. "Damned coach needs to pull his head out of his ass. Who calls a running play on third and long?"

"I'd say a coach who has a lot of faith in their running back."

"Ours averages under a yard a carry," Billy grumbled.

Laughing, Slate took off his ball cap and wiped the sweat from his forehead. "So does that mean you're ready to concede the fact that I have the best high school football team in Texas?"

"Hell, no."

Slate tugged the hat back on and grinned. "So where have you been keepin' yourself? Faith was real upset when you canceled dinner on Friday night." His hazel eyes twinkled. "Luckily, she hasn't heard the gossip about you being at Bootlegger's." Before Billy could try to explain, Slate slapped him on the back. "Not a problem, buddy. I can't blame you for wanting to hang out with a bunch of pretty cowgirls instead of an old married couple. Of course, it sounds like you didn't have much chance to socialize, not when you had to take Shirlene home." Slate nodded at him. "I sure appreciate you watching out for her. She's had a tough time since Lyle died."

A shaft of guilt speared through Billy. Of all the people in Bramble, Slate was the one Billy hated to lie to the most. There were times he'd actually thought about telling his friend who he really was and why he was there, but then he'd remember his pledge to his family. And regardless of how much he liked Slate, blood was thicker than water.

Besides, he wasn't responsible for the collapse of Dalton Oil or Lyle's heart attack—that had been set in motion long ago by used-up oil fields and fluctuating fuel prices. The only thing C-Corp had done was ensure that the failing company wouldn't be revived. It was a small deception. Although looking back at Slate's smiling face, it seemed like a much bigger one. Maybe it was the guilt that prompted his next words.

"Shirlene didn't look all that upset on Friday night to me. With the way she was drinking and flirting with men, it seemed pretty obvious she only married Lyle for the money."

Slate's smile slipped. "Then you've been listening to a little too much town gossip. Shirlene might've married for money, but she stayed married for love."

"And what makes you think so—the fact that she didn't divorce him in the first couple years? Maybe she just wanted it all, instead of half."

Beneath the brim of the cap, Slate's eyes narrowed. "Who are you? And what did you do with the Bubba who never has a bad word to say about anyone—especially a good-lookin' woman?"

Billy tried to slip back into the charming country boy,

but for some reason, he was struggling to connect with that side of his personality. So instead he offered a weak smile and an even weaker excuse.

"I might've tipped a few too many this past weekend at Boot's."

Slate nodded as the smile returned. "Ahh, the joy of single life."

"Missing your freedom?" Billy asked, hoping to get the conversation on a less volatile topic.

"Not a bit, my friend. I'd much rather stay home with my pretty wife and baby than suffer through a night of listening to the townsfolk's crazy talk." He shook his head. "Have you heard the one about Shirlene shacking up with some con artist?"

Billy's gaze slipped down to his bare feet. "Yeah, I heard that one."

Slate laughed and shook his head. "Crazy townsfolk."

"Yeah, they're crazy all right."

They talked for a few more minutes about the upcoming football season and Slate's daughter's amazing ability to blow bubbles. When the sun slipped closer to the horizon, Slate pushed away from Billy's truck.

"Well, I guess I better get home for supper. Faith's trying out her mama's pot roast tonight." He shot a glance over to Billy. "I'd ask you back to the house, but I won't put you on the spot."

Since Billy figured his guilt would only triple if he got to know Slate's family, he was grateful. As they walked to Slate's Yukon, Billy couldn't help making the offer he'd made more than a few times.

"The head coaching position in Dogwood is still yours if you want it."

"Dogwood is your home, Bubba," Slate said as he pulled open the car door. "Mine is right here in Bramble."

That's what Billy was afraid of.

Long after Slate was gone, Billy stood out front and stared at the road. The day had been another hot one, and he couldn't help but wonder how the Fosters and Shirlene were surviving without an air conditioner. He had thought about going back over to fix it. But since his mind was already overcrowded with images of Shirlene, he figured it was best to pay someone else to do it.

Besides, Shirlene didn't want to see him any more than he wanted to see her. She only thought of him as her annoying redneck neighbor, something that bothered him more than he was willing to admit. Especially when that's exactly what he had been angling for. He didn't want her getting the wrong idea about what had taken place on Friday night. Didn't want things getting more complicated than they already were. Obviously, she hadn't gotten the wrong idea at all. In the last couple days, he hadn't seen hide nor hair of her.

It was for the best. Billy's time was almost over in Bramble. With or without his granddaddy's remains, it was time to get back to the business of running C-Corp.

He turned and headed for the trailer, but just before he reached the front steps, a weed caught his eye. After cleaning out the yard on Friday morning, he thought he'd gotten all the weeds. But it looked as if he'd missed one. He walked over and plucked the tiny plant. Except as soon as he did, he noticed another one—and another. Until before Billy knew it, he was standing in the junk-filled yard next door.

The Navigator was gone, the yard quiet except for the

chirp of sparrows up in the elm tree. In the heat of the late afternoon, a stench rose up from the piles of garbage, a stench that burned Billy's nostrils and had his eyes watering. And if it affected him that way, how much worse would it affect little kids?

It didn't take him long to load the back of his truck with broken pieces of furniture, old mattresses, and the bags of trash he'd collected. The numerous empty vodka bottles worried him. Obviously, Ms. Foster had a drinking problem—hopefully, they didn't belong to Jesse. He had slipped through the hedge for one last armful when a truck pulled into the lot. For a second, Billy considered making a run for it. But before he could dive behind an upended sofa, the teenage boy yelled at him.

"Excuse me, sir," the tall lanky boy climbed out of the old truck and headed toward him.

Since every person in town had pointed him out at one time or another, it only took Billy a minute to recognize the boy.

"You're Austin Reeves, Slate's new quarterback," he said. He wiped his hand off on his jeans and held it out to the kid, who hurried over and grabbed it in a firm handshake.

"Yes, sir."

"Bubba Wilkes," Billy said.

Austin's eyes registered shock. "*The* Bubba Wilkes?"

Billy laughed. "I don't know if I'd go that far, son. I think you're a bigger celebrity in this town than I am."

Austin shook his head. "No way. When I first moved here, all I heard about was Bubba. Not to mention your truck. I bet Coach sure misses driving around in it."

"So he claims." Billy said. "But I think he's BSing me

a little so as not to hurt my feelings. So what brings you out to Grover Road, Austin? If you're looking for Coach Calhoun, he just left."

"Actually, I was looking for Mia. But I guess I got the wrong trailer."

The young man's words surprised Billy. Mia didn't seem like the type to hang around with the most popular boy in school—or any boys, for that matter. She seemed wary of men. Or maybe just a redneck from east Texas.

Smart girl.

"No, you didn't get the wrong trailer," Billy said. "Mia lives here, but she's not at home right now."

Nodding, Austin reached around and pulled his wallet from his back pocket. "That's okay. I just wanted to drop by her driver's license. She dropped it the other night when she stopped for gas. I've been meaning to get it back to her, but with work and practice I haven't had a chance."

"She stopped by for gas the other night?" Billy asked. "I didn't even know she had a car."

"A blue Impala."

"No kiddin'," Billy's gaze snapped over to the old bed frame and tires resting against a tarp-covered heap. "I guess I need to get to know my neighbors a little better."

"You and me both," Austin said as he held out the license with a picture of a dark-haired Mia on the front. "Because I thought Mia's last name was Foster."

Chapter Twenty-one

IT WAS HARD TO TRUST. At least, it was hard for Mia. Life had dealt her so many untrustworthy people that she couldn't help but be skeptical of a woman with a perpetual smile on her face. It was probably this skepticism that made her treat Shirlene Dalton like a dog with fleas.

"We shouldn't have spent the money," Mia said as she adjusted the seatbelt on her bony shoulder blade. "Not when we only have fifty-two dollars left."

"Fifty-two dollars and a refrigerator filled with groceries." Shirlene winked at her. "What more could a couple of footloose-and-fancy-free gals wish for?" When Mia didn't say anything, she swatted her arm. "It was only a couple burgers and some tater tots, honey. It's not like we purchased the Taj Mahal."

"That's that place in India you was teachin' me about, ain't it, Mia?" Jesse asked from the backseat.

Mia sighed. "How many times do I have to tell you that 'ain't' isn't proper English?"

"Well, maybe I ain't proper," Jesse grumbled. "But I talk just like most folks in town."

He had a point. But before Mia could come up with an answer for that, Shirlene spoke up.

"She's right, Jesse. You don't want to end up like Bubba, do you?"

"I like Bubba," Jesse stated, defiantly. "He don't work much, and he's got a cool truck with really cool bull balls."

"Jesse!" Both Shirlene and Mia spoke at the same time.

Jesse flopped back in the seat. "Well, he does. And when I grow up, I'm gonna have a truck just like his, and I ain't gonna have to listen to no meanie girls like you two."

Shirlene smiled as she turned onto Grover Road. "I don't think I've ever been called a meanie girl before."

"Well, get used to it." The words slipped out before Mia could stop them, and she shot a quick glance over at Shirlene. "I-I mean as long as you're with us, you'll have to get used to it."

Shirlene looked over at her for only a second before returning her gaze to the road. "I knew what you meant, honey."

After that, they didn't talk much. Of course, it was hard to keep up a conversation with all the noise coming from the back. Adeline had discovered her voice and babbled out baby talk. Jesse started making a weird popping noise with his mouth. And Brody hummed "Twinkle, Twinkle Little Star," sounding like a bullfrog during mating season. Couple that with the occasional grunt from the sleeping pig in the very back, and Mia wondered if at any second she might start screaming and pulling out her hair.

The racket didn't seem to faze Shirlene. Of course, from what Mia could tell, nothing fazed Shirlene Dalton.

Not getting kicked out of a beautiful mansion. Or stuck with four orphan kids. Or forced to hock a diamond ring the size of a walnut. The woman just kept on smiling as if life was a bed of roses.

Mia wished she could be as optimistic. The kids were fed and happy today, but tomorrow would bring more hardships. She had thought that Shirlene might be the answer to all her problems. But the woman could barely take care of herself, let alone an entire family. Which meant Mia would have to look elsewhere for help.

The SUV suddenly slowed down, and Mia glanced over to see Shirlene squinting out the windshield. "Just what in the name of heaven does he think he's doing?"

Mia followed her gaze, and her heart stopped. Not because Bubba Wilkes was flipping a ripped-up sofa into the back of a truck, but because Austin Reeves was helping him.

Mia hadn't seen Austin since the night she ran away. And she didn't want to see him. Not when she had acted like such a geeky nut. For a moment, she thought about opening the door and diving out into the mesquite that lined the road. Shirlene had slowed to a crawl so Mia would probably only suffer a few bumps and bruises. And physical pain was much better than dying from embarrassment beneath Austin's pretty brown eyes. Then she remembered that Austin was one of those hero kind of guys who would come running over to help if he happened to see her, which meant she'd have to suffer through the next few minutes.

She jerked down the visor and examined herself in the tiny mirror. Nothing had improved since that morning. She still had two pimples on her chin, ugly glasses, and limp hair. She pulled the glasses off before tugging out the ponytail holder. She might've kept primping if Shirlene hadn't spoken.

"Since Bubba's a little too old, I'm guessin' you've got a thing for Austin."

Mia slapped up the visor and released her breath in a huff. "As if."

Shirlene flashed a grin. "It's nothing to be ashamed of, honey. Star quarterbacks are hard to resist. When I was younger, all the girls had a crush on Slate Calhoun."

"Well, I don't have a crush on Austin," Mia stated. But Jesse ruined her reply by leaning up as far as his seatbelt would allow.

"Austin and Mia sittin' in a tree—K-I-S-S-I-N-G. First comes love, then comes marriage, then comes Mia with the baby carriage—"

Without hesitation, Mia reached back and smacked him right in the mouth. "Shut up! Do you hear me? If you embarrass me in front of Austin, I swear I'll beat the tar out of you, Jesse Rutledge!"

Since Mia never hit the kids, the entire car grew quiet as Jesse fell back against the seat in stunned shock. Adeline stopped babbling and Brody quit mid-hum. Only Shirlene seemed to take the outburst in stride and calmly pulled over to the side of the road.

"Well, of course, Jesse won't say anything, Mia. As much as he likes to tease you, he'd never do anything to hurt you. Isn't that right, Jesse?" When Jesse didn't answer, Shirlene looked back at him. "Just like Mia didn't mean to hit you. Girls just get a little crazy where boys are concerned—Lord only knows, I've done my share of crazy things over men." She frowned and glanced out the windshield. Bubba and Austin had finished loading the sofa and were now staring down the road at them.

"Now apologize to each other and let's move on," she said.

As much as Shirlene's interference annoyed her, Mia couldn't help feeling guilty over Jesse's tear-filled eyes. "I'm sorry, Jesse. Are you okay?"

Jesse tested his bottom lip with his tongue. "Yeah. You don't hit as hard as Uncle Mickey."

Shirlene's gaze snapped over to Mia, but Mia refused to look at her. And after only a moment, she popped the SUV into drive and headed back down the road. As soon as they pulled in behind Austin's old pickup, Jesse jumped out of the SUV and raced over to greet Bubba and Austin.

But before Mia could reach for the door handle, Shirlene stopped her. "Remember, honey, it's not about the package as much as how you present it." She picked up the glasses off the console and handed them to her.

"Huh?" Mia said.

Shirlene plastered on one of her smiles. "Smile, honey, smile."

But Mia wasn't good at smiling. She was much better at frowning. Which is why she settled somewhere in the middle—no facial expression whatsoever. She got out of the car, and then opened the back door to get Adeline.

"Well, if it isn't the star quarterback of the Bramble High Bulldogs," Shirlene said as she helped Brody down, then walked to the back to let Sherman out. Austin dusted his hands off and strutted over with a big smile of his own. Obviously, he was much better at presenting himself than Mia.

"If you're nice, I might give you an autograph," he said,

his pretty brown eyes twinkling in a way that made Mia's stomach ache. His gaze swept over to her for only a second before it returned to Shirlene. Mia couldn't really blame him. Why would you look at a skinny girl with glasses and acne when you had someone as dazzling as Shirlene to look at? Which didn't explain why Bubba Wilkes was looking at Mia. And not just looking, but studying her with an intensity that made her palms start to sweat.

Mia hadn't paid too much attention to Bubba so far. After meeting him, she had placed him in the category of dumb ol' country boy—the type of man who was more concerned with his big truck and hunting rifle than a bunch of runny-nosed kids. She appreciated him trying to fix their air conditioner and the ice cream he'd bought them at the Dairy Treat, but she figured that had more to do with his "hots" for Shirlene than them. Still, Mia had viewed him as harmless enough. Until now. With those intense dark eyes pinned on her, he didn't look harmless as much as calculating.

"So just what brings you out to Grover Road, Austin Reeves?" Shirlene asked.

"I was looking for Mia," he said.

For a second, Mia thought she might choke to death on her own saliva, which was weird when she didn't have any left in her mouth. With all eyes on her, she swallowed hard and tried to speak. "Me?"

"Yeah." He pulled his wallet out of his back pocket and walked over to her. "You dropped this the other night." He handed her the driver's license, a driver's license she hadn't used in over a year. Which was probably why she stared down at the picture for so long. The dark-headed girl who stared back at her didn't even look familiar.

"I like your hair better that way," Austin said.

Mia wasn't worried about what the quarterback of Bramble High thought about her hair. She was worried that he'd noticed her name. A name she hadn't even given to Shirlene because it was all anyone needed to have the sheriff knocking on their door. Just the thought had Mia panicking, and she shot a glance over at Bubba. But he appeared to be busy instructing Jesse on how to tie down the sofa in the back of Austin's truck.

"Thanks." She slipped the license in the back pocket of her jeans and tried to smile brightly. She must've sucked at it because Austin looked a little scared. Fortunately, Shirlene came to her rescue.

"Well, that was mighty nice of you, Austin. But that doesn't explain why you're taking off with my best couch."

Austin's eyes swept over to dilapidated sofa in the back of his truck. "Your sofa?" He looked at Shirlene. "You live here?"

"I sure do."

"Yeah, right." Austin laughed. "And I'm Troy Aikman."

"Then I might just have to get your autograph, after all," Shirlene said as she directed Brody away from a pile of rusty nails. "Because the truth is that I've decided that house of mine is too big for just one person. So I moved in here until I find another place to live."

"Here? With Mia's family?"

"That's right," Shirlene said.

Austin looked confused, and Mia grew even more freaked out. She'd thought that Shirlene wanted to keep the information about where she was living a secret. But it seemed the woman no longer cared about tarnishing her image. Or about making people suspicious.

"So whose idea was it to do a little spring cleanin'?" Shirlene asked.

"I was headed to the dump anyway." Bubba shrugged as he tossed Jesse the end of the rope. "I figured you wouldn't mind if I cleared out some of your garbage."

"And just who gave you permission to go poking around in my yard, Bubba Wilkes?" Shirlene asked.

"You want me to put it all back, Sugar Buns?"

She slapped a hand on her hip. "What I want is for you to leave me alone. But I can't seem to get that through your thick, hillbilly skull."

While they continued to bicker, Mia tried to find out if Austin had noticed her last name. As much as she hated the idea, she needed to get him alone. Any embarrassment she might suffer was nothing when compared to the safety of the kids.

"Austin, would you like something cold to drink?" she blurted out.

Bubba and Shirlene stopped bickering and looked at her as if she'd grown horns. Even Adeline looked up at her with curious blue eyes.

"Umm, thanks," Austin said as he placed his crumpled straw cowboy hat back on his head. "But after I drop this load off at the dump, I need to get back to town."

"I'll come with you!" The words rushed out, and she quickly tried to soften the desperation in her voice. "I mean, you can't be expected to unload this stuff by yourself."

"I planned on helpin'—" Bubba started, but Shirlene cut him off.

"You can't help anyone, Bubba Wilkes. Not when I've got an air conditioner that still needs fixin'." She hurried over and took Adeline from Mia. The baby only whimpered for a second before she cuddled up to Shirlene's big boobs. "Mia's right, Austin. You'll need some help."

Austin glanced over at Mia's wimpy arms. "Uhh, okay, I guess. It shouldn't take us long."

"Take your time," Shirlene said. "In fact, why don't you take Mia back in town with you? She hasn't gotten to meet a lot of young folks."

Austin's eyes narrowed on Shirlene for only a brief second before he nodded. "Yeah, okay." He started toward the driver's side, but stopped and came back around to the passenger's door. As he held it open, Mia got that funny feeling in her stomach again and wondered if she'd made a big mistake. There was no way she would get through this without making a complete idiot of herself. But before she could back out, Shirlene gave her a nudge toward the door.

"Go on, honey," she whispered. "Just remember that the rooster only crows for the hen he has to chase."

Chapter Twenty-two

THE DESIRE TO SEE MIA have a little fun wasn't the only reason Shirlene had pushed her off on Austin. She also had a strong desire to get Adeline all to herself. But the fantasy of cute, cuddly babies was soon wiped out by the harsh reality of bodily functions. Not more than ten minutes after Bubba and Jesse left to get parts for the air conditioner in town, Adeline turned as ripe as an outhouse in late August.

"Phew-wee, honey." Shirlene crinkled her nose. "You smell worse than Sherman after he got into the garbage."

Adeline's blue eyes studied Shirlene for a moment before rosy lips tipped up in a smile that showed off her eight tiny teeth. She looked so darned cute; the stench didn't seem quite so bad.

"Okay, then." Shirlene gave her a quick kiss on her downy soft curls. "Let's get you cleaned up." She held out her hand to Brody. "Come on, honey, you can help."

But Brody had dug a deep hole in the ground and buried Barbie up to her neck, and he wasn't about to leave his damsel in distress. Scooting away from her hand, he crossed his pudgy arms over his chest and shook his head.

"Now don't get all out of sorts," Shirlene said. "We won't leave Barbie." She reached down to grab the doll out of her burial site, but Brody wasn't having it.

"Mine," he yelled in his deep voice as he jerked the doll out of the dirt and scrambled to his feet, racing off before Shirlene could grab him.

Bubba had cleared away a lot of the garbage, but there was still plenty for a little boy to hide in. And Brody seemed to know all the best hiding places. Shirlene had no more discovered him in one place, then he would streak off and hide in another. The game had the little boy giggling with glee while Shirlene grew more frustrated and Baby Adeline more odorous. It might've gone on forever if Sherman hadn't taken pity on her. When Brody raced out from behind an oil drum, Sherman was waiting for him. He squealed and chased after the kid, sending him straight into Shirlene, who latched on to his hand and didn't let go until they were inside the house.

Things only went downhill from there.

Shirlene had watched Hope, Faith, and Mia change diapers. But seeing and doing turned out to be two different things. Especially when she opened up the diaper and the wave of stink made her eyes water. And the smell wasn't near as bad as the sight. For the second time in a week, Shirlene thought she might toss her cookies.

How could a child so tiny make a mess so big? A mess so big that Shirlene would need an entire box of those wipey things to clean it up. Her eyes widened as her gaze snapped over to the container of diaper wipes on the floor a good eight feet away. She tried to close the diaper back up but the little Velcro tabs had stuck together and refused to come unstuck.

She glanced over at Brody who stood sulking in the doorway. "Brody, honey, could you help Shirlene get the wipeys?"

Brody sent her the evil eye and didn't move a muscle.

"Please, honey," she pleaded as she tried to keep the diaper on while Adeline wiggled like a worm on a hook. "I'll give you some chocolate."

Sherman squealed at the word, but Brody was more stubborn. With a shake of his Barbie, the kid turned and ran into the other room.

With no one else to ask, Shirlene looked at Sherman. "I'll give you an entire case of Snickers if you can push that box of wipeys over here."

The pig was smart, but he wasn't that smart. Or maybe the stench had finally gotten to him. With a toss of his head, he trotted out the door after Brody. When he was gone, Shirlene looked back at Adeline.

"Just sit tight, honey." She made a dive for the container and, within seconds, had it in her hands.

But it turned out that seconds was all a baby needed to make a king-sized mess.

Shirlene didn't care about the bedspread or Adeline's clothes—as far as she was concerned, those needed to be thrown away. Adeline, on the other hand, wasn't that disposable. When the entire container of wipeys failed to do the job, Shirlene held the baby out in front of her and carried her to the bathroom.

Washing a baby was even harder than changing one. Adeline's little chubby body was as slick as a seal's and twice as hard to control. She splashed and kicked so much there was more water out of the tub then there was in it. Becoming aware of the fun his sister was having, Brody raced into the bathroom and started stripping off his clothes.

"Oh, no," Shirlene shook her head as she wrangled with the baby. "You can take a bath in the morning." But all it took was Brody's bottom lip quivering for her to change her mind. "Fine. Hop in. One more can't hurt anything."

She was wrong. Brody might want to take a bath with Adeline, but Adeline didn't want to take a bath with her brother. Once Brody was in, she started throwing a fit that rivaled any Hope had ever thrown—and everyone in town knew Hope could throw a fit—and taking the baby out of the tub only made her madder. Looking for anything to distract her, Shirlene grabbed up a brush and waved it around. When the baby stopped crying and reached for it, she gladly gave it up. She didn't know if it was an appropriate toy for an eleven-month-old, but at this point, she didn't care. After drying her off, Shirlene spread a towel on the floor and set Adeline down so she could bathe Brody.

While his sister had been throwing a fit, it looked like Brody had gotten bathed all by himself. Using an entire bottle of baby shampoo, he and Barbie were covered in a slick, golden-tinged slime that took turning on the shower to finally remove. By the time Shirlene had him rinsed and out of the tub, she turned to discover a cyclone had hit the bathroom. Toilet paper was strung from one side of the room to the next. The cabinet underneath the sink was opened and more rolls of toilet paper littered the floor, along with bars of soap and other bathroom necessities. Adeline and Sherman sat amid the disaster, the pig's big, pink ears wrapped in toilet paper and Adeline waving a tampon.

Two hours later, the kitchen and living room didn't look much better. The floor was littered with plastic bowls and pans from the bottom kitchen cabinets, crackers and dry cereal, half-full bottles and sippy cups, and the tiny bits of material Brody was cutting from the pleated bottom of the couch.

As Shirlene sat on the floor watching him, she realized she'd gotten her wish: Adeline was cuddled up against her shoulder sleeping. It was really too bad that Shirlene was too mentally and physically exhausted to enjoy it.

"What the . . . ?"

She glanced up to find Bubba standing in the doorway with Jesse. For once, the kid didn't seem to have anything to say. In fact, both he and Bubba had such shocked looks on their faces that Shirlene couldn't contain a giggle—a giggle that ended on a hysterical sob that had Bubba dropping the bag to the floor and striding over.

He leaned down and slipped a hand between her breasts and Adeline's belly. But when he tried to pull the baby away from her, Shirlene's arms tightened reflexively. "It's okay to let go now, Shirley Girl," he said in a soothing voice. "I'm just going to put her down for the night." She released her hold. And once the baby was gone, her arms flopped limply to her sides.

"Jesse, get those scissors away from Brody," Bubba said as he headed to the bedroom Mia shared with Adeline, "and get him ready for bed."

Brody didn't utter a peep when Jesse took away the scissors; he just allowed his brother to lead him to the bedroom as if he hadn't just thrown a major fit when Shirlene had tried to do the exact same thing.

Bubba came out of the bedroom with the smelly

bedspread and headed for the door, Sherman close on his heels. When he returned from outside, he was minus the bedspread and pig, but had gained one teenage girl. He must've told Mia about the state of the trailer because her eyes only widened for an instant before they returned to Shirlene.

"Are the babies okay?" she asked.

"They're fine," Bubba answered for her. "Adeline was sleeping when I got here, and Brody was playing." Shirlene was thankful he'd left out the scissors part. Although she figured Jesse would enlighten his sister soon enough. "But I think Shirlene needs a little break," Bubba said. "We'll be just next door if you need us."

Once Mia disappeared into the bedroom with Jesse and Brody, Bubba came back over and scooped Shirlene up in his arms. She was too tired to resist or form coherent speech. So she closed her eyes and let him take her where he would. He took her back to his trailer and maneuvered her through the door and into the tiny bathroom where he set her down on the lid of the toilet.

Bubba stood over her, his chocolate-colored eyes comforting. "The clean towels are in the cabinet, and the soap and shampoo are in the windowsill."

She didn't know what it was about soap and shampoo that had the tears falling, but suddenly there they were, trickling down her cheeks and dripping from her chin. Shirlene expected Bubba to run for the hills. Instead he squatted down next to her and reached out to smooth her sticky bangs from her eyes.

"Hey, now. You're all right. You're gonna take yourself a hot shower, and you'll feel just fine and dandy in no time."

"I thought it would be easy," she whispered. "They're no bigger than gnats. But then Adeline wouldn't hold still . . . and those diaper do-hickeys got all tangled up."

He nodded solemnly. "Those can be tricky."

"And all I did was turn my back for a second—just one second—and the toilet paper . . ."

He reached up and grabbed a washcloth from the rack. "Kids are as quick as greased lightnin'."

She swallowed hard and blinked back the tears. "And when they cried, I pretty much let them do whatever they wanted—even if it was bad for them."

He tipped up her chin and gently wiped off her cheeks. "I've always been a sucker for tears."

"They hate me," she sniffed. "They really hate me."

"Well, I'm not an expert, but it looked to me like they like you just fine."

She shook her head. "No, they hate me, and they have every right to. I can't even watch a couple toddlers for two hours without putting them in danger—Brody could've cut himself, and Adeline could've found something really poisonous in the bathroom cabinet."

"But they didn't," Bubba said.

"Only because you got there in time." She sniffed and attempted a smile. It was a weak effort. "It's funny, when you think about it. After all the fertility specialists, the tests and the drugs, it turns out that God knew exactly what he was doin', after all." The washcloth Bubba held in his hand stopped in mid-stroke. "It appears that Shirlene Dalton is infertile for a very good reason—I suck at being a mama."

A sob escaped, followed by another one and another one until she jerked the washcloth from Bubba's hand and

buried her face in it. Only seconds passed before she felt
two warm hands slip under her elbows and lift her to her
feet.

Bubba pulled her close to his warm chest. "What am
I going to do with you, Shirley Girl? Just when I think I
have you all figured out, you up and surprise me."

Shirlene surprised herself. She had never been much
of a crier, but she stood there crying in Bubba's arms like
a kindergartener on the first day of school. She waited for
the teasing jokes to start, but he only held her, his hands
rubbing up and down her back until she finally quieted.
When she did, he spoke softly against the top of her head.

"Being a mama isn't just about changing diapers and
keeping kids from making messes. It's about love. And it
seems to me, you've got plenty of that to give." He pulled
back and grinned down at her. "Even if you don't want to
send any my way."

Before she could absorb the sweetness of his words, he
leaned over and turned on the shower. "Now you take your
time. And if you need me to wash your back, Honey Buns,
you just holler." He tossed her a sexy wink and was gone.

Shirlene wasn't sure if it was the good cry or the hot
shower that revived her, but by the time she stepped from
the bathroom, she felt much better. She found Bubba
stretched out on the sofa in the living room watching the
smallest television she'd ever seen in her life. But it was
hard to notice the television when Bubba wore only a pair
of faded jeans and a bright smile.

"So I see you found the shirt," he said as his eyes
shimmied over her squeaky clean body in the cut-offs and
western shirt.

"It was a little hard not to, seeing as how you set it

on the back of the toilet." Her gaze drifted over all that smooth skin and rippled muscle. "I'd ask if you peeked, but I'm afraid I already know the answer."

His grin got wider as he got to his feet and turned off the television. "Now I wouldn't be as low as that, Shirley Girl." He moved into the small kitchen and opened a cupboard. "You want something to drink?"

She really did. Not only because of her harrowing night with Brody and Adeline, but because her heart rate had just tripled at the way Bubba's back muscles rippled when he reached for the bottle of tequila. Still, she wasn't about to go back to the trailer with alcohol on her breath. Not after being such a disaster as a babysitter.

"No, thank you. I've sworn off the stuff." When he shot her a surprised look, she shrugged. "At least, until I find a home for the—" she left the sentence hanging for only a brief second before adding, "me."

Bubba put the bottle back and turned. He leaned against the counter and crossed his arms, but his posture was anything but relaxed.

"So the kids don't have a mama, do they?"

Shirlene wondered if she should ask for that drink after all. But instead she walked over to the recliner and flopped down. She hated to break her promise to Mia, but she was tired of having the burden of four children on her shoulders. And for some reason, she trusted Bubba.

"No," she said. "They don't have a mama or a daddy. From what I could get out of Mia, they were living with foster parents in Houston before they ran away. Thus the name 'Foster'."

"So they aren't even sisters and brothers?"

Shirlene shook her head. "I guess not even Brody and

Adeline are related. And it sounds like Jesse had more than a few foster parents."

"Were they abused?" he asked.

"I've only gotten bits and pieces," she said. "But I think there was physical abuse, and I'm starting to wonder if there wasn't sexual. Mia has this look that's almost...."

"Haunted," Bubba finished for her. A long silence followed before he moved over to the sofa and sat down. "So what do you plan on doing with them?"

She leaned her head back and stared up at the ceiling. There was one point where she'd actually thought about adopting them herself, but tonight proved her inability to handle even two children—let alone four. She looked back at him. "I figure that there has to be someone in the entire state of Texas who wouldn't mind having four cute kids—someone who would love them like they deserve to be loved."

He stared at the carpet between his bare feet. "And until you find those people, you're planning on letting them live with you in the trailer?"

"Do I have another choice?"

"You could call Sheriff Winslow and let him handle it," he said.

She shook her head. "I can't do that. I can't trust that he won't send them back to Houston before I can get things worked out. Besides, I promised Mia."

He looked up and studied her. "And do you always keep your promises, Ms. Dalton?"

Nine months ago, she would've answered "yes," but nine months ago she'd had a husband who didn't expect anything more from her than to be happy. At the time, she thought her life had been perfect. But now she realized that expectations—from yourself and other people—were what made a person grow. Without them, you were nothing more than a stagnant puddle of water. Or a ditzy trophy wife.

"No," she said. "I haven't done a very good job of keeping my promises lately. But I plan to keep this one."

"Even if it's against the law?"

"Even then," she said as she got to her feet. "I probably should get back. I don't want Mia to worry."

"I'll walk you."

The trip back to the trailer wasn't as enjoyable as the trip from it—more than likely because Bubba wasn't carrying her. Still, when she stumbled over a tree root in his yard, he reached out and took her hand. He didn't cradle it, but rather interlocked every finger with his until their palms touched.

When they reached the trailer, she turned and tried to come up with the words to thank him. But she couldn't seem to find any that would express her gratitude. So instead she kept it simple.

"Thank—"

Her words were cut off by a pair of very warm lips. This kiss wasn't like the ones he'd given her before. It wasn't deep, hot, or hungry. This one was brief and sweet, a mere brush of moist lips as he cradled her jaw in his hand. Yet the tenderness of the kiss left Shirlene reeling. Afraid she was going to do something really stupid, she hurried up the steps. But before she reached for the doorknob, she couldn't help but look back.

Bubba stood at the bottom of the steps. A country boy in faded jeans and bare feet. A redneck with stubbled jaw and wavy hair. A knight in shining armor who always seemed to be there when she needed him.

"Goodnight, Bubba," she whispered.

"Billy" he said. "My name's Billy."

Chapter Twenty-three

THE RINGING OF HIS CELL PHONE woke Billy from a sound sleep. Rolling to the edge of the mattress, he felt around for his shirt and pulled the phone from the front pocket. Noting the number, he pushed a button and answered.

"Damn it, Brant," he grumbled. "What the hell are you doing calling so early?"

His brother chuckled. "If you think nine o'clock is early, little brother, you've taken too much time off work."

Billy glanced over toward the window and at the bright sunlight that streamed through the sheet. The lateness of the hour should've surprised him, but since he hadn't gotten to sleep until well after two, it wasn't that shocking.

"So any luck finding the body?" Brant asked.

Billy propped the pillows behind his back. "No. Granddaddy wasn't buried in the Bramble cemetery or any cemetery within a hundred and fifty miles. But I'm not going to give up. There are a few more history books I want to read through, and I have an appointment with another historian when I travel to Lubbock for the Plains Gas meetings."

"Billy the Tenacious," Brant said. "But I think you're spinning your wheels this time, little brother. It's doubtful that the people of Bramble even buried our granddaddy. His body was probably tossed out in the mesquite somewhere to be picked apart by vultures."

Billy had thought about that—he just refused to believe it. Which probably would be described as stubbornness more than tenacity.

"Has Beau found anything of interest in Dalton's house?" Brant asked. "Lyle had relatives who lived in Bramble at the time, didn't he?"

"Yes. But Beau hasn't found anything, and I don't think he will." Billy paused. "Which is why I'm giving the house back."

"Excuse me," Brant said. "Have you lost your mind? The woman owes us a million dollars." He hesitated before he continued. "Of course, you're probably right. We'll end up losing money anyway. With Dalton closing in less than a month, Bramble will be a ghost town within a year."

"What?" Billy sat up so quickly he got a head rush. "I thought we'd talked about waiting until the beginning of the year to close Dalton Oil."

"We did, but the company is losing more than I thought, and I don't see any reason to keep it afloat. Besides, without jobs, it shouldn't take people long to clear out. Then we can tear down that town hall and give Daddy our granddaddy's plaque for Christmas." It was something Billy and Brant had dreamed about doing for a long time. But vengeance was a funny thing. Once you had it in your sights, it lost most of its appeal. Or maybe what had lost its appeal was screwing over a town filled with people Billy had grown fond of.

"We aren't Christmas shopping at a mall, Brant. These are people's lives we'll be destroying—and for what, a stupid plaque?"

There was a pause before his brother spoke. "This isn't just about a plaque, Billy. It's about a curse. A curse the Cateses have carried around for decades. But maybe you're right. Maybe we should wait for something to happen to Beckett? Or, God forbid, our little Brie?" Just the thought of something bad happening to his two youngest siblings had Billy's stomach knotting.

"Besides, we aren't doing anything to the town that wasn't going to happen eventually. No matter who had bought out Dalton, they weren't going to make it solvent. We're just jerking the Band-aid off quickly."

"For the town's sake, Brant, or our own?" Billy asked.

"Both," Brant said. "Where did this sudden change of heart come from?" When Billy didn't say anything, Brant's voice softened. "I realize you've made some friends in the town, and I don't intend to leave people without a way to support their families. I promise we'll find them openings at C-Corp—just not in Bramble." He paused. "Or does this have more to do with Lyle Dalton's wife?"

Lyle Dalton's wife. Those words placed together made Billy want to hit something. Which was crazy. But Billy had felt more than a little crazy lately. All because of a fiery-haired woman with eyes the color of a summer meadow. A woman who had shattered all his perceptions about her, and in the process, left him doubting who he was and what he wanted.

"I just don't think we should run off half-cocked, is all," Billy said. "All I need is a little more time to find our granddaddy's grave, Brant. I'm telling you that's the key to the curse—not leveling an entire town."

"But why take a chance, little brother? The Cates family's paid long enough, don't you think?"

The phone clicked dead, and Billy stared at it for a few moments before allowing it to drop down to the mattress. He wanted to be mad at Brant, but he couldn't be mad at a man who had lost so much. Brant wasn't a bad person. He was just a person who wanted something or someone to blame for the loss of his family. And Billy couldn't hold that against him, especially when he'd been the one to give his brother an outlet for all his rage and anger. The one who came to Bramble, Texas, looking for his own outlet for the pain. At the time, it had seemed like a good idea. Instead of waiting around for the next horrific thing to happen, he'd felt as if he was doing something to stop the string of bad luck. Now he wondered if maybe all their bad fortune had nothing to do with a curse and everything to do with fate.

Maybe the Cates family was just too stubborn to accept it.

But it was too late to change the course of events he'd put into play. Dalton Oil would fail, and Bramble would become a ghost town. Not even Colt Lomax's company, Desperado Customs, would change that. And Brant was right. It wasn't like they had caused Dalton Oil to fail—but they hadn't done anything to stop it.

He reached for the phone. He might not be able to help Bramble, but he did have the means to correct another injustice. The phone only rang twice before it was answered. Although it wasn't exactly the voice Billy had expected to hear.

"Mine!" The gruff voice that came through the

receiver almost broke Billy's eardrum. He really needed to see about getting the kid a speech pathologist. A three-year-old should have a bigger vocabulary than just one word. And while they were at it, maybe they could bring the kid's octave up a few notches and teach him to play with gender-correct toys.

Before Billy could say anything, Shirlene's faint voice came through the receiver. "Can I see that for a second, honey? Just for a second, and then you can have it back." Brody must've conceded the phone because it wasn't long before Shirlene's voice came on, loud and clear.

"Okay, I get it. My credit is going to be ruined if I don't pay my bill—except I hate to tell you this, honey, but my credit is already in the crapper so it really won't make a difference. But I promise, as soon as I hit a windfall, you'll be the first bill I pay—well, after the Visa bill and Mastercard, seein' as how they hassled me first."

Billy couldn't help but smile. Not because Shirlene was in such financial straits, but because the woman could keep such an optimistic outlook even when things weren't going her way. Not her husband's death, or eviction, or four orphans, or numerous bill collectors could keep Shirlene Dalton down.

Bad luck wasn't a curse to Shirlene, just a mere inconvenience.

Billy smiled as he slipped into the voice he used for all his business meetings, deep and professional with very little twang. "Good mornin', Ms. Dalton."

She released her breath in an exasperated sigh. "Oh, it's you. Run out of little puppies to drown, Mr. Cates?"

"Actually, I was just headed to the pound to get some more."

"I'd laugh, if I didn't believe you," she said. Her words were followed by Adeline's baby gibberish, and Billy figured she must be holding the baby. Obviously, the other night hadn't completely soured Shirlene on the little girl.

"But I'm not calling to talk about what I do for entertainment," he said. "I'm calling to tell you that I've decided to give your house back."

There was a long pause before she spoke. "Suffering a bit of guilt, are you, honey?"

"I guess you could say that," he answered truthfully. Although it hadn't been a bit of guilt—more like an entire avalanche. Mr. Peabody had called him yesterday to say Shirlene was flat broke. Broke enough that she had to sell her diamond ring to the highest bidder just to buy groceries for a bunch of orphans. And if that wasn't enough to make Billy feel like the biggest heel in Texas, he didn't know what was.

"Well, thanks for the offer, Mr. Cates," Shirlene said. "But I don't need any handouts."

Billy swung his legs over the mattress and got to his feet. "This isn't a game, Ms. Dalton. And even if it is, you win. The house is yours, free and clear."

She laughed. "And you expect me to fall for that? Not likely. Do you plan to let me move back in just so you can have the pleasure of tossing me out again? Well, I'm not falling for it. You can have the house. I'm fine and dandy just where I am."

His anger spiked. "You call being broke and living in a beat-up trailer with no air conditioner fine and dandy! Have you lost your mind, woman?"

She only hesitated for a moment. "How did you know my air conditioner doesn't work?"

Damn. He flopped back down on the mattress and ran a hand through his hair. "A lucky guess. Most old trailers don't have working air conditioners. But that's beside the point, Ms. Dalton. I'm offering you a chance to move back into the comfort of your home—a home with refrigerated air—and you're refusing me? That's just plain stubborn."

She laughed. "I've been known to have such a streak. It's just been a while since I showed it off. And I must say it feels kind of good."

"Well, it won't feel so good when you have to hock another one of your diamonds."

"My... you do have a way of getting information, don't you, Mr. Cates?" she said in that sassy voice of hers. "Of course, with the way Twyla's been flashing her hand around, it couldn't be that hard. But just so you don't have to spend any more time worrying about little old me, I've found another way to make money. In fact, I need to cut our conversation short because my sugar daddy just arrived."

Billy sat straight up in bed. But before he could get any words out, the crazy woman hung up. He stared at the phone. Her sugar daddy? She had to be kidding. There was no way she'd found a sugar daddy that fast, especially when she'd been kissing him no more than a day earlier. Of course, she hadn't been kissing him as much as he'd been kissing her. One minute, he was noticing how nicely their hands fit together, and the next, he was kissing her like the sex-crazed womanizer he claimed he was. It was pathetic, and one of the reasons he'd decided to keep his distance from Shirlene Dalton.

Which didn't explain why he got dressed in record time and hurried through the hedge with his open shirt flapping.

When he got there, Shirlene was standing in the yard talking with a man Billy had never seen before, a man who didn't seem like the sugar daddy type. He wore a pair of overalls and drove a white van with a trailer hitched to the back. Still, the man couldn't seem to keep his eyes off Shirlene. Not that Billy blamed him. No matter what the woman wore—tight jeans and stilettos or cut-offs and bare feet—she exuded a raw sex appeal that only a eunuch could ignore.

And Billy was no eunuch.

It had been barely a day since he had seen her, an entire day where he had tried to convince himself that his interest in Shirlene had more to do with proximity than real desire. But if that was true then why did his heart hitch when she glanced over?

"Billy," she said. It was the first time she'd said his name, and his heart did another crazy flip. It was nothing compared to how it felt when she flashed him one of her dazzling smiles. His breath got all jiggy, and it took a real effort not to walk right over and kiss the daylights out of her. Instead, he directed his attention to the man. Billy's disapproval must've registered because the man took a step back.

"This is Owen Carlisle, Billy." Shirlene shifted Baby Adeline to her other hip. "He's a picker."

Before he could ask her what the man intended to pick, the front door of the trailer opened, and Jesse came barreling out, followed by Brody, the pig, and Mia. Everyone greeted him, including the pig—everyone but Mia. Since returning from her date with Austin, the teenage girl seemed even more intimidated by him. He could only assume that she knew he'd seen her driver's license and was worried he'd turn them in. He probably should. But lately there were a lot of things he should be doing that he wasn't—like staying the hell away from Shirlene Dalton.

"What's a picker?" he asked.

"You know," Shirlene said. "Like that television show where those two men go to people's junk piles and buy things off them. In fact, that's where I got the idea to call someone out to look at my junk."

Owen Carlisle smirked, and Billy suddenly had the strong desire to wipe the expression off with his fist. Instead, he found himself walking straight over to Shirlene and staking a claim he had no business staking by hooking an arm around her waist.

He held out his other hand. "Nice to meet you, Owen."

"Same here," the man said, although he didn't sound any more convincing than Billy. No doubt, before Billy got there, he figured Shirlene's junk would be easy pickin's. But Billy wasn't about to let that happen. And neither was a nine year old with an aptitude for sales. The man had no more than pointed at an old gas station sign, then Jesse jumped in and started wheeling and dealing.

"Is there a reason your hand's on my waist?" Shirlene asked as the kids followed the picker around the yard.

Billy looked down, and for a moment, he got lost in the vibrant green of her eyes. He was brought back to his senses when Adeline reached out and grabbed for the snaps on his shirt. Catching her hand, Shirlene pulled it back and pressed a quick kiss on the tiny fingers.

"I see you and Adeline have formed a truce," he said, as he struggled to pull his gaze from Shirlene's full mouth. It wasn't easy, especially with it tipped in a soft smile.

"As long as she saves all the dirty diapers for when Mia's watching her, we're golden."

Billy's laughter was cut off when he noticed Owen standing by the old Chevy. Shirlene followed his gaze, and they both walked over to find the man low-balling Jesse.

"Two thousand is a fair price for this old car, son," Owen said. "And I won't go a penny more."

"Five," Billy jumped in.

Owen shot him an annoyed look before countering. "Five and half. And that's final."

"Twenty." Billy quickly put an end to the bidding. If he couldn't get the stubborn woman to take her house back, at least he could give her enough to last her a while.

Shirlene shot him a surprised look. "Cash money?" When Billy nodded, she grinned and lifted a hand. "Sold to the cute redneck from east Texas."

Before Billy could even absorb the fact that Shirlene had just called him "cute," Owen pointed to the tarp in the corner. "What about that car?"

Billy had looked beneath the tarp soon after talking with Austin and written down the VIN number for Mr. Peabody to look into. As he watched, all the color drained from Mia's face. The young girl looked so scared that Billy started to jump in. But it was Shirlene who came to her rescue.

"I'm afraid that's not for sale, Mr. Carlisle. But I've got an old pickup over here that you're gonna love."

The picking continued, and by the time Owen Carlisle was finished, most of his cash was in Shirlene's hand. Billy and Jesse helped him load up the trailer, but before he climbed into his van, his eyes swept over to Brody.

"What about the Colt?"

Confused, Billy followed his gaze to the little boy who stood there with the holster dragging halfway down his hips. But it wasn't Barbie weighing the holster down. It was a gun. And not a plastic toy gun, but the real thing.

"Oh. My. God." Shirlene said as both she and Mia rushed over to grab the gun. But Billy got there first and easily lifted it from the holster before the kid started screaming.

"Mine! Mine!"

It was one thing to scream for a girl's toy and another to scream for a dangerous weapon, and Billy didn't waste any time correcting the stubborn boy. "That's enough, Brody. This isn't a toy."

Brody's deep voice cut off, and he watched with big eyes as Billy flipped open the chamber and checked for bullets. The chamber was empty and more than a little rusted. Brant was the gun collector in the family, but Billy knew enough about guns to know this was a Colt Single-Action Peacemaker. One of the first made.

"Well, I'll be a monkey's uncle," Shirlene said as she walked over and stared down at the gun. "Colt has been looking all over for that ever since it went missing during one of mama's binges—"

She cut herself off, but it was too late. Her words explained all the empty vodka bottles and filled in one more piece of the puzzle that was Shirlene Dalton. She wasn't a spoiled gold digger, after all, just a woman who had lived through hard times and fought her way out of poverty with a strong will and a bright smile. Billy had to fight down the urge to pull her into his arms. Instead, he sent her a smile.

"Family heirloom?"

"Something like that." She studied the gun. "It belonged to my great-great-granddaddy, Wynn Murdock, when he was the sheriff of this town."

Chapter Twenty-four

SHIRLENE HAD GOTTEN HER WISH.

"Bubba" Billy Wilkes was gone. Instead of jumping for joy, Shirlene found herself as somber and mopey as Mia. She didn't know how it had happened, but somewhere along the line, she'd formed an attachment to the hillbilly from east Texas. It made sense that she would miss having a man around to fix things. She just didn't think she'd miss Billy's outrageous flirting and country boy charm. But she did miss it, missed it so much that she made up every excuse she could think of to go over to his trailer.

But the lot was empty, the trailer locked tight. The man who had cradled Adeline against his chest and ruffled Brody's hair every time he walked past him—treated Jesse as if he was a man instead of a scared little boy and showed Mia only respect—was gone. It took Billy going back to the green hills of Dogwood for Shirlene to realize that the folks of Bramble had been right all along: Billy was a good ol' boy.

Rolling to her back, Shirlene stared up at the ceiling.

The cool breeze from the air conditioning vents fell across her bare legs. Before he left, Billy had fixed the air conditioner. And replaced the front door and locks. And had the old truck and car frames the picker hadn't bought towed off to the junkyard. The only thing he'd forgotten to do was say goodbye.

It shouldn't have bothered her. He didn't owe her anything. Still, it hurt. She had started to think of Billy as a permanent fixture, someone who would always be there. Someone who belonged in Bramble as much as she did. And not just Bramble, but right next door where she could call on him whenever she needed him.

She kicked at the covers, and Sherman grumbled awake. But all it took was a couple of scratches between his ears to get him back to sleep. She wished she could go to sleep as easily. All she could do was lie there and wonder what Billy was doing at that very moment. No doubt the man was at some east Texas honky-tonk whooping it up with some small-town slut.

Except after everything she had learned about the man, the image wouldn't jell. What did jell was a picture of Billy with a pretty hometown girl. A girl with small breasts and little experience. A girl who was smart enough to appreciate the man in her arms. Shirlene pinched her eyes closed, but the image of Billy kissing such a perfect woman wouldn't go away. She was so busy beating herself up for being an idiot that it took her a few minutes to notice the rumble that came through the open window.

A deep rumble that could only come from a big diesel engine.

Shirlene's eyes popped open as the noise grew louder. Jumping up from the bed, she jerked open the door just in time to see Billy's truck drive past. She was halfway through the hedge before she realized she wore nothing but panties and Billy's sleeveless western shirt. But before she could turn around and head back inside for her bra and cut-offs, a cowboy stepped out of the monster truck and headed to the front door. A cowboy in jeans without holes, a pressed western shirt with the sleeves intact, and a sexy Resistol cowboy hat pulled low on his head.

"Billy?" The word popped out of her mouth, and the cowboy hesitated with his hand on the doorknob. Realizing it was too late to turn back now, she stepped out into the open. He studied her for a long, uncomfortable moment that had her fidgeting with the hem of the shirt and crossing one big toe over the other. Finally, he released the doorknob and came back down the steps. As he approached, she struggled to catch her breath. She had seen Billy Wilkes in ripped shirts, camouflage, and nothing but skin. And he had looked mighty fine in all of those. But there was something about the starched shirt and cowboy hat that had her breath halting in her chest.

Especially when he stopped no more than inches away.

"Who did you think I was?" he asked. It was funny, but there was something about his somber voice that reminded her of Mr. Cates. Or maybe it was just the different clothing that had her confused.

"I wasn't sure," she said.

Billy just stood there in the shadows looking tall, dark, and hot. It took a real effort not to reach out and smooth down the collar of his shirt.

"So we haven't seen much of you lately," she said, her voice slightly shaky.

"I've been busy."

She tipped her head and tried to make out his eyes in the shadow of the hat. "And just what kind of business would have Billy Wilkes all spit and polished?"

"Does it make a difference? I thought you didn't want any part of me, Ms. Dalton."

The brutal honesty of his remark had her taking a step back. Her heel landed on a rock, and she stumbled before Billy's warm fingers closed around her arm and steadied her. The action brought him closer. Close enough to be engulfed in his heat.

"And what happened to the hardheaded man who doesn't take 'no' for an answer?" she asked rather breathlessly.

"Well, maybe I finally figured it out." He gave her the once over. "So you mind telling me what you're doing running around half naked?"

She took a steadying breath that didn't do much to steady her pounding heart. "Only if you answer my question about where you've been the last three days. Of course, it's probably not that hard to figure out seeing as how Billy Wilkes is only interested in three things— hunting, fishing, and women. And since it doesn't look like you're dressed for the first two, I'll have to go with the last."

His hand tightened on her arm. "If I said I was with a woman, would you turn back around and go home?"

"Yes."

"Fine. I was with a woman."

She might've believed him if he'd released her arm. But instead he pulled her closer. With her heart banging out a polka, she reached up and smoothed down the collar of his shirt, her fingers brushing the soft curls at the back of his neck. "Liar."

His breath caught. "I'm all wrong for you."

"I couldn't agree more, honey." She leaned in and rubbed her cheek against the scratchy stubble on his chin as she whispered in his ear. "All wrong."

He released her arm, and his hands slipped around her waist. "It will cause nothing but trouble."

"No doubt." She licked his earlobe before sucking it into her mouth. He rolled his head closer, the brim of his hat grazing the top of her head.

"So what do you want, Ms. Dalton? Spell it out so there won't be any excuses later." His breath fell hot against her neck.

"I want you to stop calling me Ms. Dalton for one thing." She tipped back her head as he kissed his way up her neck. "And I want you to stop talking to me like I'm a stranger and go back to being the obnoxious hillbilly who loves to tease the hell out of me." His lips hesitated before they resumed the soft little nibbles that were making it hard to think. She became even more mindless when he tugged up her shirt and his warm, bare hands skated down her hips to cup each cheek of her bottom through her panties.

Moaning, she stepped up on the tops of his boots so she could brush her hips against the hardness beneath the fly of his zipper. "And I want a tour of Wilkesville."

She thought he would laugh, but instead a deep growl came from his throat as he effortlessly lifted her into his arms. She hooked her arms around his neck and watched as a big smile settled over his face. Her Bubba was back.

"I've got to warn you, Shirley Girl," he said as he maneuvered her up the front steps. "I might not last past the first attraction."

Once he kicked the door closed behind them, she

pressed her lips to the bare skin in the opening of his shirt. "Then I guess I'll have to get an all-night pass, now, won't I?"

This time he did laugh, and he was still laughing when he set her down on the floor next to the bed. He went to take his cowboy hat off, but she stopped him.

"I like it."

He tugged it back on before pulling her into his arms. "Into a little role playing, are we?"

"I might be." She tugged his shirt out of his jeans before ripping open the snaps. "You ever seen the movie, *Butch Cassidy and the Sundance Kid*?"

He slipped the shirt off his shoulders. "Is Troy Aikman the best quarterback that ever lived? Of course, I've seen it. Every Texan worth his weight in cow manure has seen that movie—" He stopped in the process of toeing off his boots. "Ahh, Sundance and the schoolmarm scene." He kicked his boots to the side and reached for his belt buckle, but Shirlene beat him to it.

"All women dream of naughty outlaws with big guns," she said as she tugged his belt from the loops. "Didn't you once tell me that you have a big gun you'd like to show me?" She ran her fingertips over the bulge beneath his fly. When he groaned and tipped his head back, she popped open the snap and slid the zipper down.

Billy's gun was big. She'd seen it at half-mast, but fully aroused it was a little intimidating. Intimidating and extremely arousing. There was something so sexy and vulnerable about a man standing there with his desire so blatantly exposed, and Shirlene couldn't help but take the pulsing flesh in hand and give it exactly what it was begging for.

"Lord have mercy," Billy breathed as she learned the feel of him—the soft skin of his shaft, the ridged dome of the tip.

It had been too long since Shirlene had touched a man—too long without the sensual sensation that went with learning the textures of a body so different from her own. And she wanted to learn Billy's textures, to glide her hands over every square inch of skin. Not just her hands, but her mouth, and her tongue.

Kneeling on the floor, she continued to stroke her hand along the shaft as she took the tip in her mouth. She was a little out of practice, so it took her a while to find a steady rhythm. But if the primal noises he released were any indication, Billy didn't seem to notice. He tipped his head so far back his hat fell to the floor. Moments later, he pulled her back to her feet. She started to protest, but he cradled her face between his hands and silenced her with a soft kiss.

"Next time, Baby. This time I want to be in you."

Since his words were so sweet, she didn't argue. She just stood there smiling while he finished getting undressed.

"Don't tell me you're planning on keeping my shirt on," he said as he tossed his jeans and underwear into a corner. "I like you in it and all, but...."

Shirlene wasn't modest about much, but her unfettered breasts were one of the things she was modest about. It didn't help that Billy had left the light on in the kitchen, and it spilled across the floor and directly on her. Or that his body was so damned tight and perfect. She thought about asking him to turn off the light. But before she could get the words out of her mouth, his warm fingers slipped into the opening of her shirt.

"You aren't shy, now are you, Shirley Girl?" He sweetly kissed her mouth as a snap popped. "Because there's nothin' to be shy about." Two more snaps followed. "It's just little ol' me." The rest came undone, and he slipped the shirt off her shoulders.

But before he could lean back and take a look, Shirlene crossed an arm over her chest and started rambling like an idiot. "I know they aren't as perky as some girls. And they might look a little like two overripe melons hanging from the vine, but you can't expect gravity not to kick in—"

He placed a finger over her lips. "I hate to be the arrogant kind of asshole who brings up other women during sex, but you need to check out a couple of *Playboys,* sweetheart." His finger blazed a trail of fire down her chin and along her neck, stopping just shy of her breasts that swelled above her arm. "If you had, you would know that you're every man's fantasy." His finger dipped into the softness of her cleavage. "And you wouldn't be so cruel as to let me get this close to my fantasy and then keep me from doing all the things I've only dreamed about, would you, honey?"

She took an uneven breath. "What kind of things?"

His eyes crinkled in thought. "Well, I'd love to tell you, but don't you think it would be better if I just showed you?"

Before she could answer, he had her panties off and had eased her down to the edge of the bed. Kneeling before her, he coaxed her legs apart and moved so her thighs cradled his ribcage. The sight of his hard stomach inches from her hot center distracted her so much she wasn't aware that he had removed her arm until his warm hand encased one breast.

She might've pulled away if he hadn't been so gentle. He held her breast as if it was as breakable as Hope's mama's fine china, as if any sudden movement might cause it to scatter into a million pieces. Then slowly he began to caress her, his rough fingertips barely touching as they skated over her flushed skin. Her nipple tightened with need, but he chose to ignore it, teasing her with feather-like touches until she thought she might go insane. Then he firmly took her in hand and lowered his head. The wet heat that settled over her nipple had her hips lifting from the mattress as he pulled her into his mouth and teased her with his tongue. When he finished with one breast, he moved on to the other until Shirlene locked her legs around his torso and tugged on his hair.

He lifted his head, his eyes a sweet chocolate glaze. "Are you telling me you're ready, Shirley Girl?"

She answered him by reaching down and taking him in hand. And after only a few strokes, he was reaching for the nightstand. His movements were clumsy and endearing as he placed the extra large condom on. Until that moment, she hadn't really given much thought to how he would fit. But any apprehension she felt was quickly put to rest when Billy eased her back to the mattress and slipped inside of her. It was a snug fit, but a perfect one. Billy seemed to fill all her empty spaces, spaces Shirlene hadn't even known needed filling.

"You okay?"

Shirlene looked up at the man who hovered above her, a man who had turned out to be so much more than she had ever imagined. Reaching out, she brushed a lock of hair off his forehead. "What? You think this west Texas girl can't handle an average-sized boy from the sticks?"

He grinned, but it faded when she adjusted her hips for a deeper fit. With his hands braced on either side of her shoulders, he started to move. The down stroke held the bliss of expansion, the upstroke, the tingle of contraction. It was an explosive combination that had her hips rising to meet each thrust and her hands grasping his butt cheeks. He allowed her to control the tempo, moving faster when her fingers tightened and slower when they relaxed. And when she moaned and went tumbling over the edge of an intense orgasm, he rode the wave with her, prolonging her climax with deep, smooth thrusts. It wasn't until the last tingle of sensation melted from her body that he went after his own satisfaction. She watched as his handsome features tightened in ecstasy before all strength drained out of him, and he slumped down on top of her.

The weight of his body felt good, and she curled her arms around his waist. A moment later, he lifted his head and looked down at her. A smile tipped the corners of his mouth, but his eyes were serious.

"Regrets?"

She shook her head. "Not a one."

He nodded. "Good, because the tour's only starting, Shirley Girl."

Chapter Twenty-five

IT WAS STILL DARK when Billy woke. He stared at the sheet hanging over the window. Seeing as how he felt more relaxed and content than he had in years, he wondered what had awakened him. A slight shift of heated skin against heated skin gave him his answer, and he turned his head and looked down at the naked woman cuddled against his side. He had failed to turn the kitchen light off, and a shaft of light fell over her, highlighting her creamy skin and flaming hair.

Going to bed with Shirlene Dalton was a monumental mistake. Their relationship was complicated enough without adding sex to the mix. Not only was he playing her for a fool with his country-hick charade, but now it looked as if Shirlene might be the key to ending The Cates Curse. But even knowing this, he couldn't bring himself to pull away from the warm cocoon of her arms. His mind might be telling him that making love to Shirlene was a big mistake, but his body was telling him something else entirely.

And not just his body, but something deep down inside him.

Billy reached out and brushed the hair back from her forehead. She was so damned beautiful, each feature perfectly sculpted to take a man's breath away. High forehead, straight nose, smooth skin, and full lips that drove him insane. They were slightly parted, and he could hear the soft sound of air being pulled in and out of her lungs.

And what a set of lungs she had. The mere sight of her standing there in nothing but a pair of cotton panties had almost caused a premature disaster, and it had taken the batting averages of most of the Texas Rangers to keep from diving into those sweet breasts like a sex-crazed fifteen-year-old. Even now he couldn't help lowering the sheet to get a peek of her glorious bounty. Or leaning over to take a quick taste. Except a quick taste soon turned into some uncontrollable gluttony.

"Mmmm," she hummed, her fingers gliding through his hair. He lifted his head to a smile that put the finishing touches on his hard-on.

"Good mornin'," he said.

She leaned up to kiss him, but before her lips met his, a noisy sparrow had her glancing over at the window. "What time is it?" She rose up on her elbows. "I need to get back to the trailer before the kids get up."

"Shhh." He nuzzled her neck. " 'It is not yet near day. It was the nightingale, and not the lark, That pierced the fearful hollow of thine ear. Nightly she sings on yond pomegranate tree. Believe me, love, it was the nightingale.' "

Shirlene pulled back and stared at him as if he'd lost his mind. Looking at the beautiful woman before him, he figured he had. "Bubba Wilkes quotes Shakespeare?" she said.

He reached out and caressed one perfect breast. "I took a drama class in high school for the easy A. I had a major crush on Juliet so I volunteered to play Romeo. But believe me, one kiss wasn't worth the year of razzing I took from the football team and my brothers over those damned tights."

Shirlene laughed. "Well, I played Juliet in high school, and I think you just stole my lines."

"No kiddin'?" He pulled the sheet off her and dropped it to the floor. "Then maybe I should give it another try." His gaze trailed down her body to the deep auburn hair between her sweet white thighs. " 'But soft! What light through yonder window breaks? It is the East, and Juliet is the sun…' "

Fifteen minutes later, Romeo and Juliet had died their "deaths" and were headed back toward Shirlene's trailer. Shirlene might not have any regrets, but Billy sure did. He had made a vow that he would stay as unattached as possible. He'd broken the vow with the people of the town, and now he'd broken it with a descendant of the very man who had started it all.

Sheriff Wynn Murdock.

But when they had reached the bottom of the steps that led to her trailer door and she turned to him, he didn't see an enemy. Just a woman he couldn't help pulling into his arms and giving one last kiss. She melted against him like butter in a cast iron skillet, and several moments passed before he could bring himself to pull away.

Pink edged the horizon with the promise of dawn, and he rested his cheek against her head and waited for the sun.

"Do you believe in fate?" he asked.

She pressed her lips against his collarbone. "Fate as a wicked force that takes away all human decision? Or fate as a divine plan?"

"Aren't they one and the same?"

She pulled back and looked at him. "I hope not. I'd much rather think of my life as being planned out by a loving god, then by a random roll of the dice."

"So you can blame God for the bad things that happen to you, instead of people?" He brushed the hair off her forehead.

Shirlene laughed. "People would be shocked at the skeptical man living in the good ol' boy body of Bubba Wilkes." She gave him a quick kiss. "And no, I don't blame God for the bad things that happen to me. Instead, I like to think of God as my own personal GPS. He guides me toward the right path, but it's up to me to follow his instructions. Although I have been known to veer off course a time or two."

"Was Lyle on course or off?" he couldn't help asking, or feeling a swift kick in the stomach when her eyes turned misty.

"On course. But I didn't realize it for years. I figured I'd planned it all—a grand scheme to leave a hard life behind me." She smiled softly. "But Lyle was exactly what I needed to calm the wildness of my youth and to teach me that love transcends age and physical beauty."

"So you loved him."

She nodded. "Very much." Her eyes refocused on him. "And what about you, Billy Wilkes? Have you left broken hearts all over east Texas?"

"No. The last steady girlfriend I had was in college, but we both were ready to call it quits when I graduated."

"College?" She tipped her head. "Hmm, you never fail to surprise me." The admiration in her green eyes had the truth bubbling up to the surface.

"Listen, Shirlene," he said. "I'm not who you think I am."

She blinked before her smile returned. "I know. And I want to apologize for not seeing it sooner. My mama always said not to judge a book by its cover." She leaned over and kissed his neck. "Although you've got a mighty fine cover, Billy Wilkes."

It was hard to keep focused when her lips were so hot and sweet. But he wanted to tell her—no, he needed to tell her. Except before he could, the front door opened and Jesse peeked his head out. Shirlene jumped back like a scalded cat.

"Hey, what are y'all doin' up so early?" Jesse stepped out on the steps in his droopy underwear, his eyes sleepy and his hair shooting straight up on his head. "Swattin' flies again?"

Shirlene looked confused. But before she could question Jesse, Billy jumped in. "We're just talking."

"Oh." Jesse's didn't seem to be in any hurry to leave. He just stood there staring at them as he scratched his head and, then, his balls. Realizing they weren't going to get to continue their conversation, Billy turned to Shirlene.

"I'll call you later."

She nodded and sent him a dazzling smile before heading up the steps. Billy was halfway through the hedge when he realized his mistake. He couldn't call Shirlene, not unless he wanted to break the news of him being Mr. Cates via caller ID. No, he'd have to catch her alone, which could be problematic considering she was surrounded by four orphans.

Billy returned to the trailer with every intention of going back to bed. But sleep proved to be elusive, especially on sheets that smelled of Shirlene Dalton. So he rolled out of bed and took a cold shower. With little else to do, he headed over to see Beau.

When Billy arrived, Kenny Gene or Sheriff Winslow were nowhere to be seen. Austin must've relayed the news about Shirlene living out on Grover Road. Still, Billy took a few minutes to check out the trees that lined the driveway before he walked around back. On his way to the patio doors, he glanced over at the swimming pool. There was his little brother stretched out on a lounge chair in nothing but his boxers, his straw cowboy hat resting over his face and a cooler of beer within hand's reach.

At ten in the morning, it was a little early for drinking. But considering it had only been four months since Beau had finished chemo, Billy couldn't fault him. That didn't mean he was about to let his brother lie there without a little hassling. Billy circled the pool area and came up behind him. His plan was to grab the chair and tip it over, rolling his brother straight into the pool. What he didn't count on was Beau's quick reflexes. On the way into the water, he reached out and grabbed Billy's shirt. And when Billy's boot got stuck in the leg of the chair, he went head first into the pool right after his brother. He surfaced with his cowboy hat still on his head, but only had time for a quick breath before Beau pushed him back under. The horseplay continued until Billy caught Beau in a headlock and made him cry "uncle."

"So I thought you weren't due back from Lubbock for another couple days," Beau said as he lifted the lounge chair out of the pool.

"I decided to come back early." Billy fished his hat from the water and placed it on his head before swimming over to the steps and sitting down on the edge of the pool to pull off his boots. He scowled at the soaked leather of his Lucchese custom boots. Or maybe it wasn't the soaked leather that had him so upset as much as the reason behind his quick return from business meetings in Lubbock. A green-eyed, redheaded reason that had him as jittery as a cat with a firecracker attached to its tail.

"So I guess the meetings didn't go all that well?" Beau asked as he retrieved his hat.

Billy stood and stripped down to his jockeys. "Plains Gas isn't any more solvent than Dalton Oil, so it was a waste of time."

Tugging his hat back on, Beau climbed out of the pool. "So how's Aunt Milly?"

"As crazy as ever." Billy stretched out on a lounge chair to dry off. "She now thinks that William's ghost visits her every night. And that house of hers has more crap in it than Brant's."

"Our brother does like to collect things, doesn't he?" Beau stretched out on the lounge chair next to Billy. "He's been bugging me to check out antique shops in the area— he's especially interested in any civil war weapons."

Shirlene's Colt Peacemaker popped into Billy's head, but he kept his mouth shut. As much as it bothered him to keep a secret from his brothers, he wasn't about to throw more fuel on Brant's fire. Especially when it already burned out of control.

Of course, Brant wasn't the only Cates brother burning out of control. Billy had no more than closed his eyes when images of Shirlene, all naked and willing, rippled through his mind like the wind on the water of the swimming pool. Then suddenly she was there, lounging on the chaise next to him in nothing but a teeny-weeny bikini and miles of soft skin and supple cleavage. He was so caught up in his fantasy that he jumped when Beau spoke.

"You like her, don't you?"

It was weird how brothers could get in your brain without you even giving them permission. Billy didn't know if it had to do with genes or growing up together, but it wasn't the first time that a brother had read his mind, and it probably wouldn't be the last. But he wasn't about to let Beau know that.

"Who are we talking about?"

Beau shot him an exasperated look. "I'm not an idiot, Billy. If your reaction to the painting wasn't enough, then your reaction at Bootlegger's was."

"I just didn't like the thought of a woman driving drunk." Billy tugged his hat lower.

Beau handed him a beer from the cooler. "Well, I'm glad to hear it's nothing more than common courtesy, big brother. Because I'd sure hate to see that gold digger get her hooks into you."

Billy wasn't sure how it happened. One second he was lounging back about ready to take a sip of beer, and the next he was in Beau's face. "Don't fuckin' talk about her like that." He shook the bottle of beer at his brother until foam came out of the top. "She's not like that."

An idiotic grin split Beau's face as he nonchalantly relaxed back on the lounger. "That's what I thought."

The grin, coupled with his brother's words, annoyed the hell out of Billy. But what annoyed him the most was his reaction, especially since he had been the first one to call Shirlene a gold digger. Talk about being out of control; Billy had really lost it.

He released his breath and sat back. "Look, I'm sorry. I guess I didn't get enough sleep last night."

The smug grin got even bigger, but Beau didn't say a word. He just sat there drinking and smiling until both their beers were gone and their skin had started to turn pink.

"So what do you think she'll do when she finds out?" Beau asked as he handed Billy another beer.

It was the same question that had been rolling around in Billy's head for most of the night. Twisting off the top, he downed half of the beer before he answered. "I figure she'll hate me—along with Slate and the rest of Bramble."

Beau nodded as he stared out at the land surrounding the estate. "It kind of grows on you, doesn't it? It's not as green as Dogwood, but there's something about the barren wildness that pulls at a person. If you stare at it long enough, you can almost see a dusty cowboy riding the range, or a group of outlaws running from the law." Beau glanced over at Billy and grinned. "Or an east Texas redneck driving his monster pickup."

Billy reached out and tapped the brim of Beau's hat. "You've been out here alone for too long, little brother. You're starting to sound as crazy as Aunt Milly."

Beau's smile dropped. "You can't stop Brant, Billy. Ever since he lost Amanda and BJ, revenge eats at him."

"And you think I don't know that, Beau? I was there when he found them, remember? I witnessed the carnage and his pain so I understand his need for revenge. Hell, I wanted revenge, too. But these people aren't responsible for the things that have happened to our family—and I'm starting to wonder if anyone is. Maybe the Cates Curse was just something our crazy forefathers thought up to explain acts of God."

"Maybe." Beau's piercing blue eyes stared back at him. "But that doesn't change the fact that Dalton Oil is going under or that Shirlene Dalton will blame you."

Chapter Twenty-six

"As I TOLD YOU BEFORE, Kyle, we ain't had any runaways in Bramble since Floyd Miller's cows got loose," Sheriff Winslow said into the cell phone. "But if you're dead set on sendin' someone on a wild goose chase, you go right ahead." After he hung up the phone, he didn't waste any time returning to the conversation he'd been having with Rachel Dean. "So Beauregard Williams is now Beauregard Cates?"

"That's what Ruby Lee told me." Rachel Dean poured Harley more coffee. "I guess she overheard Mr. Peabody talkin' on the phone." She placed a hand on her hip and shook her head. "Now there's a strange one. I ask you, what kind of man don't eat red meat? No wonder Mr. Peabody looks like one of them el-bean-os."

Harley nodded. "A man's got to have meat." His eyes narrowed. "Well, that's sure enlightenin' news about Beau. I never did think the man was a criminal. 'Course he doesn't look old enough to be runnin' Dalton Oil either."

"According to Ruby, he don't run it," Rachel said. "His

brothers do. I guess he's got three. One's even got himself a helly-copter."

"She did it again," Cindy Lynn fumed. "Shirlene has gone and found herself another sugar daddy."

"Well, I can sure understand it." Rachel set the coffee pot down. "Beau's smile makes a woman melt like lard on a slab of oven-fresh bread. After goin' without sex for a good nine months, Shirlene didn't stand a chance." She stared out the window for a few seconds. "'Course for livin' with the man, she sure don't seem to like his company all that much. Every time I see her, she's with those Foster kids and Bubba."

"Well, maybe Beau is only good at one thing," Twyla leaned on the counter. "My ex—the second, not the first or the third—couldn't put two words together. But Lordy that man was good between the sheets."

"Well, it doesn't matter if he's a talker or a lover," Harley stated. "If he's goin' to be tastin' the pie, he needs to pay the cook."

A mumble of agreement spread through Josephine's Diner.

"You thinkin' we should form a plannin' committee, Harley?" Rachel asked.

"That's exactly what I'm thinkin', Rachel." Harley got up from his stool and hitched up his pants. "We'll give Cates a few more weeks of enjoyin' our scenery. But if he hasn't popped the question by then, we'll need to do a little intervention." His mustache twitched. "Late September would be nice. Nothin' like a weddin' to fill up a lazy autumn afternoon."

"Speakin' of weddin's," Twyla said. "If Beau ain't a criminal, you think you could relieve Kenny Gene of his deputy job, Sam? Every time I get a few minutes to talk about weddin' dates, he has to go runnin' off to do his official duty."

Sheriff Winslow nodded as he stabbed another bite of biscuits and gravy. "As soon as I'm done with my breakfast, I'll head on out and get him. Lord only knows what kind of trouble that boy is gettin' into."

"I shore could use me one of them beers."

Kenny Gene glanced over at Rye Pickett, who was crouched on the ground next to him, and he had to admit that his best friend looked like he'd been rode hard and put away wet. Sweat dripped in long trails through the green face paint Kenny had forced him to apply, and the shirt beneath the camouflage hunting vest was soaked clear through. Even the sprigs of mesquite in his cap looked wilted from the harsh sun that beat down on their heads.

Looking back at Beau Williams and the stranger who were stretched out on loungers not more than fifty yards away, Kenny had to agree that an ice cold beer and a splash in the pool sounded tempting. But Sheriff Winslow had given him a job to do, and he wasn't about to let a little thing like scorching heat and dehydration keep him from it.

"Law enforcement officers ain't got time to worry about things like comfort, Rye," he said as he pulled his own sweat-soaked shirt away from his neck.

"Well, then I guess I ain't cut out to be a law enforcement officer because I'm about done hangin' out here sweatin' my balls off. Besides, Beau shore don't look like a criminal to me." He spit a stream of tobacco to the ground, almost hitting a lizard that scurried from a rock.

Kenny shook his head. "That's the difference between civilians and law enforcement officers, Rye. A cop can tell a criminal from a hundred yards away. And this man is a scoundrel if ever I've seen one. Why, just look at the way he was playin' *Brokeback Mountain* with that stranger right beneath Shirlene's nose."

"Brokeback what?" Rye stared back at him in confusion.

Kenny swallowed hard. If word ever got out that he let Twyla talk him into watching that movie with them fellers who liked to run buck-naked through the woods, he'd never be able to show his face in town again. Especially if anyone ever found out that he had actually liked the movie—not the buck-naked part as much as the thought of camping out in the wilderness without a woman nagging him about setting a wedding date.

"Never mind." Kenny lifted his binoculars and stared through the lens trying to make out the features of the man who was stretched out next to Beau. But all he saw was a long crack and a blurred image. Obviously, Wal-Mart-Special binoculars would not survive a drop from a tree. When he lowered them only a few minutes later, the stranger in the cowboy hat was completely gone and only Beau remained.

"I think that feller has the right idea. I'm leavin'." Rye pulled off his cap and jerked the mesquite branches out of the top.

"You can't go," Kenny said. "We've still got some surveillance to do."

"You'll have to do it by yourself, Kenny. I'm headed to Bootlegger's for a cold one." He slapped his cap back on his head and crawled off on his elbows and knees.

Once he was gone, Kenny looked back at the swimming pool. It had been over a week since he'd had anything good to report back to Sheriff Winslow. Or to Twyla, who was more into his deputy duties than Sam was. After he had told her about Beau moving in with Shirlene, she'd given him more sex than she had since Christmas. The thought had him fidgeting in his sweat-drenched clothes, and without Rye there to distract him, his mouth suddenly felt as dry and parched as Sutter Springs in late August. He reached for his canteen, but it turned out to be as dry as his mouth. While screwing the cap back on, his gaze swept over to the red-and-white cooler of beer by the lounge chair. And when Beau got up and went inside, the desire for a beer became too overwhelming to resist.

By the time Kenny reached the gate, he was as close to dehydration as a man could get. But just as he lifted the latch, Beau stepped back out the patio doors. Luckily he was talking on the phone, and Kenny had time to dive into a mesquite bush.

"...maybe he's right, Brant. Maybe it's time to let this revenge thing go—I mean the entire town will suffer when we close Dalton Oil's doors. Do you want that on your conscience? Because I sure as hell don't." Beau grabbed the cooler and turned back to the door. "And if we do this, it won't just hurt the town, Brant. It will hurt Billy. I think he loves—"

His words were cut off when the door clicked closed behind him.

Kenny waited only a moment more before he untangled himself from the bush and raced toward his truck.

Damn, he was going to have some hot sex tonight.

Chapter Twenty-seven

EVEN THOUGH SHIRLENE HAD GOTTEN very little sleep the night before, she couldn't seem to sit still once she got back inside the trailer. A giddy energy consumed her, causing her to attempt things she'd never attempted before. By the time Mia and the kids had gotten up, she'd scoured the oven, cleaned out the refrigerator, and started breakfast. While her cleaning skills were adequate, her cooking skills were dismal. The pancakes she whipped up were thin as paper, filled with eggshells, and burnt on one side. Still, the kids seemed to love them.

The rest of the morning, she dusted and mopped, and did three loads of laundry. But the giddy energy remained. So after lunch, she herded everyone into the Navigator for a trip into town. Not only did she want the kids to have new clothes for Founder's Day on Saturday, but she wanted to put a little distance between her and Billy Wilkes.

"Now aren't you glad you came?" Shirlene said to Mia as she pulled the Navigator into a space right across the street from the park.

Mia only crossed her arms and slumped farther down

in the seat. It had been like pulling teeth to get the teenager out of the trailer. Shirlene couldn't remember much about her teenage years, but she sure didn't remember being such a worrywart. If Mia wasn't worrying about money, she was worrying about the townsfolk finding out they were runaways. And if she wasn't worrying about those things, she was worrying about Adeline learning to walk, or Brody's lack of speech, or the pimples on her face. Even now, she flipped down the visor and checked her chin out in the mirror.

"Would you stop frettin', honey," Shirlene said. "Austin's not going to care about a few pimples."

Mia flipped the visor back up. "As if I care what he thinks." She shot Shirlene one of those belligerent looks. "I thought the rooster only crows for the hen he has to chase? It didn't look like Bubba had to do much chasing to get you to crow."

Before Shirlene could do more than sputter, Jesse unbuckled his seatbelt and shoved his head between the bucket seats.

"Billy and Shirlene sittin' in a tree. K-I-S—"

Shirlene didn't hit him, but she did slap a hand over his mouth. Except when she started to deny his words, she realized she didn't have a leg to stand on. She and Billy hadn't been kissing in a tree—they'd been having sex in his trailer. Just one more thing you shouldn't do when you had a passel of too-smart-for-their-own-britches kids around. But if she'd learned anything in the last week, it was that sugar can get a kid's mind off just about anything.

"Who wants ice cream after we get done shopping?!" she yelled. She was rewarded with squeals from every kid and pig in the car. Everyone but Mia, who sent her a sour look as she climbed out of the SUV. Shirlene figured she'd just have to live with that.

What was also hard to live with was Mia's miserly ways. They had no more than stepped foot in Duds 'N Such when the teenager gave Shirlene a budgeted amount she could spend. For a woman who hadn't looked at a price tag in over ten years, it was more than a little humiliating to be relegated to the sale rack. Still, Shirlene had to admit it was kind of fun to try to put together cute outfits for each of the kids without going over Mia's budget, and she was delighted when she ended up with money left over. Figuring she deserved a reward for her efforts, she picked out an inexpensive sundress for herself. But before she could set it on the counter with the rest of the clothing, her gaze drifted over to Jesse.

The boy was standing in the boot section, ogling a pair of ostrich-skinned boots. He didn't pick up the boots, or even touch the bumpy leather. He just stood there with his hands shoved deep in the pockets of his jeans, and his eyes glazed over with desire. It was a look Shirlene understood all too well. How many times in her youth had she stood in Duds 'N Such coveting something she couldn't afford? But before she could figure out how to get Jesse those boots without causing Mia to throw a fit, a deep voice cut into her thoughts.

"I've missed you."

The hanger slipped through her fingers, and she turned to find Billy standing too close, the brim of his Resistol hat inches from her forehead. His deep brown eyes held a look that made her breath hitch, and it took everything she had to keep her voice steady when she finally spoke.

"You just saw me a few hours ago."

"I know," he said in a low whisper that fluttered the hair by her ear. "And that's a few hours too long." Her heart did a funny little two-step, and she found herself swaying toward his firm lips. But before she could do some K-I-S-S-I-N-G, Brody slipped between them and tugged on the leg of Billy's jeans until Billy reached down and lifted the boy into his arms. The action was so natural and effortless that it brought a lump to Shirlene's throat. It grew when Brody reached up and touched the brim of Billy's hat, and without hesitation, Billy took it off and placed it on the boy's head.

"I've got to tell you, son, cowboys don't carry around naked dolls in their holsters. How about if I buy you that toy tractor over there?" Before Brody could even open his mouth, Billy answered for him. "I know—mine."

Shirlene actually giggled, sounding just like a thirteen-year-old standing next to Justin Bieber. The sound shocked her so much she completely forgot about Jesse's boots and the pretty flowered dress and, instead, hurried over to the counter to pay for their purchases.

Mia didn't comment as she watched Justin ring up the clothing, but her perpetual frown lifted slightly when she discovered Shirlene had spent under the budgeted amount. Unfortunately, Shirlene didn't get to savor the small victory. She was too concerned over her strange reactions to Billy. The man stood a good twenty feet away, examining the boots Jesse had been looking at, and still Shirlene's heart felt as if it was about to thump from her chest. It was crazy. Sure the sex had been great—better than she had ever had in her life—but that was no reason for her to feel as if she might pass out at any moment from lack of oxygen.

He was Bubba Wilkes, for God's sake, an ordinary country boy from east Texas.

But no matter how much she reasoned with herself, she couldn't stop the windfall of emotions that assailed her when Billy glanced over and sent her a soft smile. A smile that brought back midnight whispers and sweet kisses with a man who seemed anything but ordinary.

Worried that her knees would give out at any second, Shirlene grabbed the bags and headed for the door. "Come on, y'all. I'm just dyin' for a big ol' scoop of chocolate ice cream."

But the chocolate fix didn't help—nor did putting some space between her and Billy. All it took was him exiting the store with a large bag that he stopped and deposited in the back of the Navigator, for the dopey feelings to return. She was lucky she could even talk when he strutted across the street with his hat tugged low on his forehead.

"You bought Jesse those boots, didn't you?" she said as he sat down next to her.

He bent his head and slid his tongue over her Rocky Road, causing her stomach to take a sudden dip. As he savored the flavor, his eyes squinted over to the bench in front of the pharmacy where Jesse sat happily eating his ice cream while talking a mile-a-minute to Moses Tate. "A boy needs a pair of boots that fit about as much as a beautiful woman needs a pretty dress."

Before Shirlene could melt to the cement in a puddle, Mia got up from the table next to them with an ice cream-smeared Adeline perched on her slim hip.

"I'm taking the kids over to the park to play."

"Why don't you let us do that, Mia?" Billy held out his hands, and Adeline practically dove into them. "It looks to me like all the young girls are sitting on the bleachers watching the boys show off their baseball skills."

Mia glanced across the street, and her face grew even paler. As much as Shirlene wanted to come to her rescue, she knew Billy was right: The girl needed to learn how to be a teenager, no matter how painful the lesson.

"Go on, honey." Shirlene held the last of the drippy ice cream cone down to Sherman who inhaled it before licking her fingers clean. "Just remember that a smile goes a long way."

With a roll of her eyes, Mia trudged across the street. When she was gone the space between Shirlene and Billy seemed to get even smaller. Needing something to do, she picked up a napkin off the table and wiped off Adeline's mouth. The baby jerked her head away, smearing strawberry ice cream on the collar of Billy's shirt. Shirlene went to wipe it off, but when her knuckles brushed against the smooth skin of his throat, she jerked her hand back as if scalded. Confused by her reaction, she turned her attention to Brody's sticky face.

"So I guess the regrets have caught up with you."

The softly spoken words had Shirlene glancing up into Billy's eyes. But their intensity had her looking away again. "It's not that," she whispered.

Warm fingers curled around her chin as he turned her back to face him. "Then what happened to the sassy woman who showed up in my yard in nothing but a shirt?"

She tried to come up with a good lie, but she failed miserably. So she gave him the truth. "She's confused." She swallowed hard. "And scared."

His eyes flickered, and his fingers tightened on her chin. She thought he would question her, or at least give her some type of reassurance. Instead he only nodded and got to his feet. Somehow she respected him more for not giving her pretty words that might make her feel better now, but would only make her feel worse when he left town.

But as the day progressed, she realized that it didn't matter. With or without pretty words, she would be upset when Billy went back to Dogwood. And so would the kids. While Shirlene struggled with being a caregiver, Billy was a natural. If he wasn't pushing Brody in a swing, he was tossing Adeline in the air, or playing catch with Jesse, or hooking Mia into a conversation with Austin after the baseball game was over. It appeared that Billy was a man worth missing.

"This seat taken?"

Shirlene glanced up to see Moses Tate standing there. Over his wrinkled western shirt, he wore a faded jean jacket that had to be hotter than Hades in the late afternoon heat. But his bald head didn't seem to be sweating, although the lips around his puckered mouth looked a little parched.

"It's taken now, honey." Shirlene moved over on the park bench to let the man sit down next to her. It took a while. Moses was slower than molasses in winter. When he was finally seated, he turned and nodded at Adeline, who was fast asleep in Shirlene's arms.

"That's one of them Foster kids, ain't it?"

"Adeline," Shirlene said.

Moses nodded. "Jesse told me that they was livin' out on Grover Road close to where you used to live."

"Yes, sir."

He studied the baby with those piercing eyes. "Ain't seen much of their mama."

"She works a lot. So I'm helping out," she said, although she was getting darned sick of lying. Hopefully, the paperwork would come through soon so she could quit.

Moses squinted at her. "Know a lot about babysittin', do ya?"

The old man's perceptive eyes made Shirlene more than a little uncomfortable, and she forced a laugh. "Not near enough, honey."

Fortunately, he didn't continue with his line of questioning. And when his head bobbled on his narrow shoulders and his chin touched his chest, Shirlene figured he'd nodded off to sleep. She'd figured wrong.

"Dad-gum fools," he grumbled. "Can't even see what's right in front of their faces. I knew Faith wasn't Hope the moment she walked into Bootlegger's. And it wasn't just her ugly hair that gave her away. She don't act nothin' like Hope—not the walk, or the talk, or the way she looks at Slate Calhoun.

"And I'll tell you something else," he pulled the squashed cup from the pocket of his jacket and spit a stream of tobacco into it, "I knew that Colt Lomax was the father of Hope's baby. Hope has had a thing for Colt since she was runnin' around in them droopy diapers. 'Course nobody asks me. And if a person don't ask, I'm not one to tell."

His eyes squinted. "Take that Beau feller, for example. He waltzes into town, and nobody pays him a lick of attention until he shows up with you. Then they come up with some harebrained idea that he's after your money. When the truth comes out and they find out his name is really Cates, you'd think they'd put two and two together?

But no sirree. Instead they start talkin' about weddin's."
He shook his head. "Durn fools are missin' the entire dad-
gum boat. But I know—my pappy was there when it happened. And I'll tell you one thing; it's no co-winkie-dink
that those boys bought out Dalton."

It was hard to keep up with Moses Tate, but she
couldn't ignore the part about the wedding. "Whose
wedding?"

"Why, yours and that Cates feller."

Shirlene's eyes widened. It was one thing to let the
town get all worked up about other people's weddings,
and another for them to get worked up about hers. She
wasn't ready to get married. Her eyes wandered over to
Billy, who was letting Brody run through the sprinklers.
And even if she was, it wouldn't be with Beau.

She got to her feet. "If you'll excuse me, Mr. Tate. I
think I'll go on over to Josephine's and get me a glass of
lemonade. Would you like one?"

"We ain't got time for lemonade, Missy. Not when
there's about to be a shootout at the O.K. Corral."

"Right." Shirlene winked. "I'll have my gun oiled and
ready."

It didn't take her long to locate Mia. She was standing
off to the side of the group of sweaty teenage boys and
giggling teenage girls, looking awkward and uncomfortable. When she saw Shirlene she almost looked relieved.

"Could you keep an eye on Adeline for me, honey?"
Shirlene said as she handed off the sleeping child.
"There's something I need to take care of."

"What's wrong?" Billy walked up with Brody, who
was dripping wet and grinning from ear to ear.

"Nothing I can't handle," she said before heading

toward the town hall. She should've known that Billy wasn't the type to let things go. He caught up with her right in front of the town hall dedication plaque.

"What's going on, Shirlene?"

She shook her head. "The crazy people of this town have gotten it into their heads that I'm going to marry Cates."

"Which one?"

She stared at Billy as if he was crazy as the townsfolk. "What difference does it make which Cates? Beauregard Cates. His brother." She glanced over at the brass dedication plaque with its dark, engraved letters. "Or William Cates. I'm not marrying any—" She stopped midsentence, and her eyes traveled back to the plaque.

Billy's hand tightened on her arm. "Shirlene, you need to listen to me for a second."

But Shirlene wasn't listening. Her mind was too busy trying to piece things together. It only took a second.

"Cates," she breathed. "Moses was right. It couldn't be just a coincidence. Which means that Dalton Oil was bought out by the descendants of a man who was killed right here in Bramble." Her eyes narrowed. "But why? Why would the Cates brothers want to own something with such bad history?"

Since there was only one person who would have the answers, Shirlene pulled her phone from the pocket of her cut-offs and searched for the number she'd put in her phone before leaving Mr. Peabody's office. Billy released her arm and took a step back, but she barely noticed as she pushed the button. As it started to ring, she prepared the questions she wanted to ask in her head, questions about why Mr. Cates had come to Bramble and why he had bought out the bank and evicted her from her home. She figured she knew the answer to that one. She had a Colt Peacemaker to prove it.

She was so wrapped up in her thoughts that it took her a moment to realize that Billy's phone was ringing. She might've thought it was a coincidence if it hadn't stopped at the same time that Mr. Cates's voicemail picked up—and if she hadn't looked up into a pair of eyes that held so much sadness it took her breath away.

With her gaze pinned to his, she hung up and pressed the button again. The ringing that came from his back pocket had the phone slipping through her numb fingers to the hard concrete between her feet.

"You?" she whispered. He reached for her, but she jumped back. "You're Mr. Cates?"

He stared at her, his only acknowledgment a slight nod.

She shook her head, unable to believe it. Or maybe she just didn't want to believe that the man she'd given herself to was the same man who had evicted her from her home. A man who had played both sides of the fence as well as any seasoned actor.

"So 'Bubba' was nothing more than a lie."

He looked away from her. "My brother, Buck, called me Bubba."

"And liar?" She tried to speak over the lump in her throat. "Did he also call you liar? Imposter? Lowdown, rotten scoundrel?" Her fists tightened as she stepped closer. "Or do you have an explanation for pretending to be a good ol' boy from east Texas? Come on, Bubba, where's your fake smile and hillbilly anecdotes now?"

When he only stood there, she reached out and punched him hard in the chest. "Go on, tell me a funny story about your big ol' family, or all those women who can't wait to get their hands on Wilkesville."

Unable to stand the sight of him for a second longer, Shirlene whirled and headed for the street. But just as she stepped off the curb, Sheriff Winslow's squad car came barreling around the corner with sirens blaring and pulled up in front of the jail. Before Shirlene could do more than blink back the tears, Beau Cates was being pulled out of the backseat in handcuffs.

Chapter Twenty-eight

WITH HIS GAZE PINNED ON SHIRLENE, it took Billy a moment to register the sound of the siren. And another to realize Beau was getting out of the backseat. He wasn't the only one who hurried over to the squad car, either—the siren had attracted the townsfolk like bees to honey. People came out of the buildings all up and down Main Street to surround the flashing lights. Before Billy could maneuver around the folks to get to his brother, Mayor Sutter came chugging out the side door of his office.

"What's all the commotion?" When the mayor saw Beau, his handlebar mustache waggled. "Now, Sam, I told you not to force things. I thought we were going to give Beau another week before we brought out the shotgun."

"This ain't about a shotgun weddin'," Sam said as he steered Beau up the path that led to the town jail. "This is about him being a good-for-nothin', lowdown snake in the grass who intends to close Dalton Oil."

"What do you mean, close Dalton Oil?" Rossie Owens stepped up. "Why would he want to do a thing like that?"

"Because he wants revenge," Shirlene pushed her way through the crowd, glaring at Billy as she did.

"You that bad in bed, Shirl?" Twyla asked.

Shirlene ignored the question. "Revenge for Beau's great-great-granddaddy being shot in our town." She looked back at Billy. "Isn't that right, Bubba?"

"Somebody was shot in Bramble?" Rachel Dean asked. "Why, nobody's been shot here since William Cates. And why are you askin' Bubba? He ain't gonna know nothin' about that seein' how he's from east Texas."

"An East Texan who happens to be a direct descendant of William Cates," Shirlene stated.

Rachel's eyes widened. "No foolin'?" She looked back at Billy. "You're William's relative? Why, honey, if I'd known that, I'd have given you a chicken-fried steak on the house."

Rossie came up and slapped Billy on the back. "And all the Cuervo you could drink."

Shirlene released a loud groan. "He didn't come here for drinks on the house or chicken fried steak. He came here to close down Dalton Oil and ruin our town."

"Now, Shirl," Kenny Gene hopped in. "I hate to disagree, but I was there when Beau Cates here was talkin' to his brother. And he's the one plannin' on shuttin' down Dalton, not Bubba."

Shirlene stomped her foot and pointed at Billy. "That is his brother, Kenny Gene!"

Kenny scratched his head. "Why, that don't make no sense, Shirl. If Bubba was brothers with Beau then he woulda brought him along fishin'. And I ain't never fished with Beau." He looked at Beau. "Right, Beau?"

Beau grinned and shook his head. "No, Kenny, you're

right. I haven't gone fishin' with you. But once this is all over, I hope to."

Kenny's face brightened. "Well, I shore would like that, Beau. You fish with live bait or eggs—'course I've seen Bubba catch a fish with nothin' but a piece of Velveeter cheese—"

"Oh, for the love of Pete." Shirlene looked around at the crowd circling them. "Don't you people get it? Bubba Wilkes isn't your friend. He's been playing you—" she swallowed hard, "and everyone for fools. He's not here to go fishing or hunting or tell you a bunch of hillbilly stories. He's here to wipe Bramble off the map."

A murmur went through the crowd, and Billy figured that the tar and feathers would be brought out at any minute. But instead the townsfolk surprised him again.

"Now, Shirl." Mayor Sutter stepped forward, hitching up his pants over his big belly. "I realize you've had it tough lately, what with Lyle dying and Hope and Colt being in California. And I'm sure it's frustratin' to discover that the man you've been shackin' up with is a low-down scoundrel." He shot a mean glare over at Beau, who seemed to be thoroughly enjoying himself. "But you can't take your frustration out on Bubba."

Shirlene's shoulders drooped, and Billy figured it was time to speak up. Before he could, a man pushed his way through the crowd, a man Billy needed no introduction to. Especially when Shirlene threw herself into his tattooed arms.

"Colt!"

The dark-headed man hugged her close and smiled. "If I had known how much you'd miss me, Shirl, I would've taken you with me." He tried to pull back, and when his sister continued to cling, the smile slipped. "Hey, what's wrong?" He looked around the group. "What happened?"

"That's exactly what I'd like to know." A pretty petite woman moved out from behind Colt. At first, Billy thought it was Faith Calhoun with Daisy Mae. But when an identical woman stepped up with another baby, Billy figured it out.

"Well, hey, Hope." Harley Sutter rushed over to hug the woman with hair much longer than her sister's. "How was your trip to California? You see any of them movie stars?"

"Don't try to sidetrack me, Uncle Harley," Hope said as she handed the baby to him. "What in tarnation is goin' on here? I leave town for no more than a few days, and a riot breaks out?" She pointed a finger at Beau. "And why is that poor man handcuffed?"

Everyone started talking at once as fingers were pointed at Billy and Beau. But the flapping mouths closed when Hope released a noise so shrill and loud that the kids in the crowd covered their ears and Sherman shot out of nowhere, squealing with delight as he trotted over to Hope.

While she squatted down to greet him, Billy glanced over at Shirlene. If looks could kill, Billy would be as dead as his great-grandpappy. And he couldn't blame her. He deserved her hatred, but damned if it didn't hurt. He felt like he had been kicked in the stomach by a mule, and he would give just about anything to have five minutes alone with her to try and explain. But if the look on her face was any indication, she wasn't going to give him five seconds, let alone five minutes. It probably didn't matter, anyway. He had no good explanation for all the lies he'd

told. He looked around at the faces he'd come to know—
and even love. No, he had no explanations. All he had was
the truth.

"My name is William Wilkes Cates," he said in a voice
loud enough to carry to the people who stood in the back.
"And I'm a direct descendant of the William Cates who
was shot and killed right here in Bramble in the summer
of 1892..." The words came out much easier than Billy
had thought. In fact, once he'd relayed the entire story
from William's murder to the demise of Dalton Oil, he
felt almost cleansed. Not of guilt. He had that in spades.
But of the burden of lies he'd carried with him for so long.

"...so it's not Beau that should be in handcuffs, but
me," he stated. "I was the one who deceived you. I was
the one who found out about Dalton Oil's troubles and
planned to use it for revenge."

In the silence that followed, Billy could've heard a
pin drop. The usually talkative people of Bramble were
struck speechless. They just stood there staring at him as
if they couldn't quite believe their ears. It was Slate who
finally separated from the crowd and walked over—Slate
who threw a punch that made Billy's head snap back.

"You sonofabitch!" Beau charged forward, but Billy
shook it off in time to step between him and Slate.

"I deserve more than that, Beau," he said.

"Damn straight, you do," Slate said, his fists clenched
and eyes snapping. "This town welcomed you with open
arms and your thanks is closing Dalton Oil?"

"Dalton would've closed anyway," Beau came to
his defense. "Billy isn't responsible for that. That was
Mr. Dalton's doing."

"But it was you who evicted Shirlene from her home,

wasn't it?" Faith said so softly Billy could barely hear her. "You who refused to give back her things."

This time it was Colt who stepped up, but Hope placed a hand on his arm and stopped him. "He's not worth it, Colt." She turned to Billy. "I think you've worn out your welcome in this town, Mr. Cates." She glanced over at the town jail. "And if you're not out by sundown, I'm sure the sheriff can find you and your brother a place to spend the night."

"Let's go, Billy." Beau came up, his hands no longer in cuffs.

Billy nodded and, as if by some divine power, the crowd parted to let them through. As he walked away, he tried not to look at the confused, hurt faces of the townsfolk. It was difficult. He would miss them—all of them, from Rachel Dean to Moses Tate, who slept soundly on the bench in front of the pharmacy.

With Beau following close behind, Billy was almost to his truck when a child's screams stopped him in his tracks. He looked down the street to where two state patrol cars were parked. One officer was trying to control a fighting Jesse, while the other was helping a woman in an ugly pantsuit place Brody into the back of a plain blue sedan where Mia was already sitting with Baby Adeline.

Billy forgot all about leaving Bramble as he set a track record getting to the officers.

"What's going on here?" He tried to keep his voice calm, but it was difficult when a hard knot of fear had settled in his stomach.

"You need to stay out of this, sir," the officer said, but his words ended on a grunt when Jesse kicked him in the shin. The tactic gained the boy his release, and he hurried over to Billy and clung to him like moss to a tree. It was the first time Jesse had ever hugged Billy, and it made the knot in his stomach tighten even more. It also pissed him off.

"You'd better have the correct legal documents, officer," he said between his teeth, "because if you don't, I'm going to have your badge."

Before the state trooper could answer, Shirlene came running up, her eyes filled with fear and desperation.

"Mine! Mine!" Brody screamed, holding out his chubby arms to her. That was all it took for Shirlene's fear to be replaced with a determined look that made the woman in the ugly pantsuit take a step back.

"Just what do you think you're doing with my children?" she said as she pulled a sobbing Brody from the woman's arms. Since she towered over the woman by a good foot, Billy understood why the woman didn't argue with her.

Shirlene turned to the officers. "And get Mia and Adeline out of the back of that car."

"I'm afraid I can't do that, ma'am," the shorter of the two officers said. "These children are runaways and wards of the state. They've been missing from their foster home for months, and we're here to take them back."

"No, they ain't," Kenny Gene chimed in, alerting Billy to the fact that the entire town was now circled around them. "Them kids are the Foster kids. They live out on Grover Road with their mama."

The state trooper looked thoroughly confused. "So you're saying," he pointed to Shirlene, "she's their mother?"

"She ain't their mother, she's Shirlene Dalton—" Kenny Gene started, but Pastor Robbins cut him off.

"Their foster mother." The man moved out of the group of townsfolk. In his board shorts and Hawaiian shirt, he stood out like a hooker in church. "I'm the one who has been helping her with all the paperwork."

"Shirlene a mama." Harley Sutter shook his head as he bounced Daffodil in his arms. "That's almost as big of a surprise as Hope turning out to be Faith."

"It ain't that big of a surprise, Harley," Rachel Dean said. "Everyone knows how much Shirlene has wanted children of her own. And seein' as how these kids trail after her like a bunch of cute little ducklin's, it looks like she found them." She wiped at the corner of her eyes with her big man hands. "And if that ain't the sweetest thing, I don't know what is."

The woman in the ugly pantsuit pulled open the car door and took out a thick folder. "But I have no records saying they have new foster parents. Their foster parents are Barb and Mickey Primple out of Houston."

"No, they ain't!" Jesse yelled as he pulled away from Billy. "They're just two mean folks who shouldn't have kids! And we ain't goin' back there never again! We're livin' out on Grover Road with Billy and Shirlene!"

His yelling got Brody to start screaming, which got the entire town all talking at once. Again it was Hope who put an end to the ruckus with one of her loud hog calls. But this time, Sherman didn't race over to her. Instead, he remained right next to Shirlene as if he knew she needed his comfort.

"Are you sure you have the right children?" Hope asked once the crowd had settled.

The woman opened the folder and proceeded to hold up a picture of each of the children and read off their names—names with surnames that didn't match. "Mia

Michaels, age sixteen. Jesse Rutledge, age nine. Brody Phelps, age three. And Adeline Rhodes..." She hesitated.

"Eleven and a half months."

Billy glanced over at Shirlene. The smile had fallen, and her eyes were green, glistening pools of unshed tears. Tears that made his heart wrench. Especially when she fought so hard to keep them contained.

"She'll be one in another week." Shirlene's voice shook. "I was planning on giving her a party—you know, the kind with her very own cupcake that she could smear..." She bit down on her bottom lip. "So you see, you can't take her." She looked over at Billy, and a tear trickled down her cheek. "Tell her, Billy. Tell her that she can't take my baby."

Billy's hand tightened on Jesse's shoulder. "No one is taking anyone," he stated as he stared down first one officer and then the other.

The short state patrolman held up his hand. "I don't know what's going on here. All I know is I have my orders. I have to get these kids back to Houston. You can take it up with the judge there."

"My name is William Cates, and I own C-Corp," Billy said. "I'm also a close friend of Judge Myers. If you'll just let me make a few phone calls, I can get this all figured out without you taking the kids anywhere."

The woman's eyes narrowed in confusion. "C-Corp? But I thought it was an employee of your company who called with the children's whereabouts in the first place."

Shirlene stared at him. "You turned in the kids?"

"No." Billy shook his head. "I would never do that." But he could tell by the look on her face that she didn't believe him.

The state trooper grabbed Jesse's arm and pulled him toward the patrol car. "Come on, son."

Watching little Jesse try to fight off the officer was the final straw.

"Let him go!" Billy yelled as he reached out for the officer's arm. The other state trooper went for his gun, and Beau grabbed Billy from behind.

"Don't do anything stupid, Billy," Beau said.

But it was too late. Billy had already done plenty of stupid things. One more wasn't going to make a difference. Unfortunately, before he could shake his little brother off, Colt and Slate grabbed his arms. Still, Billy fought—fought as Jesse was forced in the car and Brody was taken from Shirlene. Fought until he was face down on the hot asphalt and had to watch as his last hope of redemption drove away.

Chapter Twenty-nine

THE DOOR OF THE OLD CHEVY CREAKED OPEN, and Shirlene wasn't surprised to see her brother. Colt, Hope, and Daffodil had been living in Shirlene's guest house until their new home was completed. But since Shirlene no longer had a guest house, they were now sharing the trailer with her. At one time, she would've welcomed the company. Now all she wanted was to be alone.

"Move over, Sherman." Colt eased the pig out of the way so he could sit down on the cracked leather seat. Sherman grunted his disapproval, but quickly resettled against Shirlene's thigh as her brother slammed the door.

For a few moments, Colt slouched down in the seat and stared out the windshield. There wasn't much to see. Just the ramshackle back fence and the branches of the elm tree swaying in the darkness.

"So where are we headed?" he finally asked.

It was a good question. One Shirlene didn't have the answer to. She had come out to the car hoping to figure out the tangle her life had become; instead she felt more knotted than ever. Still, she put on a brave front.

"How about Paris?"

Colt shook his head. "Last time you took me there, I had to suffer through your bad French accent for an entire month—along with your refusal to eat my pancakes unless I called them crepes."

Shirlene stroked Sherman's ears. "I don't know how you put up with me."

Colt's hand settled on her shoulder, his strength and love communicated through the tight grip of his fingers. "Because you were the best kid sister a brother could ask for." When her gaze slid over to him, he held up his other hand. "Don't get me wrong; you had your moments. But most the time you were this happy-go-lucky little girl who refused to let a drunken mama, or a surly brother, bring her down." His hand tightened. "It was your positive nature and unconditional love that kept me sane."

"Whoever said you were sane, Colt Lomax?"

He flashed one of his rare smiles. "Now there's the spunky sister I love and adore." When she didn't answer his smile with one of her own, he grew somber. "We're going to get them back, Shirl. Pastor Robbins is working on it as we speak."

"But how, Colt?" She put her greatest fears into words. "How can I get the children back when I don't have a job or a big enough house for all of them to live in? You and I both know that no court in the country is going to give me those kids."

He released her shoulder and looked back out of the windshield. "Hope and I have been talking. If the courts won't give you the kids, we're willing to adopt them."

His words should've made Shirlene feel happy. After all, Colt and Hope were wonderful parents. But instead of feeling relieved, she just felt resentful. Hope and Colt had a baby. The Foster kids were hers.

Except they weren't hers, and it was a waste of time to even fantasize about it. She had wanted a good home for the children, and this was her chance to get one. Which meant she needed to release her own selfish desires and appreciate the gift her brother was offering her.

She turned to him. "You won't be sorry, Colt. Adeline is the cutest and best little baby—well, except when she's hungry. She needs to eat at least five meals a day—but not carrots. She hates carrots. And Brody is precious as long as you don't mess with Naked Barbie or give him a pair of scissors. And Jesse—well, Jesse is Jesse. He's ornery as sin, but sweet as the dickens and can sell a soccer ball to a one-legged man. And then there's Mia. The girl's been through a lot, but any teenager who can feed and take care of an entire family by herself for close to a year—"

Colt held up a hand. "You don't have to convince me, Shirl. If you love them, I'll love them. And seeing as how you refuse to move out of this pile of tin, you'll be close enough to our new home to help with the kids every day. Although I don't know how long we'll be living in Bramble if Dalton Oil goes under." His hands tightened into fists. "I should've kicked William Cates's ass while I had the chance. And considering he's cooling his heels in the town jail, I still might."

Earlier that afternoon, Shirlene might've egged her brother on. But now she no longer cared about punishing Billy. She just wanted him gone. Gone from her life and gone from Bramble. She didn't want to see those lying eyes or hear his lying words ever again. But no matter how much she knew he was a lowdown rotten scoundrel, there was something about his actions today that hadn't added up. Why would a man who had called Children's Protective Services fight so hard to keep the kids in Bramble?

Billy had fought. The state trooper had barely placed a hand on Jesse when Billy had started swinging. Shirlene had wanted to fight, too, but she refused to upset Brody when she knew the situation was hopeless. So she had smiled and talked softly to the little boy as she placed him in the car seat, trying her best not to look in his confused, tear-filled eyes. But even after the car had pulled away, the memory of those eyes remained with her. As did Mia's. And Jesse's. And sweet Baby Adeline's.

"Come on, Shirl," Colt said. "Let's go inside. Pumpkin will want a kiss from her aunt before she goes to sleep."

Shirlene shook her head. "You go on. I'll be there in a minute."

Most brothers would've argued. But that was the nice thing about Colt. He understood the importance of solitude.

"Say 'hi' to those Frenchies for me," he said before he slipped out the car door.

After he disappeared inside the trailer, Shirlene only hesitated for a second before she reached for the door handle and climbed out. When she slipped through the hedge, there was no sexy cowboy to greet her. Just an empty lot filled with ruts from an oversized truck, a truck that still sat in town waiting for Billy to be released from jail in the morning. She wondered where Billy had found the outrageous truck. No doubt he had bought it off some poor redneck who didn't care that it would be used to deceive an entire town.

While Sherman rooted around in the yard, Shirlene

climbed the steps to the front door. It was dark inside, but she didn't turn on the lights. The half moon shone brightly through the thin sheets tacked over the window. She stayed away from the bedroom, and instead moved into the living room and sat down in the lopsided recliner. She stared at the small blank screen of the television for a few minutes before the door to the other bedroom caught her attention. It was funny, but she'd never been in the room—never even looked in it.

The room was filled with hunting and fishing equipment—a gun vault, fishing poles, waders, and camouflage vests. And she couldn't help but wonder why a wealthy oil and natural gas tycoon had gone to such extremes to fill the room with country boy clutter. Her gaze fell on the large picture propped against the closet. It was covered with a sheet and seemed so out of place in the room that Shirlene couldn't help but be curious.

Walking around mud-spattered boots and tackle boxes, she reached out and grabbed one edge of the sheet. The material slid easily to the floor, revealing the painting beneath in the soft moonlight. With her hand poised in mid-air, she stared at the nude painting.

It had been a while since she'd looked at it—or maybe she had never really looked at it. It was just another thing Lyle had bought her, something else to fill the nooks and crannies of her mansion. But she looked at it now, carefully studied each feature of the naked, laughing woman who stared back at her.

The artist had painted the picture from a photo Lyle had taken on their honeymoon. Shirlene had been on a margarita high at the time. And she suddenly wondered if she hadn't spent most of her married life under the influence.

She had loved Lyle, but her life with him hadn't been perfect. In fact, it had been lonely. More lonely then she had been willing to admit. Lyle had loved her, but his first love had always been Dalton Oil. And hers had been herself. At least it had been until four orphans showed up. Four orphans and a man who gave her something she hadn't even realized she needed—companionship.

Maybe that was why the woman in the picture looked like a stranger, an old friend Shirlene had once known but who had long since moved away. And with time and distance, Shirlene was better able to see her friend for what she was—a little girl from Grover Road pretending to be a wealthy socialite.

A woman who was as fake as Bubba Wilkes.

"He took it with him the very first day I showed it to him."

Shirlene jumped and glanced over her shoulder to see Beau standing in the doorway, his silver hair gleaming in the moonlight.

She looked back at the painting. "I don't know why. The man thinks I'm nothing more than a spoiled trophy wife."

Beau stepped into the room. "At one time, I wouldn't have denied it. But a man who thinks that about a woman doesn't usually steal their nude painting and store it with his most prized possessions."

"You don't have to lie anymore, Beau," Shirlene said as she slipped the sheet back over the painting. "I know who Billy really is."

"Do you?" he asked, and when she turned she found him examining a container of salmon eggs. He set the jar down and looked at her. "Because I don't think you do,

Shirlene." He waved his hand around. "This is Billy. And so is the thick country twang, and the genuine smile, and the big monster truck. Billy really is a good ol' boy from east Texas. A good ol' boy who loves his family and is willing to do whatever it takes to keep them safe."

"Even ruin a town?"

He released his breath. "Even that. I think Billy would do anything to break The Cates Curse."

"The Cates Curse?" She lifted an eyebrow. "Are you drunk? Or is this some story you made up to get Billy out of jail?"

"Neither, but by the time I finish telling you this story, you might think I'm crazy—or at least, my family is." When she didn't say anything, he continued.

"The Cates Curse has been passed down for generations—a family legend that was given credit by the string of bad luck that seems to haunt the Cates. Thinking to outrun the curse, my daddy left Lubbock when he was nineteen and moved to Dogwood where he met my mother. The move seemed to work until my oldest brother Buck got hit by a train when he was coming home from the prom one night. We all tried to pass it off as a bad accident until Brant's family was killed in a tornado.

"Billy had been traveling with Brant at the time, trying to get C-Corp on its feet. He went with Brant to identify the bodies of Brant's wife and his son. Billy went a little crazy after that—became obsessed with history and The Cates Curse. Still, I don't know if Billy would've ever come to Bramble if I hadn't been diagnosed with cancer."

Beau's words painted a picture more detailed than the one across the room, and Shirlene couldn't help but be pulled in.

"Are you dying?" she asked in a soft whisper.

Beau grinned. "I sure hope not—at least, not yet."

"But how is ruining Bramble going to fix the curse?"

"We both know that it won't," he said. "But I think it gave Brant a purpose to live again, and Billy was willing to go along with anything that might save his brother—until he started to become attached to Bramble. And not just the town, but the people."

"Has it made a difference?" she asked. "Are you going to keep Dalton Oil open?" Even in the dim light, she could read the answer on his face. "That's what I thought." She tried to move past him, but he took her arm.

"Just give him a chance, Shirlene," Beau pleaded. "If anyone can fix it, Billy can. He's a genius at figuring things out."

"If he is such a genius, Beau, he never would've lied."

Sherman's loud squeals had Shirlene pulling away from Beau and heading for the door. By the time she got down the steps, she understood what had the pig so excited. Jesse stood in the yard, his Superman shirt ripped and his chest pumping in and out as if he'd run for miles.

"Jesse!" She raced across the yard and tried to pull him into her arms. But he wasn't having it.

"Don't touch me!" he yelled as he jerked away. "I hate you! You pretended like you liked us, but it was all a lie."

"That's not true, Jesse," she tried to soothe him. "I like you—in fact, I love you. You, and Brody, and Mia, and Adeline are everything to me."

Tears trickled down the boy's cheeks, causing Shirlene's heart to rise to her throat. "Then why didn't you fight for us? Why did you let them take us without a fight?"

She swallowed back her own tears. "It's not that simple, Jesse. You can't fight the law."

He stared back at her, his voice shaking. "Billy did. They stopped him, but at least he tried. He fought until he couldn't fight no more." He glanced up to see Beau coming down the steps. "Billy!" He raced over, but came to a skidding stop when he saw who it was. "Where's Billy? Is he inside?" He tried to rush past Beau, but Beau held him back.

"Sorry, buddy, but Billy isn't in there. He's in the city jail."

Jesse's legs finally gave out, and he slumped down on the dirt at Beau's feet, his sobs harsh and heartbreaking.

Unsure of what to do, Shirlene stared down at him. Jesse was hysterical, and suddenly she felt pretty hysterical herself. Hysterical because the boy was right. She hadn't fought to keep them. She'd just stood there and let a strange woman take her kids. Just stood there waiting for someone to come to her rescue. Except it wasn't up to some knight in shining armor. Or her brother. Or even the town. It was up to her. She was the only one who could earn the children's respect. And this time it would take more than handing over an expensive ring. This time it would take courage and action.

Shirlene glanced down at the pig who sat at her feet. "What do you say, Piglet? You want to go kidnap a group of orphans?"

Chapter Thirty

BILLY FELT LIKE he had the one time he'd tried to ride a Brahma bull and failed—sore, achy, and pissed that he'd been unable to achieve what he'd set out to do.

Shirlene hated him. And the kids were gone.

He lifted the Naked Barbie off the bed next to him. Brody had entrusted the doll into Billy's care so it wouldn't get wet in the sprinklers and, in the excitement of the day, had forgotten to reclaim it. Billy had worked so hard to get the kid to quit playing with the doll. Now, damned if he wasn't torn up about the little boy having to do without it.

Even firing Mr. Peabody hadn't made him feel any better.

What had the uppity man been thinking when he'd reported the kids to Children's Services? Of course, it wasn't his fault as much as Billy's for having him look up the VIN number of the Impala in the first place and for waiting until tonight to call Judge Myers. He just hadn't wanted to upset the apple cart. To disrupt the dream he'd been living in with Shirlene and the kids. A dream he'd started to believe in.

Until reality woke him.

Billy stared down at Barbie's skinny body and ran a finger over the hard curves that were nothing like Shirlene's sweet, soft ones.

"I knew a feller once who had one of them blowup dolls."

The Barbie clattered to the floor as Billy came to his feet and stared at Moses Tate, who had somehow gotten into the room without Billy knowing it. The old man stood on the other side of the bars, his eyes squinting down at the doll.

"Used to let her ride next to him in his pickup like she was his girlfriend or somethin'. 'Course that came to a terrible end one day when Earl got out for gas and that darned thing floated right out after him. Dolly might've survived if Tinker Jones' coon hound hadn't gotten after her." He shook his head. "Ripped her up like a garbage bag, leaving poor Earl with nothin' but a tiny pair of pokey-dotted panties."

Billy cleared his throat. "That's quite a story."

"No better than the one you told us today," Moses said. "You had me fooled, boy. I'd figured out Beau, but I never figured on you."

"I'm sorry, sir."

Moses shrugged. "I figure family sticks up for family, and what we did to your family was a cryin' shame."

"I still had no right to deceive you." Billy sat down on the bed and ran a hand over his face.

"Nope, you didn't. But it ain't nothin' I can't forgive." He shot him a sly look. "'Course, sorry might work for me—with one foot in the grave, I can't afford to hold a grudge—but a simple sorry ain't gonna work for that gal's broken heart."

Billy didn't need to ask who he was talking about. "I

know, and I intend to get those kids back to her as soon as I get out of here."

"I wasn't talking about the kids, son—anyone with half a brain knows you love those kids as much as she does." He pointed a finger that was as bent and gnarled as a hickory stick. "What you have to prove is your love for her."

Billy stared at the old guy. "Love her? Shirlene Dalton?"

"Well, I ain't talkin' about that nekked doll on the floor."

"But..." Billy got up from the bed and started to pace. "I don't...I mean I like her—no, I more than like her. She's sassy, and funny, and the kindest woman I've ever met." He kept pacing, now talking to himself more than to Moses. "And when she smiles, it's like the sun just popped up over the horizon—like your day has just started, and you didn't know it until you looked into those beautiful green eyes. And when she kisses you, it's like you're a big piece of chocolate cake and she's a chocoholic. It makes you feel about ten feet tall. Like you could do anything you set your mind to—anything at all."

He stopped pacing and stared at the picture of the Texas state flag as the truth finally sank in. "I love her." He looked back at Moses. "I love Shirlene Dalton."

Moses grinned, displaying his purplish gums. "I know, son. But it ain't gonna make no difference if we can't get you out of there." He held up a ring of keys that weighed so much it caused the old guy to take a couple shuffling steps back. "Damn, Sam and his key fetish. It's likely to take us all night just to find the right one. 'Course I figure that will give me plenty of time to tell you the story I came to tell you."

But before Moses could start on another story, a loud

clank drew their attention to the window. Billy walked over and opened it to find Kenny Gene standing there holding a tow rope that had already been attached to the bars.

"I'm breakin' you out, Bubba," he said loud enough to wake up the entire town. "I know it will ruin my chances of becomin' a dep-u-tee. But since I broke my binoculars, I ain't got the right equipment, anyway."

"Well, I sure appreciate that but—" Billy started, but Kenny was already on his way to the truck that was parked on the grass just outside. The engine revved, and the truck shot across the lawn, spitting chunks of turf behind it. Billy might've taken cover from flying plaster if he hadn't noticed that the tow rope wasn't attached to Kenny's bumper.

"Darn fool," Moses muttered as he worked his way through the key ring. Billy watched his shaky hands for a few seconds before he turned back to the window to see if Kenny had finally noticed he wasn't dragging the bars behind him. A face popped up in the window. A face that had Billy jumping back in fear.

"Hey, handsome," Rachel Dean said. At least, Billy thought it was Rachel Dean. It was hard to tell with her hair twisted up in curlers and the layer of green goop on her face. "I couldn't sleep a wink thinkin' about your poor ol' granddaddy, so I got up and made you some of my cinnamon buns. I ain't never been much of a cook, but..." she winked and Billy couldn't help but think of the little insurance lizard on those television commercials, "I figured a man like you would know good buns when he saw them." She tried to fit the plate through the bars, and when that didn't work, she tried handing them to him. But between the size of the buns and her man hands, it was a lost cause.

"I'll just bring them in," she said, right before her head disappeared.

"Good Lord, Rachel," Harley Sutter's voice drifted over to Billy. "You like to scare me to death. What are you doin' traipsin' around in the dark?" The man's head appeared, his handlebar mustache almost reaching from one side of the small window to the other. "Well, hey, Bubba, how you doin', son?"

"Just fine, sir," Billy answered, although he was more than a little confused by all these midnight visitors.

"How's that room treatin' you?"

"Snug as a bug in a rug." Billy glanced around the jail cell that looked more like the guest room at his Aunt Clara's—from the brass bed and crocheted toilet paper cover to the rag rug and patchwork quilt. The hallway door flew open, and Rachel Dean came flopping in wearing a chenille robe that had seen better days and a pair of red galoshes.

"Well, hey there, Moses, I didn't know you was visitin'." She held out the plate of cinnamon buns, but the old man shook his head.

"If they're as hard as your cookies, my gums can't take 'em."

"I sure wouldn't mind one," Harley said before he disappeared from the window. He wasn't gone for more than a few seconds when the top of a head appeared.

A head Billy recognized immediately. Or maybe it wasn't the head he recognized as much as the teased, towering hair.

"Hey, Bubba," Twyla said. "I figured you might be lonely, so I came by to keep you company."

"He don't need company," Kenny came running back up. "He needs to be broke out. So get out of the way, woman."

"Don't you tell me what to do, Kenny Gene," Twyla snapped. "We ain't married yet." Her hand with the huge diamond ring popped up in the window. "Ain't it purdy?"

"I'd ask what's going on here," a deep voice interrupted. "But since you always seem to be in the middle of a town ruckus, big brother, I figure it's par for the course." Beau's face appeared. Billy had to admit it was a welcome sight.

"You bustin' out, Billy?" he asked with a smirk on his face.

"At this rate, the answer would be no."

Beau laughed. "Well, I'll see what I can do about that."

Fifteen minutes later, Beau was on the other side of the bars along with half the town. But Billy was no closer to breaking out. Moses couldn't seem to find the right key. Of course, with everyone gnawing on Rachel's cinnamon buns and trying to help, it couldn't be easy.

Billy sat on the bed, holding a cold washcloth to his eye. He should be irritated with their ineptitude, but instead he couldn't help smiling. It seemed the people of Bramble weren't the type of folks to hold a grudge. Even with a man who might be responsible for the town's demise. It was endearing, and at the same time, filled him with more guilt than a sinner in Sunday school.

"That's sure a shiner you got, Bubba," Rye Pickett said. "You get that from Slate or Colt?"

"It looked to me like Colt's knee when Billy was tryin' to beat up those police officers," Rossie Owens said.

"Well, they deserved to be beat up." Rachel Dean released her breath in a huff. "It just don't seem right that some strange folks would take our kids. I don't care if they did have the right paperwork."

"They didn't just have paperwork, Rachel," Sheriff Winslow spoke around a mouthful of bun. "They had guns with bullets."

"You call them guns," Rye Pickett jumped in. "Why those was nothin' more than pea shooters."

"Well, pea shooters or not," Harley said, "I agree with Rachel. The Fosters are part of our community, and we should've done what Bubba did. We should've fought for them. Possession is nine-tense the law, you know. And once they get to Houston, we might never get them back."

"Unless they don't make it to Houston."

Everyone turned and looked at Beau, who was checking out his front teeth after trying to take a bite of one of Rachel Dean's buns. When he finally noticed everyone looking at him, he explained. "If Shirlene has anything to do about it, those kids will be back here by morning."

Billy came up off the bed and moved over to the bars. "What do you mean, Beau?"

His brother grinned broadly. "Only that your girlfriend has decided she's not going to wait around for a judge. I think she's planning on kidnapping them back tonight—with the help of a young redheaded escapee who knows exactly what motel they're staying the night at."

Billy grabbed the bars and shook them. "And why the hell didn't you tell me this before?"

"Because I knew you'd do exactly what you're doing. You'd overreact. Besides, there's not much you can do when you're locked up in jail."

"So why didn't you go with her? She needs someone watching out for her." Billy reached through the bars for his brother, but Beau jumped back just in time.

"Believe me, the woman who raced off in the Navigator didn't look like a woman who needed watching out for. She looked like a she-devil on a mission. Besides, I tried going with her, but she flat out refused—something about not trusting the Cates boys as far as she could throw them. You sure did a number on her, Billy."

"I don't want to hear that crap right now, Beau," Billy growled. "I want you to get me out of this jail cell so I can go get her before she ends up in jail herself."

Rye puffed up like a toad. "No one's gonna arrest our little Shirlene. I'll make sure of that."

"They sure aren't." Harley looked at Beau. "You said you knew where the kids are, son?" When Beau nodded, he herded him toward the door. "Then what are we waitin' for? Time's a wastin'."

"You're not goin' anywhere without me, Harley Sutter," Rachel said as flopped toward the door. "Those kids might need some tender lovin' care."

There was a chorus of agreement as everyone shuffled out.

"Wait!" Billy called after them, but his only response was the click of the door as it closed.

"Don't you worry, boy," Moses said. "I'll have you out in a jiffy." His hands shook so badly that he dropped the keys to the floor. Billy was about to go after them when an engine revved followed by the creak and grating noise of shifting bricks and stucco. With a loud clang, the bars disappeared, along with the window and half the bricks in the wall.

Billy raced over to the opening. And there was Kenny grinning and waving out the window of Billy's monster truck.

"We just needed a little more power, is all!"

Chapter Thirty-one

MIA SHIFTED ON THE HARD MOTEL MATTRESS, careful not to wake Brody, who was curled against her side. It had taken forever to get him to sleep. While Adeline had worn herself out crying, Brody had continued to sob until Mia had made up a tall tale about them going on a nice little vacation and Billy taking care of Shirlene and Barbie while they were gone.

She reached out and stroked her fingers through Brody's hair. For a second, one brief wonderful second, she'd thought her life had finally taken a turn for the better—thought she had finally found her happily-ever-after. She should've known better. Happily-ever-afters were just something you told children to put them to sleep so they would have enough strength to survive the next day. Except Mia was tired of surviving. She wanted to rest, to lie down and go to sleep and never wake up. And maybe she would do that after the babies were safe.

Maybe she would do that.

Mia had just closed her eyes when someone pounded on the door. She sat up, part of her hoping it was Jesse, and the other part hoping he'd escaped the life she was destined to live.

"W-what?" Ms. Buddager sat up in bed, sounding confused and disoriented. She was one of the nicer case workers Mia had had to deal with. She seemed genuinely concerned about kids—making arrangements to stop for the night so Mia could get the babies out of their car seats and soothe them and frantically calling the police when Jesse ran off. It only took her a moment to switch on the lamp by the bed and slip her feet over the edge of the mattress.

"Who is it?" Ms. Buddager asked when she reached the door.

"Room service," a nasally voice replied.

"Well, for heaven sakes, I didn't call for room service." She slid the chain back. Mia started to warn the woman that it was doubtful that this motel even had room service. But before she could say anything, the door was pushed open, and Shirlene stood there with Jesse. In her hand was Brody's toy gun. She pointed it at Ms. Buddager. The woman moved against the wall and lifted her hands.

Mia slipped out of bed. "What are you doing?"

Shirlene flashed a big smile. "I'm gettin' my kids back."

For a moment, Mia felt a bubbling excitement. But it fizzled quickly when reality took hold. "It doesn't work like that, Shirlene. You can't just take us back—they'll only come and get us again."

"I've been thinking about that, and I figure that Lyle Dalton knew enough people in high places to help us out." Shirlene waved the cap gun. "And until we can talk to those people, I'm sticking to you like glue. Even if I have to travel all the way to Houston with you and beat the tar out of Auntie Barb and Uncle Mickey."

The thought of Shirlene taking down her foster parents had Mia smiling. Or maybe it was the fact that Shirlene was willing to fight for them after all.

"Why, Lord have mercy," Shirlene said. "Mia Michaels knows how to smile. I thought that frown was permanently affixed." She looked over at Ms. Buddager. "Sorry, honey. I know you're just doing your job, but I love these kids, and I refuse to let them go back to an abusive situation."

"Abusive?" Ms. Buddager dropped her hands. "The Primples were abusive?"

Shirlene looked over at Mia. "I realize you're the kind of person who likes to carry the entire load on your shoulders, but don't you think it's about time you released it to someone else?"

Mia might've found the courage to tell Ms. Buddager all the things she'd been keeping to herself all these years if there hadn't been a commotion outside the door. Jesse raced over and pulled it open. The sight that greeted Mia completely took her by surprise. The entire town of Bramble seemed to be standing outside.

"What in the world?" Shirlene took the words right out of Mia's mouth.

"We came to get our kids," Mayor Sutter said as his big stomach led the way into the room.

"We sure did." Rachel moved up next to him, looking so scary that Jesse took a step back. "We ain't gonna let strangers come in and take what's ours." She winked. "And y'all are ours."

Mia struggled to fight back the tears as Ms. Buddager finally moved away from the wall.

"Well, I'll be. This is the first time I've had to deal with something like this." Ms. Buddager shook her head. "Unfortunately, I can't hand these children over without going through the proper channels." She glanced at Shirlene. "But I give you my word they won't go back to the Primples." Her gaze drifted down to the gun. "Or to a woman who brandishes guns."

"Even if those guns only shoot caps?" Billy pushed his way into the room. His shirt was ripped, and his hair all mussed. One eye was puffed up, and there was a knot on his stubbly chin. Mia still wasn't sure that he hadn't turned them in, but she had to admit he looked pretty pathetic. Pathetic but determined.

He pinned Ms. Buddager with a steely stare. "I realize you're only doing your job, but these kids belong with Ms. Dalton." He looked behind him. "Which is exactly why I brought along my good friend, Judge Myers."

A man pushed his way through the crowd and scowled at Billy. "Good friend might be a stretch, Billy Cates, seein' as how you woke me up from a sound sleep and practically ordered me to get on your helicopter and fly here."

"You can hate me later, Judge. For now, you need to get this woman to release these kids into Shirlene Dalton's custody."

Judge Myers looked at Shirlene. "How are you, Ms. Dalton? I don't know if you remember me, but we met at a Houston benefit." He studied her tattered western shirt, cut-offs, and flip-flops, then looked down at his wrinkled shirt and jeans. "We were both dressed a little differently at the time."

Shirlene smiled. "Of course I remember you, honey. And please call me Shirlene. Most folks do."

"Cap, you say?" He stared at the gun, and a smile flirted with his lips. It dropped only seconds later. "I wish I could just hand these kids over to you, Shirlene, especially when it looks like you're ready to go to any lengths to keep them. But we both know that that's not how things work. There's paperwork that needs to be filled out, and red tape that has to be cut."

Pastor Robbins moved to the front of the crowd. "I've got the paperwork right here, sir." He held out a stack of papers and the judge looked them over before handing them to Ms. Buddager.

She examined them and then looked back at the pastor in shock. "How did you get them completed and signed so quickly?"

Pastor Robbins looked over at Shirlene. "After Ms. Dalton came in to talk with me, it wasn't so hard to figure out what orphans she was talking about. Especially when every time she came to town, she brought them with her. So by the time she got me the paperwork, I'd already done some research and gotten the ball rolling, so to speak."

Ms. Buddager shook her head. "But still, it usually takes months."

Pastor Robbins smiled and glanced up at the ceiling. "Let's just say, I've got connections in high places."

"So I can have the kids tonight?" Shirlene asked.

It took a moment for Ms. Buddager to pull her gaze away from the ceiling. "I'll have to check out your living conditions."

Mia felt her heart sink. Even Shirlene looked a little sick to her stomach.

"That shouldn't be a problem," Billy stated. "Everyone knows that Shirlene Dalton lives in the biggest house in town."

"She sure does," Mayor Sutter agreed. "With plenty of room for an entire brood of children."

Ms. Buddager's gaze wandered around the room filled with expectant faces. "Well, in that case..."

Jumping in the air, Jesse let out a whoop that woke up Brody. After Mia picked him up to soothe him, the little boy stared in wide-eyed wonder at all the people in the room. When his eyes landed on Billy, Billy pulled the Barbie from his back pocket and held it out to him.

"I think you forgot something, son."

Brody grinned and reached for the doll, but his hand dropped when he noticed Shirlene. Both hands came up as he bellowed in his loud, deep voice.

"Mama! Mama!"

For a split second, Mia felt a stab of jealousy. But it left quickly enough when Brody cuddled up against Shirlene, who wasn't even trying to hide the tears that trickled down her cheeks.

Too bad Ms. Buddager had to go and ruin the moment with her next words.

"You need to realize that this is only temporary, Ms. Dalton. Adoption has an entirely different set of paper work and requirements. And they frown on single parents, especially with four children."

The judge nodded. "She's right. One child would be a possibility—maybe two, but four..."

"What about three?" Mia finally spoke. "They'd let Shirlene adopt three kids, wouldn't they? I mean, Jesse is old enough to help her with Brody so all she'd have to worry about is Adeline. And I'm sure Ms. Buddager could find me another home until I'm eighteen."

A stunned silence followed, and it was hard not

to fidget beneath all the eyes pinned on her. Then suddenly an arm encircled Mia, and she was tugged close to Shirlene's big breasts.

"Not a chance, honey," Shirlene spoke loud enough for every person in the room to hear. "We're a family. And everyone knows that families stick together."

A chorus of "amen" had tears leaking from Mia's eyes.

Hope was a funny thing: It had a way of rekindling even when you thought it was completely snuffed out. And as much as Mia tried to ignore it, a small flame flickered to life in her heart. A flame that soon burned as bright as the smile on Shirlene Dalton's face.

Chapter Thirty-two

THE FOUNDER'S DAY ACTIVITIES WERE held in Confederate Park in the center of town. Big oil-drum grills were lined up behind the playground, offering up burnt hot dogs and undercooked hamburgers, while Josephine's smoker sat in the far corner, puffing out the fragrant smell of smoking cherry wood and barbeque spices. A number of booths and activities had been set up along the pathways leading to the gazebo, a gazebo that resembled a purple fairytale castle with its strings of twinkle lights and the civil war cannons positioned on either side.

Sitting on a blanket beneath a shade tree, Shirlene tried her best to smile at the people who stopped to chat. But it was hard to smile when images of the last time she'd been in the park kept popping into her brain—images of Billy playing with the kids while she had looked on like a lovesick idiot. She was still an idiot. Because no matter how much she tried, she couldn't seem to forget the man. Not his dopey smile. Or his stupid hick talk. Or his sweet kisses.

Even if they had been nothing more than a pack of lies.

"Mama!"

Shirlene looked over at the face painting booth where Colt had taken Brody and waved at the beaming boy with the Spiderman webs painted across his chubby cheeks. Ever since the night at the motel, Brody had called her mama. He'd even taught it to Adeline. The word brought a warm feeling to her stomach, but a tightening to her heart. The kids might be living with her now, but for how long? As Ms. Buddager had said, the rules for adoption were much different from the rules for fostering. Still, Shirlene wasn't going to worry about it today. The kids deserved some fun, and she was determined to see that they had some.

"Come on, Piglet," she said as she gently nudged the sleeping pig awake. "Let's go see where Faith and Slate took Adeline." But just as she got to her feet, Harley Sutter's loud voice rang out through the park.

"If I could have y'all's attention." The mayor of Bramble stood on the steps of the gazebo, a bullhorn held to his mustached mouth. "I need everyone to head on over to the town hall for a very special presentation."

Since the folks in Bramble loved presentations about as much as they loved weddings, the entire park headed across the street. Shirlene glanced around for the kids. Mia had gotten Adeline from Hope and was heading over to the town hall, while Brody was being carried over by Colt. Which left only Jesse unaccounted for. And knowing how easily the boy could find trouble, Shirlene weaved her way through the crowd searching for him.

When she reached the maples in front of the town hall, she realized she'd been right. Jesse had found trouble. Trouble in the form of a handsome, lean cowboy who had Shirlene taking a step back. His intense brown gaze slid over to her, hitting her harder than a punch in the gut, and she turned with every intention of collecting the kids and getting the hell out of there. Unfortunately, the crowd closed in, pushing her closer to the man and the large tarp-covered object that had been placed in front of the town hall dedication plaque.

"I'd like to welcome y'all to the Founder's Day festivities," Harley's voice reverberated through the bullhorn. "As you know, it was over a hundred years ago that we first dedicated our town hall with a beautiful plaque made by Will—" A high-pitched squeal came from the horn, and Sherman answered with an ear-splitting squeal of his own, leaving Harley with no other option than to turn off the horn.

"Beg pardon," he said before he continued in a voice that needed no amplification. "Well, I guess we don't have to go into the particulars, but needless to say, we feel real bad about what happened to your great-granddaddy. And we wanted to acknowledge the sacrifice your folks made all those years ago. Especially considerin' how hard you and your brother have been workin' to keep Dalton Oil open."

Harley handed the bullhorn to Kenny Gene, who was grinning like a Cheshire cat, then motioned to Billy and his brother. Shirlene hadn't noticed Beau standing next to Billy and Jesse, looking as handsome and cocky as ever. As he followed his brother over to where Harley stood, he flashed her a dazzling smile. She ignored it and turned back to Harley.

"Hope you like it, boys," Harley stated as he motioned for Kenny to take off the tarp. It took more than a few moments, which only seemed to heighten the anticipation of the crowd. Finally, Rye Pickett stepped up and helped, and the tarp was pulled free to the "oohs" and "ahhs" of the townsfolk.

Shirlene didn't know what she expected. But it wasn't a life-sized piñata of Billy Wilkes. The color of the eyes was a little off, but the features were almost perfect, as was the height and the width of the papier mâché body dressed in the tissue-paper western shirt and jeans. The only differences between the piñata and the man standing next to it were that the piñata had a John Deere cap and a fishing pole.

"We didn't have a picture of your great-granddaddy, so we had to improvise," Harley said with a truck full of pride in his voice. "Of course, this isn't the permanent one. We're havin' a bronze one made in Lubbock. But until we get it, Darla was nice enough to offer her skills at papier mâché." Since Billy and Beau seemed speechless, Harley continued. "Now I know you'd rather have your granddaddy's bones, but we looked high and low and couldn't find a headstone or a grave anywhere around Bramble with William Cates's name on it."

A loud snort pulled everyone's attention to Moses Tate, who stood by the flag pole squinting out at the crowd.

"That's because he ain't buried here, you durn fools."

"So where's he buried, Mr. Tate?" Kenny yelled through the bullhorn.

While the rest of the town covered their ears, Moses seemed unaffected by the volume. "Don't have a clue. All I know is you ain't gonna find no bones around Bramble because William Cates didn't die here."

A mutter of confusion rose up from the crowd, and Billy stepped forward.

"Are you saying my grandfather never came to this town?"

Seemingly unconcerned with the bomb he'd just dropped, Moses took his time pulling the squashed plastic cup out of his shirt pocket and spit a stream of tobacco in it. After he wiped off his mouth, he shrugged his bony shoulders.

"I ain't sayin' that a'tall. According to my grandpappy, that much is true. William Cates did come to Bramble to deliver the plaque he'd made. And he did end up fightin' with the mayor over the money owed him. But that's where the story takes a turn. Cates wasn't shot down in the middle of the street. Instead he and the mayor came to one of them compromises: When the town hall was finished, Cates would deliver a new plaque with the right dates. And for makin' the trip from Lubbock, the town would treat him to a night at Miss Hattie's Henhouse."

A startled gasp had Shirlene looking over at Ms. Murphy, whose face was even paler than usual. Obviously, the woman was offended by just the mention of the legendary brothel.

"It was there that William Cates got in a fight during a poker game," Moses said. "There that he was shot dead and his body disposed of by Miss Hattie in an attempt to keep things quiet."

"But why would they want to keep it quiet?" Beau asked.

Moses' gaze snapped over to Beau. "You think your grandmammy would've liked hearin' that her man died in a whorehouse?" While Beau blushed, Moses looked back at Billy. "I'm sorry, son. I planned on tellin' you the night I came to break you out of jail." He shot an exasperated look at the crowd. "But folks kept interruptin' me."

"So Sheriff Wynn Murdock didn't kill my grandfather?" Billy said.

"That I couldn't say. My grandpappy was upstairs when the shootin' broke out downstairs in the poker room. Since most the men in Bramble showed up at Hattie's on a Saturday night, I guess it's possible."

Billy shook his head. "I understand why they lied about what happened, but why didn't they send the body back to Lubbock for a proper funeral?"

"Probably because none of the towns within a day's ride had a mortician. And in west Texas in August a body can turn ripe purdy darn quick."

A stunned silence followed, as if no one knew what to say or do. As usual, it was Kenny Gene who finally spoke, this time without the bullhorn.

"So does this mean we ain't gonna do our other surprise?"

Harley only hesitated for a second before he hitched up his pants and shook his head. "'Course not. One doesn't have nothin' to do with the other. Besides, I think findin' out we aren't responsible for Bubba's granddaddy's death is cause for celebration."

His words were barely out of his mouth before Twyla and Cindy Lynn hooked their arms through Shirlene's and pulled her from the crowd. Still stunned by Moses' story, she didn't put up a fight until Harley took her hand and joined it with Beau's.

"I realize she isn't as good a gift as a statue, but she's a fine woman with a heart of gold."

Shirlene stared at him for only a moment before the truth hit her. "Are you crazy?" she yelled as she jerked her hand back from Beau, who seemed in no hurry to relinquish it. "You can't just give people away!"

"Of course, you can." Twyla flopped a veil on Shirlene's

head. "My daddy gave me away three times. Although he swears the next time he ain't takin' me back."

"Well, no one is giving me away." Shirlene tried to rip the veil off, but it was firmly attached to her hair with some kind of wicked clip.

"Now, Shirl." Darla rammed an ugly purple bouquet at her. "Don't get all bent out of shape. We all know you've been shackin' up with Beau for the last couple weeks. And you can't let a fox into the henhouse without makin' him pay for the eggs."

Beau's laughter rang out, but it fizzled when his big brother spoke.

"She's not marrying Beau."

Darla's hand dropped, and Twyla stopped fussing with the veil. As mad as she was at Billy, Shirlene was thankful for his timely interruption. If the crazy townsfolk would listen to anyone, it was their "Bubba." Except instead of reasoning with the crowd, he took off his hat and spoke directly to her. And it was hard to look away from the sincerity in his dark eyes.

"I know you don't want to talk to me," he said in a soft voice. "And I don't blame you. I acted exactly like the lowdown scoundrel you called me, and there isn't one thing I can say that will change that. But before I leave, I need to apologize. To you," he looked out at the crowd, "and the entire town. You folks treated me like family while all I could see was revenge—revenge for something you weren't even responsible for. I'm sorry for that. You *have* become family to me, and I'll never forget my time here in Bramble."

Sadness settled over the faces of the townspeople. Shirlene knew how they felt. The thought of never seeing

Billy again had her heart aching, and it took everything she had inside to keep her knees from giving out as he turned back to her.

"But I'm especially sorry for what I did to you, Shirlene. All the lies and games." His eyes seemed to stare straight through her. "But you need to know that they ended the moment you stepped into my arms. From that moment on, everything I felt was real—more real than anything has ever felt in my life. Because the truth is . . ." He reached out and ran the back of his knuckles down her cheek. "I love you, Shirley Girl, and I will until the day I die."

Mumbles of confusion filtered up from the crowd, quickly followed by a wave of excited chatter that had Twyla readjusting the veil, and Darla wrapping Shirlene's hand around the bouquet.

"Shirlene and Bubba," Rachel Dean sighed. "I don't know why I didn't see it before."

"It does makes sense." Harley beamed. "They're two peas in a pod."

"Two doves on a telephone line," Darla gushed.

"She did it again," Cindy Lynn huffed. "She up and got herself a sugar daddy."

"Yippee!" Jesse let out a loud whoop and punched the air. "Billy's gonna be my sugar daddy!"

"No." Shirlene released the bouquet, and it hit the cement with a thump as loud as the breaking of her own heart. "No, Jesse. Billy's not going to be your daddy." Tears welled up in her eyes as she turned to the town. "Because I'm not marrying Billy Cates. You see, I've had Bubba-lovin'. And believe me, it ain't all that."

The townsfolk were so stunned that anyone would turn

down Bubba Wilkes that they didn't even try to stop her as she shoved her way through the crowd and raced down the street. Shirlene didn't know where she was going; she just knew she had to get away before she did something really stupid. Like allow the town to marry her to the biggest liar in east Texas.

Ducking into the alley way between the bank and the hardware store, Shirlene hurried behind the trash bin and leaned back against the brick wall. Tears dripped down her cheeks, and she let them. In a minute, she would brush them away and go back out to face the town. Of course, she should've known that a minute was too much to ask for. Especially with a best friend who had run track in high school.

Hope came around the corner of the dumpster. With all the excitement and a houseful of kids to take care of, this was the first time they'd been alone since Hope had returned from California. And Hope didn't waste any time getting down to the nitty gritty.

"Geez, Shirl." She leaned back on the opposite wall and wiped the sweat from her brow. "I leave town for a few days and just look at how much trouble you get into."

She counted off on her fingers. "You get evicted from your house. Have a heated affair with a young man barely out of diapers. Stumble upon a band of orphans. Hold up a bank. And steal my pig right out from under my nose."

"I did not have an affair with Beau Cates," Shirlene sniffed. "Or steal your pig."

Hope's blue eyes shifted down to Sherman, who had followed Shirlene into the alley and was now snuffling around for something to eat. "I don't know what you'd call it when he refuses to leave your side."

"He's just worried about me, is all." Shirlene squatted to scratch the pig's head.

Hope slid down the wall and sat on the ground across from Shirlene. "So you love Billy, don't you?"

If it had been anyone else asking the question, Shirlene might've been able to lie. But it was hard to lie to a woman she'd confided in for most of her life.

"Yes." She snorted. "Which just goes to show you how screwed up I was after Lyle's death. I probably would've fallen in love with just about anyone who gave me the time of day."

"But you didn't." Hope stared back at her, her blue eyes all-knowing. "Are you just going to let him go?"

A tear trickled down Shirlene's cheek, but she quickly brushed it away. "I don't have another choice. I'm not willing to spend the rest of my life with a man I can't trust as far as I can spit. I deserve better than that. And so do my kids."

"I trust Billy."

The softly spoken words had both women turning. Faith stood in the opening of the alley, her big eyes sincere and as watery as Shirlene's.

"We all lie, Shirl," Faith said as she moved closer. "I lied when I pretended to be Hope—first to the entire town and then to Slate. And Hope lied about doing well in Hollywood and her feelings for Colt. You even lied when you tried to keep everyone from finding out that you'd spent all of Lyle's money. Not to forget all the lies you told to keep the Foster kids from being sent back to an abusive situation."

Hope got to her feet. "I hate to say it, but my little sister's got a point. We're all willing to lie if the justification is big enough. What matters is taking responsibility for our lies and doing what it takes to make things right. And Billy Cates has done a damned good job of making things right. Not only did he stop the kids from being hauled back to Houston, but he's gone against his big brother and is making every effort to save Dalton Oil."

A loud rumble drew their gazes to the street. And Shirlene watched as a monster truck drove past with flags flapping. But Billy didn't even glance her way. His gaze was riveted on the road ahead.

A road that led away from Bramble . . . and her.

A sob broke free. And before Shirlene knew it, she was crying like Baby Adeline when she was forced to take a nap. Hope and Faith were at her side in an instant, but Shirlene wasn't the type of woman who took sympathy well.

Holding up a hand, she spoke between sobs. "I'm okay, really. I just haven't gotten very much sleep in the last couple days—what with Adeline cutting molars and Brody getting used to a new house." She took a deep breath and released it before she sniffed back the tears and tried to send both women the most convincing smile she could.

"See, I'm just fine." Her voice broke, and Faith blinked back her own tears while Hope studied Shirlene like a parasite under a microscope.

"Truth or Dare, Shirl?"

"What?" Shirlene stared at her friend in confusion.

"You know the game," Hope said. "You've made me play it enough over the years. So answer the question, truth or dare?"

Shirlene sniffed. "You know I always choose dare, honey."

Smiling, Hope took her hand and squeezed. "I also know you've never chickened out on a dare yet."

"And never will," she confirmed with a weak smile.

Suddenly Hope looked as close to tears as Faith. "So here's your dare, Shirl. I dare you to go after what you want. You've always told me that people make their own happiness, so I dare you to make yours. I dare you to forget the past and concentrate on the future. I dare you to go after the man you love."

Chapter Thirty-three

THE FOLLOWING DAY, Billy pulled up in front of the southwestern-style home Slate Calhoun had built. With Beau only moments behind him, he didn't waste any time climbing down from the truck and heading toward the double doors. But before he reached the small courtyard, he glanced over the stucco wall of the side yard and spotted a crumpled cowboy hat. Moving around to the gate, he slipped inside and was immediately greeted by Slate's dog, Buster.

"Hey, boy, how you doin'?" Billy leaned over to scratch the dog's ears as the black Labradoodle danced around his legs. He glanced up to see Slate leaning on a shovel in the shade of a cedar tree.

"You need something, Cates?" he asked.

Billy straightened, his eyes trained on the shovel. "A few seconds of your time would sure be appreciated." When Slate only stared back at him, Billy took off his cowboy hat and rolled the brim through his hands. But the speech he'd planned on giving suddenly seemed windy and redundant. So he tried to condense it, and ended up sounding like the dumb country boy he was.

"Growing up, I never worked real hard at making friends. With four brothers, I always had plenty of people to play with." Billy cleared his throat. "So I never knew what it was like to have a best buddy that wasn't related—a buddy to complain about my crazy family to, or just talk about similar interests. I didn't figure it out until it was too late—something I regret."

Slate continued to stare at him, and Billy realized it was a lost cause. No stupid speech was going to make Slate forgive him. So he gave up on words and dug in his front pocket for the keys to the truck.

"Here." He tossed the keys over to Slate who reached out and caught them. "Take care of her for me." Tugging his hat back on, he headed to the gate.

"I'm afraid I can't do that," Slate said.

By the time Billy turned, Slate had dropped the shovel and taken a few steps closer.

"You don't want the truck?" Billy asked.

Slate pushed his crumpled straw cowboy hat up on his forehead. "No, I want the truck. But that's not really what you're talking about it, is it?"

Damn, maybe Billy didn't want a best friend after all. He released his breath and rested his hands on his hips. "Fine. I'd sure appreciate it if you looked in on Shirlene for me from time to time."

Slate quirked an eyebrow. "I could do that, but we both know that's not what Shirlene needs. She doesn't need a friend looking in on her. She needs a man who'll be there for her night and day. For her and those kids."

"You were there in town yesterday. She doesn't want me."

"You're right. She doesn't want the man who set out

to ruin Bramble." Slate dusted his hands off on his jeans. "But she might want the man who decided to reorganize Dalton Oil and see if he can't save it. The man who took care of the lien against her house. And the man who is pulling every string imaginable to make it possible for her to adopt those kids."

Billy stared at him. "Who told you?"

"Colt." Slate grinned. "He called your brother Brant to read him the riot act."

"And how did Brant take that?" Billy couldn't help but smile at the thought of the two stubborn men locking horns.

"Not well. It seems he's a little perturbed with his brothers for outvoting him in the last shareholders' meeting." Slate shook his head. "I can understand you changing your mind about closing Dalton Oil, but how did you get your other brothers to go along with you? Even if your grandfather didn't die in Bramble, it will still take a boatload of money to get Dalton back on its feet."

"Beckett was easily bribed with the promise of a new custom chopper made by Desperado Customs—something I hope Colt will agree to. And Beau already likes Bramble. Or maybe I should say Shirlene."

"So is Beau going to be the one who stays in Bramble and oversees the reorganization?" Slate asked.

"Not likely."

"But you're not."

Billy's smile dropped. "No. I think Bramble needs someone they can trust."

"They trust you, Billy." Slate stared off at the miles of open space behind the house before he looked back. "And as crazy as it is, so do I."

The sound of tires rolling over the gravel had Billy glancing back at the driveway. He swallowed hard. "I can't live here without her."

Slate studied him for only a few seconds before he stepped over and placed a hand on his shoulder. "So take care of yourself, man."

"You do the same." Billy nodded. "And I expect you to keep me posted about that genius kid of yours—and your mediocre football team."

"Shiiit." Slate followed him out the gate with Buster on his heels. "You wish your team was as mediocre." He stood in the driveway and watched as Billy climbed into the rental SUV. Beau had already started backing out when Slate yelled.

"You are my friend, Billy Cates, and you better damned well not forget it."

Billy spent the rest of the day at Dalton Oil, going over the plans for restructuring. By the time he got back to the trailer, he was dead in his boots. He probably should've spent his last night in west Texas at the same motel Beau was staying in. But he couldn't quite bring himself to do it. If this was to be his last night, he wanted to spend it here.

He pulled the rental SUV into the lot and turned off the ignition. For a few moments, he just sat there, staring at the beat-up trailer. It was funny. But the first few times he'd stayed in the pile of aluminum siding, he'd been more than happy to leave it behind. Now he felt a deep sadness. And maybe it wasn't the trailer he would miss as much as his neighbors.

His gaze shifted over to the hedge, and he opened the

door and got out. It was a short distance to the ground. Much shorter than the stretch it took to get out of his old truck. He already missed the stupid thing. Maybe he'd buy himself another one when he returned to Dogwood. Although none would carry the memories of a sexy redhead in turquoise stilettos or a sassy Daisy Duke in cutoff jeans.

The lot next door looked completely different than it had a few weeks earlier. All of the junk had been cleared away, and the only things in the yard were a small plastic kiddie pool and the old Chevy. Billy had planned on having the antique car towed to Dogwood for Brant, but now he wondered if he shouldn't just leave it right where it sat. The car belonged here as much as the elm tree that grew next to it. As much as the old junk that had once filled the yard.

As much as Shirlene.

Just her name made his stomach cramp and his heart beat faster. And for a second, he visualized her in the yard hanging clothes, or chasing after Sherman, or playing with the kids. He thought about climbing the steps of the trailer and taking one last look inside. But he didn't think his heart could take it, so he turned and walked back to his trailer.

Leaving the lights off, he made his way to the bedroom. He tossed his cowboy hat to the top of the chest of drawers and had just reached for the top snap of his western shirt when he heard the distinctive click of a gun hammer being pulled back. For a split second, he wondered if he'd underestimated the people of Bramble and if he would end up just like his great-grandpappy. The possibility seemed even more likely when he turned to see the shadowy outline of the woman standing in one corner.

A woman holding a very big gun.

"I guess that's not Brody's cap gun," Billy stated as he tried to keep his heart from bumping out of his chest. And it had nothing to do with the deadly weapon pointed at him.

"Nope." Shirlene stepped closer, and Billy wondered if a heart attack was possible at thirty-four. He had thought she looked good in cut-offs and his shirts but it was nothing compared to how she looked in the slinky black dress and red high heels. Every drop of moisture evaporated out of his mouth as she stopped in front of him, her scent enveloping him like a steamy wave of east Texas humidity. The moonlight that filtered in through the window glistened off the ripe cherry of her full lips.

"So finish," she said, her breath falling hot against the skin of his throat.

It took more than a few seconds to find his voice. "Excuse me?"

"The clothes." She waggled the gun inches from the fly of his jeans. "Finish taking them off."

He narrowed his eyes. "If we're reenacting *Butch Cassidy and the Sundance Kid*, shouldn't I be the one with the gun?"

"Let's just say that history repeats itself." She sat down on the bed and leaned back on one elbow, the slinky material of the dress riding up on her thighs. "Slowly. Snap by pearl snap."

About a million questions raced through his mind, but Billy wasn't born with corn mush for brains. If a beautiful woman asks you to strip—you strip. Except stripping for a woman was a lot harder than Billy expected. Or maybe what was hard was doing it for a woman who held your entire world in her hands. His heart was thumping to beat the band, and his hands shook as badly as Moses Tate's. With fingers that felt like bratwurst sausages, he struggled to get even one snap undone. Frustrated, he jerked too hard, and the entire front of the shirt popped open.

"Do you understand the word slow, Cowboy?"

He might've come back with a clever quip if she hadn't crossed those mile-long legs. She swung a sexy stiletto, pulling his gaze to the toes that matched her lipstick.

"Or maybe your problem isn't speed as much as finesse," she said with a waggle of the gun. "Didn't your mama teach you not to blindside a woman with love words in front of an entire town?"

The air left his lungs, and his Adam's apple took a ride up and down his throat. "I guess she never got around to it, seeing as how I've only said those words to one woman."

"And what about all those women who wanted a tour of Wilkesville?"

Normally, he would've candy-coated the truth. But lying was no longer an option. "I can't tell you I wasn't willing to give tours. I just wasn't willing to invite them to live there."

The foot stopped swinging, and the barrel of the gun lowered. "And what exactly would be the criteria for asking a woman to live there?"

He knew his next words would be the most important words he would ever speak in his life, but damned if his brain hadn't turned to corn mush. Still, he did the best he could with little oxygen and a heart attack imminent.

"She has to be confident. The kind of woman who wouldn't let a bad haircut or comic book t-shirts detract from her beauty. And she'd have to be a fighter. Someone who won't give up when life throws a few obstacles in her path—like the death of a husband she loves and the eviction from her home by a villainous scoundrel. A woman with a heart big enough for four orphans and an entire town—and hopefully for a stupid hillbilly who loves her more than he could ever put into words. Marry me, Shirley Girl."

Shirlene stared up at the man who had filled her fantasies and dreams since the very first night she stumbled into his bed. His wavy, dark hair was flat from his cowboy hat, and his shirt hung open to reveal the hard muscles beneath. But it was his face that held her attention, a face that had become more familiar than her own. A face that usually held a smile, but that now just held the somber look of a man who had made mistakes and was sorry for them.

A man who loved her and who she loved in return.

Happiness flooded her. The giddy kind of jump-up-and-down happiness that Shirlene had felt very few times in her life. Billy's love was like dark chocolate ganache on a great big quadruple-layered cake. All she wanted to do was dive right on in and start licking it up.

But first things first.

She waggled the gun at him. "So where were we?"

"What?"

"Ahh, yes. I believe you were about ready to get to those jeans. Although you might want to take the boots off first, honey."

Billy's eyes narrowed as he placed a hand on his hip. "Are you kidding me? I just asked you to marry me and all you can think about is re-enacting some scene from a movie?"

She bit back a smile and tried to look innocent. "Well, you can't expect me to make my home in Wilkesville after a measly couple of tours, now can you?"

The anger left his face. "How much time are we talking about?"

"All the time we want. The kids are as snug as bugs in a big mansion of a rug with my brother and Hope watching over them."

His eyes lit up. "Then in that case, Sugar Buns, I'm going to give you the grand tour." He slipped the shirt off his shoulders and let it fall to the ground.

With his gaze pinned on her, he toed off his lizard-skin boots before pushing his jeans down his slim hips. In the moonlight, every lean line of muscle stood out like one of those smooth marble statues they had in Rome. All except the muscle Billy displayed when he slipped off his underwear.

No Greek god had ever boasted something as big as Billy's.

Shirlene studied the bobbing length of him as desire sizzled a shaft of heat straight through her. "I guess they grow 'em big in east Texas."

Instead of answering, Billy leaned down and removed his socks before stepping up against Shirlene's legs. The gun slipped from her hand, and before she could pick it back up, he reached down and pulled her to her feet.

"Say it." His hands cradled either side of her face, one thumb caressing her bottom lip. He leaned in and brushed a kiss over her mouth. "Say it, Shirley Girl."

She hooked her arms around his shoulders and stared back into those rich brown eyes. "I love you, Billy Wilkes Cates. And I'll love you until the day I die."

The dopey, country boy smile she'd come to adore slipped over his face. "Fair enough," he said, "because I plan on doing the same thing."

His next kiss was deep, wet, and skillet-fried. When he had her feeling as if she'd just climbed off the biggest roller coaster at Six Flags—all shaky-kneed and thrilled—he grabbed the hem of her dress and lifted it over her head. Since she didn't have a stitch on under the dress, naked flesh met naked flesh, and they both sucked in their breaths.

With his eyelids at half-mast, he stared down at her bare breasts pressed against his chest. "I guess they grow 'em big in west Texas."

She tipped back her head and laughed while Billy trailed kisses down her neck.

Much later, after she'd received a grand tour of Wilkesville and then some, Shirlene lay in Billy's arms, feeling as content as one of the Widow Jones's cats after a big saucer of cream.

"So when's the weddin'?" Billy asked, his lips brushing the top of her head.

She yawned and burrowed closer to his chest. "I think the weddin' committee has it planned for the third week in September. After summer heat, but before the high school football playoffs."

Billy pulled back and stared down at her. "You mean the town has already planned it?"

"Right down to my ugly flowers and bridesmaids' dresses."

"But that's crazy," he said. "They were all there when you turned me down flat."

Shirlene smiled brightly up at him. "Welcome to

Bramble, Billy Cates. Which brings up a good point. Where are we going to be living?"

Surprise was evident in his eyes. "You'd move to Dogwood?"

"I'd move to the ends of the earth to be with my country boy."

Her reply gained her a deep kiss before he pulled back and spoke. "Well, I can't say we won't be spending a lot of time in Dogwood—my family is pretty close-knit. But I think during the school year, the kids need to be here in Bramble. This is their home, and they've been through enough upheavals in their lives."

This time Shirlene gave him a kiss. When she pulled back, she couldn't help asking, "What if it turns out that Wynn Murdock killed your grandfather? Will your family ever be able to forgive me?"

He eased her on top of him. "I think my family is going to love you as much as Beau does—" He hesitated. "Well, hopefully, not that much. I'd hate to have to beat the tar out of all my brothers."

"I think you're being awful optimistic, Billy Cates," she said. "Especially if my relative was the one who started The Cates Curse."

After adjusting her legs until she straddled him, he sent her a wicked smile.

"What curse? Because from where I lie, Sugar Buns, my life looks like nothin' but blessin's."

Epilogue

"I SHOULD BE MAD AT YOU, you know?" Shirlene gathered her Vera Wang wedding dress around her and sat down on the rickety steps. "Josephine went to all the trouble to make my favorite chocolate cake, and you ruined it by being a gluttonous pig."

Sherman snorted and flopped down at her feet, remnants of chocolate icing still clinging to his upside-down, heart-shaped snout. Shirlene laughed and scratched his head. Even if he had jumped up on the table and devoured half her wedding cake before Billy and Jesse had gotten to him, she couldn't hold a grudge. Sherman was family. And everyone knew you forgave family just about anything.

"It was a beautiful weddin', wasn't it, Piglet? The First Baptist Church looked so pretty, and Pastor Robbins' vows were so beautiful. And you couldn't ask for a better place for a reception." Shirlene looked out at the crowd of townsfolk that filled the lot around her trailer.

Beneath a canopy of September stars and strings of colored Christmas lights, her friends and family seemed to be enjoying themselves. Numerous folks were on the dance floor Kenny Gene and Rye had put down, including Colt, who whirled Hope around like a purple top in her ugly maid-of-honor dress. Over by the refreshment table, Faith stood talking to Billy's mama and daddy, who had made the trip out from Dogwood. Billy's parents each held a baby. But since Daffodil and Daisy looked so much alike, Shirlene wasn't sure who was who until one let out a bloodcurdling scream that rivaled her mama's hog calls.

Billy's brothers, Beau and Beckett, were there as well. Beckett looked exactly like Billy, right down to the sexy, brown eyes and wavy hair. He stood next to Beau, listening to a story Kenny Gene was relating, completely unaware of the looks being tossed his way by all the flustered women. Brant and Brianna were the only ones who hadn't come from Billy's family. Shirlene had been upset, but Billy said to give them time. They were the stubborn ones in the family and would come around eventually.

A flash of lavender caught Shirlene's eye, and she turned to see Mia headed for the hole in the hedge. The young girl had yet to warm up to the town and was no doubt hiding out. Still, she looked so much happier since Shirlene and Billy had signed the adoption papers. Her long bleached hair was gone, and short jet black curls framed a face that was no longer as haunted as it had once been. Before she slipped through the hedge, Mia stopped to get after Jesse for something. But Jesse paid no attention to his sister and tore off across the yard with one of Tyler Jones's kids, the tail of his tuxedo shirt flapping behind him.

Shirlene didn't worry about Jesse. The boy was a survivor and would no doubt own half of Texas by the time he was twenty. And Brody wouldn't be far behind him. In the last few weeks, the three-year old's vocabulary had grown from one word to thousands. He talked more than Kenny Gene. Even now, the little boy was sitting at one of the picnic tables between Harley Sutter and Naked Barbie, shoveling in the emergency store-bought cake and chattering up a storm.

"Are you about ready to call it a night, Mrs. Cates?"

Billy's familiar twang poured over Shirlene like a gentle summer rain, and she turned and looked up into the soft chocolate love of her husband's eyes.

"Mmm, Mrs. Cates," she said. "I like the sound of that."

"No more than I do, Shirley Girl," Billy said as he adjusted his arms around a sleeping Adeline before placing a kiss on her golden curls. "Addie's all tuckered out from dancing. I swear I didn't know a little sprout could last so long. She must've sweet-jabbered every man in town to take her for a spin." He winked. "It appears she's as big a flirt as her mama."

"More like her daddy." Shirlene rose to her feet, causing Sherman to grumble when he was forced to move.

Hooking an arm around her waist, Billy pulled her close. "Not anymore, Cinnamon Muffins. I've met my match."

"Damn straight." Shirlene leaned in to give him a kiss, but the loud rumble of a truck had her turning toward the road.

The crowd separated as a monster truck pulled into the lot, its deep-treaded tires rolling right up to the steps. The door swung open, and Slate Calhoun jumped down, wearing a sexy tuxedo and a Stetson—and a wide grin.

"Damn, I love this truck," he said as he tossed Billy the keys.

Billy laughed. "I'll tell you what, Calhoun. You win another state championship this season, and I might just let you borrow her."

Slate's eyes lit up. "Now that's a deal."

After handing out kisses to all the kids and multiple instructions to Billy's parents, who would be staying with them while Billy and Shirlene were on their honeymoon, Shirlene allowed Billy to help her up into the truck.

Once the door was slammed, he turned to her. "So how come you haven't asked me where I'm taking you on our honeymoon?"

She shrugged. "Maybe because I don't care where we go or what we do. There's only one thing I need in life."

"And what's that?"

Shirlene flashed him her brightest smile. "A little Bubba-lovin'."

Billy pulled her close and growled, "Mine."

The town of Bramble watched as the truck wheeled around the lot and headed down the dirt road with beer cans clanking. The words that were shoe-polished in the back window, *Hitched For Good*, had barely disappeared in the darkness when Harley spoke up.

"Well, I guess that settles that."

Rachel Dean swiped at her eyes. "It sure does. Faith, Hope, and Shirlene are all married off."

Sheriff Winslow heaved a sad sigh. "Won't be much excitement around town now."

"Pert near none at all," Rye Pickett agreed.

Kenny Gene's face fell. "Does that mean the party's over?"

No one answered. They all just turned and shuffled back to their warm beers and Solo cups of sweet tea. Only one person remained. One person who stood with his ninety-year-old eyes squinted at the road.

"Dad-gum fools," Moses Tate grumbled to the chocolate-smeared pig at his feet. "They don't even realize that the eldest Cates ain't gonna give up until he finds them bones and has his revenge. 'Course," he shrugged, "if people don't ask, I ain't one to tell."

The pig smiled.

He knows there's something
special about her kiss...

Please turn this page
for an excerpt from

Going Cowboy Crazy

Chapter Two

SLATE CALHOUN SAT BACK in the dark corner and watched the woman in the conservative pants and brown sweater take another sip of her beer as if it was tea time at Buckingham Palace. Hell, she even held her little pinkie out. If that was Hope Scroggs then he was Prince Charles. And he was no pansy prince.

Still, the resemblance was uncanny.

The imposter swallowed and wrinkled up her cute little nose. A nose that was the exact duplicate of Hope's. And so were the brows that slanted over those big blue eyes and the high cheekbones and that damned full-lipped mouth. A mouth that had fried his brain like a slice of his aunt's green tomatoes splattering in hot bacon grease.

The kiss was the kicker. Slate never forgot a kiss. Never. And the few kisses he'd shared with Hope hadn't come close to the kiss he'd shared with this woman. Hope's kisses had always left him with a strange uncomfortable feeling; like he'd just kissed his sister. It had never left him feeling like he wanted to strip her naked and devour her petite body like a contestant in a pie-eating contest.

But if the woman wasn't Hope, then who the hell was she?

He'd heard of people having doubles—people who weren't related to you but looked a lot like you. He'd even seen a man once who could pass for George W. in just the right lighting. But this woman was way past a double. She was more like an identical twin. And since he'd known Hope's family ever since he was thirteen, he had to rule out the entire twin thing. Hope had two younger sisters and a younger brother. And not one of them was a looka-like whose kisses set your hair on fire.

The woman laughed at something Kenny said, and her head tipped back, her entire face lighting up. He'd seen that laugh before, witnessed it all through high school and off and on for years after. Hell, maybe she was Hope. Maybe his lips had played a trick on him. Maybe he was so upset about losing last night's game that he wasn't thinking straight. Or maybe, it being a year since her last visit, he was so happy to see her that he read something in the kiss that wasn't there.

It was possible. He'd been under a lot of stress lately. Football season could do crazy things to a man's mind. Especially football season in West Texas. Which was why he had planned a two-week Mexican vacation after the season was over. Just the thought of soft rolling waves, warm sand, and cool ocean breezes made the tension leave his neck and shoulders.

What it didn't do was change his mind about the woman who sat on top of the bar with her legs crossed—showing off those sexy red high heels. Hope didn't cross her legs like that. And she hated high heels. She also hated going to the beauty salon, which was why her long brown hair was down to her butt. This woman's hair was styled in a short layered cut that made her eyes look twice as big and was highlighted the color of Jack Daniels in a fancy crystal glass.

Of course, Hope had lived in Hollywood for five long years. Maxine Truly had gone to Houston for only two years and had come back with multiple piercings and a tattoo of a butterfly on her ass. So big cities could screw you over. He just didn't believe they could change someone from an outspoken extrovert to an introvert who hadn't spoken a word, or even tried to, in the last hour.

Laryngitis, my ass.

That couldn't be Hope

But there was only one way to find out.

Pushing up from his chair, he strolled around the tables to the spot where her adoring fan club had gathered. It didn't take much to part the sea of people. Hope might be the hometown sweetheart, but he was the hometown football hero turned high school coach. In Bramble, that was as close as a person could get to being God.

As usual, Kenny Gene was talking to beat the band. Sitting on the barstool next to her, he was monopolizing the conversation with one of his exaggerated stories.

"...I'm not kiddin', the man blew a hole the size of a six-year-old razorback hog in the side of Deeder's double-wide, then took his time hoppin' back in his truck as if he had all day to do—hey, Slate."

Slate stopped just shy of those pointy-toed shoes and trim little ankles. Slowly, he let his gaze slide up the pressed pants, up the brown sweater that hugged the tiny

waist and small breasts, over the stubborn chin and the
full mouth that still held a tiny trace of pink glittery gloss,
to those sky blue eyes that widened just enough to make
him realize he hadn't made a mistake.

The woman before him wasn't Hope.

But he was willing to play along until he found out
who she was.

"Kenny, what the heck are you doing letting Hope
drink beer?" He pried the bottle from her death grip as
he yelled at the bartender. "Manny, bring me a bottle of
Hope's favorite and a couple of glasses." He smiled and
winked at her. "If we're going to celebrate your homecomin', darlin', then we need to do it right."

"I wanted to order Cuervo, Slate," Kenny defended
himself. "But she didn't want it."

"Not want your favorite tequila, Hog?" He leaned
closer. "Now why would that be, I wonder?"

Before she could do more than blink, Manny slapped
down the bottle of Jose Cuervo and two shot glasses, followed quickly by a salt shaker and a plastic cup of lime
wedges. He started to pour the tequila but Slate shook his
head.

"Thanks, Manny, but I'll get it." Slate took off his
hat and tossed it down. Stepping closer, he sandwiched
those prim-and-proper crossed legs between his stomach
and the bar as he picked up the bottle and splashed some
tequila in each glass—a very little in his and much more
in the imposter's. He handed her the salt shaker. "Now
you remember how this works, don't you, sweetheart?"

"'Course she knows how it works, Slate," Twyla piped
in. "She's been in Hollywood, not on the moon."

Slate didn't turn to acknowledge the statement. He

remained pressed against her calf, the toe of her shoe teasing the inseam of his jeans and mere inches from his man jewels. His body acknowledged her close proximity but he ignored the tightening in his crotch and continued to watch those fearful baby blues as they looked at the salt shaker then back at him.

"Here." He took the shaker from her. "Let me refresh your memory, Hog." Reaching out, he captured her hand. It was soft and fragile and trembled like a tiny white rabbit caught in a snare. He flipped it over and ran his thumb across the silky satin of her wrist, testing the strum of her pulse. As he bent his head, the scent of peaches wafted up from her skin, filling his lungs with light-headed sweetness and his mind with images of juicy ripe fruit waiting to be plucked.

Easy, boy. Keep your eye on the goal line.

With his gaze pinned to hers, he kissed her wrist, his tongue sweeping along the pulse point until her skin was wet and her pupils dilated. Then he pulled back and salted the damp spot he'd left.

"Now watch, darlin'." He sipped the salt off, downed the shot, then grabbed a lime and sucked out the juice— all without releasing her hand. "Now you try. Lick, slam, suck. It's easy."

She just sat there. Her eyes dazed and confused. He knew how she felt; he felt pretty confused himself. His lips still tingled from touching her skin, and his heart had picked up the erratic rhythm of hers.

"Go on, Hope," Kenny prodded. "What's the matter with you? Don't tell me, you forgot how to drink in Hollywood?"

That seemed to snap her out of it, and before Slate

could blink, she licked off the salt, slammed the shot, and had the lime in her mouth.

A cheer rose up, but it was nothing to what rose up beneath Slate's fly. The sight of those pink-glitter lips sucking the lime dry made his knees weak. And so did the triumphant smile that crinkled the corners of her eyes as she pulled the lime from her mouth. A mouth with full lips like Hope's but with straight even front teeth. Not a slightly crooked incisor in sight.

Relief surged through him. The hard evidence proved he wasn't loco. It also proved his libido wasn't on the fritz. He wasn't hot after one of his closest friends; he was hot after this woman. This woman who was not Hope... unless she'd gotten some dental work done like they did on *Extreme Makeover.*

He mentally shook himself. No, she wasn't Hope. And if it took the entire bottle of tequila to get her to fess up, so be it.

He poured her another shot and had her salted and ready to go before she could blink those innocent eyes. "Bottoms up."

She complied, demonstrating the lick-slam-suck without a flaw. She grinned broadly when the crowd cheered, but she didn't utter a peep. Not even after the next shot. Damn, maybe she was Hope; she was just as mule headed. And could hold her liquor just as well—although she did seem a little happier.

"Do a Nasty Shot," Sue Ellen hollered loud enough to rattle the glasses behind the bar.

Slate started to decline, but then figured it might be just the thing to get to the truth. Besides, he'd always been a crowd pleaser.

"You wanna do a Nasty Shot, Hog?" he asked.

She nodded, all sparkly-eyed.

For a second, he wondered if it was a good idea. She'd almost set him on fire the last time she kissed him. Of course, that was when he thought she was his close friend and her enthusiasm had taken him by surprise. Now he knew she was a fraud. A sexy fraud, but a fraud nonetheless. Knowing that, he wouldn't let things get out of control. He would get just aggressive enough to scare her into speaking up.

"Okay." Slate lifted her wrist and kissed it, this time sucking her skin into his mouth and giving it a gentle swirl with his tongue. Her eyes fluttered shut, and her breasts beneath the soft sweater rose and fell with quick little breaths.

The man muscle beneath the worn denim of his jeans flexed.

This was definitely a bad idea.

Unfortunately, with the entire town watching, he couldn't back out.

Lifting his head, Slate cleared his throat. "Remember how this works?" He covered the wet spot with salt. "Same premise, but this time we lick and shoot at the same time. Just leave the sucking part to me. Here." He uncrossed her legs and stepped between them, which prompted a few sly chuckles from the men. "For this, we need to get just a tad bit closer."

Those long dark lashes fluttered, and her thighs tightened around him. Slate's breath lounged somewhere between heaven and hell, and his hand shook as he poured a full shot for her and a little for himself.

"Okay, darlin'." Luckily, he sounded more in control

than he felt. "You ready?" He dipped his head and pressed his mouth to her skin.

She hesitated for just a second before she followed. The silky strands of her hair brushed his cheek as her lips opened and her tongue slipped out to gather the salt, only millimeters from his. Even though they didn't touch, an electric current of energy arched between them so powerfully that it caused them both to jerk back. Those big baby blues stared back at him, tiny granules of salt clinging to her bottom lip.

His mind went blank.

"Tequila, Coach," Rossie Owens, who owned the bar, yelled.

Snapping out of it, he straightened and grabbed up the full shot, then downed it in an attempt to beat back the rearing head of his libido. She followed more slowly, her wide confused eyes pinned on him.

"The lime, Slate," Kenny laughed. "You forgot the lime."

Hell. He jerked up the lime and sucked out the tart juice, not at all sure he was ready to go through with it. But then people started cheering him on, just like they had in high school when they wanted him to throw a touchdown pass. And, just like back then, he complied and reached up to hold her chin between his thumb and forefinger as he lowered his lips to hers.

It wasn't a big deal. Slate had kissed a lot of girls in his life. Including one whose eyes were the deep blue of the ocean as it waits to wash up on a Mexican shore. Except he hadn't noticed that about Hope. Hope's eyes were always just blue. Yet, this woman's eyes caused a horde of descriptive images to parade through his mind. All of them vivid . . . and sappy as hell.

Luckily, when he placed his lips on hers all the images disappeared. Unluckily, now all he could do was feel. The startled intake of breath. The hesitant tremble. The sweet pillowy warmth.

"Suck!" someone yelled.

Her lips startled open, and moist heat surrounded him. Shit, he was in trouble. He parted his lips, hoping that once he did, she would pull back and start talking. But that's not what happened. Instead, she angled her head and opened her mouth wider, then proceeded to kiss him deep enough to suck every last trace of lime from his mouth, along with every thought in his mind. Except for one, how to get inside her conservative beige pants.

Slate pulled his head back. Get in her pants? Get in whose pants? He didn't know who the hell the woman was. And even if he did know, he sure wasn't going to get in her pants in front of the entire town. He liked to please people, but not that much.

Ignoring the moist lips and desire-filled eyes, Slate dropped his hand from her chin and lifted her down from the bar. When he turned around, the room was filled with knowing grins. He thought about explaining things. But if he'd learned anything over the years he'd lived in Bramble, it was that when small town folks got something in their heads, it was hard to shake it. Even if it was totally wrong. Which was why he didn't even make the effort. He just grabbed his hat off the bar as he slipped a hand to the petite woman's waist and herded her toward the door.

It wasn't as difficult as he thought it would be. Which was just one more reason the woman wasn't Hope. Hope was too damned controlling to let anyone herd her anywhere. Just one of the things he didn't particularly miss.

Once they were outside, Slate guided her a little ways from the door before he pulled her around to face him.

"Okay. Just who the hell are you?"

Her gaze flashed up to his just as Cindy Lynn came out the door.

"Hey, Hope. I was wonderin' if you could come to the homecomin' decoratin' committee meetin' on Monday afternoon. I know decorations ain't your thing, but everybody would love to hear about Hollywood. Have you met Matthew McConaughey yet? One of my cousins on my father's side went to college with him in Austin and—"

"Hey, Cindy." Slate pushed the annoyance down and grinned at the woman who, on more than one occasion, had trouble remembering she was married. "I know you're probably just busting at the seams to talk with Hope about all them movie stars, but I was wondering if you could do that later, seeing as how me and Hope have got some catching up to do."

"I'm sure you do." She smirked as she turned and wiggled back inside.

Realizing Cindy Lynn would be only one of many interruptions, Slate slapped his hat on his head and took the woman's hand. "Come on. We're taking a ride."

She allowed him to pull her along until they reached the truck parked by the door. "This is your truck?"

Slate whirled around and stared at the woman who sounded exactly like Hope—except with a really weird accent. He watched as those blue eyes widened right before her hand flew up to cover her mouth.

The hard evidence of her betrayal caused the temper—he worked so hard at controlling—to rear its ugly head, and he dropped her hand and jerked open the door of the truck. "Get in."

She swallowed hard and shook her head. "I'd rather not."

"So I guess you'd rather stay here and find out how upset these folks get when I inform them that you've been playing them for fools."

She cast a fearful glance back over her shoulder. "I'm not playing anyone for a fool. I just wanted some answers."

"Good. Because that's exactly what I want." Slate pointed to the long bench seat of the truck. "Get in."

The sun had slipped close to the horizon, the last rays turning the sky—and the streaks in her hair—a deep red. She looked small standing so close to the large truck. Small and vulnerable. The image did what the Mexican daydreams couldn't.

He released his breath. "Look, I'm not going to hurt you, but I'm not going to let you leave without finding out why you're impersonating a close friend of mine. So you can either tell me, or Sheriff Winslow."

It was a lame threat. The only thing Sheriff Winslow was any good at was bringing his patrol car to the games and turning on his siren and flashing lights when the Bull-dogs scored a touchdown. But this woman didn't know that. Still, she didn't seem to be in any hurry to follow his orders either.

"My car is parked over there," she said, pointing. "I'll meet you somewhere."

"Not a chance. I wouldn't trust you as far as little Dusty Ray can spit."

She crossed her arms. "Well, I'm not going any place with a complete stranger."

"Funny, but that didn't stop you from almost giving me a tonsillectomy," he said. A blush darkened her pale skin. The shy behavior was so unlike Hope that he almost smiled. Almost. She still needed to do some explaining. "So since we've established that we're well past the stranger stage, it shouldn't be a problem for you to take a ride with me."

"I'm sorry, but I really couldn't go—"

Kenny charged out the door with the rest of the town hot on his heels.

"Hey." He held out a purse, if that's what you could call the huge brown leather bag. "Hope forgot her purse."

Slate's gaze ran over the crowd that circled around. "And I guess everyone needed to come with you to give... Hope her purse."

"We just wanted to see how things were goin'." Tyler Jones, who owned the gas station, stepped up.

"And say goodbye to Hope," Miguel, the postmaster, piped in.

There was a chorus of goodbyes along with a multitude of invitations to supper.

Then someone finally yelled what everyone else wanted to. "So what are you gonna do with Hope now, Coach?"

What he wanted to do was climb up in the truck and haul ass out of there. To go home and watch game film—or better yet pop in a Kenny Chesney CD and peruse the internet for pictures of Mexican hot spots. Anything to forget he'd ever met the woman, or tasted her skin, or kissed her soft lips, or stared into her blue eyes. Blue eyes that turned misty as she looked at the smiling faces surrounding them.

It was that watery, needy look that was the deciding factor.

"Well, I guess I'm going to do what I should've done years ago." He leaned down and hefted her over one shoulder. She squealed and struggled as the crowd swarmed around them. Then he flipped her up in the seat and climbed in after her.

"What's that?" Ms. Murphy, the librarian, asked as she handed him a red high heel through the open window.

After tossing it to the floor, Slate started the engine. It rumbled so loudly, he had to yell to be heard.

"Take her to bed."

The woman next to him released a gasp while poor Ms. Murphy looked like she was about to pass out. Normally, he would've apologized for his bad behavior. But normally he didn't have a beautiful imposter sitting next to him who made him angrier than losing a football game.

He popped the truck into reverse and backed out, trying his damnedest to pull up mental pictures of waving palm trees, brown skinned beauties, and strong tequila. But they kept being erased by soft white skin, eyes as blue as a late September sky, and the smell of sun-ripened peaches.

The town of Bramble, Texas watched as the truck rumbled over the curb and then took off down the street with the stars and stripes, the lone star flag, and Buster's ears flapping in the wind.

"Isn't that the sweetest thang?" Twyla pressed a hand to her chest. "Slate and Hope—high school sweethearts together again."

"It sure is," Kenny Gene said. "'Course, there's no tellin' how long Hope will stay."

"Yep." Rye Pickett spit out a long stream of tobacco juice. "That Hollywood sure has brainwashed her. Hell, she couldn't even remember how to drink."

"Poor Slate," Ms. Murphy tisked. "He'll have his hands full convincing her to stay and settle down."

There were murmurs of agreement before Harley Sutter, the mayor, spoke up. "'Course, we could help him out with that."

Rossie Owens pushed back his cowboy hat. "Well, we sure could."

"Just a little help," Darla piped up. "Just enough to show Hope that all her dreams can be fulfilled right here in Bramble."

"Just enough to let love prevail," Sue Ellen agreed.

"Just enough for weddin' bells to ring." Twyla sighed.

"Yep." Harley nodded as he hitched up his pants. "Just enough."

Sometimes you *can* go home
again... This town's sexiest
rebel is baaaack!

Please turn this page
for an excerpt from

Make Mine a Bad Boy

Chapter One

IT WAS A DREAM. It had to be. Where else but in a dream could you be an observer at your own wedding? A silent spectator who watched as you stood in the front of a church filled to the rafters with all your family and friends and whispered your vows to a handsome cowboy you've loved for most of your life. A cowboy who kissed you as if his life depended on it, before he hurried you down the aisle and off to the reception, where he fed you champagne from his glass and cake from his fingers, before taking you in his strong arms and waltzing you toward happily-ever-after.

It was a dream.

Her dream.

"Hog, you gonna eat that piece of cake?"

And just like that the dream shattered into a nightmare.

Hope Marie Scroggs pulled her gaze from the dance floor and looked over at Kenny Gene, who was staring down at the half-eaten slice of wedding cake on her plate.

"Because if you ain't," he said. "I sure hate to see it go to waste." Without waiting for an answer, he speared the cake and crammed a forkful into his mouth, continuing to talk between chews. "That Josephine sure outdid herself this time. Who would've thought that raspberry jam would go so good with yeller cake?"

The fork came back toward her plate. But before he could stab another piece, his girlfriend, Twyla, slapped his hand, and the plastic fork sailed through the air, bounced off one of the ceramic pig centerpieces, and disappeared beneath the table.

"Kenny Gene, don't you be eatin' Hope's food! She needs all them noot-tur-ents!"

Hope didn't have a clue what Twyla was talking about, and she didn't care. All she wanted to do was recapture the dream. But it was too late. Too late to ignore the fact that she wasn't the one who whirled around on the dance floor in the arms of Slate Calhoun—the handsomest cowboy in West Texas.

But it should've been.

It should've been her dressed in her mama's three-tiered lace wedding dress. Her who sipped from his clear plastic Solo cup. Her who licked Josephine's Raspberry Jamboree Cake from those strong quarterback fingertips. Her arms looped over that lean cowboy frame. And her face tucked under that sexy black Stetson, awaiting a kiss from those sweet smiling lips.

Her.

Her.

Her.

Certainly not some damned Yankee who had come to Bramble, Texas, looking for her long-lost, twin sister only to steal that same sister's identity like a peach pie set out to cool. It wasn't fair, and it wasn't right. Not when Hope was the one who had done all the prep work. The one who suffered through all the cheerleading practices and homecoming parades and hog-calling contests all to make her family and the townsfolk proud.

And then some citified wimp with ugly hair shows up, and their loyalties switched like Buford Floyd's gender, and she was expected to grin and bear it? To pretend that everything was just fine and dandy? To act like she didn't give a hoot that her life had just been spit out like a stream of tobacco juice to a sidewalk?

Her anger burned from the injustice of it all, and all she wanted to do was drop to the ground and throw a fit like she had as a child. And if she'd thought it would work, she would have. But it was too late for that. The vows had been spoken; the marriage license signed.

Besides, she was Hope Marie Scroggs, the most popular girl in West Texas, and she wasn't about to let anyone know just how devastated she was that the dreams of her wedding day were being lived out by someone else.

Someone who, at that moment, looked over at her and smiled a bright, cheerful smile with white, even teeth that reflected the lights shooting off the huge disco ball hanging from the ceiling. How could some sugary sweet Disney princess have lived in the same womb with her for nine months? It made absolutely no sense whatsoever. Nor could she figure out why she smiled back—though it might have been more of a baring of teeth because Faith's smile fizzled before Slate whirled her away.

"Your fangs are showin', honey." Her best friend, Shirlene, slipped into the folding chair next to her with a soft rustle of gold satin.

Since her daydream was already stomped to smithereens,

Hope turned to Shirlene and lifted a brow at the mounds of flesh swelling over the top of her bridesmaid's dress.

"Better than havin' my boobs showin'."

Shirlene didn't even attempt to tug up the strapless confection that put Hope's grotesque purple maid-of-honor's dress to shame. "Admit it. You've always been jealous of 'the girls'." She flashed a bright smile at Kenny and Twyla as they got up and headed for the dance floor.

"The girls?" Hope's eyes widened. "Those aren't girls, Shirl. Broads, maybe, but not girls."

Shirlene laughed. "Okay, so you've always been jealous of 'the broads'."

Hope shrugged. "If you had my teacups, you'd be jealous too."

"I don't know about that. I get pretty tired of lugging these suckers around."

"I'm sure Lyle doesn't mind helping out with that." She glanced around for Shirlene's husband. "Where is Lyle, anyway?"

"He's got a meetin' in the morning, so he wanted to get to bed early."

"A meetin' on a Sunday?"

For just a brief second, Shirlene's pretty green eyes turned sad before she looked away to fiddle with the purple ribbon tied around the fat ceramic pig. One of the same pigs that had been pulled out for every town celebration since they were made for Hope's fifteenth birthday. "That's the problem with marrying a wealthy man. They're so busy making money; they don't have time to make babies."

"Are you still trying?"

Shirlene shrugged as she retied the ribbon in a perfect bow. "Lyle thinks it's God's will."

"You could adopt, you know."

"I know, but maybe Lyle's right. Maybe this West Texas girl is a little too wild to be a good mama." Releasing her breath, she flopped back in the chair, causing her broads to jiggle like Aunt Mae's Jell-o mold. "Geez, we make a pathetic pair, don't we, Hog? Me a lonely, childless housewife and you a jilted woman."

Hope looked around before hissing under her breath. "I was not jilted, Shirl."

"I don't know what you would call it, Hog. Everyone in town was there when you accepted Slate's proposal—a proposal, I might add, that was never made."

Her jaw tightened. "You know as well as everybody else that Slate proposed to me."

"Years ago. And we both know he was never serious." She hesitated and sent Hope a pointed look. "And if I remember correctly, neither were you."

Unable to look back at those perceptive green eyes, Hope stared out at the dance floor where Slate continued to whirl her sister around. "I always planned on marrying Slate."

Shirlene snorted. "If I had a dime for every one of your plans, Hope, I'd be rich enough to lure the Dallas Cowboys away from Jerry Jones."

"As if you're not already."

"True." The contagious smile flashed as Shirlene reached over and picked up a champagne bottle. She filled a cup for each of them before lifting hers. "Here's to wild West Texas women—we might be down, but we'll never be out."

Finally giving in to a smile, Hope lifted her cup and tapped Shirlene's. "Damn straight." But before she could take a sip, the mayor, Harley Sutter, came chugging up and took the cup from her hand.

"No time for drinkin', Hope." He handed the cup to Shirlene and pulled Hope up from her chair. "Not when the entire town wants a dance with their sweetheart."

Since Hope had never been able to disappoint her hometown, she rolled her eyes at Shirlene and allowed Harley to pull her out to the dance floor. Unfortunately, the two-step had ended, and the band struck up one of those stupid wedding songs that only worked in a room filled with drunks. Still, she pinned on a smile and tried to act like she enjoyed impersonating a flustered chicken.

"Glad to see you so happy, Hope," Harley said as he flapped his arms above a belly that was more keg than six-pack. "You know what they say, 'Home is where the heart is.'"

Unless some Disney princess stole it right out from under your nose, Hope thought as Harley swung her right on over to Sheriff Sam Winslow.

"He's right, Hope," Sam said as he flapped. "Hollywood has had our sweetheart long enough. Though I bet they ain't gonna be real happy to lose such talent. That hemorrhoid commercial you did sure brought tears to my eyes. It had to be real hard to get such a look of complete discomfort." He swung her around. "But you sure nailed it, Hog. Myra raced out and got a tube that very night."

"A tube of what?" Rachel Dean stepped up.

"Hemorrhoid cream," Sam answered, before stepping away.

"Oh, honey," Rachel Dean clapped her man hands,

then jerked Hope into a swing that almost snapped her spinal column, "I got hemorrhoids when I was pregnant. And I'm tellin' you right now, there ain't no cream on God's green earth that will help with that hellish burnin'.'"

Not wanting to talk about hemorrhoids or pregnancy, Hope gladly turned to her next partner. Although her pinned-on smile slipped when she stared up into a pair of dreamy hazel eyes. As she struggled to regain her composure, the silly song ended and a waltz began.

"Could I have this dance, Miss Scroggs?" Slate asked.

The word "no" hovered on her lips. But, of course, she couldn't say no. Not unless she wanted him to know exactly how hurt she was.

"Only if you keep those big boots off my toes, Cowboy."

"I'll do my best." Slate flashed the sexy grin that made women melt. Hope didn't melt, but she felt thoroughly singed. Or maybe just annoyed that she didn't get to claim the body that went with the smile.

His best turned out to be worse than Hope remembered. After only two steps, her toes were smashed under his boots, and she was forced to do what she'd always done when they danced: Take the lead. Except now he didn't follow as well as he used to.

"Listen, Hope," he said. "I realize this has been hard on you. You come back to Bramble expecting... well, I don't exactly know what you were expecting, but it sure couldn't have been a twin sister you didn't even know you had. Or a wedding that had been planned without you knowing—our wedding, no less." Slate chuckled. "Crazy townsfolk."

She looked away. "Yeah...crazy."

"But you want to know what is even crazier," he

continued. "All it took was one look from Faith—or maybe a kiss that knocked my hat off—and I was a goner. A complete goner."

Hope wished that she was a goner. Gone from this man. And this room. And this town. If the pits of hell opened at that very moment and swallowed her up, it would be a relief.

But that didn't happen. So all she could do was guard her toes and try not to act like she gave a darn that her wedding plans had disintegrated just like her dreams of becoming a movie star. Thankfully, the slow ballad ended, and Slate was pulled away as Harley bellowed.

"Come on all you unhitched folks! It's time for the garter and bouquet toss!"

Hope tried to make a run for it, but the town pushed her forward, swarming around a chair that had been set up in the middle of the dance floor. A chair where her sister sat and waited for Slate to dip that head of sun-kissed hair and, using nothing but his teeth, tug the light blue garter down a leg identical to her own.

"I love a man who knows what to do with his mouth!" Rachel Dean yelled, and whooping and hollering broke out loud enough to shake the sturdy stone building.

With the town's attention focused elsewhere, Hope attempted to inch her way to the door. But she should've known better, especially when she had such an ornery best friend.

"Now don't be gettin' any ideas about leaving, Hog." Shirlene positioned her body between Hope and the exit. "Not when everyone expects you to get up there and catch that ugly bunch of silk flowers Darla hot glued together."

"Ugly?" Darla clasped her hands to her chest. "Well,

I'll have you know that I paid a pretty penny for those at Nothin' Over a Buck."

"Of course, you did, honey." Shirlene sent her a wink. "If anybody can stretch a buck, it's you."

The words seemed to pacify Darla, and she smiled brightly as Shirlene slipped an arm around Hope and leaned down to speak in her ear.

"Now I know you want to go home and wallow in self-pity. But we both know that this town isn't going to let you get away with that. So just bite the bullet and get in there and do me proud." She gave her a loving pat on the back before she shoved her into the middle of the dance floor. And by the time Hope caught her balance, Shirlene had disappeared in the crowd of single ladies.

It was a pathetic group. There was Twyla who had already been married three times. Rachel Dean who came close with two. The librarian, Ms. Murphy, who was smart enough to avoid marriage all together, but still, had to endure the crazy ritual every time someone had a wedding. Hope's two younger sisters, Jenna Jay and Tessa. And a couple other giggling girls.

Her twin sister stood to the side, holding her "Nothin' Over a Buck" bouquet and grinning like the seven dwarfs were all coming over to the castle for dinner. Of course, who wouldn't grin if they had just wrangled the best-looking man this side of the Mississippi while their sister was forced to fight for the leftovers?

Well, Hope wasn't fighting.

She was all fought out.

She didn't care if Darla's hot-glued flowers were made out of solid gold. She wasn't going to lift a finger to catch them. Not one finger.

"Ready?" Faith looked directly at her, and Hope experienced the same strange phenomenon that she always experienced when her twin sister looked at her. It was like looking into a mirror. Not just externally, but internally. Everything Hope felt was reflected right back at her. Hurt. Confusion. Anger. Self-pity. It was all there in the familiar blue eyes.

Thankfully, Faith broke the connection by turning around and giving Hope something else to think about. Like how to avoid the large bouquet of silk flowers that she launched over her shoulder.

Hope figured it wouldn't be hard, not when Twyla had perfected the wide-receiver dive that won her numerous silk-flower trophies and a bunch of good-for-nothing husbands. But as the bouquet sailed through the air, Twyla didn't move one under-developed muscle toward it. Nor did Rachel. Or Ms. Murphy. Or Jenna Jay. Or Tessa. Or any of the giggling girls. Instead, everyone just watched as the purple batch of flowers tumbled end over end straight toward Hope.

She took a step back.

Then another.

But the bouquet just kept coming. If it hadn't been heading for her like a heat-seeking missile, she might've turned and run. But she wasn't about to take her eyes off Darla's creation, not when her own maid-of-honor bouquet was a good solid five pounds of hardened hot glue. So, instead, Hope widened her stance and prepared to deflect the floral grenade with an arm.

It would've worked too, if her watch hadn't snagged the yard and a half of tulle netting surrounding the flowers, something Hope didn't realize until she lowered her arm and felt the dead weight.

Like a preschooler doing the hokey-pokey, she shook her arm to try and get it loose. But the bouquet refused to budge. And after only a few seconds of crazy arm waving, she realized it was no use and let her arm drop. She expected a wave of catcalls and whistles, but what she got was complete silence.

Confused, she glanced up to find the entire roomful of people staring.

Except not at her.

Few things could pull the town's attention away from their sweetheart. Yet something had. Something that had nothing to do with ugly silk flowers and five pounds of hot glue. Something that so intrigued the town they had completely forgotten Hope Scroggs existed.

A chill of foreboding tiptoed up Hope's spine, and her stomach tightened and gave a little heave as she slowly turned around.

Just that quickly, things went from bad to worse.

A man stood in the open doorway with his shoulder propped against the frame as if he didn't have a care in the world. As if he didn't stick out like a sore thumb from the other men who were dressed in their Sunday best of western pants, heavily-starched shirts, and polished cowboy boots.

This man looked like a desperado who'd come off a long, hard ride. Road dust covered his round-toed black biker boots with their thick soles and silver buckles, partially hidden by the tattered hem of his jeans. Jeans so worn that they molded to all the right nooks and crannies, defining hard thighs and lean valleys. A basic black t-shirt was tucked into the jeans, stretching over miles of muscle and hugging the hard-knots of his biceps.

But even with a body that could tempt a bible-banger on Sunday, it was his face that held Hope's attention. A face made up of tanned skin, hard angles, and a thin layer of black stubble. Come to think of it, everything about the man was black—including his heart. Everything but those steel gray eyes. Eyes that scanned the room as if looking for something.

Or someone.

Hope ducked behind Kenny Gene and stealthily peeked over his shoulder, watching as the man pushed away from the doorjamb and weaved around the tables—thankfully, in the opposite direction. The smart thing to do would be to slip out the door before he saw her. And she might've done just that if his fine butt in those buttery jeans hadn't distracted her.

It was a shame, a darned shame, that the man was such a mean, ornery lowlife.

A mean, ornery lowlife who stopped right in front of . . .

Faith?

It made no sense, but there he stood, those unemotional eyes drilling her sister with an intensity that caused the Disney smile to droop.

"It seems I missed the weddin'," he stated in a deep, silky voice that didn't match the rough exterior. "So I guess the only thing left to do . . ." Those big biker hands slipped around Faith's waist, "is kiss the bride."

Then before Hope's mouth could finish dropping open, he lowered his head and laid one on her twin sister. Not a gentlemanly peck, but a deep, wet lip-lock that left little doubt that a tongue was involved. It was that tongue that forced Hope's true nature to return from the depressed, self-pitying cocoon it had been hiding in since learning Slate was in love with Faith. That lying, conniving tongue that caused her long withheld emotions to spew forth in a geyser of liberating anger.

"Colt Lomax!" Hope screamed, loud enough to shake the tiles from the ceiling as she shoved her way through the crowd. "Get your filthy hands off my sister!"

THE DISH

Where authors give you the inside scoop!

♥ ♥ ♥ ♥ ♥ ♥ ♥ ♥ ♥ ♥ ♥ ♥ ♥ ♥ ♥ ♥

From the desk of Vicky Dreiling

Dear Reader,

HOW TO RAVISH A RAKE stars shy wallflower Amy Hardwick and charming rake William Darcett, better known as "the Devil." I thought it would be great fun to feature two characters who seem so wrong for one another on the surface but who would find love and happiness, despite their differences.

Miss Amy Hardwick is a shy belle who made her first appearance in my debut historical romance, *How to Marry a Duke*. When I first envisioned Amy, I realized that she was representative of so many young women who struggle to overcome low self-esteem. Amy doesn't fit the ideal image of the English rose in Regency Society, and, as a result, she's often overlooked by others. But as I thought back to my days in high school and college, I remembered how much it helped to have girlfriends who liked and supported you, even though you didn't have the flawless skin and perfect bodies airbrushed on the covers of teen magazines. That recollection convinced me that having friends would help Amy to grow into the woman I knew she was destined to become.

Now, during her sixth and quite possibly last London Season, Amy is determined to shed her wallflower image forever. A newfound interest in fashion leads Amy to draw designs for unique gowns that make her the fashion darling of the *ton*. All of her dreams seem to be coming true, but there's one man who could deter her from the road to transformation: Mr. William "the Devil" Darcett.

Ah, Will…*sigh*. I confess I had a penchant for charming bad boys when I was in high school and college. There's a certain mystique about them. And I'm certain that the first historical romance I ever read featured a charming bad boy. They really are my favorite type of heroes. So naturally, I decided to create the worst bad boy in the *ton* and throw him in sweet Amy's path.

William Darcett is a younger son with a passion for traveling. He's not one to put down roots—just the occupation for a bona fide rake. But Will's latest plans for another journey to the Continent go awry when he discovers his meddling family wants to curb his traveling days. Will refuses to let his family interfere with his carousing and rambling, but a chance encounter with Amy in a wine cellar leads the wallflower and the rake into more trouble than they're prepared to handle.

This very unlikely pair comes to realize that laughter, family, and honesty are the most important ingredients for everlasting love. I hope you will enjoy the adventures of Amy and Will on their journey to discover that even the unlikeliest of couples can fall madly, deeply in love.

My heartfelt thanks to all the readers who wrote to let me know they couldn't wait to read HOW TO RAVISH A RAKE. I hope you will enjoy the fun and games that finally lead to Happily Ever After for Amy and Will.

Cheers!

♥ ♥ ♥ ♥ ♥ ♥ ♥ ♥ ♥ ♥ ♥ ♥ ♥ ♥ ♥ ♥

From the desk of Amanda Scott

Dear Reader,

What happens when a freedom-loving Scotsman who's spent much of his life on the open sea meets an enticing heiress determined to make her home with a husband who will stay put and run her Highland estates? And what happens when something that they have just witnessed endangers the plans of a ruthless and powerful man who is fiercely determined to keep the details of that event secret?

HIGHLAND LOVER, the third title in my Scottish Knights trilogy, stars the fiercely independent Sir Jacob "Jake" Maxwell, who was a nine-year-old boy in *King of Storms*, the last of a six-book series beginning with *Highland Princess*. Lifting a fictional child from a series I wrote years ago to be a hero in a current trilogy is new for me.

However, the three heroes of Scottish Knights are friends who met as teenage students under Bishop Traill of St. Andrews and later accepted his invitation to join a brotherhood of highly skilled knights that he (fictionally) formed to help him protect the Scottish Crown. I realized straightaway that the grown-up Jake would be the right age in 1403 and would easily fit my requirements, for several reasons:

First, Jake has met the ruthless Duke of Albany, who was a villainous presence in Scotland for thirty-one years (in all) and is now second in line for the throne. Determined to become King of Scots, Albany habitually eliminates anyone who gets in his way. Second, Albany owes his life to Jake, a relationship that provides interesting twists in any tale. Third, Jake is captain of the *Sea Wolf*, a ship he owns because of Albany; and the initiating event in HIGHLAND LOVER takes place at sea. So Jake seemed to be a perfect choice. The cheeky youngster in *King of Storms* had stirred (and still stirs) letters from readers suggesting that an adult Jake Maxwell would make a great hero. Doubtless that also had something to do with it.

Jake's heroine in HIGHLAND LOVER is Lady Alyson MacGillivray of Perth, a beautiful cousin of Sir Ivor "Hawk" Mackintosh of *Highland Hero*. Alyson is blessed (or cursed) with a bevy of clinging relatives and the gift of Second Sight. The latter "gift" has caused as many problems for her as have her intrusive kinsmen.

Alyson also has another problem—a husband of just a few months whom she has scarcely seen and who so far seems more interested in his noble patron's affairs than in Alyson's Highland estates or Alyson herself. But Alyson is trapped in this wee wrinkle, is she not? It is, after all, 1403.

In any event, Jake sets out on a mission for the Bishop of St. Andrews, encounters a storm, and ends up plucking Alyson and an unknown lad from a ship sinking off the English coast two hundred miles from her home in Perth. The ship also happened to be carrying the young heir to Scotland's throne and Alyson's husband, who may or may not now be captive in England.

So, the fun begins. I hope you enjoy HIGHLAND LOVER.

Meantime, *Suas Alba!*

Amanda Scott

www.amandascottauthor.com

♥ ♥   ⬜   ♥   ⬜   ♥   ♥ ♥   ⬜

From the desk of Dee Davis

Dear Reader,

I've been a storyteller all of my life. When I was a kid, my dad and I used to sit in the mall or a restaurant and make up stories about the people walking by or sitting around us. So it really wasn't much of a leap to find myself a novelist. But what was interesting to me was that no matter what kind of story I was telling, the characters all seemed to know each other.

Sometimes people from other novels were simply mentioned in another of my books in passing. Sometimes they actually had cameo appearances. And several times now, a character I had created to be a secondary figure in one story has demanded his or her own book. Such was the case with Harrison Blake of DEADLY DANCE. Harrison first showed up in my Last Chance series, working as that team's computer forensic expert. It even turned out he'd also worked for *Midnight Rain*'s John Brighton at his Phoenix organization, even though the company was created at the end of the book and never actually appeared on paper.

Interestingly enough, Harrison, although never a hero, has received more mail than any of my other characters. And almost all of those letters are from readers asking when he's going to have his day. So when A-Tac found itself in need of a technical guru, it was a no-brainer for me to bring Harrison into the fold. As he became an integral part of the team, I knew the time had come for him to have his own book.

And of course, as his story developed, he needed help from his old friends. So enter Madison Roarke and Tracy Braxton. Madison was the heroine of the first Last Chance book, *Endgame*. And like Harrison, Tracy had been placed in the role of supporting character, as a world-class forensic pathologist.

What can I say? It's a small world, and they all know and help each other. And finally, we add to the mix our heroine, Hannah Marshall. Hannah has been at the heart of all the A-Tac books. A long-time team member, she's always there with the answers when needed. And like Harrison, she made it more than clear to me that she deserved her own story. With her quirky way of expressing herself (eyeglasses and streaked hair) and her well-developed intellect, Hannah seemed perfect for Harrison. The two of them just didn't know it yet.

So I threw them together, and, as they say, the plot thickened, and DEADLY DANCE was born.

Hopefully you'll enjoy reading Harrison and Hannah's story as much as I did writing it.

For insight into both Harrison and Hannah, here are some songs I listened to while writing DEADLY DANCE:

Riverside, by Agnes Obel

Set Fire to the Rain, by Adele

Everlong, by Foo Fighters

And as always, check out www.deedavis.com for more inside info about my writing and my books.

Happy Reading!

♥ ♥ ♥ ♥ ♥ ♥ ♥ ♥ ♥ ♥ ♥ ♥ ♥ ♥ ♥

From the desk of Katie Lane

Dear Reader,

Before I plot out the storyline and flesh out my characters, my books start with one basic idea. Or maybe I should say they start with one nagging, persistent thought that won't leave me alone until I put it down on paper.

Going Cowboy Crazy started with the concept of long-lost twins and what would happen if one twin took over the other twin's life and no one—save the hot football coach—was the wiser.

Make Mine a Bad Boy was the other side of that premise: What would happen if your twin, whom you didn't even know you had, married your boyfriend and left you with a good-for-nothing, low-down bad boy?

And CATCH ME A COWBOY started with a melodrama. You know the kind I'm talking about, the story of a dastardly villain taking advantage of a poor, helpless woman by tying her to the railroad tracks, or placing her on a conveyor belt headed toward the jagged blade of a saw, or evicting her from her home when she has no money to pay the rent. Of course, before any of these things happen, the hero arrives to save the day with a smile so big and bright it rivals the sun.

For days, I couldn't get the melodrama out of my mind. But no matter how much the idea stuck with me, I just didn't see it fitting into my new book. My heroine had already been chosen: a favorite secondary character from the previous novels. Shirlene is a sassy, voluptuous west Texas gal who could no more play the damsel in distress than Mae West could play the Singing Nun. If someone tied Shirlene to the train tracks, she wouldn't scream, faint, or hold the back of her hand dramatically to her forehead. She'd just ask if she had enough time for a margarita.

The more I thought of my sassy heroine dealing with a Snidely Whiplash–type, the more I laughed. The more I laughed, the more I wrote. And suddenly I had my melodrama. Except a funny thing happened on the way to Shirlene's Happily Ever After: My villain and my hero got a little mixed up. And before I knew it, Shirlene had so charmed the would-be villain that he stopped the train. Shut off the saw. Paid the rent.

And how does the hero with the bright smile fit into all of this? you might ask.

Well, let's just say I don't think you'll be disappointed. CATCH ME A COWBOY is available now.

Enjoy, y'all!

Katie Lane